Forever Night

by

Stephen B King

Forever Night

Cover Art by *Jennifer Greeff*

The Wild Rose Press, Inc.
PO Box 708
Adams Basin, NY 14410-0708
Visit us at www.thewildrosepress.com

Publishing History
First Edition, 2022
Trade Paperback ISBN 978-1-5092-4525-3
Digital ISBN 978-1-5092-4526-0

Previously Published 2015 Totally Entwined Group (UK)
Published in the United States of America

"It's okay, I won't bite," said this angel in disguise, and I took her small, warm hand in mine. Zap—the surge of electricity as we touched rocked me to my very core, and I knew at that moment that this was a woman I had to get to know, if only I knew how to make that happen. She squeezed back as I gripped her hand and smiled at me with a hint of mischief, a smile of pure joy at my embarrassment. As our eyes locked, she winked at me and shook her head so her long blonde locks shimmered in the colored light.

"I'm Tank, I mean, sorry, I'm Paul," I muttered back, realizing how completely stupid I looked and sounded. She would think I was pathetic, I knew with a sinking heart, and who could blame her?

"Tank?" she asked, but gave me the biggest, most incredible smile, and I swear in that one moment I blushed three shades redder. My God I was making a mess of this, but to my incredible relief Sam came to my rescue, joined in and helped me out.

"That's his nickname, Mandy—can we call you Mandy?"

She ignored the question and just stared at me. "Why would anyone call such a handsome man Tank?"

Oh my God, that question made me turn to mush and sweat broke out on my forehead. Surely she was toying with me. What could such a woman ever see in someone like me?

Praise for Forever Night

"Great book! Intense, and the type of book you do not want to put down."

"This book was fascinating and horrifying like watching a train wreck. I have never had a book affect me so much. The writer had me envisioning the cold eyes of the killer."

"The journey that you are taken on will be strange and scary, that keeps you wanting to read more. The author did a great job on the book by keeping you wanting more as you read, there was a lot of details on the person that story was about. Great job"

Dedication

Forever Night has been a part of me for what feels like years and has been a labor of love and angst. I would be very remiss in not thanking people who were invaluable along the way.

My wife Jacqui has been a never-ending supporter and has urged me to pick up a pen and write the stories I bombard her with for a long, long time. Without her there pushing me, none of this would have been possible. My daughter Tania has been with me from the very first when Forever Night started out life as a poem, trying to depict the bizarre mindset of a deranged killer who lives among us, yet very well disguised. She told me she loved all twenty verses and wanted to hear more. I will never forget her words, "Dad, this is really good, but what happens to him next?" Without her proofreading, helping, researching, pushing and prodding, and reading chapter by chapter as I created the tragic story of Paul 'Tank' Williams, again, FN would have stayed a poem and been buried for all time.

She also was the first person to tell me I was getting my tenses wrong.

When I finally thought it was finished (boy did I have a lot to learn about finishing a book because it was a long way from being finished) I sent it out into the world and nervously waited for agents and publishers to tell me it was crap, because I genuinely felt it was. To my delight, Sarah Smeaton, a senior editor at TEG, wrote back and said, "I love what you're doing with this story, but your tenses are all wrong. If you can fix it up I would like to publish it." Thanks, Sarah, I will be forever indebted to you. Then the hard work began and I had the pleasure of working with Shannon Combs, another senior editor with TEG, and I began to bombard her email with ideas, whines and complaints and she was always a friendly shoulder to lean on. Thanks, Shannon, and everyone else at TEG for bearing with me, and helping me bring to life the story of Forever Night.

Last, but not least, thank you to Leonard Cohen, whose masterful use of words has inspired me for years. If I could write one hundredth as well as he does, I'd die a happy man.

Book One

I walk among you, well disguised
I look for truth; you give me lies
I rarely speak; you do not hear
You run and hide, and live in fear.

Forever night, your beating heart
Is in my hand; my blade is sharp
The witch is dead, will hurt no more
The scarlet rains upon the floor.

Foreword

During the ten-month reign of terror carried out by the man who became known as the 'Perth Ripper,' I was a senior journalist for the West Australian daily newspaper and was responsible for most of the reporting locally and internationally at the time.

Like everyone else, I was morbidly fascinated by the case. We have been reasonably sheltered here in Australia in general, and Perth, more specifically, has not suffered with the dearth of serial killers seen in other countries. Partly this could be because of the rigidly strong firearm laws we have, or perhaps our lifestyle creates a more relaxed mentality; who can say why? While we are not immune, the incidence is much lower, thankfully.

When I studied journalism at university, I gained a second degree in criminal psychology, which was a good fit for crime reporting, and since then, what drives some to become serial killers has always held a special interest for me.

In the aftermath of 'The Ripper' case, I was fortunate enough to obtain a copy of the journals describing his past, including his childhood. I also held interviews with the survivors, which led me to write this book because there is a story to tell here. My research paints a tragic picture, not only for the victims and families but also of someone who rose above a horrific childhood to become a decorated war hero. He met the love of his life only to then have everything unravel due to circumstances he himself could not possibly control.

Chapter One

"Amanda," I whispered, close behind her after returning from the bathroom. She stood before the sliding glass doors to her balcony. She was staring out at the night-lit cityscape. I blew warm air gently across her neck, through her long blonde hair, the heady scent of her green-apple shampoo in the air of the warm breeze through the adjoining window assailed my senses. Her beauty reflected back at me in the glass and was on display to everyone who looked toward her seventh-floor apartment window.

The radio played a great old song by someone I couldn't remember, She giggled and turned. "I'm not Amanda, silly. Who is she?" Her eyes sparkled with mirth and the three glasses of wine she had drunk earlier. I'd had only ice water, wanting to keep control, knowing tonight would be special.

I admit I had made mistakes in the past, but this time it *was* her. I was absolutely convinced of that *and* that she was lying. I looked down at her blue eyes from my towering height, then allowed my questing gaze slowly to drift lower to her lips, ruby red as she licked them, her throat so milky. Her cleavage showed the rise and swell of her breasts above her perfectly flat tummy. I imagined where her belly button was, wondered if it was pierced, and remembered it certainly used to be. I decided to play safe and sink my knife about an inch higher.

Why do they always deny it? I asked myself.

"Oh my God. No!" she screamed, her lovely eyes pleading when she saw the knife.

"You're nothing but a liar, Amanda," My left hand held her hair, bunching it up at the back of her head.

"I'm…not…Amanda," were the last words the deceitful cow spoke. Even in death, she lied. I had lost all feelings for her long before and felt nothing now I'd finished the mission I came to do.

A momentary panic flickered, then her eyes—earlier sparkling—now dimmed and faded. I let her slip to the floor. She was just a crumpled heap in an ever-widening pool of her own blood as it soaked into the carpet.

I was reminded of a similar scene in some long-ago gore-movie scene—Deep Red, or Blood Red, or some such film. It had "Red" in it anyway. I always liked that movie, even if I couldn't remember the title. I squatted by her side and tilted her head so her dead eyes faced the window and she could watch the sunrise a few short hours later. I'd always been considerate, and she loved the sunrise; Amanda had once been my wife.

Some times were easier than others. In my experience, you can never pick which it's going to be. Planning only goes so far. Sometimes they see it coming, and they beg and plead, scream or offer anything I want as a way of escaping their fate. But it was always pointless. It made no difference to me, and there was nothing Amanda could have said or done that would have let her escape once she became my mission. That had been predetermined—she chose her course, not me. I had done so much for her, made her my queen, idolized her in every way, and would have died for her. Why had she had treated me so badly? How could she have been so unfaithful? Then, the final insult, she had run away and hidden from me. *How dare she?*

I lifted her dress, gathering it at her waist. Lifting her with one hand and yanking with the other, I pulled off her powder-blue panties. Naturally, they were filmy and lacy, befitting the type of woman she was. Fortunately, her blood had not stained them, but they snagged on her high heels as I pulled them off—they always seem to do that! I smelled her scent before placing them, bunched up, in my left pocket. They would provide me pleasure later as I relived tonight over and over in my head. This would keep the voices quiet, hopefully forever, now my quest was ended.

I admit that I had made errors in the past; sometimes I get confused, though I believe anyone would if they'd been through half the things I had. But, this time I knew it was her. There was no doubt. Right now, the voices, sometimes quiet—sometimes screaming in my head—were gone. For the first time in weeks, I could hear myself think, and even if it didn't stay that way, at the very least the silence would give me some respite. The headaches never left me...unlike the voices—they just varied in intensity.

I realized I was aroused and wondered if it was the deed performed or the smell of Amanda's panties that had turned me on. I shrugged, not caring which. I'm not sick, you understand, not sick at all, despite what the papers say about me. I knew my cause was just—Amanda had lied to me and cheated, and now she was dead, as she deserved to be; that was enough for me.

I went to work with my knife, leaving my message clear to anyone who could see what happens to unfaithful women like Amanda. On previous occasions, the newspaper headlines had called it *mutilation*, but they'd never divulged what type. I lived in hope that they would one day. I did enjoy reading about myself in the papers and seeing my exploits on the TV news.

I cannot describe the euphoria and the sheer joy of 'being,' knowing that finally, I had tracked down and found the woman who had destroyed my life. As repayment, I had taken hers. I had spent months searching, thinking I had found her previously, and now, I had.

"We could have had a life together, Amanda. It could have been perfect. This is *your* fault, not mine." I shook my head, looked down at her, then squatted at her side again and cleaned the stiletto knife—a keepsake from a war in a distant land—on the shoulder of her once-white dress. I pushed the blade back into the handle as I stood. She had been beautiful, the most beautiful woman in the world to me.

She had gotten her blood on me, but I am resourceful and always prepared. *'Adapt, adapt, adapt,'* our drill sergeant had screamed at us during training. I crossed to my backpack, undid the flap, and pulled out track pants, T-shirt, trainers, and a plastic bag. I undressed and re-dressed in a matter of moments and slipped everything else, excluding the knife, into the plastic bag and back in the backpack. I tucked the knife into my sports sock—just in case I needed it again in a hurry. I also put the wig and fake mustache I had worn into a special plastic bag that I kept inside the side compartment.

From the front pocket, I took out my leaving disguise, which was a baseball cap with long straggly blond hair stitched to the sides and back, eyeglasses with clear glass but thick rims, and a stick-on goatee beard. I bought it from a joke shop some months before, but it looked so remarkable once applied I considered growing one once my mission was complete.

Now to clean up.

When I arrived earlier at Amanda's, or Heather as she'd liked to call herself while hiding from me, I had excused myself to her bathroom. There I put on thin white rubber gloves, so I did not have to worry about fingerprints on other than the bathroom door handle and light switch. I'd been careful not to touch anything else. She had made it all too easy, being at the window with her back to me when I'd returned. I guess there was always the possibility of leaving some DNA somewhere, but my earlier training was invaluable. We had studied how often cases are closed, even after years, because of a DNA sample inadvertently left at a crime scene. We were told there was always *transference*, often minute, that brought even the cleverest of criminals undone.

I crossed to her laundry, where I found what I needed under the sink. I took a damp cloth and bottle of ammonia spray, though bleach would have done just as well, but the spray bottle made it easier. I retraced my steps to the bathroom, spraying as I went—the carpet, the door handles inside and out, and everywhere inside the bathroom, just in case. I knew the ammonia would contaminate any DNA sample I'd left behind, although I looked very carefully for short dark brown hairs of mine or from the wig, even though tracing me through wig sellers was unlikely.

When I was sure I'd been thorough, I took the small plastic coin bag with stray hairs I had collected from random places from my right pocket. The train, buses, even the back of a chair at my doctor's surgery where I found them; I was always on the lookout for stray hairs. I held the bag up to the light, removed one, and carefully placed it behind the tap on the basin. Smiling to myself, I flipped the light off after wiping it, then shut the door.

I retraced my steps to Amanda's body, squirting the ammonia as I went, then squatted and scoured her white dress for any of my hairs. I had been very careful, and my hair being short meant it was unlikely any had fallen out, but I hadn't gotten this far without being cautious. Once satisfied, I placed two more hairs from my stash, one inside her bra on her left breast, the other in a fold of her now crimson dress, across her stomach to the side of the wound.

I felt so good at my cleverness I almost giggled at the thought of the efforts of the forensics officers who would try to match the hair samples. Wouldn't it be funny if one matched a known criminal? From the same pocket, I took out another plastic bag which held a scrunched-up, used tissue that I had taken from the bin at the bus stop. I gently rubbed the damp cloth over Amanda's lips and the fingertips of one of her hands before placing it back in the bag. That, along with my clothes, would go into the charcoal barbeque on the balcony of my home. I would burn them to ashes later.

Nearly done, I stood and moved over to my backpack and put it on. I slipped on the cap, glasses, and goatee, then gave a liberal dosing of the cleaning spray to the area where I'd changed clothes. I was suddenly struck with a case of the giggles as I recalled the sing-song voice of the TV ad jingle for the product. I stopped in my tracks, trying to remember the name of the actress with the stupid look on her face in the ad, but I couldn't. My memory was deteriorating since being wounded, and

I often had trouble recalling the simplest of things. I shrugged and then walked backward to her front door, still spraying. I took one last look around as I slipped the bottle and cloth into my backpack, feeling safe in the knowledge no one would know it was gone.

It seemed to me the police were mostly stupid or was it that I was just smarter? *The latter*, I thought. I turned off the light and left. The radio was playing a song I didn't know, but it sounded very much like a band I should be able to remember.

Heather, nee Amanda, lived alone, and it could be days before she was missed and found. By then, the ammonia would have done its job and evaporated, so there would be no physical evidence of my presence at the scene, just the hairs from three different people and saliva from a fourth, and possibly traces of the spray. The air conditioning might confuse the time of death, but that was unlikely, technology being what it was. I knew I was so much smarter than the task force set up to find me. Now I was finally finished my mission; she was dead, I could retire, and they would never find me.

I left the apartment and walked with a stooped gait and limping on my left leg to the elevator so I would look shorter on the CCTV camera views in the building. The description given in the media on previous occasions was always that of a limping man who looked nothing like me by the photofit. If they knew any more, they were keeping it from the press, but I didn't think they did. I was too smart for them.

I knew the location of the cameras in the building, having checked a few days before, and I had been very careful to hide my features when arriving with Amanda. I had not touched her and had kept my distance in the lift, stood stooped, and walked with a limp, telling Amanda it was just a temporary cramp from sitting in her little car on the drive back. How typical of her to drive a sports car—*easier to attract men*, I thought with disgust.

I had arranged for her to meet me at the bar instead of me picking her up. She believed me when I'd told her my car was in the workshop. We'd returned to her place after eleven p.m., and I knew there would be very few, if any, people around to see me. The CCTV in a building like this was usually grainy and hopefully would give no clear image of me. Planning, planning, and more planning, these were always my watchwords.

Hands in pockets to hide the gloves, I used my elbow to call the elevator, and I didn't encounter anyone leaving. I slipped out into the night, overjoyed at my work, knowing my mission was complete, and knew I would escape detection. The world was rid of one more slut; the cops should thank me, not hunt me.

I whistled a tune as I headed to the multistory car park where I had left my older-model white sedan and realized it was the same song as earlier on my lips, which made me smile even more. My car was one of hundreds, if not thousands, on the road, with the number plates 'borrowed' from a late-model SUV a few days earlier in another car park. They would be tossed into the river tomorrow after putting my own plates back on. *Maybe it's time to upgrade the Car*, I mused, *get a decent one, settle down with a dog, pipe, and slippers*. Then a bout of the giggles hit me at the absurdity of that thought.

I turned the corner and almost fainted. Up ahead, I saw Amanda, arm in arm with a man. Her long blonde hair was flying in the breeze as she laughed at some private joke between them. I closed my eyes, shook my head, looked again, and exhaled a long sigh of relief. Her hair was light brown, not blonde. It was just a trick of the light from an electrical goods store they were walking in front of. The bitch was dead after all, and the voices were still quiet in my head.

I started whistling again, crossed the road, and increased my pace, eager to get home. I thought tonight would be the night I could get all the way to the next level in my latest video game, *Death and Destruction, Los Angeles.* I could hardly wait.

****

It was nine days later when I saw the article about Heather De Santo in the paper. Her tearful parents told her life story while the picture of a smiling young woman peered out at me. I read what a distraught friend said about her and her sister, who had been on holiday in England, rushed back to console their parents. I read the police report, complete with their promise of an early capture of the madman who had murdered Heather.

The screaming headline read *The Ripper Kills Again—Number 10.* The newspapers loved a good rhyme, and after I read it twice all the way through, I groaned deeply.

There was no escaping the fact that Heather wasn't *my* Amanda after all. I had made another mistake. The voices started, mocking me, murmuring for now, but soon I knew they would get louder and louder inside my head. *"Find the bitch, kill the bitch. Find the bitch, kill the bitch."* I sighed, trying to ignore them and the burgeoning headache. I turned the page and went back to my cornflakes.

Chapter Two

Detective Inspector Dillon Bradley left the commissioner's office after the briefing, though it had been much more like an ass-kicking than any briefing he had ever been to before. He was dejected, angry, and even more morose than usual. Dillon was tall and slowly fighting a losing battle with his weight at forty-eight years old. He was slightly rotund with gray hair around the temples, which gave him an authoritative, distinguished look. Some said in certain lights, he resembled a middle-aged, overweight famous movie star.

He had just been given a warning that if he did not make significant progress in the 'Ripper' case *very* soon, he would be relieved of his command and probably sent back to the vice or drug squad. Either one would probably spell the end of both his career and quite probably his marriage.

His marriage was far from happy as it was, but being the head investigator of the Major Crime Task Force for the biggest homicide case in Western Australian history gave Kathy, his wife, at least some status. He knew how important that was to her, with her charity work and wide circle of socialite friends. Her pride in him had been in very short supply in recent months, yet he had no idea why. Thirty years of marriage had mostly been happy, but recently she treated him as if he was an annoying stranger who could do nothing right.

If he was transferred to vice or the drug squad, he was sure it would all be over. She would lose too much face in her circle and leave him. She was unbearable now, and he dreaded to think how bad life would be without her if it happened. While he still had feelings for Kathy, he realized he loved his house just as much and had no desire to lose half of it and everything else and start all over again at his age. It was cynical thinking, but as a happy home life was pretty nonexistent these days, he forgave himself that.

Dillon hadn't needed Commissioner Pollock, who had never been in the field or led a large investigation— had never even arrested someone—to tell him that the city was in a state of panic. Blonde-haired women lived in fear, with now ten of them brutally murdered. His own daughter was blonde, for goodness' sake, though she lived in Melbourne and should be safe, as all of the victims had been in Perth. But even she had an edge of fear, mixed with a morbid fascination, in her voice when they spoke on the phone about the *Ripper*.

Many women locally felt vulnerable and scared for their lives, with some suspecting every male they came across. The newspapers and TV reports were not helping with sensationalist headlines and reporting. He had lost count of the number of times he had seen the headline: *Police still have no leads in the Ripper hunt.* It always amazed him that not having any news could be made into news itself. If there was a silver lining, it would be for the hair dye companies' profits, for all the women changing their hair color in an attempt to avoid being targeted. There was still a section of the female population who refused to be scared, daring fate and the

Ripper to step in, as if they wanted to meet him to prove they didn't live in fear. Not that anyone deserved to be murdered and mutilated like that, but sometimes he wondered at people's stupidity in putting themselves at risk.

There was some talk in the letters to the editor section of the newspaper that vigilante groups should be patrolling the streets. That was just madness, but highlighted the terror people felt. If the police couldn't track down this maniac, how could a bunch of well-meaning amateurs? That said, he understood the helplessness members of the public were feeling, and the desire of people to want to do something, anything, to catch the man.

The thirty members of his task force were working twelve hours a day, six days a week. Dillon had had to force some officers to take time off to spend with their families. They all shared anger at the brutal killer and horror at the mutilations he inflicted on the victims' bodies. Their passion to catch him was unlike anything Dillon had seen in a squad before. It was, in many ways, like hunting a ghost, though.

It was true they did have some information that had not been released to the press, some lines of investigation ongoing, even a few that looked promising, but there was so much they didn't know. They didn't have any witnesses, or forensics that made any sense at all. There was no CCTV worth anything, and no idea who, when or where he would strike next. In a city of one-point-eight million people, this man lived in plain sight, yet was still very well hidden. In his heart, Dillon knew that if they got rid of him, whoever took over as lead would have no more success than Dillon had had, unless and until the killer made a mistake.

They had combed the background of all of the victims, looking for any similarities or coincidences to find some common denominator. They had no idea where the victims had met their killer. They had interviewed neighbors, friends, work colleagues and families, trying to find anything to give them a lead.

There had been reenactments, TV interviews and calls for witnesses with no result other than the usual crackpots and time-wasting dead ends. There had been no discernible pattern on a map where the victims had met, lived or worked—as far as they knew, they hadn't known each other. There was not a single moment they could find where any two of them had even been in the same building at the same time. Still, they kept digging deeper and deeper, knowing that sometimes it could be the most inconsequential thing that linked all the victims together in their murderer's eye.

The prepared psychological evaluation was next to useless, but did give them some background information into the whys and wherefores of the murderer's past, and what sort of person he was likely to be. Dillon was sure that once they caught him, the profile would be crystal clear. To him psyche evaluations were like the prophecies of Nostradamus in that they only made sense after the event. Other than a vague outline and conjecture about the type of person they were looking for, they were no real help in identifying the killer.

What Pollock wanted from him was something to take to the media to show what a good job they were doing and reassure the public. Publicity had been one of the commissioner's strong points. He loved being in the limelight. What could be achieved by replacing him as head was a mystery. Pollock could make no useful suggestions as to any lines of inquiry they could make. *'Just fix it or else,'* Dillon had been told in no uncertain terms.

He looked at his watch and wondered what he would do for lunch. The commissioner would be off to somewhere nice, no doubt, while everyone in the task force worked through their lunch break, or ate a hurried sandwich at their desk. Dillon realized that he wasn't hungry after all. He went back to his office and once again looked at the piles of paperwork awaiting his attention. Ten homicides created so much information to administer. He sat down, turned and faced the window, looking out across the city to the parklands and cricket ground and thought about Marci.

He needed her *distraction*. He didn't want to, he was always so guilty afterwards, but he yearned to feel needed by someone, because his wife acted as if she despised him. He took out his mobile and recalled Marci's number. He wondered why hookers often had a name that ended in 'i' or 'y', as the phone rang. He ran through some he knew from his days in vice, Mandi, Traci, Cyndi. Marci answered and he lost his train of thought with her sweet voice that he found so sexy.

Marci had short black hair so Dillon thought she should be completely safe, safe from the Ripper anyway. As a prostitute, she faced danger every day but that was different, and for her, an acceptable risk.

Dillon had, some time before, helped her out of a bind, not just with the police but a pimp who'd threatened to carve his initials on her face. She had told Dillon that she owed him more than she could ever repay, and would never forget that debt. She had added that so as far as she was concerned, he could see her every day if he wanted to.

"I'm coming over about six tonight, is that okay?" he asked.

"Of course it is, darling, bring a bottle of wine. You know what I like," she answered, as he knew she would.

Dillon didn't know if she would cancel a 'date' she had scheduled once she got off the phone with him. She was a very popular woman who provided the full 'girlfriend' experience and received a high price, but never charged Dillon. They didn't exchange other pleasantries; they never did on the phone—and he broke the connection. He slipped the phone into his pocket and sat back farther in his chair, thinking of what they would be doing later. It would be the kind of sex that had been sadly missing in his marriage.

He was still like that later, frozen, though his thoughts had returned to the killer they were hunting. He was mentally going through Heather De Santo's file for the hundredth time when his phone rang. It was Kathy. There was no hello or pleasantries and Dillon could hear the undercurrent of indifference with him in her voice when she spoke. He sighed to himself at the thought of another night with her at home, and her constant fault-finding in him.

"I'm cooking roast chicken for dinner. Will you be home on time?" she asked.

He tried to be pleasant back. He always tried his best. "Hi, love, chicken sounds great but I don't think I'll get away on time, probably home about eight-thirty to nine. Could you keep it warm for me? There's no need for you to hold off eating yourself."

"I don't know why I bother," she replied and hung

up, as had been typical of Kathy lately.

She didn't tell him if she would keep his dinner warm or not and he wondered if he should call back and ask. If he did he knew it would lead to yet another row and, as angry as he was, he just couldn't face that. Dillon realized he was clenching the phone so tightly his knuckles where white and his hand trembled. He resisted the urge to throw it across the room just as Detective Sergeant Mike Knowles knocked and entered. He held some papers in his hand and had a look of stifled excitement in his eyes.

Mike was a good officer who was incredibly fit; he regularly competed in triathlons. With his short crew cut, he looked every inch the sun-bronzed Australian athlete that he was. "I think I may have something," he said.

Dillon pointed to the left-hand chair in front of his desk, then very slowly replaced the phone receiver in its cradle. Still trying to bring his temper under control, he raised his eyebrows and nodded for Mike to continue.

He placed the first print on Dillon's desk, which showed a picture of their killer with Heather De Santo in the elevator. His head was bowed to one side and his left hand was held over his mouth, making any identification impossible. Despite all of the media warnings, she was willingly taking her murderer up to her apartment. Dillon just looked back. They had all seen this picture before.

"How did he know the camera was there?" Mike asked.

Gritting his teeth and trying his best not to bark back—he hated rhetorical questions—Dillon attempted to refrain from taking his bad mood with Kathy out on his favorite staff member. "What makes you think he did, Mike?"

"De Santo lived in a good building. There are three cameras that should have got us something, but he is facing away from all of them. I wondered if it was just coincidence, luck or maybe something else," Mike went on, his voice getting quicker. "Would a guy who has killed ten women without leaving any forensics be smart enough to leave false evidence and not know where the cameras were?"

"Go on."

"If he knew where they were, then he had to have been there to check it out before. Luckily for us, this building has a digital recorder that stores images for about a month. So, I went back a few days at a time and I found this, and this, and this." He put three pictures down, which were not crystal clear, but showed a man with a similar build, wearing gray overalls and a gray cap pulled low, with a full black beard, looking up at each camera. There was no emblem on the pocket, so while at first glance he appeared to be a workman, the lack of company logo was suspicious.

"Do you think he looks like him?" He placed the last picture down. This one showed the tall, long-haired blond guy wearing a T-shirt, track pants, and a cap with a football team logo, filmed limping as he left the building. This man was currently their prime suspect.

Dillon pulled open his top drawer and grabbed a large magnifying glass. He spent the next few minutes going over the five prints in silence. He went from one to the other and back. Finally, he sat up straight in his chair, the first smile in weeks on his face. "Good work, Mike. This would never hold up in court, obviously, but I think you may be right." He looked again, and the more he did, the more he thought that despite the changes in outward appearance, this could be the same guy.

Dillon's mind raced with possibilities. If the Ripper was stalking his victims before killing them, then they could have been chosen at random from different locations. If his stalking was to the extent of checking for cameras before the crime, there would be more man-hours needed going back prior to each victim's death, searching available CCTV and re-interviewing everyone, hunting for anyone who may have noticed this man checking out where the victims had lived and worked. Possibly he had made a mistake and not worn a disguise on one of those as he had on the two occasions with Heather De Santo. A lot of background checking had already been done, but this level of pre-planning put things into a different perspective.

The profiler had put forward the possibility the victims had been killed merely because they all had very similar features. They had no connection to one another or the killer that police could discover, but if they could get more pictures or descriptions of the man from his prior reconnaissance of the victims, they could draw up a composite with an artist and see what he looked like undisguised. Finally, they had a direction they could take, and more important than anything else, for him personally, it might buy him more time with the commissioner.

"There is one more thing, boss. This is just a feeling, and I'm not sure I should say anything, but, err, well, as we don't have much else to go on, I think it's worth investigating…"

"Spit it out, Mike," Dillon urged.

"I think he is military. Ex-army is my guess." Quickly moving on, Mike knew Dillon only wanted facts and evidence rather than unsubstantiated theories.

"I've studied the film repeatedly, and when he arrived and left the apartment for the murder, he had a limp, but this guy." He tapped his fingers on the print of the man in gray overalls taken before the murder. "He doesn't. He holds himself tall, with his back straight. Just the way he walks, it's like he's got a steel rod up his backside. I think he's spent years marching on parade. Another thing, you can't really see it from the still pictures, but on the video, he is so alert and always checking the terrain. It seems more than just nerves. To me, it's like this guy has been trained by the army. I'm absolutely sure of it."

Dillon knew Mike had been in the army for seven years and thought if anyone could spot a fellow soldier, Mike could. Dillon was one of those bosses who always knew everything about his team. He would often ask after wives or children by name from only having heard of them once. While some people were good with faces and terrible with remembering names, Dillon seemed to remember everything about everyone. His memory was legendary, as was his attention to detail.

Mike sat back in his chair, waiting for the ax to fall, but instead, Dillon got up from his chair. "Show me what you mean, Mike." Without waiting, Dillon walked out of his office, heading for Mike's desk and his computer station in the squad room.

For the next few minutes, he watched as Mike pointed out on-screen what were, to him, signs of the suspect's bearing and military gait. Dillon had to admit his arguments were sound. He would not have noticed for himself, but once it was pointed out, it looked obvious. It was subjective, that was true, and it could be open to criticism, but when you believed it, you saw more details that confirmed the theory.

As head of the investigation team, Dillon had to ensure his men didn't go off half-cocked in the wrong direction. At the same time, Mike Knowles was a seasoned investigator and had been years in the army himself. Dillon decided that Mike's instinct should be pursued, and it wasn't as if they were swamped with other avenues to investigate.

Thanks entirely to Mike's intellect and gut feeling, they had two new directions to investigate. One was trying to build a usable composite picture for Pollock to take to the media, and the second was checking out men who had left the army. The obvious possibility, which had to be reined in without further proof, was perhaps someone who had suffered post-traumatic stress disorder. The more he thought about this, the more it made sense, but they needed to find further corroboration. Certainly, stress alone would not make a man kill blonde women, so there had to be a reason he targeted who he did.

They had no idea why the killer mutilated the victim's vaginas after death. The possibility, no matter how slim, of an emotionally crippled ex-soldier whose blonde wife had abandoned him perhaps seemed as if could be some light at the end of what had been a very long tunnel.

The lack of useable evidence, fingerprints, or DNA from the ten murder scenes could also point toward a military mind in terms of the way each killing had been planned with precision. The profiler had indicated they were looking for a fully functioning sociopath with psychopathic urges whose type of personality was capable of strategic planning to the last detail.

"Let's get the team together, Mike. You've done well here." He clapped him on the shoulder. They had work to do.

Chapter Three

Journal Excerpt #1, My Childhood and Family
I am keeping this journal because I think my story should be told after I find Amanda and kill her. Once the mission is achieved, I will disappear, and the world will be rid of that hurtful bitch. Then I will send this journal to the newspapers and let them show her deceitful nature and how she drove me to this. People can then understand that everything that happened was her fault, not mine. I just did what had to be done; after all, the army trained me well.

****

I hated my father and loathed my clingy mother, as anyone would with my upbringing, but I don't agree that that makes me deranged as the newspapers say I am. It burns me up that they say such bullshit about me when they don't know me or that I have a clear mission and a purpose for what I do. I have made mistakes along the way, that is true, but I am determined to succeed, and my parents, as bad as they were, just set me up to succeed in adult life. The direction I chose to take is justified. They just gave me a 'win at any cost' mentality and nothing more.

If I can also show how inept the police force is, then so much the better. My fame—or should that be infamy? —will live on and be a beacon for others. When Amanda is dead, I won't tell anyone that I've stopped killing so that all the other lying sluts out there will think I'm still active and will be warned. I like to think that maybe it will stop some from becoming evil like she did, and not only would I have got the revenge I deserve, but I would have done a great community service. That thought is sweet indeed.

My father was a Vietnam veteran, Colonel Jack 'Ramrod' Williams, and a career military man, as was his father before him, as well as two uncles. If you cut my family, we bleed khaki. I don't remember my grandfather. I don't think I ever met him, but if I did, he was probably as big an asshole as my dad was.

Father's idea of parenthood, when he was home, which wasn't often, thankfully, was to treat me like one of his soldiers from a very young age. Everything I did had to be done with military precision. By the numbers, hut one two three, or it was a beating. By beating—I mean a caning—across my bare bum, thighs, and back, often until I bled. I can still hear the whistle through the air and feel the pain of being hit with whatever was close to hand if he didn't have his favorite cane nearby. If I dared cry, it was always more stripes for that indiscretion too. I grew up being hurt frequently by him and punished more if I shed a tear or yelled out. That was 'girly' according to him. I learned at a young age to 'toughen up.'

I don't remember at what age the beatings started, but I was probably three or four. I do remember the time he laid a hand on me after I had spilled some milk on the carpet. There was no warning. He slapped me across the face and cut my lip open, which caused me to drop the cup, which made an even bigger mess. He picked me up, put me over his knee, and spanked me hard. It felt like it went on and on and on. I relived that episode in nightmares for months afterward and was petrified every time I held a cup for years.

I could often tell when I was going to get a beating. It was in his eyes. He would snap, and when he did, no amount of pleading or tears would stop him. That only made it worse. Running away didn't help either. He was fit and would chase me and hurt me twice as much when he caught me. Later, after I grew up a bit and got quicker, he would then wait for my return. It didn't matter how long I was gone. The beating would always be worse for running, and he never forgot when a beating was owed, with interest.

My mother never tried to stop him, not that I ever saw anyway. I'm not saying she enjoyed watching him hurt me—possibly she did, or maybe she was scared of him too. I never witnessed him hitting her, but as a child, when I heard noises from their squeaky bed along with the moaning and grunting, I imagined he was hurting her in some grisly way. Regardless of whether he was hurting her or not, I despised her all the more for not trying to stop him and protect me. He was a monster at the drop of a hat for any real or imagined indiscretion of mine, and she was worse.

I hated him and was very careful not to upset him or get my jobs wrong and make him angry. I lived a very quiet life when he was around, hoping and praying he wouldn't notice me. Yet no matter how hard I tried to please him, I always did something wrong or didn't perform a task well enough for his lofty standards. If I dared drop something, felt unwell, didn't finish a meal, left a crease on my bed, or something, there was always a reason that he could find. Then his eyes would cloud over, and I knew I was in deep trouble.

Sometimes I'm sure I didn't do anything wrong, but he would punish me anyway. He was always yelling that it was 'for my own good.' And his personal favorite, he was 'making a man out of me.' I lived in fear, and it was just wonderful when he went away on a posting. The beatings would stop, and my back and bottom would heal. But he always returned, and as I got older, the worse he became each time.

As I entered my teenage years, he stopped using the cane so much. Instead, he used his fists, although even then, his personal favorite was still the thick bamboo garden stake he kept in the shed for special occasions. I used to cringe when I heard him say, 'I'm gonna shed you, boy, and make a man out of you.' And he would drag me by the arm into the shed at the back of the garden. He had cable ties by the boxful that he used to secure my wrists across his workbench before 'making a man out of me.' But I never understood how that made a man a man. All it did was make me scared.

My school grades were perfect. They had to be. Nothing short of that would do for him. I didn't dare do anything other than be top of my class and excel at everything I tried. But no matter how well I did, he never praised me or rewarded me for a great end-of-term report. I would stand before him, trembling after handing over my assessment, which always described me as the perfect student, though timid. He would just nod at me so that I knew I had been dismissed. If he ever had beaten me for handing over a good report, I would have been lost as it would have been impossible for me to do any better.

It was that striving to be the best at everything I did

that led me to success in the army, but my army story is for later. Looking back, it was only a fear of failure that stopped me from committing suicide—I remember that I thought about it often. I also contemplated running away many, many times, but I knew if he found me and dragged me back home, then I would really be in trouble.

I had no school friends. Students like me just didn't attract them unless it was other nerds. What I did attract were bullies, but no bully was ever as hard on me as my father, although they tried. They would steal my lunch, punch me unexpectedly, and even flush my head down the toilet if ever they caught me in there at recess or lunchtime. That particular torture caused me to use only the bathroom at home, a habit I found very difficult to break in the army later on.

One particular favorite of the group was to get me in a circle and push me around and around until I fell down dizzy then they would kick me, and some even spit on me. They called me 'Beaky' or 'Teacher's Pet,' and one time, they forced me over into a pile of dog droppings. From then on, they called me 'Dog Shit Williams.' Then, I was in more trouble when I got home as my school uniform was dirty or torn. School was hell on earth, and in the early days, I always hoped my father would take me and protect me from the bigger, stronger boys, but he never did. And, if I came home with a black eye or bruising, he would beat me for not being 'man enough' to stand up for myself—I couldn't win, so I didn't try.

My bedroom—I was an only child—had to be spotless, my pajamas folded neatly, slippers placed just so under the bed, and my drawers packed with clothes folded with all pomp and ceremony. Not that I had many toys, but the few I did have always had to be put away the moment I finished playing with them. Life was clinical, with everything having a place in his orderly world.

I had my list of jobs to do. Other kids got pocket money for doing chores, and I got caned if I didn't do them perfectly. He never hugged me, told me he loved me, or kissed me goodnight. He would not allow me to be scared of the dark, and in truth, I grew up fearing him rather than the darkness or things that went bump in the night. No matter how unwell I got, I would never tell him as he did not have a sympathetic bone in his body. His cure for any illness I had was to punish me. For all of that, I lived each waking moment when he was home on leave trying to please him, but I don't think I ever once did.

My mother hid her drinking from him when he was home and drank like a fish when he wasn't. She lived in fear of him, too, I think. I guess that's why she drank. When he was away on deployment, she smothered me with love and kindness to such an extent there were times I became physically ill. Her breath always smelled of white wine, which was her preferred choice, and she would always hug me to her oversized breasts and press my face between them. She stroked me all over, touching me everywhere, while I struggled to breathe, and she called me over and over 'My little Jackie Boy,' even though Jack wasn't my name but my father's.

The nasty times often would start with her rubbing soothing lotion into the sore areas on my back, buttocks, and thighs after a beating and my father had gone out. But the rubbing went on and spread to other areas, and no matter how much I squirmed or wanted her to stop, even begged and pleaded, she wouldn't. I would eventually get physically excited by that. How could I not? But that excitement made me want to vomit. I knew in my heart she shouldn't touch me like that, but I could hardly tell my father, could I?

When he was away, she made me sleep with her naked and hold me to her, and I felt sick in my stomach every night as bedtime neared. It was horrible, though I tried to hide that from her. At least she didn't hurt me—far from it, she wanted to 'make me feel better.' She did often find fault with me, but a stare from her would be all it took to make me scared. My worry was, what if she told Dad when he got back? Life was one nightmare after another, living in a permanent state of fear, loathing, or wanting to throw up. Some things happened in bed with my mother, which to this day I cannot think about and I will not write about because they were dirty things.

My father wanted to make a man of me, and he succeeded. I did become a man eventually. I plotted how I could get my revenge on him for years. He came back from a posting somewhere; he never told me where he had been or what he did in the army. We rarely spoke in a normal conversation about things like that, but he had been gone three months that time, and I had hoped he was dead.

I saw him from my bedroom window, standing alongside the cab, paying the driver with his suitcases on the ground at his feet. My insides turned to mush, and my skin became clammy with cold sweat. He always beat me on his first day back, always, and I was sure that day would be no exception unless I got him first.

I was sixteen, very nearly seventeen, and had filled out a lot while he had been away. I was on holiday from *school and no longer skinny but tall and more muscular. I had grown into a younger version of him. I knew the beatings needed to end that day, or I would die trying to make them stop. I was beyond caring either way. I didn't care about dying at that point; living had always been the problem for me. Just getting through each day, trying not to be bullied at school or beaten or coddled at home, it all seemed like differing levels of the same misery. While growing up, my thoughts were frequently filled with death and suicide. I drew pictures of it, wrote awful poems, and imagined horrible ways of ending my own life or his. A comforting thought was always that my mother and father would suffer knowing it was they who had caused my death, but then the fear of not succeeding crept in, and I was again powerless to do anything about it.*

On that fateful day when he returned, I became very calm, calmer than I would have thought possible. I raced out to the shed and grabbed his bamboo garden stake, which felt thick and comforting in my hand. My mother was out—I didn't know where. I ran back into the house and waited inside the back door, ready to do or die, the cane held at the ready like a Samurai sword.

When he walked into the kitchen, I hit him across his face with all the strength I possessed. I will never forget the sound of the swish through the air, the whack as his weapon of choice made full contact with his skin and bone, and the startled look as it hit. I watched, amazed as blood squirted out from his broken nose in one direction, and his briefcase flew across the room in another, to crash into the china cabinet and smash two of Mum's cups. Without a pause, I laid into him, time and time again, not saying a word or giving him time to do or say anything. If he held his arms up to protect his head, I hit him across the stomach, groin, or sides. With one blow, I'm sure I heard a rib crack, then when he lowered his arms, I hit him across the face again. He ran at me, but I saw him coming, and I braced myself and kicked him as hard as I could between his legs. He went down in a screaming crumpled heap, and I stood over him, hitting as hard and as fast as I could with the cane until my arms tired and my adrenaline depleted. This was no whipping or caning as he had administered to me over the years. This was a beating, and I felt wonderful. Eventually, I stopped and looked down at him on the floor, my nemesis defeated at last. I was panting, out of breath, as he cowered in a fetal position, scared and crying, bloody and hurt. I cannot describe how wonderful it was finally to hurt him back.

For the first time in my life, I knew happiness, even joy. I knew I had at last won. My father was beaten. My tormentor lay crying and bleeding on the kitchen floor. The sight of his blood was thrilling and made me want to make him bleed even more, lots more. I think that if I had a knife in my hand, I would have stabbed him a thousand times, but I could hardly stand from weakness after the adrenalin rush. I was completely out of breath and realized I had to leave, so he did not see I was almost at the point of collapse.

I threw the cane on top of him, left the house, and didn't return until well after dark. I caught a bus and went to the beach where I walked on the sand and swam in my underpants because I hadn't taken a towel or bathers. My heart soared more than I knew possible. That was the first day of the rest of my life, a corny saying I had seen on a poster once and had never known what it meant until that day.

My father and I never spoke again, but he also never tried to hit me. Even when he was dying of cancer much later, I wouldn't visit him in hospital. For me, he had died years before in the kitchen. My mother also changed that day. She became distant and treated me very warily as if she was scared of me. I remember how angry that made me with her. How dare she be scared of me? It only made me hate her all the more. She was so frightened, she never took me to her bed again, so it was a double victory for me.

Often days would go by without a word being spoken to me or to each other in my presence. Meals would be served and eaten silently, the only noise coming from the TV in the corner. I think they were the happiest times of my life. I came and went as I pleased, my clothes were always cleaned for me, and my meals were prepared. Life was fantastic. Violence had made it that way, and I had learned that violence was good if you were the giver and not the receiver.

One evening I was walking home past a lane, and a dog suddenly growled at me and made me jump. Without a thought, I kicked it in the side and loved the sound of bones breaking and of it yelping. I kicked it some more and enjoyed that experience too. This was the new me. I was never going to be scared of anything ever again.

A few days later, with my new confidence, bravado, and newfound love of inflicting pain, I went to the local skate park. I knew this was where the bullies who had made my time at school a misery hung out. They went there to smoke cigarettes and try to get girls to do dirty things with them. I said nothing as I approached, and they didn't notice I was there until I was on top of them.

I had been smart enough to come from the direction of the summer evening sun.

Frankie, or Devo as he liked to be called, was sitting with his back to a gum tree. He had just taken a drag from a smoke when I kicked him in the side of his head as hard as I could. This knocked him flat on his side. Blood squirted from a badly gashed lip and cuts on the inside of his mouth from the teeth I had broken. I had been sure to wear my thick, sensible school shoes so I could cause as much damage as possible. Instantly his mates were on me, and I fought hard. I was hurting them as much as I could, kicking, punching, and even biting like an animal. I had tasted blood and yearned to make them bleed more.

I'd like to say I beat up all of them and lived happily ever after, but it was not to be so. Those guys were tough, and I got seven kinds of shit kicked out of me. Over the years, I had grown used to being punched by my father, so the pain didn't stop me. It just made me fight harder. There were seven or eight of them hitting me, and had it not been for some adults who were walking nearby who came to my rescue, I may well have been killed by them.

I remember being held down, my arms pinned, and Devo kicking me in the balls as his damaged mouth bled all over me while others punched me in the face. That was the worst, and I was all done by then. I remember he kicked me three times, and on the last kick, I passed into the darkness.

I woke up in the hospital—an ambulance had been called by my saviors—and I slowly recovered over the next few days. My father didn't visit, and I was glad about that because I had lost a fight and knew he would have disapproved. Sickeningly, it seemed I still wanted his approval. My mother came every day and took me home in her car when they let me out. My nose had been broken, I had six stitches above my eye, and I couldn't sit still for weeks. It seemed to take forever to feel normal again. But for all of that, I liked what I had done and spent nearly all of my spare time planning how to get them back. It had taken eight of them to defeat me, and I lay awake at night plotting how I would get each of them alone and kick them in the balls twenty or thirty times.

Those guys never bullied me again. There were easier pickings at school, and they now knew I would fight back regardless of the odds or how much they hurt me. In the melee, I had hurt some of them too, which they were not used to. It was much better for all of us from that day on. I ignored them, and they ignored me. My plans of revenge stayed as just plans.

The police interviewed me, but I told them I didn't know who my attackers were. I don't think they believed me, but I also think they didn't really care either. A skateboard park fight—they had better things to do. Life went on.

I had a part-time job at the local hardware store, so I never had to ask for money from my parents. Clothes were bought for me, by my mother, without me asking. When I finished school and graduated dux, my parents didn't even attend the graduation. After the ceremony, I went home and applied to join the army. While waiting for the interviews and physical testing, I started working in the hardware shop full-time.

I never really stopped to think about why I joined the army. Was it a last-ditch effort to win my father's approval? I don't know. I never told him I was joining up, but maybe deep down, I still yearned for him to say he was proud of me. But of course, he never did.

I breezed through army interviews and physicals. My family history and school results also served me well, and when I was accepted, I still didn't tell my parents. When induction day came, I packed my bags without a word and left home for Kapooka Army Base. I never returned to the house where I had endured so much misery.

When my mother contacted me two years later to tell me my father had stage-four lung cancer, I felt nothing for either of them. I could have gotten leave to visit him, but I didn't want to. I went on with my life, and he died. I didn't feel the need to go to the funeral either. I hated him as much that day as I ever had. I also think he didn't expect or want me to visit him. He wouldn't have wanted me seeing him frail, weak, and dying. He was always too proud for that.

By then, I had moved on, and the life I was living was good. I had finally found a home, some happiness, and a purpose where violence was a way of life. In fact, the training was all about killing in various ways.

Chapter Four

Dillon stood before the team, Mike Knowles by his side, as he outlined tasks for everyone. He formed them into ten teams. One victim was allocated per team. They were to go back and look for any evidence of a possible stalker for up to four weeks prior to each murder. Armed with the most recent CCTV pictures, they were to re-interview everyone connected in hopes someone remembered something. Of course, the passage of time in some of the murders made that difficult, but they were hopeful. Any and all CCTV was to be reviewed, going back as far as possible to find any sighting of the Ripper undisguised.

They had exhausted all avenues at Heather De Santo's apartment and her workplace. Her colleagues checked out fine, and she had no workplace affairs or intimacy that anyone was willing to admit to. Everyone described her as a nice person who wouldn't hurt a fly. She'd enjoyed being single and her free and easy lifestyle.

They now knew she met her killer earlier that night at a Northbridge bar, but no one working there remembered any specifics about the man she had been with other than the fact he was a big guy with brown hair and a mustache. The bar had been busy, and no one could remember anything that made Heather or her date stand out from the crowd. It seemed they left together, but no one could agree on a time, and driven to her apartment. The car had been examined by forensics, but there were no usable prints found. The exterior passenger-side door handles had been wiped clean, and her killer had been careful not to touch anything inside. He must have rubbed the inside handle on exiting.

The search of her personal belongings, computer, and apartment didn't throw up any information as to how she knew her killer or where she had made contact with him. Dillon's best guess was they had met, as far as De Santo was concerned, randomly, and a first date arranged. None of her friends, family, or work colleagues knew anything about a new man in her life, but Heather seemed to keep very much to herself normally. She didn't use a diary other than a work-related one. Consequently, the task force had no other leads.

It had been slow going, as they knew it would be, just like the other murders previous. But with the pictures they now had of the man in the uniform, Dillon impressed upon them that this was the break they had been hoping for and that they could use it to build up a better description of the offender if they could find corroboration. They knew the murderer used disguises to hide his appearance, but they still had no idea how he chose his victims or why other than the remarkable resemblance they had to each other. With more witnesses to work with, the artist could remove the items of disguise, and hopefully, they could get a picture of the man they could go to the press with. When they had that, Dillon told them an arrest wouldn't be too far away with a media blitz he was planning. As it was, the papers and TV were screaming for more information from them on a daily basis.

Four of the women had been married, two in relationships, and three had children. Three of the singles had been listed on Internet dating sites, but the list of men they met had been interviewed with nothing to show for it. The women's jobs ranged from nurse, administrative assistant, librarian, shop assistant, process worker, and one was a fly-in, fly-out cleaner at a mining camp.

The department knew these weren't random killings—there was a reason, as far as the killer was concerned. The psychological profile they had built told them that victim selection was important to the offender because of some previous hurt, either real or imagined. Clearly, the resemblances between all victims showed a commonality, but they knew there had to be some trigger other than the fact they were all short, blonde, and very attractive.

Mike Knowles was working on the possible military angle and had requested a list of all discharged soldiers going back five years in Western Australia. He was focused in particular on anyone who had shown violence toward women or who had psychiatric problems, causing his discharge. Perhaps, they hypothesized, he had suffered post-traumatic stress disorder. This was going to be some list in itself. However, that too helped everyone on the team feel they were making progress and that the net was tightening ever so slightly.

It was imperative this information be kept from the press until they had more information to run with, and Dillon threatened everyone with a fate worse than death if any of the current investigative avenues were leaked to the media. He was aware of the political fallout, and he did not want to put the army offside by announcing something that could be a dead end. The army was touchy about returned soldiers with stress— understandably so—so it was very much a case of treading warily until they had more information.

"Why are you all still here? Get on with it," he yelled, then turned and left them to it.

On the one hand, Dillon was pleased they were getting somewhere and now had a direction. On the other, he was a very unhappy man on the home front. Kathy had called and insisted he be home on time that night as she had something she had to discuss with him. He feared the worst, worried she knew about his dalliances with Marci or had gotten fed up with the hours he worked, the lifestyle he led, or that she had met someone else and wanted a divorce. He felt miserable and dreaded going home.

****

An American Navy Seal who I had discussed revenge with in a bar in Iraq once told me about the Native American Indian theory that went something along the lines of if you sat by a river long enough, your enemy would come by in a canoe and you could shoot arrows at him. I believed this to be true, not literally, but if you were searching for someone and you waited long enough in a central place, sooner or later, they would come.

I was sitting at an outside table of a Hay Street Mall café at twelve-fifteen when I spotted Amanda, and this time I was absolutely positive it was her. I had stayed a few days inside my apartment, too sick to leave. The headaches had become unbearable after I'd discovered I had killed the wrong woman again, and the voices were relentless. But after two days in my dark bedroom, hardly eating, drinking water by the bucket, and consuming various over-the-counter painkillers, I'd recovered to the point that I could function again.

I was getting worse, and I knew it. The headaches were coming more frequently and more severely. The doctors had warned me they would, but I did not want to go back in case they didn't let me out again. If it was going to be the death of me, fine. Death didn't offer any fear or mystery to me, as I had seen plenty of it. When I died, it would be on my terms, and I still had a mission to complete.

Experience told me that when the pain had eased to a dull roar between my ears, I would be starving. So, that morning, feeling better again, I decided to venture into the city and catch an afternoon movie. *American Sniper* had just been released, and I wanted to see it. I stopped for lunch at a café near the theater and had just finished my chicken with salad tortilla wrap when Amanda hurried by.

She was across the road, so she didn't see me, and even with a lot of people between us, I knew it was her. There was not one iota of doubt in my mind. At once, I was elated, angry, and ice cold. I saw everything, just as I had been trained, almost in slow motion. She was wearing washed-out jeans with fashionable worn-through holes in them, a white polo shirt, and in the sunlight, I could make out the darker shade of a red or purple bra she wore beneath. White trainers, fashionable sunglasses, and an expensive-looking bag with shoulder strap completed the picture. She looked fantastic. Even after everything she had done to me, I still yearned for her with every fiber of my being. But my need to kill her was stronger.

She wore her long blonde hair tied in a ponytail, and momentarily I was transported back to a time long ago. The cold, wet night in Sydney, at the house she had shared with two other girls where we had made love for the first time. Her hair had been tied back then too.

I stood immediately. My thigh connected with the table, and my black coffee spilled everywhere. I walked away, grabbed my laptop bag from the seat alongside me, and threw the carry bag strap over my shoulder, never taking my eyes off her. I stayed on my side of the road, pulled my sunglasses down, and tugged my cap lower over my face. I wasn't wearing a disguise and had to be careful she didn't turn and recognize me. I was keeping pace with her but slightly behind her diagonally.

Although she stopped and looked into the odd window or two, she walked with a purpose, and while I followed, I thought about the dilemma I faced. If she had driven into the city, she would have parked in a parking station, and when I shadowed her back there, she would drive away, and I would be stranded. It was beyond the realms of freak happenstance that she would be in the same car park I was. If she had arrived by bus or train, how could I escape her seeing me without a disguise and still follow her home? Worse, if she was meeting someone and she left with them, I would lose her, possibly forever. I was out of my comfort zone. Things were moving beyond my control too quickly. I didn't like it, but I had no choice other than to watch and wait to see what developed. Meanwhile, the voices that had been quiet started chanting in my head, *kill her, kill her,* over and over again. I decided then that if I had to, I would kill her in public and worry about the consequences afterward.

The headache of the last three days suddenly was gone. My thoughts were clear. Save for the voices, I began to think about plans for each eventuality, all the while walking along, watching her incredible body from behind, remembering when it had been mine to touch and hold.

Amanda suddenly turned and entered a building. I glanced up at the sign, *Sebastian's Restaurant*. She was meeting someone for lunch. Obviously, it would be a man. My anger with her went up another notch. Maybe I would just walk in and kill them both where they sat. I wished I had a gun with me to make it easier. I crossed the road, stopped at the window edge, and casually looked at my watch. I glanced around so that if anyone had noticed me, it would look as if I were waiting to meet a lunch date myself.

My curiosity grew. I had to know who she was with. I turned and cupped my hands over my eyes to shield them from the sun and looked inside through the window, searching for her. There she was, her back to me, at a table with three other women. Immediately my pulse rate slowed. There was no lover present. It seemed they would be there a while, so I looked around for somewhere to wait with a vantage point. Across the road was an Internet café with a vacant computer by the window—perfect.

I crossed the road and entered the café. I changed a twenty for coins, fed the slot, fired up the screen, and opened the local newspaper's online site. I then settled back in my seat to pretend to read it. I was kept company by a couple that looked like backpacker tourists and a well-dressed middle-aged woman sending an email. I spent most of the time looking out the window, waiting,

41

calming the voices, knowing that she would be dead soon, one way or another. I had finally found her, and she and I would soon both be at peace.

I reached into my laptop bag's front section and took out the knife, making sure I wasn't being observed, and placed it in my jacket pocket. I tucked the bag under the chair, hoping that no one would wonder why I was in an Internet café if I had a laptop with me. If I had to follow her back to the parking station, I would just kill her there. Upon reflection, I realized that Amanda would never take public transport. That just wasn't her. If I could manage to get her at knifepoint into her own car, we could go somewhere quiet, and I could take my time. If it looked like that wouldn't work, then I would do it right there, quick, and get away before anyone could do anything. I had no compunction about killing any well-meaning bystander who tried to interfere. She was going to die. There was nothing surer in my mind.

Time dragged by, and I kept feeding the slot coins to maintain my spot on the computer by the window. I watched and waited and hoped that her last meal was at least a good one. I smiled to myself at the thought.

****

With time on my hands, I allowed my mind to wander while keeping watch and drift back in time. I thought back to our first meeting at a bar on the North Shore in Sydney. I had been on leave with two other guys from my unit. They had been intent on trying to pick up every good-looking woman they came across—and some not so good-looking—and failing miserably. I had been content to tag along, trying to fit in and just enjoy being on leave with a good bourbon buzz.

At that time in my life, I had never had a girlfriend.

The very thought frightened me. At school, I had been too busy studying. Then the army. Well, I supposed it was fair to say I lacked any sort of self-confidence and found women very scary. I tended to think of women as I thought of my mother, and that made me want to vomit. I swallowed bile and let my mind drift back in time.

I could kill people, as I had been trained to do, without any qualms, but the thought of being alone with a woman terrified me. The exception to this was, of course, the prostitutes I had used from time to time. That was different. There was no emotional commitment. It was purely physical, and they were just there to fulfill a need. I delighted in hurting some of them in minor ways and had sex brutally with them, which made me feel better about the whole thing. With hookers, comparisons of my mother did not intrude too much, and slapping them around a bit would usually make the residual thoughts disappear. They always seemed to be fine with it, especially when I paid them more than the going rate, which only really increased my loathing of them and reinforced my ideas that women were just sex objects to be used and abused.

Anyway, there we were, three sheets to the wind on beer and bourbon, in a bar with decent music playing. We were hard and extremely fit, with two of us on the prowl for a pickup. I watched as Johnno took off across the bar to try his luck with a table full of women out for a drink after work, shaking my head. After five minutes or so, he beckoned us over. Sam took off faster than a rifle shot, so what else could I do but follow? I would have looked stupid staying back at the bar by myself. I had spent all of my time in the army with my mates trying to fit in, mimicking whatever behavior passed as normal to enable me to feel some sort of acceptance. The reality was that I was wishing in my head I had stayed back at the hotel and played computer games or watched a gory movie instead of being out bar-hopping.

One of the girls patted an empty seat by her side, looking straight at me. She was stunningly beautiful, gorgeous face, long silky blonde hair, and the deepest blue eyes you could just fall into. Even though she was sitting down, I could see that her body was to die for. I towered over her, and as I went around to her side of the table to sit, I realized just how small and diminutive, yet so perfectly proportioned she was. I had seen lots of good-looking women in my time—they seemed to be everywhere—but this was the first time one had shown the remotest interest in me. Next to her, I felt like a lumbering, clumsy oaf.

She wore a shiny bright yellow shirt. The bar had some ultraviolet lights, and the buttons seemed like torches in the purple light, forcing me to look at her breasts. The shirt was happily stretched, and the space between each fastening gaped open. She was, without a doubt, the most beautiful woman I had ever met. To say I was instantly petrified would be the understatement of the year. I had absolutely no idea what to say or what was protocol for this sort of situation. I had never experienced it before.

She smiled and held out her hand to me, saying, "Hi, I'm Amanda," and all I could do was dumbly stare back at her hand until the laughter of my two mates woke me from my hypnotized state, and I could feel myself turning beet red.

"I think the sarge"—I had attained the rank of sergeant by then—"is in love," Johnno yelled above the *chatter and background noise of the bar. I could have punched him.*

"It's okay, I won't bite," said this angel in disguise, and I took her small, warm hand in mine. Zap—the surge of electricity as we touched rocked me to my very core, and I knew at that moment that this was a woman I had to get to know, if only I knew how to make that happen. She squeezed back as I gripped her hand and smiled at me with a hint of mischief, a smile of pure joy at my embarrassment. As our eyes locked, she winked at me and shook her head, so her long blonde locks shimmered in the colored light.

"I'm Tank. I mean, sorry, I'm Paul," I muttered back, realizing how completely stupid I looked and sounded. She would think I was pathetic, I knew with a sinking heart, and who could blame her?

"Tank?" she asked but gave me the biggest, most incredible smile, and I swear in that one moment, I blushed three shades redder. My God, I was making a mess of this, but to my incredible relief, Sam came to my rescue, joined in, and helped me out.

"That's his nickname, Mandy—can we call you Mandy?"

She ignored the question and just stared at me. "Why would anyone call such a handsome man Tank?"

Oh my God, that question made me turn to mush, and sweat broke out on my forehead. Surely she was toying with me. What could such a woman ever see in someone like me?

Johnno now joined in the fun at my expense. "Well, Mandy, it's top-secret, we could tell you, but we would have to kill you to avoid being thrown in jail." He laughed loudly at his own joke, as he often did. Sam and

I didn't. We had heard them all numerous times before.

Sam leaned in close to Amanda. I never called her Mandy, ever. Amanda is such a beautiful, even musical name. He said, "Mandy, we call this big lug Tank because he is a natural-born hero. He took out a tank single-handed in the desert while our group was trapped and under heavy fire. He would never tell you himself, as he barely talks at all, but he saved quite a few lives that day, including us two muppets because we were pinned down. They even gave him a medal. He can fight Arabs by the bucket, but he's scared stupid of a beautiful woman like you."

That set off the whole table laughing, everyone except Amanda and me. She looked at me with something like awe, and I stared back at her, wanting to run away at a million miles an hour, yet at the same time, all I wanted was to reach out and touch her some more.

I glanced down, and we were still holding hands, neither of us seeming to want to let go.

She beamed such a golden smile at me and said, "I'm very happy to meet you, Tank, I mean, Paul." She still didn't let go, and I couldn't have, even if I tried.

She lowered our hands onto her thigh, and I reveled in the feel of her warm skin under her black skirt and again felt a jolt of lightning from my hand all the way to my toes.

So that was how we met, and it was perfect. We drank, we laughed, and she told me about her dead-end job as a travel agent for a company she couldn't stand. She wanted to go traveling herself instead of sending other people, and she was so beautiful to me that I believed she deserved to see exotic places.

I told her about the army and how we only had two

weeks' leave before heading back. She wanted to know about Afghanistan and seemed to hang on my every word. She listened intently, relishing talk about the army lifestyle. What I considered to be my normal everyday life, she found to be the most interesting thing she had ever heard. Time and time again, I found myself wondering if this was real or a dream. Never before had any woman shown interest in me or what I did, but that said, I had never really been in a situation to meet such a woman.

We stayed at that bar, grabbing some snacks to eat, and when the band started up, Amanda wanted to dance. As small as she was and as big I was, she dragged me up to the dance floor. She did not give a fig for my protestations that I could not, and had never, danced before in my life. My resistance made no difference. Amanda wanted to dance with me, and Amanda was going to get what she wanted. That became a way of life for us, her getting what she wanted. I could never deny her anything.

Up until we danced, she had been sitting down the whole time. Her pencil skirt hugged her tightly, and even in three-inch heels, she barely came up to my chest. Her long blonde hair flew all around her as she moved, while I shuffled my feet and tried to make it look as if I could dance, but I felt like a complete clod. I was sure my mates were laughing at me, but when I glanced back, they weren't. Sam was kissing one of Amanda's friends, and Johnno seemed as if he was asleep in the chair.

Between songs, she moved close to me and snuggled in, and I put my arm around her, both wanting the next song to start to hide my embarrassment but at the same time not wanting to take my hand off her. I loved the feeling of being so close to her. Her hair smelled wonderfully clean, and it was the first time I had ever noticed a woman's perfume. I have no idea what it was called, but I never forgot that smell.

She stared up at me, moved even closer, and murmured, "It's okay, Tank, you won't break me. You can touch me." Her smile was radiant.

The buttons on her shirt were under stress when she danced, threatening to pop off as she moved to the music. I swear I had never seen anyone so unbelievably beautiful, so sexy, and I knew I never would again. When she shimmied side-on to me, through the gaping holes, I could clearly see the white bra trying to contain her breasts. She saw me looking and laughed all the more. Amanda always saw the fun side of everything that happened in life. She moved in close and whispered, "Do you like them?" She laughed, moved away again, and her eyes sparkled, holding a promise of things to come.

The drinks flowed, the band played on, and we became closer, touching more. The delightful tease of promises made continued, and with it, I felt myself slowly growing more confident with her. I was completely besotted. In fact, I was stone cold in love.

* * * *

My daydreams in the Internet café were suddenly interrupted by a white people mover taxi that pulled up across the road and tooted its horn. The next instant, the restaurant door opened, and the four women walked out, laughing and chatting without a care in the world, and climbed into it. Before I could do anything, the cab pulled away from the curb.

Fuck, fuck, fuck. I raged inside my head. I jumped up and raced outside to see the taxi's plate just before a car turning left from the street behind obscured it completely. Fate was kind. I got it and committed it to memory. It was a black-and-white cab. All I had to do was track down the driver and make him tell me where he'd taken the women. I was mad as hell at my rotten luck but calmed down, breathing deeply and slowly. My headache reared up again, and the voices were screaming incessantly at me. I would get her. I had to get her. It was just a matter of when.

Chapter Five

Journal Excerpt #2, The Army
Kapooka Army Base, New South Wales

I admit that I lied about my childhood and early family life for my entry interviews and evaluations to join the army. Not because I thought that I was insane because of it, but simply because I felt at the time it was better to tell them what I believed they wanted to hear. In the back of my mind was the feeling that there was nothing to be gained by maligning my father to them. He was, after all, a serving colonel. Yes, by anyone's definition, my childhood was bad. I knew that, and in my heart, I also knew that what my parents did was wrong, but I'd escaped unscathed. Part of me thinks that tough love from them made me stronger and more determined to win at all costs, and that attitude was one that the army interviewers liked a lot.

When I had lain in my bed at night as a child, I had imagined what a good childhood was and pretended my parents loved me. When the psyches had asked me all those questions about my upbringing, it had seemed natural to tell the fantasy life rather than the real one. It really had been too easy to fool them, and if you want my opinion, the army was short of men and women wanting to sign up. Unless you had Lunatic tattooed across your forehead, they weren't really interested in declining physically fit applicants. There was little point in knocking back recruits. There were so few of us mad enough to want to join up. We were in short supply, or so it seemed to me.

Plus, let's not forget that my father, bastard that he had always been to me, was someone to be reckoned with in the army. No one in their right minds would want the job of telling him his son wasn't fit for active duty. Colonel Jack Williams' temper was apparently legendary.

I can't tell you how many times I had to grit my teeth and smile when someone said, "Oh, you must be Jack Williams' boy." As if I were his possession, or minion, which in many respects I suppose I was up to the time I had taken the cane to him. I wanted, of course, to punch them till they bled. Sometimes I found myself imagining cutting them open with a bayonet or firing a gun into them at point-blank range over and over again, but training, discipline, and an indescribable need to stay in the army won out. I had learned to just smile back and say, "Yes, sir," then make up a whole load of bullshit about how well he was doing, what a great dad he was, and what a fantastic family I had been fortunate to grow up in. God, it made me sick, but I had been determined to not only get on well with everyone I could in the army but be the best recruit they'd ever had. In some ways, I think I succeeded in that.

One memorable occasion was when an officer who had been stationed with my father in Vietnam not only got me crapping on about how wonderful life was with Dad, but then he asked me with a nudge and a wink how my sexy mother was. I very nearly threw up all over him. Somehow, though, I kept it down and said she was doing just fine, thank you, sir, and smiled back. I had learned a lot back then about how to smile to hide my feelings. I even practiced in front of the mirror to make sure I looked as if I meant it. I had perfected the smile because I realized by watching everyone around me that was what people who'd had a normal upbringing did. I tried to fit in and convince them I'd had one too. So, I had to perfect my smile and make it look natural. Laughing came harder for me, but I seemed to be teamed up with other misfits and eventually, even laughing became second nature, though everyone still thought of me as the strong, silent type. Although I can't say things seemed particularly 'funny' to me, but laughing was what people did, so I learned to as well.

I had grown into a big bulky lad, like my father, but had never done any exercise to get that way—that was one good thing he passed on to me, a strong physique. But now, there were exercise, training, and fitness demands that I came to love. I excelled at everything. It was as if all those years of not exercising now came out in a rush, and I reveled in pushing myself harder and harder every day.

At week eight, I had set a new record for the assault course, and when I looked at myself in the mirror after a shower, I liked what I saw. I was an imposing figure not to be messed with, sporting a crew cut hairstyle and bulging muscles, which made me feel even tougher. My fitness level had increased dramatically. I marched well, ran fast, fought hard, then they had taught me to shoot and how to kill. While I won't say I became a marksman, I shot well and rarely missed a target. Every weapon they gave me I loved, almost in a sensual way. I had found my true calling.

I know that sounds a bit sick, thinking of a weapon

in a sexual way, but lots of other army guys felt the same. I'm quite sure of that by the glint in their eyes. The army is all about killing, adapting, and surviving. We had been taught to love our rifle, care for it, and the day would come when it would look after us. A weapon was always dependable. People were not. At least they never had been in my experience.

Week eight had also seen bayonet training, and something stirred inside me as I learned to stab and kill an opponent. Though I hadn't known it then, of course, this helped me later in life, and while I loved all aspects of firing guns—'This is a weapon, this is my gun, this one is for killing, and this one's for fun,' a drill sergeant had yelled at us—the knife became my weapon of choice. There was something wonderful about being so close you could stare into someone's eyes as you slid a knife into them and watch them die. It's quiet and very personal, unlike shooting someone from a hundred meters away. Killing someone either way didn't bother me, but I preferred the more personal touch, both in combat and later on my mission too.

At that point, I hadn't killed anyone, but I had found myself thinking about it all the time, even fantasizing, you could say. One night I had happened across a stray cat when I was by myself. I had gone out at the back of the barracks to practice the assault course in the dark. I checked to make sure there was no one around, then I killed it, just to see what it felt like. To be honest, it didn't give me any pleasure, and I was disappointed at that, but neither had it made me feel guilty. It had been, after all, just a stray cat, and I probably had done it a favor, even though I took my time in ending its miserable life. That hadn't been the only animal I killed; I had found a few *more, but any feelings I got lessened over time, and I looked forward to being sent overseas where I could kill something bigger—a human being. My dreams about my first kill were regular and vivid.*

Army life meant being awake at six every morning, and I fell into bed at ten every night feeling tired, sometimes even exhausted, but so very, very good. I generally slept like a baby and flew out of bed at reveille because I was ready for whatever that day had to offer. The food was great—much better than anything my mother had served—and while sleeping four men to a room took a bit of getting used to, get used to it I had. Bunking with other guys also helped with something else I hadn't been used to; mateship. Teamwork and looking after one another had been drummed into us, and so I discovered another first; I had friends, and these friends, if needed, would die for me, and I would die for them. This then became my real family, and I felt at home, finally.

For the first time in my life, I had felt valued, respected, needed, and wanted. I had been hellbent on doing every job, task, and lesson, no matter how menial or dirty, not only well but incredibly so. We were being constantly evaluated and tested, but once again, my father had set me up for a life of evaluation. At least the army hadn't beat me with a cane if I hadn't performed. The habits of a lifetime served me. Failure in anything they had asked of me hadn't been an option. It had been unthinkable.

One Saturday night, we were given a pass to go into Wagga Wagga. This was the nearest town to the base. By then, I was in a group of six who had become mates and, not having had alcohol for weeks, we got very untidy at one of the local pubs. The single women knew the town was visited by fit men who had been locked away for weeks, and it was a very good, fun night. Though, I'd had no interest in women myself. I had perfected my smile by then, so I blended in well, but I didn't want to talk to any of the girls who were out for some fun with an army guy.

Some of the local men got upset and jealous with their girlfriends who had been chased by us and they decided they had to teach us a lesson and show their women that they were the real men. As the four of us who had remained until closing time left the pub, we were picked on in the car park by seven or eight thugs. One of them hit Mark with a beer bottle without warning, splitting his cheek open, and he went down, holding his face in his hands, screaming.

Something snapped in me. A red rage descended, and I waded into them, kicking and swinging punches. I was intent on not just hurting, but breaking bones, even killing. If I'd had a weapon, I would have used it without a thought. These were scum who had hurt a friend and member of my team. All I was able to think of was my father hitting me when I was younger. In the melee, I felt blows raining on me, but not one of them hurt until much later in the barracks when the cuts and bruises showed. Nothing could stop me as I sought to hurt the bastards who had ambushed us without warning. I admit, I enjoyed fighting them, urging them to come get me, and I fought like a caged tiger smelling blood for the first time. Each time I had made one of them hurt, it had urged me to make them bleed more.

The other two men with me hadn't slowed in fighting either, but they were more measured and controlled. Perhaps they had been fearful for their safety and not getting hurt, but I didn't care, and it was them who pulled me off one of the attackers when the others ran away or lay unconscious on the gravel. Their voices filtered through the red fog, and with them holding my arms, I stopped fighting, breathless. The bloodlust departed as quickly as it had arrived, and once the adrenaline rush faded, I was exhausted.

Looking back, it was as well they stopped me because I could have just as easily killed one or more of them. At the time, I hadn't cared, and my life could have turned out very differently. Lying in bed later that night, I thought about it and realized another valuable life lesson. If I was going to hurt someone, I had to keep control and keep the rage inside. While it's fine to enjoy inflicting pain, I thought it should be at my discretion and under my control, and I need to rein myself in. It didn't matter to me that I had hurt them. They deserved it. If I'd had a knife with me, I knew I would have used it without a thought. Although it had been early in my training, I was coming to grips with the fact that life was there to be taken, and the strong always take from the weak

We got Mark up on his feet and hurried away, anxious to avoid a police investigation. Our basic first-aid training helped us patch up one another back at the barracks. I had ripped my shirt and had a major scuff on the toe of my shoe, which meant they were useless. What I'd been wearing had been covered in blood, some mine but mostly from others, and everything had to be replaced on my next leave. We all had cuts and bruises, but nothing too serious. Mark's cut cheek hadn't needed stitching, and luckily he had avoided a fracture or concussion somehow, but the last time I saw him, he still had a scar.

The next morning at parade, the drill sergeant stopped before the four us and shook his head. I'm sure he had seen recruits return from leave battered and bruised many times before. He had barked in the guttural voice we all had known, loved, and hated, 'I hope you did the platoon proud and gave as good as you got.'

'Yes, Sergeant,' we all fired back.

He lowered his voice, but if anything, that made him sound only more menacing. 'Don't you ever turn up to my parade again looking like you've gone ten rounds with Mike Tyson, now drop and give me fifty each.' We immediately fell to the ground and frantically started our push-ups, grateful to have escaped further punishment. But, I filed away in my memory bank another life lesson. Sometimes violence was condoned, at times, even applauded.

The next time leave passes came around, we four were put on night guard duty, perhaps as much as to keep the townsfolk safe as to punish us. I shrugged and got on with it. I loved my army life, just loved it, and nothing would spoil it, least of all extra duty. For me, that was a reward.

The rest of basic training passed without anything worth reporting. Marching out parade day arrived, and I was the only one not to have family there to see it. I didn't care. I had graduated with very high results and was about to be transferred to the next stage of my life; officer and military police training.

****

Dillon reverse parked his car in the two-car garage, climbed out slowly, and pressed the close button on the remote control. He walked to the adjoining door, unlocked it, and entered the house to the sound of the radio filtering through, playing a song by one of kathy's favorite female singers. Kathy had seen her concert at the Perth Arena a few months before.

He had a heavy heart as he entered, calling out to Kathy he was home, and heard her answering back from the kitchen area, telling him where she was. Her voice was neutral, almost happy, compared to how she had spoken to him lately—was that a good thing or bad? He detoured to the bar fridge and took out a beer. He opened the bottle and flipped the lid off into the bin below the opener, which was mounted on the end of the bar.

"Hey, babe," he said as he sat on a stool at the breakfast bar, placing his Phone and keys on the counter as he did. "How was your day?"

Kathy turned and smiled thinly. *Smiling?* he silently questioned, and Dillon noticed how she was dressed. She wore a nice top and skirt rather than the tee and track pants she usually had on. Kathy liked to be comfortable around the house, yet she wasn't dressed to go out. Even though she didn't have makeup on, she looked nice. This made Dillon even more worried. Maybe she was leaving him tonight and had worn clothes for the occasion.

"Mine was all right. How was yours?" Dillon felt close to freaking out. This was not like her at all. She spoke to him the way she had back when they had been happy. Dillon, like a lot of police officers, rarely spoke in detail of his job, preferring to leave his stresses and strains at work. Kathy was well aware of that, so her asking seemed to be more from nerves than a genuine interest in his day.

"Same old, same old," he replied then sipped from his bottle. Her next comment nearly floored him.

"If you feel up to it, I thought we might go out for dinner, and if you don't feel up to it, order pizza in. Nothing fancy, just a steak at the local pub would be fine. We haven't been out in quite a while, just the two of us."

Dillon looked more closely at Kathy's face. Her eyes seemed milky. *Has she been crying?* he asked himself. "You're right, hon. We haven't been out for a long time. It's a great idea. I'll get showered and changed, and we can go when I finish this beer if you like?" He paused but decided he had to know, so asked, "Is everything okay, love? What was it you wanted to talk to me about?" He sat back, sipping slowly as he waited for the rockets to rain down, cannon fire to shred him to bits, and Hurricane Kathy to blow away the debris.

She moved from in front of the sink and approached him, still on her side of the breakfast bar. She put her elbows on the top, bowed at the waist, took his left hand in her right, and said, "I owe you an apology, a very, very big one, Dillo." Dillo was her pet name for him, a blast from the much happier past. "I know I haven't been very nice to live with lately. I don't know why you've put up with me. I do love you." Two tears trickled from her eyes and down her cheeks.

Now he was petrified, on several fronts all at once. She hadn't told him she loved him in years, apart from on his birthday or in a Christmas card, where it would be written. If he told her first, she would reply with an obligatory "I love you, too." Secondly, she hadn't used her pet name for him for a very long time. Thirdly, and way more important than the other two, Kathy *never, ever* apologized. It was impossible for Kathy to be wrong about anything. A true Aries, he had been told, not that he believed in astrology. Even if in a debate when she was proved to be wrong, she would simply change the subject and move on rather than say sorry. But now she was apologizing?

"I love you too, babe. What's wrong?" He squeezed her hand in his and waited.

The dam burst, and out it came in a torrent along with more tears. "I know I haven't been myself, but I couldn't stop it. I've not been sleeping. I get hot flushes all the time, then I'm cold like I have a fever. I'm irritable over nothing, and it seemed like everything you said or did was wrong. I took everything out on you, Dillon, and I'm so sorry." She paused and sobbed. He waited for more, still not daring to say the wrong thing. This was a side of his wife that was new to him, and he was stunned to witness it.

"So, a few days ago, I went to the doctors, and I got the results of the blood tests. I've started early menopause." With that, the tears really came. Her shoulders shook, she dropped his hand from hers and buried her face.

So many emotions hit him at once—happiness she wasn't leaving, sadness she was hurting, concern for her health, guilt for Marci, and anger at himself for not being more supportive. He got up from the barstool, walked around the breakfast bar, and hugged her tightly. One hand on her short hair, the other at her side, he let her cry. He knew nothing about menopause except it was the end of a woman's ability to have children, not that they wanted any more, and he did have an awareness that it could create havoc with a woman's hormones. Like many men, the rest was a mystery to him, though a friend had once said to him that husbands deserved a medal for staying with a menopausal wife.

They didn't go out for dinner, instead ordered pizza delivery. They ate it with a bottle of red wine, and talked well into the night. Dillon listened to her problems and vowed to be a better husband for her. He also promised himself he would end things with Marci. He and Kathy rekindled feelings they hadn't explored in a long time, and they kissed and cuddled on the couch.

The doctor had prescribed medication, which would help alleviate her symptoms, but she told him that knowing what the problem was would help her understand her own faults and treat him better. He responded that he now understood her issues, and by learning from her that in some cases, it could last years, he would be more understanding and considerate. In that moment, Dillon believed that their marriage was strengthened after the long-overdue discussion, yet, it was to be the calm before the storm.

Chapter Six

I waited, pacing up and down the street for half an hour, the plan crystallizing in my head. I had to wait enough time so that wherever Amanda was going, the taxi driver had delivered her and moved on. Otherwise my plan would fail immediately if she was still in the cab. I had gone into the nearest public toilet and taken from my bag my thick-rimmed glasses and a stick-on mustache. I checked my new look in the mirror and decided that I was rather fetching, like a well-built schoolteacher. I smiled a few times to make sure it stuck properly and thought about how a teacher would speak and gesture. I worked out the whole persona of my adopted character as I left the toilet and resumed my pacing.

Eventually, I thought that enough time had passed, and I took out my phone and dialed the number for Perth Metro Taxi Cabs.

"Perth Metro, where to?" the bored voice said.

"Hi, it's John here." Hardly original, but sometimes the simplest was best. "I really hope you can help me, one of your taxis picked up my wife and three friends from Sebastian's on Hay Street a little while ago, and I desperately need to catch up with her. I've had some very bad news about her sister in Kalgoorlie, and I want to give it to her in person. They are twins, you see, and she's been in a car accident. Wouldn't you know it, she left her mobile phone at home today, so I can't call her directly."

"Sorry, sir, we can't give out drivers' information." I thought she was about to hang up, so I raced on hurriedly.

"No, no, you don't understand, I'm desperate to catch up with her, and I am happy to pay the driver a hundred-dollar bonus if he can return to Sebastian's. I came here to meet her, but she had already left. He can pick me up and take me to where she is. She will be so upset when she hears. I need to tell her personally, and I may need to get her onto a plane to Kalgoorlie before it's too late. Please, please help me. I do have the registration number of the cab if it helps?"

Would she be smart enough to see the gaping holes in my story? I must have sounded upset enough to have got through her iron-like veneer, and in the background, I could hear phones ringing constantly and guessed that she needed to move on.

"What time were they picked up, and what's the number?" she said, more softly.

"About thirty minutes ago. The number is AT 1575 WA. Thank you so much for your help. You are an angel."

"Stand by," she told me, and I spent the next few minutes nervously waiting until she came back to me.

"You're in luck. He is taking a fare into the city now, and he says he will be there in about twenty minutes," she reported.

I lifted my head and eyes to the sky, acknowledging my lucky stars. "I can't thank you enough."

"I have a sister myself, so you make sure she is okay." She then hung up on me to answer another call, I assumed.

Oh, I thought, *don't you worry. I will take very good care of her*. I laughed out loud, reflecting on how gullible some people were. For a fleeting moment, I wondered how that moronic woman would feel once she read the newspaper and realized she was to blame.

The driver arrived in the cab, and joy upon joy, he looked Arabic. *Fuck, could this get any better?* Having spent so much time in Afghanistan killing them, I hated them with a passion. I opened the door, climbed in the front seat alongside him, and put my laptop bag on the floor between my feet.

"Thanks for this, man. I appreciate your help. Where did they go?" I asked. I could almost see the cash register behind his eyes as he wondered if he could cheat me, take me the long way to make a bigger fare, plus the extra hundred I had offered.

"You said bonus?" Money, money, money, that was all they ever cared about.

I nodded eagerly. "How about two-hundred cash if you take me to where you took them?" I opened my wallet, took out two crisp green one-hundred-dollar bills, and handed them over to him. I watched with dispassionate eyes as he stuffed the cash into his shirt pocket.

"Some go to Kings Park, concert, other go house in Dianella."

I vaguely remembered some advertising for a Picnic on the Green Concert that evening. There would be thousands of people there.

"Okay, the house in Dianella, did the blonde woman go there?" But he stared blankly back, and I realized suddenly that three of the woman had been blonde. "Just take me there."

I put on my seat belt. It wouldn't do to pick up an on-the-spot fine from a passing cop. I settled back in the lumpy seat and looked ahead, my hand in my pocket, tightly gripping the handle of my knife. Adapt, adapt, adapt was the core training principle of the army. History showed us that the best planning in the world generally went south at some part of an operation. Adapting to changing circumstances was my specialty, and I had a dilemma. The taxi driver. He had to die, no question about it. If I didn't kill him, he might be able to identify me, and he was the only person to be this close to me. Then, of course, there was the camera above the rear vision mirror. My picture would be stored somewhere electronically, but who knew where the recorder was in the car? It could take me forever, especially if it was wireless technology, and while I was searching for it, I would have his dead body in the car. The pictures could be stored back at the base for all I knew.

My headache, having faded for a while, returned with a vengeance like an ebbing and flowing tide as I sat there thinking during the drive. *Damn the headaches. Why did they always get worse when I needed them the least?*

Killing the driver really would be simple. From this position, the knife could be out, blade ejected and slipped in between the ribs into his heart, causing death in seconds. It would be child's play really, but then what? I would then need time to rip the vehicle apart and find the recorder, not a terribly easy thing to do on a suburban street. For all I knew, the pictures could be transmitted via the navigation system, streaming live to a nameless server. Then I realized there was another problem. The navigation unit could store the routes taken. It was still daylight, and I could not risk the driver's body being found and spoiling the rest of my mission. I had to focus on my goal. After all, the house we were heading for probably wasn't Amanda's. I only had a one in four chance of that, which was not good odds.

I had a very bad premonition about everything, and I realized I was being rushed because of my own impatience. I knew I should try to regain control of the situation and my emotions. Every other time I'd thought I'd found her, I made time to plan and ensure that I got away afterward. Knowing I left no clues made reading of the police's ineptitude in finding me much more enjoyable. I wasn't interested in some sort of suicide mission unless it became necessary. I wanted to live to fight another day for as long as I could, though the headaches getting worse told me that mightn't be for too much longer. If what the doctor had said was true and my time left was going to be limited, so for my own peace of mind, I needed to find and kill Amanda. That would quell the voices in my head, then I could sit back and enjoy the remainder of my life. Surely there would be some time for just me and my wants and needs beyond revenge against Amanda. Perhaps I could spend some time traveling? That was ironic in itself because traveling was what Amanda had always wanted to do.

Before any of that could happen, though, I had this taxi driver problem to contend with. No matter how I looked at it, I was going to have to be patient and let him live. Damn, I so wanted to kill him. Once I had the address of the woman, I could reconnoiter the area and come back in a few days' time. It would mean that possibly the driver wouldn't even remember he had delivered the killer to the victim. Also, by then, the close-up pictures of me in the cab would have been deleted or overwritten. Patience. I needed patience.

My headache was now edging toward epic proportions, and I rubbed my temple, not that it helped. The voices were demanding to *kill, kill, kill,* and were getting louder. Soon they would be screaming. As much as I wanted to heed the voices and get the job done, I realized it wouldn't work. We were very close to Dianella.

"Brother," I said, "I don't want to worry her, so point out the house to me and go by, then drop me at the end of the road, and I will walk back." He didn't care, just nodded, and before too much longer, after a few left and right turns, he pointed at a fairly nondescript duplex house located on the driver's side of the street, number 36b McMillan Drive. Farther down the road, he pulled over. I got out without a word and watched as the luckiest cab driver in Perth pulled away from the curb. He would never know how close he had come to death that day. The knife felt warm in my hand as if it was angry it wasn't going to be used.

I turned back up the street, reached up for the blue baseball cap on my head, and pulled it down. I changed my fake spectacles for dark sunglasses, hunched my shoulders to make myself look shorter, and walked back down the quiet tree-lined street. My eyes darted everywhere as I took mental notes, looking for where I could park and use as a vantage point, but there wasn't one. As I drew in line with 36b, I saw a recent model Hyundai Elantra under the carport. It looked like a woman's car, which hopefully meant she was single and lived alone. Then I was past it and was happy to see there was no vehicle in the carport of the adjoining 36a. Now

I looked for somewhere close by where my car could be parked when I came back. I noted a house on a corner about two-hundred meters away. The side had a high corrugated fence with a weeping willow tree hanging down over the top. Perfect.

I reached into my laptop bag, took out a foil packet of painkillers, and dry swallowed four of them. Hopefully, once they kicked in, I would have some peace. I walked on, head pounding. Absentmindedly I put my right hand up, under my cap, and rubbed one of the scars beneath my hairline that was itching again. A permanent reminder of the Afghan conflict, where, on a lonely mountainside, the shrapnel from a mortar shell had hit me and brought an end to me serving my country and very nearly my life.

I intended to get to Morley Galleria Shopping Center, where I could pick up a cab among the last of the shoppers unnoticed. Then return to the city, retrieve my car, and go back to my apartment and sleep. I had some planning to do when I woke. I hoped I could get home before the pain got to the stage of affecting my eyesight, as it did on occasions.

****

The investigation continued on with its renewed vigor. Slowly the teams continued to put together the interviews and reviewed all of the CCTV footage available up to a month before each killing. The intent was to see if they could find any vision of the killer any better than they had previously. They knew to search for disguises and the general build of the attacker prior to the murders, and working with the best police artist in the department, they had come up with several possible pictures of the man. Variations of him wearing a cap and without hair, and with short hair showing, a cap being a common theme of all the sightings. These pictures had a prominent place on the working whiteboard in the squad room. The man appeared positively evil with short hair, perhaps not surprisingly, as he had slaughtered ten women.

Because they knew of this murderer's love of trying to disguise his features, it didn't mean the unadorned artist's impressions were how he looked now. But every police officer on the force had copies of the pictures and description of his height and build. Sooner or later, he would be spotted. Possibly at a random breath test or traffic stop, because since circulating the picture, all traffic cops had been instructed to increase random pullovers and study drivers' faces carefully. Yes, it was a long shot, but there was a general feeling that they were due some luck in this case soon.

Hundreds of large, short-haired men had been interviewed but with no success. The team had also gone through all of the army discharges to Perth over the last five years. Those men were being tracked down and interviewed. Again, nothing thus far, but the overall sense that something would break soon was very real and tangible. The vibe around the squad room was that it was just a matter of time.

Chapter Seven

Maria Christiansen sat up in bed suddenly and listened intently. Something had woken her, and she strained to listen to the house to see if the noise was repeated. Eventually it came again. *Tap, tap, tap, tap,* coming from what sounded like the laundry side of the house. She glanced across at the sleeping, huddled form of her husband to the alarm clock, glowing green, showing two thirty-five a.m.

Was it a faucet dripping, or perhaps something touching the window and moving in the breeze? *Tap, tap,* the noise came again. She sighed. She knew she would be unable to get back to sleep with that continuing. She realized too that Erik wouldn't wake up and that he would only ridicule her if she roused him. He was a bear when he was tired, as she had learned from their eleven years of marriage. She decided to go and check for herself what was making the noise. The last thing she wanted was their eight-year-old daughter, Heidi, who had been suffering occasional nightmares recently about sharks, of all things, to wake up. Sometimes it was even hard to get her to go to swimming lessons in the pool, and any talk about going to the beach would bring hysterics. They just hoped that, like other childhood fears, it would pass in time.

She softly got out of bed so as not to disturb Erik. Her nipples hardened automatically in the cool night air as she only ever slept wearing panties. She put on her slippers, then a black satin robe, tying it at the front as she crossed to the bedroom door. First stop was across the passage to her daughter's room.

The door was slightly ajar as she peered in and saw Heidi bathed in the moonlight filtering through the window, fast asleep. Gently she closed the door and walked softly down the passage toward the laundry, all the time listening intently for the noise to reoccur. She passed the junction where the bathroom was off to her left and moved on. Suddenly, hands encased in latex gloves grabbed her from behind in a vise-like grip. One closed over her mouth, stifling the scream in her throat, the other around her waist, and she was lifted off the floor.

My God, she panicked. He was huge and very strong. She struggled and kicked him, but no matter how much she fought, it was pointless. Her feet bounced off his shins. She made a decision that if she was to survive, she had to stay calm. She stopped fighting him and silently hoped Erik would hear something and, for once in his life, wake up.

He backed into the bathroom, holding her to his body. He closed the door quietly behind them. *He must have done it with his foot,* she thought. She suddenly realized she couldn't breathe. His massive hand was not only over her mouth, but he had her nose between his thumb and finger too. She reached up and tried to prise his fingers away so she could breathe, but the rubber gloves made it hard to get a grip. Desperately she tried to move the fingers holding her so tightly, and when that didn't work she once again tried to kick him. It was like hitting a brick wall. Her panic level increased several more notches. She couldn't breathe. He was crushing her body against his. She tried everything to break free and failed, but her movements became slow and weakened.

As things were going gray, she was aware of him leaning back against the wall, one of his legs wrapped around hers tightly to stop her from kicking out and hitting the glass shower screen. As consciousness left, her last thought was, *I'm going to die.*

When she woke up, the first thing she noticed was how cold she was, and realized that her robe had been removed and she was standing, but sagging in the shower cubicle. Her wrists had been tied securely above her head, with something very thin and tight. Her hands were numb from loss of blood. She looked up and saw what appeared to be cable ties digging deeply into her skin and securing her to the showerhead. She tried to move her feet and couldn't. She glanced down and, to her horror, saw that they had been secured with the belt from her robe and were tied to the tap. While she could stand, she did not have enough slack to move her feet forward or kick out.

Her mouth had what felt like sticky tape over it, but her nose was clear, allowing her to breathe. She thought about trying to scream but realized it wouldn't be heard, except by her attacker, and that might make things worse than they already were, if such a thing were possible. She was petrified. This was what happened in movies, not in real life. She could do nothing but wait, fearing for her daughter and husband. She frantically tried to think of what to do if and when her attacker returned.

It could have been hours, but probably wasn't, before the bathroom light came on, blinding her. Maria scrunched her eyes closed and then blinked rapidly to adjust to the light. She was close to hysteria; her heart crashed like giant surf waves on a beach. She almost passed out again as her breathing increased with terror, and the tape stopped her from getting enough air into her lungs.

When eventually her breathing returned to as normal as was possible and her eyes adjusted, she opened them to see a man sitting on the toilet seat, elbows resting on his knees, watching her from behind cold, lifeless gray eyes. He wore a red cap, and blood dripped from the once-white latex gloves. Her eyes widened, and the hulk of a man noticed where she was looking.

"Your husband tried to be a hero. He must love you very much, so I had to subdue him. He is tied up asleep now on your bed, and it's up to you whether he lives or dies. Your daughter is still asleep in her room, untouched. If you tell me exactly what I want to know, I will let you free, and you can go to them. If you don't tell me or try to lie to me, firstly, I will kill your daughter, then your husband and I will show you their bodies before I kill you. Do you understand? Nod if you do."

There was not one ounce of emotion in his words, and his eyes were dead, though horribly bloodshot. Maria knew with absolute clarity that he would do what he'd said he would. Her mind raced. What on earth could he want from her and her family? She nodded frantically, eyes wide with relief. Her first fear had been that he would rape her, but he barely seemed interested in her nakedness. She next thought that maybe this was going to turn out without them all being killed. She had no idea what he wanted from her, being a normal everyday suburban housewife, but whatever he did want, she would gladly give.

73

"Last Saturday, you had lunch with three women at Sebastian's on Hay Street in the city. I want to know about the short woman with the long blonde hair who met you there. Her name is Amanda, and she was the last to arrive." His voice was cold and distant.

Maria's eyes showed confusion, and she frantically shook her head. She experienced a surge of relief, but it was mixed with pure terror as she didn't have the faintest idea what the man was talking about.

The stranger stood and slowly walked toward her. Staring into her eyes, he whispered with a menace that chilled her to the bone. "Don't test me. If you lie to me, I will know."

He ripped the tape from her mouth, and her words poured out in a torrent. She desperately tried to assure him of her honesty, "Please, please don't hurt me or my family. I have no idea what you are talking about. I've never been to that restaurant in my life—" Her words were cut off by a vicious punch to her stomach. She couldn't breathe, and pain alone would have made her fall but for the cable ties holding her up. Blood started seeping around her wrists as they cut into her skin as she sagged. Her world turned black, but she fought to stay awake. She was the only hope for saving her family. She had to convince him she was telling the truth.

The man shook his head. "Why do you women always lie?" he asked.

Chapter Eight

Journal Excerpt #3, After Basic Training
Duntroon, Canberra

I don't know why they selected me for Officer-Armed Forces Police Investigator training at the Military College at Duntroon. Yes, I had excelled in all aspects of my basic training, including all of the classroom lessons and exams, and finished top of the intake, and I suppose that was the reason, but policing? More likely, though, it was something my father had done through his connections. Possibly to stop me from going into a branch of the army that would send me to dangerous areas. While I don't think my father gave a damn either way, I knew deep down I still wanted him to care and to be proud of me. I could imagine my mother possibly having had some input too. Her love was clingy and possessive, even sickening, but I knew that, in her way, she did love me and would want me to stay safe.

Anyway, my new family, the army, wanted to send me there, and that was good enough for me. I had become a shadow of my former self. I was incredibly fit, strong, agile, and trained in killing people in all sorts of ways—I couldn't have felt happier.

For the best part of the next year, I worked hard at my new academic studies in order to go as far as they wanted me to. I was not only studying the law, investigative technics, and forensics, but also trying to cram for a Bachelor of Science degree that I was told would help further my officer career. I had never seen myself as officer material, but I did want to fit in more than anything else and to be appreciated. For a while, I worked hard, night and day, to win the acceptance that I craved. Being the army, they didn't lighten up on the physical fitness side of things either. No matter what path you follow, you are after all, a soldier first and foremost. I was training hard on that front too. After the car park fracas, I was determined to learn to fight better, harder, and hurt more effectively without losing my cool. I wanted to be able to hurt opponents without killing them, unless I chose that. I was interested in developing the control that I had lacked back in the car park brawl.

I took up boxing, although I did tire of that after a while, and switched to martial arts. I enjoyed Tai Kwon Do as the sparring was full-on and by wearing pads, the blows could be absorbed. I grew more self-confident, knowing that if push came to shove, I could fight and fight hard and hurt anyone I chose.

The days were long, physically demanding, and mentally exhausting. For a while, it was great as I gave everything to be the best I could be at all that they wanted me to do.

It would have been six or seven months in when I began to tire of the amount of studying I was doing. Slowly I became disillusioned with it all. True, I loved the police investigation side of things and had learned a lot. Of course, unknown to me at the time, that would hold me in great stead later as I learned about evidence gathering and how to avoid leaving any.

By the time eight months came around, I was desperately looking for a way out. I wanted to get back to just being a soldier and get posted somewhere I could use my skills. I approached the commanding officer, who refused to listen. He told me I was doing well and that they were very happy with all of my results. He also pointed out, in no uncertain terms, that it was not for me to pick and choose which part of the army I wanted to be in. It wasn't a democracy, and I would bloody well do as I was bloody well told.

For the first time since joining up, I was disappointed and angry at the army, though I had been schooled enough in discipline that I learned not to show it. I thought about all he had said, long and hard, and was in two minds. Firstly, I loved my army life, and I viewed it all as my adopted family and wanted to please them. But he also reminded me of my father, and the same rebellious side of me that had welled up that day in the kitchen was there again. I accepted the reprimand and left his office cool, calm, and collected. The greatest talent I had taught myself was to keep my true feelings well-hidden. I needed a plan, and it came to me about four weeks later.

The army is a conundrum, really. On the one hand, they teach you violence and the art of killing in lots of forms, yet on the other, they demand strict obedience to those of a higher rank. Even if that higher rank is an idiot, and the army has lots of those. I suppose it's just like any other walk of life.

Our drill instructor and physical trainer was one such man. For some reason, he singled me out for a range of insults which all revolved around my father. I never wanted to think about, let alone see, my dad ever again, and once he knew that, it made it all the more fun to make me his personal whipping boy. I truly don't know *why he disliked me so much as I had never been anything other than a hard-working, diligent trainee in all of his classes. He treated me with disdain and was forever giving me more push-ups, laps around the oval, or climbing the ropes in the gym a dozen more times. All the while, he would say things like, 'You're a daddy's boy,' or 'Why not tell Daddy you're being picked on.'*

I took it all, naturally, but then the day came when I thought I could kill two birds with one stone. I coldheartedly planned my revenge and, at the same time, knew I could get out of officer training. In the middle of gym class on a Thursday midmorning, he made me do twenty more push-ups than everyone else for doing something too slowly for his liking. He screamed at me, 'Hurry up, daddy's boy!' That would turn out to be the last time he did.

"Please, sir, don't call me that." *I let the menace in my voice be heard clearly. Every other person in the gym heard me and stopped what they were doing to watch something unthinkable unfold.*

In an instant, his nose was touching mine, and a bead of sweat trickled down my temple as he screamed at the top of his voice. 'You fucking weasel, Williams. Don't you fucking tell me what I can and can't fucking do, you cunt. Who the fuck do you think you are? I own your fucking ass and if you fucking well don't like it, go and fucking tell your fucking daddy all about it, daddy's boy.'

That was when I hit him. Not my best punch, not by a long shot. I could have hurt him a lot more had I wanted to, but I didn't want to. I wanted him to hit me back, which he did right on cue. I did have the pleasure of hearing the breath get knocked out of him as my perfectly timed punch made contact with his solar plexus. He then acted on instinct and hit me back, knocking me to the floor with a very good punch to my face. Blood streamed from the broken nose he had inflicted on me. Everyone in the gym came running to pull him away from me as I writhed on the timber gym floor, acting as if I'd been hurt far worse than I had. If only he knew he had been duped into doing exactly as I wanted. Deep down inside, I was laughing at him.

After being seen to by the doctor, I was locked up but felt enormously consoled in knowing that my nemesis was in another cell down the hall. The next day, both of us were standing at attention in front of the commanding officer while the riot act was read to us. He knew exactly what had transpired by interviewing the others who had been there. He would also know all about the taunts and my asking for it to stop before the two punches were traded.

He turned to me first. "Williams, what do you have to say for yourself?"

Here I had to be careful, but I had rehearsed over and over in my head what I would say. "Sir, it's a misunderstanding, sir. I had got up from doing push-ups a little out of breath and stumbled into Sergeant Little. He put his hands up to steady me and accidentally caught my nose, and I fell backward, sir." My eyes stared straight ahead as I stood at attention, without a flicker of emotion on my face or in my voice.

"Do you think I'm stupid, Williams? Do I have Colonel Stupid on my name badge?"

"No, sir, not at all, sir, but that is what happened, sir."

I didn't waver, and I felt the sergeant's eyes boring

into me, not believing what he had heard. I had given him a lifeline, and he knew it. While I was guilty of insubordination and striking, there could be no excuse for him hitting a subordinate back. His career was over if I told the truth.

At the same time, the army, and in particular the commanding officer, didn't want the stain of a full-blown investigation and dismissal on his watch. The armed forces at that time were trying to lose their reputation for bullying and sexual assaults, which recently had been in all the newspapers.

He turned to the sergeant next to me. "Well, Sergeant?"

Now the sergeant faced a dilemma. He could side with me and save his job to torment some other poor bastard, or he could be a man and admit he'd punched me. Inside I smirked because I knew I was so much smarter than the lot of them. There was no way he would own up to it now that I had said it didn't happen in the first place.

"Sorry, sir. It happened so fast it was a bit of a blur, but I am very sorry for Williams' nose, sir."

The silence went on and on, with the colonel looking from the sergeant to me and back again as he thought about what he was going to do about this. Eventually, he cleared his throat, "Gentlemen, let's be perfectly clear about this, off the record. Is this what you are both going to say? Williams, if you've been bullied, I do not want you to lie because you think it will go better for you. You could argue provocation, and from what I've heard, you would win. I don't want you to lie because you are worried about being victimized."

"I stumbled and fell, sir," I replied.

"Little, we aren't finished. Wait outside."

He saluted, which was not returned, then turned and walked out, softly closing the door behind him.

"At ease, Williams." I relaxed and knew it was all going to be fine.

"Williams, does this have anything to do with our last conversation a few weeks ago? Is this your way of getting out of officer training?" Now I had to be very careful. He was no dummy, unlike my sergeant.

"Sir, while it is true I have come to believe this officer path is not suited to me, I do think I would be a terrible officer, sir. But I also think I am an excellent soldier, and I do want to be more front line. I would never usurp your authority and try to trick you. I have too much respect for your rank and the army, sir. I have been thinking a lot lately about volunteering for SAS training, sir." That was it. I had served, and now the ball was in his court. He smiled and sat back on the edge of his desk.

"You planned this, you bastard, didn't you? No, don't answer that. You would only insult my intelligence if you did. You place me in a very tricky situation, Williams. Little has to be punished. Today's army will not tolerate his style of bullying, but with the story you've chosen to tell, I can't do that."

"Sir, I will make a good soldier, sir. I hope a great one. This is my life and my family, but I won't ever make a good policeman or officer. In my opinion, Sergeant Little has learned his lesson. He had a problem with me and me alone for some reason because of my father. With the other men, he is good, sir, very good, even. I know better than anyone that my father is a bastard, and if Sergeant Little was ever under his command, I can

understand him wanting to take it out on me. Please, sir, let me try out for the SAS. I would be gone from Duntroon, and everything else can stay as it was."

"The SAS would chew you up and spit you out, son. Although come to think of it, maybe you are suited to them. Hmm, if you're not and they fail you, it might bring you down a peg or two and teach you a lesson that you need to learn. You think you're pretty smart, don't you? No, don't answer that."

He stood up slowly, turned to his window, and looked out at the parade ground.

"I will consider this matter. You are dismissed, Williams. Send Little in."

I saluted at his back, smiling as I did. I knew I had won. I turned and left, closing the door behind me. I looked at my attacker, the poor bastard I realized he suddenly was. He would now be a hated man on the base, and I would be a hero. I motioned my head back toward the office. The sergeant stood, and our paths crossed.

He stopped and said, "I was with your father in Darwin, and he is a cunt. But you're all right, Williams. I'm sorry I took it out on you." He held out his hand for me to shake. I looked down at it, then back up into his eyes.

"I pulled that punch, and you fell for it, hook, line, and sinker. If I ever see you again, I won't hold back." I winked and walked past him, noticing Gloria, the secretary, smiling at me. Apparently, the whole base knew the story, and she, it appeared, was on my side. Once again, my use of violence was vindicated.

Three days later saw me packing my bag. I had won, though I never doubted that I would. I was off to sunny Western Australia. The SAS barracks at Swanbourne for a try-out, just as a plain soldier again. I looked forward to what my new future would hold.

****

Nothing was going right for me. I swore and cursed that taxi driver. He had sent me to the wrong house. When this was all over, I was going to look him up, and he would be one more Arab fucker that I killed.

Remembering back to sitting in the cab as we'd driven by the house, he'd just pointed to his side of the vehicle. The two houses were next to each other with a common wall between them. I had assumed the one on the right, and he had let me think that. He could have been more specific. It was *his* fault, not mine. I imagined him laughing his head off at sending me to the house next door as he'd driven away.

Thanks to the woman, I now knew it was the one on the left. I was so angry I could have screamed and smashed up the entire house in a rage, but that was not my way. I breathed deeply. I kept calm, despite the headache and voices in my head, took stock of the situation, looked at my watch, and made a decision.

My headache again was agonizing, and I rifled their bathroom cabinet for something to take to ease it while I thought things through.

As I swallowed six generic painkiller tablets I'd found, I looked in the mirror and saw the bleeding corpse hanging from the showerhead behind me. It had taken a while, but I had finally realized the mistake and put her out of her misery by turning her to the wall and slitting her throat. Then I swung her back, pulled down her underwear, and used my knife to disfigure that part of her that she used, like all other women, to trap men and cheat on them. She wasn't Amanda, but they were all tarred with the same brush. All sluts, every last one of them.

Her husband was already dead. I had lied to her about that. I wasn't about to take chances this close to my mission endgame. Once I had made her secure with the cable ties, I had gone into their bedroom and killed him instantly. He had never really known much about it.

The daughter presented me with a problem. I was, after all, not heartless and didn't want her to wake in the morning and find both her parents dead. Even though I knew she would one day grow up to become a slut like her mother and the rest of them, she didn't deserve that. My original plan had been to blindfold her and tie her up, then once I was clear, call the police myself from a call box so she could be saved. But all of that changed when I knew the prey I had come to kill lived next door. When it all came out, I was going to make sure that taxi driver knew he was to blame for a young child losing her life— I wanted to see how he liked that.

I walked into the kid's bedroom, and with my mantra permanently in the front of my mind—*adapt, adapt, adapt*—I did what I had to do. I felt vindicated because I knew in my heart this was the driver's fault, not mine. I did it as painlessly and as quickly as possible.

I cleaned up, making sure I had left no trace of me behind with my usual efficiency. I put on my backpack and left via the back door into the rear garden. The night air was wonderful, and I took a moment to appreciate it, noting that the headache that continually dogged me these days had eased off just a touch so I could think clearly again. I picked up a chair from the outdoor setting under the patio and took it over to the side fence. I positioned it and, using it as a ladder, quietly jumped over. I landed not two meters from a big dog's kennel.

Too late to do anything else, I took the knife out of my pocket and sprung the blade, not a moment too soon. The dog, a big black thing, came out of the kennel growling and, teeth bared, leaped at my throat.

I raised my arm in front of me to give him something to bite and not only fend it off but hold it in the right position. The teeth pierced my skin in several places, a few centimeters down from my elbow as he shook his head from side to side, sinking deeper and growling. I reached under its throat, stabbed deeply, then twisted to the right. His warm dog blood flooded over my hand, and with one last whimper, he died.

Fuck, can this night get any worse? I asked myself. I froze and listened carefully for any sounds, hoping the neighbors hadn't heard. I almost giggled when I remembered the nearest ones were already dead. Nothing, I heard nothing, and I exhaled a sigh of relief.

My arm was bleeding quite badly and was very painful. Australia didn't have rabies, though of course I'd had shots for everything possible in the army anyway. But I had to attend to the blood streaming from my arm. In the moonlight, I saw that while the teeth had sunk deep and the edges of the wounds were ragged, there was no flesh missing. He hadn't ripped me apart or taken a chunk of meat out of me, thankfully, though no doubt there would be my blood and DNA left inside its mouth.

I crossed to the washing line, where towels were gently moving in the breeze, and in seconds I had cut some strips and used them to tightly bind my arm like a tourniquet. Next, I looked around and saw the coiled-up garden hose, which I turned on to a slow setting and washed my arm, then soaked the ground over which I had bled. Once satisfied, I left the hose to run over the worst-affected area so any DNA of mine would be further degraded.

After drying my arm on another towel and using it as a bandage, I told myself to get my act together and stop being a baby. Time was getting away from me. It would be light soon. Then I did a circuit of the garden, checking windows and the back door for a way in. Naturally, I couldn't buy any good luck. The house was locked up tight. For the second time that night, I went to an opaque bathroom window and took out the wide cloth sticking tape from my backpack. I peeled lengths off and stuck them over the window.

I found a rock in the garden bed and wrapped it up in another towel off the line so as to muffle the sound I was about to make. With one short sharp blow, I broke the window and then stopped to listen for anyone who might have heard me. Nothing, not a murmur, from anywhere. All was still silent. Maybe my luck was turning. I released the breath I was holding slowly and very gently pulled the tape off. Shards of glass came with it.

Soon, all the glass was removed and laid out on the ground so it resembled shiny crazy paving. I climbed in and again stopped to listen to the sounds of the house to make sure I hadn't woken anyone. I quickly did a search of all of the rooms to see how many occupants I had to contend with. Again, I thought I was finally getting some luck. The rest of the house was empty, so no more children would die that night by my hand. All I could hear was the sound of faint snoring coming from the main bedroom.

I looked at the luminous hands of my diver's watch.

It was now after four a.m., and time was running out. I gently opened the door and stepped through, noting the two shapes under the bedclothes. Of course, she had a man. *Sluts can't go without a man, can they?* The anger was slowly building in me again, and the voices started up loudly, telling me to *kill the bitch, kill the bitch.* I closed the door and went to work.

Chapter Nine

The front page of the West Australian newspaper was as sensational as always.

Ripper Slaughters Five in Two Houses on Same Night. Tally Climbs to Fifteen, Perth Living in Terror.

Below the caption was a large picture of a street. It seemed much like any other in Perth, except it had been cordoned off with police cars and blue-and-white checker tape, which had been strung between trees.

A Dianella residential street is in lockdown today as the Police Major Crime Task Force scours for clues after a wave of brutal killings in two homes located side by side. One was home to a family comprising of a husband, wife, and eight-year-old daughter. Next door belonged to a thirty-four-year-old single woman who was sleeping with an unidentified male friend at the time. She also lived with her pet dog, a crossbreed Labrador-German Shepherd.

Neighbors, family, and friends are being questioned, but reliable police sources say they have no clues or know why the Ripper has changed the type and number of victims. The senseless slaughter of an eight-year-old girl has made seasoned detectives physically ill, and this reporter witnessed officers visibly distressed at what they saw inside the houses.

Task Force Commander Detective Inspector Dillon Bradley would not comment when he arrived at the houses but then left announcing there would be a full media release later. He did assure the public that the police were closing in on a suspect and had several strong leads they were working on.

The names of the victims have not been released, but sources say the family includes a forty-year-old male Australian citizen, originally from Scandinavia, his wife of twelve years, and their daughter. Their neighbor is said to have been a single woman with a boyfriend who happened to be spending the night. Police suspect the family was killed first and included torture of the wife, before the killer moved next door. Police speculate the killer possibly suspected they had heard or seen something. The unidentified boyfriend was murdered, and the woman was also tortured before being killed and mutilated.

The unnamed woman's dog was also killed and was found in a puddle of blood, giving weight to the theory that perhaps the barking dog awoke the owners, which led to their deaths.

Only one woman fit the existing profile of previous victims, that being long blonde hair, but sources say the police believe the mutilations are the same.

Turn to page three for a full list of victims and a timeline of the Ripper's victims to date.

****

Journal Excerpt #4, SAS Training

Swanbourne Army Barracks. Perth. Western Australia

Fortunately, when I arrived in Western Australia, I had around three weeks until the SAS selection process began. I knew that fitness was a major component of the testing, so I trained nonstop. By the time day one rolled around, I intended to be fit and ready—but I was to learn that for the SAS, fitness has a whole new meaning. I trained twice a day, two to three-hour sessions, for seven days a week, in whatever weather was thrown at me.

Day after day saw me with a fully loaded backpack of around forty kilos, running, jogging, or marching in the soft sand of Swanbourne Beach. Knowing that a test protocol involved being in the ocean worried me a little. Swimming never having been something I did well, so when I wasn't on the beach working out, I was in the water. I taught myself to swim and tread water wearing my boots, fatigues, and a backpack.

I'd never enjoyed swimming as a child, and I would certainly never win races for the regiment, but I was trying to ensure I would survive the selection rounds. Treading water fully dressed and wearing boots, I'd been told unofficially, was a must and a way of cutting recruits who were not fit enough. At night, after dinner, I would go to the gym and lift weights for an hour. Not necessarily heavy weights, as I didn't want to be a weightlifter, but a very fit soldier. I did lots of reps, sometimes combining weights and cardio. I would fall into bed by ten, my muscles aching, then be up at six a.m. to do it all again.

The SAS specialized in recon missions and working behind enemy lines. They are often small strike groups against specific targets or advance observation posts to guide bombing operations and so on. Fitness was based on getting to the target by running, walking, climbing, swimming, or however was needed. Then doing the job when the operation could last hours, sometimes days, before evacuating. There was no such thing as having a rest when being chased by the enemy across hostile terrain. *You succeeded or died. Failure was not an option, and in the field, you would live or die because of your physical and mental fitness and determination to succeed.*

I was confident I would make it through the selection process as I stood on parade with nineteen other candidates, all of us determined not to drop out or be cut. We all knew that during this first phase, fifteen to twenty percent of us would be leaving.

The course was designed to whittle the numbers so that only the best remained. It was also psychologically challenging to know some of us would be cut, and we all looked at each other, wondering which of us would make it and which wouldn't. To me, they all looked tough, mean, and fit, and I steeled myself to be better.

My upbringing and insatiable desire firstly to please my father and secondly to excel at everything I did for fear of punishment got me through the barrier testing. That was a series of physical tests that were brutally demanding. When that phase was finished, our numbers were down to seventeen.

Mental toughness and dogged determination were qualities that were not just wanted but demanded by the SAS instructors and trainers. Some tests were designed to make you fail. Our responses to failure, at what point that occurred, and how hard we tried to avoid the inevitable were all tested severely. Quite simply, some exercises went on until you could not continue any longer. The applicants who failed the earliest were dropped.

We were moved to the Special Forces Training Center at Bindoon, which is located a couple of hours northeast of Perth, for the next phase, which was to last twenty-one days. The focus here was to test our physical and mental strength further, as well as endurance and our ability to keep calm in stressful situations. A lot of testing was done under simulated combat conditions with live ammunition being fired around us. Teamwork was vital, and in some cases, more so than individual performance. Sleep and food deprivation were other areas tested. We were dropped into the bush by helicopter with nothing but a compass and a knife and a deadline to be at a pickup area. That was just one of the many challenges to get through.

Injuries, mostly minor, were commonplace, as the purpose of the exercises was to simulate as much as possible true wartime conditions. One of our number fell down a craggy cliff, broke a leg, and had to be airlifted out. But only after he was found four hours after he didn't reach the evacuation point. While the army didn't want injuries, they were testing us to see if we were fit enough and mentally prepared to fight under the worst possible conditions and survive. There were no half measures. We didn't have to imagine it was harsh. It just simply was harsh. There was a tremendous sense of achievement in completing a task well. For me, nothing less than being the best was an option.

For some, it was too hard. Everyone had a breaking point and had the right to cancel out at any time, and some did. There was no shame in that. The theory was that if you weren't fit enough to last the training, you wouldn't last in battle, and would die, so we were pushed to see who would break and quit first.

Others didn't reach the standard our examiners demanded be high enough, even if they did complete the task at hand. If they decided you wouldn't survive, they would come at night, generally straight after dinner, and inform those who were leaving. Those who got the word had to pack immediately and were escorted out to be returned to their unit.

The SAS motto is: Who Dares Wins, and that was something we aspired to. We lived, breathed, and slept it. It was more than a saying; it was our way of life. We were proud in knowing that if we made it through, we would be the best of the best. I think, deep down, I believed even my father would have been proud of me if I made it to the end and was selected.

Through it all, I became tired, dirty, sweaty, sometimes cold and wet, bordering on hypothermia, undernourished, and reaching the point of complete physical and mental exhaustion. I loved it and reveled in the challenges that were set day after day. Quitting was not in my vocabulary nor the SAS's. Being pushed to extremes suited me very well; my father had ensured that was my credo.

The person I had become was nothing like the cowed, weak kid who was caned by my father or emotionally coddled by my mother. I had no family life to go back to if it didn't work out, so to me, failure was not something I even considered. The tests set for endurance where failure was inevitable saw me staggering until the point of complete collapse. I wanted, no, needed, to make it through.

At one of our officer training lessons at Duntroon, we had been taught about the battle from which the saying "Don't burn your bridges" had come. A hopelessly outnumbered general sent his men forward and set fire to the bridge behind them. They had no escape, it was fight or die, and there is no greater motivator. When I turned the cane back on my father and left home without a word for the army, I had burned my bridges. There was no way back for me, ever. I had to persist, persist and persist some more until I achieved my goal in life. Nothing else mattered to me.

On the last day, only five of us remained, and one of them quit when he was told he had been selected. While he had gotten through it all, he realized it wasn't something he wanted to do anymore. He was mentally exhausted but knew it was his choice to leave, and so we were four.

Four out of twenty seemed to be about par for the course, and that night we played hard, got drunk, and felt like we were ten feet tall and bulletproof.

Back at Swanbourne, we were welcomed by SAS soldiers of all ranks as one of the team, and we knew we were part of a very select group. While some of the other army areas thought we were elitist and big-headed, only we knew why we were that way. No one knew what we had been through to earn our badge of honor and what we would go through in war for our country. That said, personally, I never really felt patriotism.

If my job was to kill people for the army or our country's politicians, I would willingly, even gladly, do it, but I never thought about a love of my country. Later, when I did kill in Afghanistan and Iraq, it didn't bother me one little bit; they were scum anyway, so far as I was concerned. But even if they weren't, I was given a job, so I did. I killed very, very well and often, though I never kept a tally. People at times have asked me how many people I killed in the army, and truthfully I don't know, but my best guess would be fifty to sixty. I never lost a minute's sleep over any of them, even the women I shot, as I did once or twice when I thought they were carrying explosives. I never felt angry at the people I killed. It was my job to do it, and it wasn't my job to feel sad afterward, so I didn't. Who cared if there were a few less terrorists in the world? Certainly not me, that was for sure.

We were given some time off before we began the next stage. That was to be an eighteen-month reinforcement phase where we would be trained in areas such as explosives, standard and heavy weapons, hand-to-hand combat, survival, patrolling, parachuting, communications, first aid in the field, and, of course, more fitness and mental training.

I had always lacked self-confidence and belief in who I really was growing up, but now I was proud of myself. I was becoming one of the most highly trained combat soldiers in the Australian Army. I could kill in a moment, without a thought or regret, if it advanced the mission or would stop it from failing. Death was a way of life. I won't say that I looked forward to killing someone, and at that point, killing for pleasure was a long way into my future. But I knew, deep down, it would not bother me in the slightest if and when I did. Sometimes in bed at night, I looked forward to what would be my first time. After all, I reasoned, that was what all the training was for, and it would be a shame to waste it.

I trained hard, loving every moment of it. I had good friends, a sense of purpose, and people who cared for me. Life was good, and soon enough came my first overseas posting to Afghanistan. I won't talk about operations there. We were sworn to secrecy, and I have too much respect for the SAS to break that vow of secrecy now.

What I will say about that time is that if there is a hell on earth, there is a fair chance it's Afghanistan. One of the guys there said in the mess hall one night, if they gave the world an enema, Afghanistan would be where they stuck the tube. I hated the place, the people, and the job we did there, but I did do that job well.

I will say one thing about the Muslims that I noticed there. They treat women as if they are second-class citizens. My only history with women was my mother, whom I despised, and occasional hookers, who were only good for one thing anyway. On that front, I was in complete accord with their thinking, although that was where it stopped.

I learned more life lessons there that shaped my destiny and ultimately helped me see women for what they truly are, but of course, that was my LBA, as I called it, my Life Before Amanda. I met her on my first leave back to Australia, in Sydney, seven months after I had shipped out.

I'd even received a medal. That was another life lesson. If you kill lots of people, they reward you and treat you like a hero, though I didn't feel like a hero. My unit had been under attack, and all of us could have been killed. I'd picked up a rocket launcher from a dead Arab and was close enough to the tank to hit it. The best bit was hearing the screams of the occupants as they'd burned, and when they tried to flee the tank, I shot them dead.

Our group did get back to the evacuation point because I'd taken out the tank. Two had been wounded, and they were carried over three and a half kilometers to the pickup. Then, three days after we got back to base, I was told I had been recommended for a medal, which I still wear to this day on a silver chain around my neck as a reminder that killing people is a good thing.

I had three tours. Two were in Afghanistan, and one in Iraq, and each was six months of hell but broken up by some good laughs. It was the chance to use all the training we had been given. Some guys were heavily affected and didn't come back, I think, because it wasn't like a war in any way you could imagine a war to be. A battle didn't seem to advance the troops, and we didn't really know why we were there, or what was hoped to be achieved, or even how long it would last. All around, people wanted to kill us. Sometimes it seemed that even those we were supposedly protecting wanted us dead. It was fucked up, but to me, it was home, and while I wouldn't say I was delighted with it, it was my job, and I needed to do it well.

All too soon, my first leave back to Oz came around, and with it, that fateful night on the North Shore when I met Amanda, and everything changed.

Chapter Ten

The squad room was abuzz. Following the Dianella slaughter, the medical examiner had recovered blood from the dog's teeth. Before being killed, it had bitten its attacker. Now they had not only had the blood type of the suspected killer, but a DNA sample was not too far away. They were waiting for it to come back from the lab, which along with the pictures from police artists, would help lead to his capture. It was only a matter of time now, as everyone seemed sure.

The blood type was O negative, another break for them, as only around ten percent of the population had that type. It would help narrow down the list of suspects as soon as they had a list to narrow down.

They had now been able to discount all of the army soldiers who had been discharged into Western Australia. They had requested a list from the army for the rest of the country. In particular, the ones who were not O negative could now be eliminated immediately, although Dillon urged caution. It was theoretically possible that the person the dog had bitten was not the Ripper. It could have been a burglar. He made them realize they could not afford to assume anything and make a mistake that could cost more lives.

If their man had been discharged but came from a different state, then naturally, he would have been discharged back to his home state. The blood types could be vital in reducing the number of suspects but could not be the only deciding factor. The killer could have later made his way to Perth, and this thought had opened another line of investigation—had there been any other victims killed by the same M.O. in other states prior?

If such a scenario were true, what had brought him to WA, and why the slaughter of Perth women? It still didn't make much sense, but as the psychologist had told them, "It is always difficult to use logic to understand an illogical person's actions. His reasons are very valid to him, even though they make no sense whatsoever to us."

The unspoken thought many of them shared was that if the maniac was ex-British or American Army, it could take months if they ever managed to track him down at all. In particular, the number of American troops returned after service didn't bear thinking about, and those governments might not release information without at least some evidence of who they were hunting. At this time, they had none, and it was looking less likely they would get such a list if their man was anything other than Australian Army. Even the Australians were reluctant to give names and files to the police, but as it was a serial killer hunt, they were *encouraged* to help by senior government people with the promise of discretion and that the men would be treated sensitively.

Now, though, with a blood test and soon DNA identification, along with the artist's impression, it was hoped they didn't need to ask for a list of everyone who'd left overseas armies, just one man. First, though, they had to exhaust all of the Australian possibilities, which Dillon thought was still their best hope, before considering other armed forces.

They had no witnesses of the man either arriving or

leaving the area. It was as if he was a ghost. Being a quiet residential street, there was no CCTV they could call on. He had arrived at the two houses unannounced, killed five people and a dog, and left the same way, back into the shadows of a sprawling city.

They had reconstructed the course of events in Dianella, now knowing that the attacker had broken in via the bathroom window of the Christiansens'. The wife had been tied up in that bathroom, and the husband had been murdered, his throat slit so deeply his spinal cord nearly severed while he slept in his bed. There was no mutilation of the man. Their killer's problem was exclusive to women, it appeared. But it did show he would murder anyone who got in the way of his killing spree. It also showed he wasn't scared of confronting a man. He was no coward. Again, to some of the investigators, it did point to a military way of thinking. The extreme planning and execution—one could almost call it a ruthless efficiency. But still, it was just feeling and instinct. There was no proof, and they all knew it was easy to make the facts fit the theory after the event. They needed to be very careful that one lead wasn't overlooked by a zealous investigation that had gone off on a wrong tangent.

From Dillon's perspective, giving the commissioner their theory and the direction the investigators were taking had got him off Dillon's back for the time being. The team had gained more time to investigate those avenues, and if they could only match the picture and profile to a discharged army vet, it would be over.

Maria Christiansen had been tortured. Why they did not know, but she had suffered over thirty shallow stab wounds before she had had her throat cut, which had ended her life. The stab wounds were not frenzied but seemed to be measured, and their depth controlled to inflict the most pain but not permit her to bleed to death. The pain and terror she must have felt were incomprehensible, and the pathologist had never seen anything quite like it. This level of violence and sadism had never been seen before in Western Australia's past. Cloth packing tape had been placed over her mouth to minimize the noise she must surely have made in the time it took her to die. She had bitten her own tongue and lips, and there was evidence the tape had been removed then replaced. She had clearly been through an agonizing and lengthy torture by a sadistic animal, who knew how to inflict severe pain along with the mental torture she no doubt had to endure.

Eventually, she had cold-bloodedly been turned to face the wall and her throat cut from behind. The arterial spray made the shower cubical resemble an abattoir. Finally, her vagina had been brutally slashed and stabbed, just like the ten women before her. That part of the attack *was* frenzied. The torture had been controlled and deliberate and had probably been performed by someone who, while they maybe didn't have intricate medical knowledge like a doctor, certainly knew about anatomy and how to torture for effect. The fact that no major arteries or veins had been cut led the investigators to think some knowledge of the body would have been needed.

The gray-colored tape placed over the victims' mouths, which had also been used to stop the sound of smashing glass, had been torn from the roll, not bitten or cut, and was the same as had been used previously. There were no fingerprints and no DNA on it, so no help there.

It was a brand sold by all hardware stores, so could have been purchased anywhere, at any time.

The killer had washed up at the bathroom sink. The victim's blood was recovered, though no other DNA had been found at the house that could be attributed to the killer. Like all of his other kills, this man was meticulous in ensuring he left no trace.

Unlike the murders of the previous victims, the torture led police to think the killer was chasing some information or, more likely, a person. They theorized it was probably a woman with long blonde hair. That seemed most likely, according to the psychologist. This theory also answered the question, why a dark-haired woman and family, if not because he was hunting for one specific target who the killer believed was known to the victims?

While Dillon theorized it would take someone with serious mental and emotional problems to commit ten murders, he believed the murderer was looking for one particular woman. In his warped and twisted mind, he kept thinking he'd found her, but then later, when he realized it was not that woman, he began hunting all over again. Dillon considered the killer may have thought the two women could tell him where he could find the one person he was searching for. Background checks so far had shown no reason why he would have selected them for torture, and police were completely in the dark as to who his intended victim was.

The theory that made sense was that the first household was nothing more than the wrong address, and on realization, the murderer went to the house next door. Officers were combing the backgrounds of both households, but so far as they could tell, they barely knew each other. That seemed to be the modern way—no one wanted to know their neighbors anymore.

So, either the killer had gone next door because he'd felt he had been observed, or perhaps the dog had been making too much noise. But then why torture that woman too? Or, after torturing Maria, he'd deliberately gone to the other house and tortured Helena Smart. Why he would do that, they had no idea. None of the surviving neighbors reported hearing the dog bark, and that further tended to make them discount the idea that the noisy dog had woken its owner, which then prompted her death. Somewhere there had to be a link. It was their job to find it, and Dillon pushed his people to do so relentlessly.

Before the killer had left the house, he had gone into the little girl's bedroom and murdered her. That affected every single member of the team, most especially the ones who were parents themselves. Two were so distraught they'd had to receive counseling and left the squad. It appeared little Heidi hadn't suffered as her mother had.

Once *The Ripper* left the Christiansen's house over the fence, he encountered the dog and killed it very quickly and efficiently. Dillon mused over this. More than anything else, this hinted that their man was a highly trained and unafraid assassin, again, possibly army trained. Taking out a large dog quietly was no small feat. When the police dog squad was used to track down offenders, the fugitives were invariably scared, and while they may try to attack a dog to flee, it would be panicked punches and kicks. They would not calmly and casually let it bite them and slit its throat while canine teeth sank deeper and deeper. It suggested that this was a cold, calculating, highly functioning assassin who could withstand the pain of a dog bite without a pause. That it was the work of a single-minded purposeful murderer was a very sobering thought for Dillon and showed a lot about the fortitude of the murderer. If and when the police did corner this man, they would need to be very mindful of how dangerous he was. This type of killer was extremely rare, and on that basis, they had requested a profiler and assistance from the FBI behavioral unit in Quantico.

Dillon believed they had beenchasing a serial killer, a smart one, but an ordinary person who, for some reason, had started murdering a particular type of woman. The killing of the dog and the torture of the two unrelated victims suggested a high level of training and purpose, yet almost a split personality. He toyed with the idea this was two different people, but had discounted it as too far-fetched.

The lesser extent of torture and quicker murder of the second woman, Helena Smart, led investigators to believe she had been able to tell the attacker the information about what or who he was looking for far quicker than her neighbor. While Helena *was* blonde, she had short hair, unlike the earlier victims who had long hair, so investigators questioned why, if *she* was the subject of his hunt, torture her before killing her?

Dillon had had a team sifting through Helena Smart's and Maria Christiansen's backgrounds. Their friends, work colleagues, and family were being questioned at length to find all long blonde-haired women they knew. They assumed if *The Ripper* had tortured them to gain information about someone who fitted his target profile, it followed that somewhere, she must have known this person, and they needed to get to her first.

Considering the sequence of events, Dillon wondered how horrifying it must have been for Helena Smart to have woken up to witness the murder of the man sleeping alongside her. They had been naked, and evidence showed showed they had made love earlier that night. Dillon knew the couple had been seeing each other for some months and were at the *serious relationship* stage as per their Facebook statuses. Having woken up to see her lover have his throat cut, she had been secured to the headboard of the bed with cable ties. They were common a brand as sold in every hardware store, and untraceable. Her mouth had been taped, then she received a series of cuts and stab wounds over her body, the same as Maria Christiansen, though far fewer.

Blood on the inside of the tape proved it had been removed and replaced a number of times, inferring questions were asked and answered before she was turned over and throat cut. Then she had been mutilated, her vagina almost obliterated, more extensively than Maria's or any of the previous victims. Dillon believed that because she had had recent sex, it may have driven her attacker to a greater rage.

The murderer had left via the front door after cleaning himself and any trace of his having been there and left the area undetected.

The Ripper was causing terror and mayhem, yet, Dillon mused, he could be next to you in a car at the traffic lights, buying sausages in the supermarket, or reading your electricity meter. He could be anyone at all. He was a sociopathic sadist who could pass unnoticed in the street because of his penchance for disguises. He could be someone's husband or brother, and they wouldn't know. Though it seemed in cases like these after the event, people would always say that they *'thought there was something funny about him'* or *'his eyes were too close together.'*

Dillon prepared himself for the press conference planned an hour later. The decision had been made to release the pictures, but not the army ties suspicion—that was still too tenuous. The public and media were hounding him and the commissioner for something, anything. With fifteen horrific murders, they were now an interstate and international news item. The pressure to stop the Ripper was enormous.

By releasing the images, they would be inundated with calls, almost all of which would be a waste of time, but each call had to be checked. They had brought in a further twenty officers for the door-to-door inquiries that they were about to unleash, but possibly, one of the sightings they would investigate could be their man. Only time would tell.

Chapter Eleven

I slept late the next day. I deserved that. I sat at my breakfast bar, sipping a black coffee, waiting for my laptop to boot up. The headache was back, despite some sleep, though I was still very tired, having gotten to bed after seven. The throbbing at my temples was incessant even though I had swallowed six over-the-counter pain killers; it matched the pain in my arm from the stupid dog bite.

I cursed my haste the previous night in not checking for a dog before jumping the fence. I was furious with myself for making a rookie error. Going in without recon, and I should have known better, went against all my training. *Well, now I have to pay the piper.* I made a mental note to slow things down and be more cautious before acting in future. I felt I was so close to finding Amanda, and I didn't want to make a stupid mistake that would end my mission prematurely.

I redressed the wound once I returned home and used an entire bottle of antiseptic to disinfect it. I hoped it would not become infected, as a trip to the hospital would be out of the question. I had intended to take the dog's head with me and burn it, so the cops didn't get my DNA. But after the bitch took so long to tell me what I wanted to know, time had gotten away from me. And there was no point denying it. I forgot it in my haste to get away from the house before people were up and about, taking early morning walks. Having donned shorts, T-shirt and trainers, sunglasses, and cap pulled low, I would have resembled any other early morning jogger but for the bloody towel over my arm.

Well, it can't be helped now. It is what it is, I thought. Logically it would still be three to seven days at best before they had a DNA result. That was assuming the dog's saliva didn't contaminate it too much, which I rather thought it might—if I was lucky. Even in the best of circumstances—in complete contrast to TV shows that showed instantaneous results—in the real world, it took much longer and was expensive. In my case, I was sure the cost wouldn't be an issue as they were desperate to stop me. I knew they would be pushing as hard as they could for speed, but I still had two days in the best-case scenario. Even then, if they did have a good clean sample and a perfect DNA result, they had to have something to match it to, and I had never been arrested or donated blood.

Of course, the army had my DNA on file; they had to because it was useful for identifying bodies recovered during combat. But the army wasn't about to put their men's DNA on a database for the cops without just cause. Realistically, it would only be relevant if they caught me, and I had determined that if they did, I wouldn't go down without a fight. I intended to take as many with me as I could. And, if it came to that, I would teach them a bloody lesson they would *never* forget. Going into battle, and killing, was my specialty, after all.

Therefore, I believed my DNA was somewhat irrelevant and wasn't going to stop my mission. I had no qualms about killing police or anyone who stood in the way of my getting to Amanda. Finding her may well be one of the last things I do anyway, so what did it matter who I took out along the way?

Of much more immediate concern was the dog bite and staving off any infection. I could not allow myself to become sick or infirm. The laptop finally booted up, and I searched *'dog bites'* and read a several medical articles. The risk of infection was high, I read, and I would need to watch it carefully. For the moment, though, it looked fine. I saw the bleeding had stopped when I had unwrapped it earlier, but when I cleaned the wounds and poured antiseptic on, it began to seep again. While the skin was broken quite deeply and looked an inflamed mess, the holes did not appear to be septic so far. I determined that before I went to bed that night, I would change the dressing and check again. I'd seen a lot worse in my time, and the ugly scarring under my hairline was testament to my ability to survive serious wounds. This was nothing, I reassured myself.

Next, I clicked on a news website and was dismayed to read the bodies had been found, *damn it!* I had hoped for more time. Details were scant at this early stage, and a press release would be made later in the evening, obviously in time for the nightly news broadcasts. I made a mental note to switch the TV on later.

I found myself smiling, just a little, at the notoriety, I had amassed and the monster the press made me out to be. Once they knew the full story, I was sure that most people would understand. And while they might not condone my actions, I was sure there would be a few men in particular who would wish to be like me in avenging the hurt and suffering an unfaithful woman could cause.

Reading further on the website, I saw an article about how the rate of marriage break-ups were increasing in fly-in, fly-out workers' relationships, and wasn't that just typical? The men go away and work in ridiculously high temperatures up north in mines, while the wives stayed home in the air conditioning and fucked anyone they pleased.

Sometimes, I thought the Muslims had it right in the way that they treated their women. They kept their bodies hidden and untouched by anyone except their husbands, and if they were unfaithful, they would be stoned to death. There was very little sex outside marriages in the Middle East, which proved this article was further validation for me. When Amanda was dead, the world would know why I'd hunted her and ended her life from the journal I was keeping.

I poured another coffee, went to my apartment window, and looked out over Scarborough beach. I watched the waves sparkle in the afternoon sun and sea breeze, and at least for a while, I was able to ignore the throbbing in my arm and clanging headache.

The lunch at Sebastian's had been with Helena's twin sister, the sister's best friend Suzi, and a new friend of Suzi's who was fairly new to Perth. The long blonde-haired travel agent was named Toni. I grinned to myself. Toni? Could it be short for Antoinette? Amanda Antoinette McMahon. I grinned. The bitch thought she could hide from me using her middle name? It was laughable; just how stupid did she think I was?

So, unfortunately, it was not as simple as going to where Toni, nee Amanda, lived. Helena didn't know where that was. She hadn't even been sure where Suzi lived, other than in Applecross somewhere. Naturally, Helena Smart did know where her sister lived. I tested her, asked her over and over to make sure she was telling the truth. Forward, backward, throwing water on her when she'd passed out. I didn't want to find out she had made up an address after I'd killed her, so she had suffered until I'd been finally convinced. Only then had I helped her on her way.

I knew most people would say I should feel guilt or remorse, but really, I didn't. I had an objective, a sacred mission, and finish it I would. I'd take whatever steps were needed, just as the army rammed into me over and over—*adapt, adapt, adapt.* I had been trained never to stop until I had succeeded, and succeed, I would. Amanda would die in my arms.

Once I'd seen the evidence of what the Smart woman had been doing earlier, I admit I lost it for a few minutes, and I accepted I shouldn't have. But that was really the essence of why I was doing what I was doing. That was exactly what women used to first of all trap a man, and made us fall for them, then used it to betray us. Maybe they couldn't help it. Who knew? So, I lost my temper a bit, so what? She was a tramp, just like the rest of them.

I had found myself a little out of breath by the time I'd finished, probably caused by the adrenaline. I still had to clean up and make sure I had left no trace of my presence, which went like clockwork. Then I changed and gotten out just as the sun had been coming up over the roofs to the east.

My thoughts turned to the sister, Georgie, Helena had called her. She'd told me her full name was Georgina, and I had to assume the cops would be questioning the family today. I would have to be careful they were not watching her for her protection when I made my move. I thought that unlikely because they had no idea I was going to go after her; I was positive of that. I knew where she lived, and I knew where she worked as a shoe shop manager at Carousel Shopping Center in Cannington. It would be too busy to take her there, yet she was married, which complicated things for an attack at her home. But nothing would stop me, certainly not a husband, though I would still need to be a little careful and most of all, patient.

I could do her just as I had the sister, in the middle of the night. But possibly, because the cops would be questioning her, they may be overly cautious. They may have police patrols watching family members for a few days, so I needed to think more and come up with a plan. I could go earlier, say in the evening, and knock on the door, possibly pretending to be one of the cops calling back to check a detail and hope to get invited inside. This idea had possibilities.

I glanced at my watch and noticed it was nearly five. The news would be on in an hour. Time for a run along the beach, which always helped me think. Fitness of body, fitness of mind, and all that stuff. I put a long-sleeved T-shirt on to hide the bandage and the cap with straggly blond hair. My sunglasses were last and barefooted. I left the apartment block for the sand and took off at a good pace.

****

The announcer said they were crossing to police headquarters for a press conference and breaking news. The picture changed to show two men behind a desk, with the usual police paraphernalia all around them. The commissioner and Detective Inspector Dillon Bradley. On the monitor screen, Dillon noticed he looked tired and drawn. Commissioner Pollock looked his usual

112

immaculate self as if he had stepped off a modeling runway. He had gray hair without a single one out of place and wore what looked like a custom-made uniform.

The commissioner cleared his throat and asked for silence, then began. "We have called you here to release some vital information and pictures of our prime suspect in the murders of now fifteen people. The deaths have culminated in the brutal slayings of Helena Smart, Michael Baldwin, and Maria, Erik, and Heidi Christiansen."

The reporters all started talking at once, asking questions, and after waiting a few seconds, he raised his hands and said loudly over the noise, "Please wait until after the announcement, and we will answer what questions we can about these heinous crimes. I will now hand you over to the head of the investigation, Detective Inspector Dillon Bradley."

"Thank you, Commissioner. I know everyone here is anxious for information about this murderer, but please be patient. We have handouts for all of you, which include our police artist's impressions of the man we are seeking, who can help us with our inquiries. For the viewers at home, please be on the lookout for this man."

The screen above and behind them on the wall changed to a series of artists' views which were also being shown on televisions all over the country. They showed the killer shaved, unshaved, short hair, long hair, with and without cap and glasses. He then went on. "We know this man uses forms of disguise to hide his features from time to time. We know he is tall, approximately one-hundred-eighty-eight centimeters, and of a solid build. Sometimes he walks with a limp, and other times not. We believe the limp is fake. The use of fake facial hair, possibly wigs or most often a cap, is used to make identification difficult so please look carefully at the pictures. This man is out there. You may know him or you may see him somewhere quite innocent. We warn everyone that if you do see anyone resembling this man you are not to approach him; he is very dangerous and armed. Please call the number on your screen. You can stay anonymous, but we need your help to track him down before he kills again."

The phone number scrolled continuously across the bottom of the screen, and again there were a dozen questions at once called out by reporters. Dillon pointed to a female reporter in the front row, who stood and said, "Do you know why he is doing this, Inspector?"

"We cannot be one hundred percent sure, no. Our police psychologist and profilers all agree he is unhinged and has a purpose that makes perfect sense to him. We think he is hunting one particular woman, perhaps someone who has wronged him somehow in the past and he feels has ruined his life. The first ten victims all looked quite similar, so we believe he either thought he'd killed the right person, only to find out later she wasn't, or it could be that he keeps killing the same person over and over again in his mind. I repeat, *he is unhinged*. One thing is for sure, he is a very sick man. However, outwardly he may appear to be quite normal, and we believe him to be fully functional in his everyday life. He could be a family member, friend, or work colleague. He may seem just a little off-center at times, but he will not come across as the raving lunatic we know him to be. For example, the Yorkshire Ripper, Peter Sutcliffe, was married, and his wife had no idea about the women he murdered. In his case, they were most often prostitutes he killed." He then pointed at the reporter next to the first.

"What can people do to be safe, Inspector?"

This caused Dillon to pause. Eventually, he said, "I cannot impress on everyone enough just how dangerously sick this man is." Again, the screen above changed, showing the pictures of the killer. "What can everyone do to stay safe? Well, avoid meeting tall, well-built men who look like our suspect for a start. If you are using a dating site or meeting a man for the first time, be careful. Meet in a public place, and if anything seems off-kilter, call for help. The fact is, we have fifteen victims now, and some of them were careful, yet he still got to them. Not only is he a deranged, sick man, he is very clever and resourceful, and he plans his kills carefully. He is, for whatever reason, driven to do what he does, and he does it well. To us, he is more than just a sick pervert who gets off on killing women. Perhaps he comes across as being pleasant, intelligent, and even personable. We know sociopaths often are. But he will stop at nothing and is totally ruthless. If you met him, you may feel his eyes are cold, or he has some mannerisms that deep down you feel are not right. Listen to your instincts.

"I urge women, especially blonde women, not to go out alone. Stay in groups or with family, be observant and careful. If something doesn't seem right, trust your feelings. If you are aware of the potential danger to yourself, don't ignore any misgivings you may have about someone who, in whatever way, resembles these pictures. I don't know how else to answer your question except to say this killer does have a type of woman he is targeting. All victims previously were short in stature, with long blonde hair and blue eyes. All were attractive and in their late twenties to mid-thirties. If this description fits you, you should be particularly careful and vigilant for any form of stalking. Contact police immediately if you feel threatened at any time. In the case of the most recent victims, we believe that one or more of them knows the woman he is looking for. So, if you know a woman who you feel meets his criteria, be mindful of that and stay as safe as possible." He nodded at someone else.

"Inspector, you've mentioned the type of woman being targeted. Pictures haven't been released of the latest victims—are those women short with blonde hair?"

"No, they are not. At this time, we can only speculate that one of these victims who were killed in their homes knew the woman he is looking for somehow. He tortured two victims, trying to find her whereabouts. Investigations are still continuing, and we want to find his intended victim urgently. Next?" he said, looking at someone else.

"Commissioner Pollock, do you feel the police have failed the community in not making an arrest so far, and fifteen people have now been murdered?"

"We have now sixty officers in total working in this task force, and these are the best people we have. Inspector Bradley and his team have my full support. They have several avenues they are pursuing, which for operational reasons, we cannot go into here. Make no mistake, we are working tirelessly to apprehend this killer, and we are getting very close. But we need your help too. If anyone sees this man or has seen him in the past, contact us immediately."

Dillon spoke up once more. "Please understand this, this man is a calculating, cold-hearted, psychopathic killer. He is mentally ill. Why or what caused his mental condition, we do not know, but we do have our suspicions. As sick as he is in what he is doing, he won't appear mentally ill outwardly. He could be literally anyone. He could be the guy who delivers your mail or repairs your car in the workshop. He isn't wearing a sign announcing that he is a murderer. He may find it difficult to fit in, but he will fit in. That's what he does. He is a chameleon. He wears disguises both physically and mentally. If he was serving you dinner in a restaurant, you would not know him unless you were looking for things that just don't seem quite right. We will catch him, we are getting close, but everyone needs to be vigilant and very careful until we do."

A voice from the back of the room yelled out, "Can you guarantee us there won't be any more murders?"

Dillon just shook his head and said emphatically, "No, I can't say that. I wish I could. But I can say we are working around the clock to catch him, and we are close. With the public's help, we hope to get him off the streets very soon. Please, everyone, if you see anything, or someone resembling this man, call Crime Stoppers. Thank you all for attending." He stood as one with Pollock, and they turned and walked out, ignoring the hail of questions being fired at them.

****

"Oh, you fucking bastard," I swore at the TV. I sat, towel around my neck, sweating after the run, looking at pictures of me. While they were reasonable facsimiles of me in various guises, it wasn't like looking in the mirror.

I would need to be careful, but that wasn't what bothered me.

I seethed with anger. *I was a psychopath? Me? How dare he say that?* I would teach him a lesson. He would regret the day he insulted me to an entire TV-watching nation. I sat and thought well into the night about how I would teach him to keep his opinions to himself. I pulled out my laptop and searched for Inspector Dillon Bradley and found a lot of listings and articles about him—the internet is wonderful. I also learned about his wife and daughter, and page after page of information appeared about them. I thought about how I would make him pay. The headache was still pounding, but I smiled faintly as an idea materialized.

Chapter Twelve

Journal Excerpt # 5, Amanda

It would be truthful to say that once we finished dancing on that first night, long ago, when I first met Amanda, I realized I had never known true happiness. I know to most people that would be an unbelievable statement to make, but it is true. The feeling of sheer excitement, just being with her was unchartered territory for me, both scary and exhilarating at the same time.

She slipped her arm around me, so I reciprocated. I was full of wonder for how she just fit into my arm, and how it felt so right that she was there, as we walked back to the table. I had nothing to gauge my feelings by— people talk about love, but I had never experienced it before. I was not even allowed a pet as a child. I hated my parents and had never had school friends, so what was love? To me love was something talked about in stupid songs or women's magazines and I never had any inkling it would ever apply to me.

It was enough to say that with that one touch from her, and in response when I put my arm around her, and touched her body, felt her warmth, I was overwhelmed with a want and yearning for her. I needed to own, possess, care for and protect her. I was excited, thrilled and almost as if I couldn't breathe and, if all that means love, then I was at once completely and utterly in love with her.

At that point, she could have done anything to me, with me or for me and I would have gladly laid down my life for her. Even more unbelievable to me was that she liked me, and I struggled to comprehend that. Much later she seemed surprised that I would think something so ridiculous. She saw me in a totally different way to how I saw myself. She liked and was attracted to me. She said she respected the fact that I wasn't trying to jump her bones like everyone else did, and she found my shyness incredibly cute. I laughed when she told me that. Me? Cute? That was not a word I could ever associate with myself.

We sat back at the table, where she slid her chair against mine and snuggled in. I felt so incredibly alive as I instinctively put my arm back around her. My thumb touched the side of her bra, and I was instantly harder than I had ever been in my life. Just the touch of her bra and I was in heaven, my mind racing with thoughts of what that bra contained. What was happening to me? What was that song? If this is a dream, I don't want to wake up—well, that was how I felt.

Out of my peripheral vision, I watched a single bead of sweat roll down her upper chest and disappear between her cleavage and it took willpower not to bend my head and lick it off. That was another totally alien concept for me. God I ached for her. She was a goddess and I was a clown. What could she ever see in me? I'm not saying I had two heads, but I believed I was well and truly punching above my weight, as they say.

Sam had lined up more glasses of bourbon and kicked Johnno to waken him. Amanda picked up my drink, took a sip, then held the glass out for me too. I took a long pull and handed it back for her to finish.

She then snuggled in tighter, turned her head into me, lifted her face and whispered in my ear, "Tank, shall we get out of here? I want to be with you, just you, and I'm done dancing." Then she licked my ear lobe and sucked it.

It was like a bolt of electricity running through my body, but in the best possible way. I shivered all the way down my spine. I had never felt anything like this and never been wanted by anyone except for my mother and that had always been horrible and sickening, and nothing, nothing at all like this. I took a deep breath and spoke, trying very hard not to sound like an overexcited schoolboy. "What did you have in mind? I'm bunking in a room with Johnno and Sam at the Hyatt, and that's not somewhere I want to take you." My voice tremored; I could hear it, which is laughable now, I know, but then I was a quivering mess. I would have crawled naked over broken glass to be with her. I had fought, shot and killed people and thought nothing of it, but I was jelly in her hands.

She squeezed my thigh and whispered again. "Well, we could go for a walk along the harbor and look at the lights, but it's raining outside. We could go for a quiet coffee and cake and play footsie under the table, or we could just save time and go back to my place. It's your choice entirely, of course, but I'd love to get out of these shoes, and clothes." She had whispered the last two words, then moved her head from my ear to look into my eyes, and hers were sparkling like fire.

I swallowed hard and stared back like the imbecile I felt I had become. She stood and said goodbye to her friends, and they smiled knowingly at me.

Johnno said in his most serious voice, "You kids just

be careful out there, okay? And remember…" Now he showed his most serious face. "Practice safe sex." He collapsed in peals of drunken laughter, but I could tell he was also jealous.

Sam joined in before winking at me and asking, "Are you going to be okay, Sarge? Would you like me to do a recon mission first, just to make sure there are no land mines?"

The pair of them started another round of laughter. Part of me wanted to laugh with them, but just for a moment, the other part of me wanted to bang their heads together for being disrespectful to this incredible woman.

Amanda defused it by looking at Sam. "No, he will be fine on his own, Sam. I want the full meal, not a snack, thanks. And, the only mine there will be is when I make him mine." She giggled and winked at him, then turned to me. "Come on, big boy, take me home."

She took my hand and led me outside after battling through the late-night crowds in the bar to the sounds of wolf whistles and slapping on the table from the guys. My face heated with embarrassment, but I was so proud to be walking out with her on my arm.

Outside in the night air, we looked up and down the street and saw the cab rank was only about seventy or so meters away. It was drizzling a very light, cold and miserable rain, but to me it was a beautiful night. She took off at a run, holding my hand, leading me, and splashing in the little puddles on the pavement.

After giving the cab driver an address in Surrey Hills, she was all over me, like a wonderful cat in heat. I was too busy touching her, rubbing her back, hips and thighs.

She moaned softly and whispered in my ear, "Don't think I haven't noticed you've been staring at my boobs all night." I flinched as if reprimanded, like a naughty schoolboy, but she carried on, having felt me tense. "It's okay, you big hunk, I liked it. You made me feel very sexy. You can touch them now, if you like."

Then she turned in her seat so that my hand, which had been on her back, slid around as if by magic to her arm, so very close to her chest. She took it in her tiny little hand and placed it over her left breast, and I was in heaven. Her hand held mine to her, squeezing it as if she were touching herself through me. While it wasn't the first woman's breast I had ever held in my hand, it was the only one I had touched that made me feel like it was the most exciting experience of my life.

I was momentarily transported back to my schooldays and overhearing excited boys talking about getting to 'first base' with a girl. It had always sounded so disgusting to me. They'd talked about it in a demeaning way, and they'd joked about different girls in the class who would and who wouldn't let their tits be felt up. I could never have known it would be so amazing.

"You like?" she whispered; voice now husky.

I was delirious. This stunning goddess of a woman desired me. I could feel how hard her nipple was through her shirt and bra, a small pebble in my palm, begging for more attention.

Frightened that I would hurt her, I was so careful not to squeeze too hard. I kissed her deeply as our tongues fought a delightful duel. Her teeth were so smooth as I explored her warm and inviting mouth.

Her hand dropped to my lap and found me achingly hard and so ready to explode. Inside my underwear, I had become painfully uncomfortable yet incredibly turned on. She squeezed me, feeling its length and girth, and moaned into the crook of my neck.

"Fuck, Tank, you're so big. Where have you been all my life?" She giggled and squeezed me harder. We kissed open-mouthed again and again, tongues making love, while I fondled her, and she felt me, our breathing ragged.

I knew that I did not want the taxi driver to see her topless, or I would have undressed her there. She would not have stopped me, as she seemed as keen for me to explore her body as I was. The kissing was enough for the moment and was a beautiful tease of a promise to come.

Up until that point in my life I'd hated to hear a woman swearing. I thought it was smutty and dirty, and I just wanted to slap whoever said it. Hookers I had been with swore and thought it was sexy. It wasn't. It was just filth. Far worse than that had been my own mother urging me in her drunken voice, "Come on, Jackie Boy, fuck your mother."

But when Amanda said the word fuck, suddenly, it was sexy, even magical and all I could do was imagine her in the most sensual way. As weird as it sounded, when she said 'fuck', it conjured up images of the most amazing lovemaking, and nothing like the smutty sex I had experienced in the past. From her mouth, anything sounded sexy, and, as I was to learn, she could say and do the most incredibly erotic things.

We pulled up in a rather rundown street in Surrey Hills and I tossed a hundred-dollar note for a thirty-dollar fare at the driver and climbed out. We dashed through the gate as the rain tumbled down harder and *splashed our way to her front door. Amanda fumbled in her handbag for a key, which seemed to take forever, then she opened the door and we fell inside, laughing.*

I once saw a movie with Michael Douglas in it, at least I thought it was him. It showed him meeting a woman and falling for her instantly, even though he was married. The moment they got inside his apartment they were undressing and madly kissing each other and had sex on the first available surface that would accommodate them. Pretty unbelievable, I'd thought at the time. Well, now I knew it was not so unbelievable, because that was how it was for Amanda and me that night.

As we got just inside the front door, her shirt came off, along with my jacket. We leaned against the back of the door, kissing with a hunger I'd never known, then a few meters down the hall she nearly fell as her skirt tangled around her feet. I was sliding it down as she was lifting the T-shirt over my head. I pulled her bra straps down and feasted on her breasts. Her hard nipples felt so right between my lips. As we passed through the doorway to her room, she was undoing my jeans and tugging them and my pants down, my erection making that very difficult. The whole scene was as funny as it was erotic and we fell onto her bed, laughing and panting.

I will never, ever forget that first time. We hadn't found time to put a light on, and this blonde-haired beauty knelt astride me, back arched, with the light from a streetlight illuminating her glistening body. My hands were holding her breasts as she screamed in orgasm, and mine following shortly after.

We made love four times that night, in different

positions. Some times were slow and loving, others hard and fast. Those times were as if it was going to be the last time either of us was going to ever have sex in our lives. When the sun rose, we woke from the sleep wrapped around each other's bodies, and both knew we were in love.

I had never considered that I was anything other than normal, though of course I knew I had had a different upbringing that had molded me into the man I was. I thought I was normal and everyone else was warped or just different. That next morning, as Amanda made us some toast for breakfast, I lay in her bed, propped up by her pillows. I was staring at her clothes strewn everywhere, and the dressing table covered in makeup, tissues and mementos of her hectic life. Her bedroom summed up her personality, and I realized just how happy a person she was. I began for the first time to think that maybe I was the different one, and possibly everyone else was normal, which was a troubling thought.

Those thoughts were interrupted by a vision of stunning beauty walking through the doorway. Her long hair was mussed all over her head, and she wore nothing but a clinging T-shirt with a huge panda bear head on it. A half-eaten piece of toast with jam on it hung in her mouth and a small tray with a cracked plate piled with toast and two steaming coffee mugs was in her hands.

Without missing a beat, she sat cross-legged at my side on the bed, her thighs spread wide Indian-style. I had a perfect view of her womanhood, framed in soft downy blonde curls, and suddenly I didn't want to eat, I wanted to be inside her again.

She put the plate on my tummy, removed the toast

from her mouth and tutted. "Not now, tiger, first we eat and drink. I'm famished. Then you can ravish me again."
Her eyes sparkled and, not for the first time, I marveled at how very lucky I was to be with her. I realized too I was hungry and grabbed the cup from her in one hand, toast in the other, wanting to eat, but wanting to make love with her again as quickly as I possibly could.

We couldn't get enough of each other for the rest of my leave and spent every moment we could together. Amanda firstly faked a couple of sick days from her work, but that progressed to calling her manager and pleading for some annual leave. She kept apologizing for the short notice and even threatened to resign if it came to it. I couldn't believe that for her to spend time with me was that important to her.

For the first time in my life, I had someone I could talk to, and I opened up about my childhood and explained no matter what, she would never be meeting my mother. While I never went into embarrassing details as to why, she understood, I think, and didn't press me for more. She was horrified at how my father had treated me and hated along with me the beatings he'd handed out. Most surprisingly, she was proud of me for eventually standing up to him. It seemed like all of the things in my life that made me feel like I didn't belong, she loved about me.

I met her mother when I took them both out for dinner. Her father had passed away some years before, and I liked her mother. I even think she liked me. She was as bubbly and happy-go-lucky as her beautiful daughter was. They both lived life like there was never enough time to do all the things they wanted to do in a day. When they were together, they did nothing but laugh about anything and everyone, but I never once felt excluded from a conversation. Amanda rarely went more than a few minutes without touching me or holding my hand, as if she needed everyone to see I belonged to her.

Amanda lived her life in a permanent state of anarchy, and that was a complete opposite to me. I had lived a regimented life since I'd been born, everything neat, tidy and in its place while Amanda's bedroom looked like several mortars had gone off in it. She had clothes everywhere, the floor was her closet, and makeup lived all over the dressing table and bathroom. It was always a joy to find her underwear in the most obscure places, and though she was meticulously personally clean and always stunningly dressed, everything around her was like a whirlwind followed her around. I nicknamed her Cyclone, and she loved it when I called her that.

Far from being put off by her untidiness, I reveled in it, as it was the essence of her, and who was I to ever to change that? The day came when she found me folding clothes up in her room. My old habits died hard. She looked at me very sternly and didn't say a word as she took the clothes out of my hands and dropped them on the floor. Never taking her eyes from mine, she pushed me back on the bed, knelt astride me, undid my jeans and yanked them and my underwear down to my thighs. Still silent, she sucked me until I was hard then moved up, pulled her panties to one side and guided me inside her warm body. We held hands while she rode me, her hair flying from side to side as she climaxed long and hard. After she collapsed on my chest she told me she loved me for the first time, and I knew my life was now complete.

As opposite as we were in some ways, we were

perfectly matched in others. She loved me talking of army life, weapons, or Afghanistan and my expected upcoming tour in Iraq. She would listen intently. We went to a shooting range with her ditzy sister Jayne and I taught them how to shoot with handguns. Amanda loved it and wanted to stay all day. She was a natural and when we got back to her place afterward she was wild with passion. She told me she had never been more turned on in her life and came multiple times that night.

She would lie in my arms, naked, which was our favorite state of dress, and we talked for hours on end. She was always fascinated, asking questions and seeking every detail I could remember about anything and everything to do with being a soldier.

Our favorite meal was what we called picnic in bed. This consisted of bread, cheeses, pickles and some smoked meats from the local continental deli, with wine, lots of wine. We ate and drank naked on these picnics and invariably never finished a meal as we ended up making love. She had an insatiable appetite for wine and life and—who would have thought it?—me.

Sadly, all too soon the two weeks' leave was up and I had to ship out and go back to the army barracks in Perth and wait for deployment. Then came another first for me, I didn't want to go. It was tearing me apart to leave her and she cried uncontrollably on our last night together. She didn't try to make me stay. She knew it was my life and supported me being in the army. In fact, she loved me all the more for it. But she hated the thought of being separated from me, and of course, I felt the same.

We promised to write emails and Skype each other every chance we got, and I promised my next leave would be with her. She drove me in her rusty hatchback to the airport, and even as red-eyed as she was, she was the most beautiful woman in the world. She wore a stunning turquoise semi-see-through top with a bra the same color underneath and white jeans. My God, she always looked fantastic in white jeans.

Sam and Johnno were waiting in the lounge, and we said our final goodbyes. I did not want to let her go, but they announced the final boarding call, and I knew I had to. Johnno and Sam walked away because Amanda was sobbing, and I was close behind. I had never cried when my father whipped me, but I cried that day as we clung to each other.

As I was getting my boarding pass checked, I turned to look at her. She was trying to be strong at the same time for my benefit. She waved at me and without thinking I left my place in the queue to run back to her.

I hugged her tightly and said, "Marry me, please. I love you with all of my heart and soul and I want to be with you for the rest of my life." Then came the most agonizing wait of my life to that point, which I suppose was all of ten seconds.

"Yes, oh yes, yes, yes!" she shouted

"Sir, you have to board now. Sir, now," the stewardess called loudly, and I looked around. I was the last one remaining, and knew I had to go.

"I will write and send you money, organize everything and I will put in for leave as soon as I can. I love you, baby." And I turned and ran to the gate and the scowling hostess, who was not at all amused at my tardiness.

"I'm sorry, but I just got engaged," I said to her.

She smiled. "Go, get on the plane, you daft bugger. We don't stop flying just because you got engaged."

With one last look back at my Amanda, I went through the gate and hurried to get on the plane, knowing it wouldn't go without me, but hating to be that person who was last to board and kept everyone else waiting.

So, that was it, back to war I went. This time we were going to Iraq, but now I had something and someone to live for, and more importantly, someone to go home to. Life had irrevocably changed for me, because suddenly, I didn't want to die.

Chapter Thirteen

Kathy Bradley knew in her heart she had been stupid and had to end it. She felt racked with guilt, the likes of which she had never experienced before. As she sat, head in hands on the cream leather couch, mentally she retraced the steps she had taken that had led to the biggest mistake of her life.

Her life with Dillon had been pretty miserable because he was working all the hours under the sun when he had been ordered to head up the *Ripper* task force to catch that monster who was murdering blonde women. He was morose with her at home and drank way too much, often falling asleep on the same couch she now sat in. Kathy knew he had been sickened by the violence of the murders, and that he had been put under intolerable pressure to catch the killer, but he wouldn't talk to her about it. He seemed instead to prefer to bottle everything up inside, rather than bother her with his troubles. If only he had known that no matter how gruesome things were, she wanted to share his life with him and hated being shut out.

Kathy had also suspected that he was seeing someone else, not that there was ever anything that she could point at as proof. *But a woman knows, doesn't she?* she asked herself. Of course, he'd denied it—well, he would, wouldn't he? *How typical*, she thought at the time, for him to not only take a mistress but confide in the woman too, leaving Kathy out in the cold.

Kathy hadn't been sleeping well. She felt frumpy all the time, always tired, sweated profusely at the drop of a hat, and they argued about the most ridiculous of things. Molehills became mountains in an instant. In hindsight, she could see she had been overly critical of him, but, dammit, he could be so bloody inconsiderate at times. Stupid things, like leaving dirty socks inside out, so she had to put her hand inside the smelly, sweaty things to turn them the right way to wash them. If she had asked him once, she'd asked him a hundred times not to do that. Of course, he always raised his eyebrows, as if *she* were the one with the problem and was just nagging him. If he just did as she asked she wouldn't have to nag, would she? It hardly seemed like rocket science. And did he ever put an empty beer bottle in the bin? Or make her a coffee if they were watching TV together at night? No, it was always she who did those things. And there was another thing, they always had to watch what he wanted to watch, as if the damn TV remote belonged to him. Granted, they were only small things, but so many small things added up to one big thing. She had felt unhappy, unloved, and unfulfilled.

For all of his faults, though, she now recognized that he was a good man and always had been. He was honest, hardworking, reliable, and in his own way, kind and loving. She knew that she could have done a lot worse in her life than Dillon and now saw that if in fact he had taken a lover, it was her frumpiness and lack of desire for him that pushed him into it. On reflection, she knew it was a shame it had taken her doctor to point out that her mood swings, lack of sleep, and irritability were all symptoms of early menopause. But she hadn't known that at the time, just that she felt so damned miserable. She was bitter and angry and thought that Dillon could have done so much more to help make her feel better about herself, but he just went on in his own way, clueless. She now knew the fault lay with her. Her husband had been the way he was when she had fallen in love with him, and he had not changed one little bit in all the years they had been together. It was she who had changed. She saw it all too clearly now, but way too late.

Then, as if to spite her further, the Gods conspired, and suddenly, inevitably it now seemed, Mark started paying her a lot of attention at work. He paid her compliments like her hair was nice after she'd had it done, when of course Dillon hadn't even noticed she had hair at all. She felt...flattered, like she was back being a schoolgirl dating for the first time. Gradually, she'd warmed to Mark, and yes, under his frequent compliments and comments, she'd even felt sexy. Feeling so miserable at home made her appreciate the attention from a much younger and strikingly handsome man, and she enjoyed the flirting.

Mark was a well-reputed ladies' man and a definite bad boy, with rugged good looks and a slim, lithe body. Every woman she knew fancied him, and jokes were often made in the ladies' toilet that he could put his shoes under their beds anytime. He was the head of accounting and admin for the charity of which she was CEO, the Children's Cancer Foundation.

They had been arranging the big annual fundraiser for the year, the Black-Tie Ball, and they had been working late nights and long hours together when it happened. They had to arrange sponsors and donations for the auction, entertainment, menus, and venue. The list of tasks they had to work together on seemed to be inexhaustible. They had eaten meals together with the clients they were coaxing money out of regularly, and one night in the city, after a meeting in the boardroom, he had taken her in his arms and kissed her.

What started out as a congratulatory kiss for sealing the deal with a major sponsor suddenly turned into something else entirely. Suddenly, she was hyperaware of his strong arms, the smell of his cologne, and the front of his body, including a substantial erection pressing against her body. And as he held her, she melted into him, and became lost in the moment.

Somewhere, in the back of her mind, Kathy had been shocked at her reaction to him. She'd realized with part horror, part excitement, that not only had she been flattered that he was attracted to her, she'd found her body had responded beyond her control. She had trouble breathing normally, and her pulse raced uncontrollably. Dillon hadn't touched her for weeks and weeks, though now she knew that had been because she treated him so poorly he had been turned off the thought of making love with her. And as she kissed Mark, she was excited in a way she hadn't experienced in many years. Kathy knew on some level she should have stopped Mark and had fully intended to, but at the time, Kathy thought it couldn't hurt to neck like kids for just a few minutes, *could it?* The longer it went on, the more she'd felt powerless to stop him going further, and deep down, she didn't want to stop him anymore. She wanted the type of gut-wrenching orgasms she hadn't felt with Dillon for a very long time. On a primal, animalistic level, she wanted to be taken and used.

She was so lost in the moment any remaining

common sense flew out of the window. She felt herself becoming wet inside her panties, unbelievably so. Her nipples were hard in his hands, and he wouldn't stop kissing her, almost distracting her from what his hands were doing. He was strong and forceful, and she felt deliciously helpless. Suddenly, she regretted not having worn sexier underwear and that she hadn't trimmed her pubic hair as his fingers delved down below her navel. Mark hadn't seemed to care about that. He was only interested in turning her on, and boy, had he done that.

He undressed her between kisses and marveled at her body, licking and sucking as he had exposed more and more of it. Kathy felt proud at his appreciation of her; she had looked after herself and went to the gym a couple of times a week to stay in shape. Mark seemed to revel in her nakedness and spent long minutes on end teasing her breasts. He made her nipples harder than she could remember them being until she thought they would burst. Mark appeared to be smitten by her body and the way she reacted to his ministrations. He made her feel young and sexy again.

Then he went down on her as if he didn't want to give her time to change her mind and stop him going all the way. That was something else Dillon hadn't done for a long time, Kathy realized. They had been standing, totally nude, when he suddenly knelt in front of her, licking and eating her, his strong hands on her buttocks, holding her to his hungry mouth. Before she had known it, she was coming hard as his talented tongue lashed her clitoris, and she'd almost passed out. Part of her had been aware when he'd carried her to a long table and laid her on it, then started licking again, and he didn't stop. She'd come a second time and held his head, lifting her lower body, coming harder than she had ever come before.

While she'd been recovering from that plateau, dazed and delirious, he'd suddenly pushed himself inside her, thrusting, all the time telling her how hot and beautiful she was. She'd been carried along on the tide of eroticism, and it seemed to her afterward that if she'd wanted to stop him, she doubted she could have. Though he was only intent on his own approaching orgasm, she climaxed again and again until he ejaculated deep inside her.

Suddenly she became aware that the air was full of the smell of his semen and her wetness. She sensed it leaking out of her, and she knew she had been wonderfully used and was deeply sated for the first time in years. She wanted to get up and go to the bathroom to clean up, but he held her and wouldn't let her go, stroking and touching her all over. He cuddled her, told her she was special, told her she was so much sexier than the younger women he had dated, and all the while, he was touching her, taking liberties with her body, sucking her nipples all over again. He'd caressed his fingers down her body until they were on her clitoris again, then rubbed his own semen all over her, used it as lubricant as he entered her first with one, then two, then three fingers. He kept her permanently turned on, not giving her time to think about what she had done, betraying her husband and wedding vows. Despite knowing she'd done wrong, she loved his attention. He was twenty years younger than her, for goodness sake, but he had treated her like his personal sex slave. Then he magically found her G-spot, a place she hadn't even known existed herself, and had only read about in women's magazines.

Kathy had been lying on her back, writhing in yet

another orgasm, while his fingers played the most amazing music inside her body. When she finished climaxing, he'd moved up her body and knelt over her, his bare buttocks on her breasts, his penis hard again, still wet from their lovemaking, the tip at her lips. She looked up at him, his face framing his manhood that had given her so much pleasure, and she felt so deliciously dirty. She had not done it for Dillon in a long time, but she'd known she would for Mark. She'd looked up into his eyes and saw how he wanted her. She opened her mouth and took him inside and she *loved* it. It was as if she were acting in a pornographic film, like everything had been exaggerated. Her cheeks hollowed as she had sucked and licked him. Her hands had been all over his body, but she'd finished with one on his bottom, the other around his shaft, milking him. She'd wanted to repay him for making her orgasm so hard.

It had been so unlike anything she had done before. This was pure sex, using and being used by each other for pleasure's sake. She had only once had Dillon's semen in her mouth, and she had nearly gagged while spitting it out, and had never done it again. This would be different. She'd known that in her heart.

Mark had told her how sexy she was, how magnificent she looked sucking him, and she had given herself completely. She loved his moans and adored the way he'd talked pure filth to her. He made her feel beautiful and slutty at the same time. She had wanted to do it for him, and show him she could be better than all the young women she knew he chased. He held her head in his hands, talked to her nonstop, his thrusts got quicker, he moaned loudly as he arched his back, and she'd panicked just for a moment.

****

Much later, driving home, Kathy suffered guilt like the weight of the world sat on her shoulders. And, if that hadn't been bad enough, then the fear hit. Things had happened so suddenly she had not once thought about the consequences. Had he had made her pregnant, or worse, given her a disease she could pass on to Dillon? *What the hell have I done? Oh my God*, she had screamed in her head as she imagined the sheer terror of going home, and it being the first time in months Dillon might want to have sex with her and he would know; it would be obvious she had betrayed him. Kathy blinked back tears, feeling more and more miserable the closer she got to home. How could she have thrown away her marriage so easily?

Somehow she'd got home, though at one point, she had considered not going at all but to a motel instead, and once there, making some excuse to Dillon. But the irony wasn't lost on her. If she did that, he might then suspect she was having an affair because for her to stay out all night would be highly unusual. Kathy had parked the car in the garage, taken a deep breath, got out and walked inside. Dillon was watching sports on TV, eating a pizza he had delivered, with a beer in hand. Wearing a scruffy tee shirt and shorts. Her husband looked the complete opposite to the lover she'd just left, and suddenly she didn't feel so bad. She feigned a stress headache and tiredness and had gone straight to the bathroom to shower before bed.

Once in her nightdress in her own bed, she found she couldn't sleep. She worried in a panic, what if Dillon found out? What if Mark opened his mouth to the wrong person and word got back to him? Would Dillon be violent? Quite possibly he would, and that made her worry all the more. She had known of other cop wives who had taken lovers and had been attacked in similar situations, but the more she thought about it, the more she realized Dillon wasn't like that. He would kick her out of the house, sure, but his attitude would be *it's over, go away,* rather than whine for her to stay; in that sense, he was a man's man and always had been. He might find her lover and beat him up; that was a distinct possibility. Dillon was many things, many good things too, but he wasn't a violent person and abhorred all violence toward women, but men…Oh yes, Kathy could imagine Mark getting hurt and Dillon standing over him, screaming obscenities.

From a practical point of view, she then worried about STDs and pregnancy and again cursed that she had not made Mark wear a condom. Looking back, she couldn't imagine when she could have done that; it all happened so fast. Clearly, had she been thinking enough to suggest that, she'd have slapped Mark's face and not had sex at all. Dillon had had a vasectomy, so she had been off the pill for years. She had lost track of her last period, no matter how hard she tried to remember. She decided she would buy a test kit to make sure that her moment of being a silly immature girl wasn't compounded by becoming a *pregnant* silly immature girl. She determined to ask for a morning-after pill from the pharmacy, just in case.

How would she face Dillon in the morning? And how would she face work? She had always despised workplace affairs and the stupid problems it caused between staff and colleagues. Now she knew she was a hypocrite, and hypocrisy was something she hated above all else. She worried and tossed and turned and pretended to be asleep when Dillon had climbed into bed with her, fearing he still might make an advance on her.

Then, inevitably, as Dillon snored, she thought back to how good it had been and how hard and often she had orgasmed. Despite all the terrible emotions running through her mind, she had again experienced a stirring in her lower tummy and a yearning to be with Mark again, to be used again as a plaything, and she had found herself smiling. Then guilt had hit all over again with further remorse that she could even smile at a time like that.

Every day afterward, she had expected Dillon to notice the change in her and confront her, yet he hadn't. While she thought she was wearing a placard saying *adulterer*, he just carried on as normal. He continued to annoy her every chance he got and complained she was a nag if she dared ask him to stop doing things that he knew she hated.

She tried to make it up to him. One night she cooked a lovely meal, got her hair done, and bought some new lingerie. Maybe, she thought, she could re-light the sexual spark missing between them. She called him at work, asked him if he could come home at a normal time for a special meal, and of course he said he would be home late again and suggested she eat alone. She couldn't help the anger and hung up on him, which she later regretted.

To make matters worse, Mark wanted her again and was trying to get her to go to a hotel with him. They would have access to a room until after the ball, he reasoned. He left flowers on her desk, sent idiotic text messages, kept telling her how sexy she looked, so eventually, of course, she'd weakened. She told herself she was only going so she could end it with him face to face. He deserved that. It was the *only* reason she was going, absolutely, definitely, and that was final. She had been silly and flattered that such a good-looking and much younger stud wanted her tired old body, but it couldn't be repeated.

Within two minutes of getting inside the door, he had his hands all over her again. She couldn't stop him, then didn't want to stop him as she'd orgasmed again and again with him. He was a drug, and she was addicted. That time she again went down on him like a woman possessed because she thought that she needed to be the sexiest, sluttiest woman Mark had ever been with. She couldn't get enough of him. She felt young again, and he had *wanted* her. In the back of her mind was also the element of danger, of being found out, and that added to the thrill.

That time he took her over and over again. His powers of recuperation were astounding. He even took her from behind, on the balcony with them both naked for anyone to see that was looking up to the eighth floor. She orgasmed hard, reveling in the blatant sexuality of their exhibitionism. He even tried to put it in her anus, offering to use the hotel's complimentary moisturizer as a lubricant. He told her it would be amazing and how sexy she would be if she let him. She stopped him, the thought abhorrent, but only just, and afterward, while driving home, she thought that maybe next time she would let him use her there too, and complete her descent into debauchery. She had just felt so incredibly alive with Mark. She thought he could do anything with her and to her, and she wouldn't or couldn't stop him.

Each time she was with Mark, sex was wonderful,

and it became a regular thing they made time for. When she was with Dillon, she felt old, tired, and worn out, yet young, carefree, and alive with Mark. Her life vacillated between a mixture of dull humdrum at home and rampant, amazing sex at work.

It had been going on for a while when the doctor broke the news to her about her menopause. She had gone to a different doctor from her usual one to check for any disease and to talk about getting the pill again, as Mark had refused to wear condoms. She didn't fight him on it, as she had adored the feeling of him being inside her. It had just been one more thing that helped her feel erotic, and she had rediscovered herself with this renewed feeling of sexiness.

Well, she consoled herself; *at least Mark couldn't have made me pregnant.* She was luckily disease free as well, but suddenly it hit her. She realized exactly what she had been doing, and why. She had been unfaithful to the man she loved. Despite his faults, he was her husband, and she loved him. It was the effects of her menopause that had made her grumpy with him all the time, and the new, different thing with Mark was just that—something new and different. It wasn't love and never could be; she knew that.

The guilt returned with all its fury, and she despised herself for what she had been doing behind the back of the man who had always stood beside her. Dillon had his faults, but he was the one she loved, she realized. All of the major problems they had were her issues, not his.

The first thing she did was talk to Dillon and tell him why she had been such a bitch. He had been wonderful and understanding, as she knew, deep down, he always was. He talked to her, held her, and later loved her, slowly and gently. While it hadn't been with the bells and whistles and screaming orgasms as she had experienced with Mark, it had been full of emotion and love. Most of all, he had listened to her and tried to understand what she was going through, and that night she had fallen in love with him all over again. And oh, didn't the guilt of her infidelity hit her hardest then. She realized that he hadn't been unfaithful to her when she'd thought he had; that had been just her moods and overwrought imagination.

The next morning, she laid in bed after Dillon had gone to work and cried silent tears. How could she have been so stupid? Thirty years of marriage, a daughter, and soon, she hoped to be a grandmother, albeit a young one. Their daughter in Melbourne was talking of children with her husband. Kathy had risked losing everything for some quick and dirty sex with a man twenty years her junior, who seemed to be the office Don Juan. What had she been thinking?

Well, at least she had been lucky. She could end it with Mark, and if she did it right, her husband would never need to know. Her infidelity would be a secret she would take to her grave, and she would spend the rest of her life making it up to Dillon.

But, she wondered, how to end it with Mark? They worked together, and the last thing she wanted was to cause a scene, especially one that would bring her workplace into disrepute. The charity was a big part of her life, and the children they helped didn't deserve the train wreck her personal life had become to derail them. It was a mess, and she spent the next few days trying to distance herself from Mark while she thought of a way out. Naturally, he had noticed and cornered her in her office one evening, as everyone else was leaving. He leaned against her door frame and asked her what he had done to upset her. He'd looked at her with puppy dog eyes, and she very nearly relented and let him take her there on the desk. Nothing got to her more than a man with that so-sad look in his eyes.

She told him he was imagining things and that she had had problems at home with Dillon. *The Ripper* investigation had become a nightmare for him with the most recent murders, but she would make some time for them to get together in the next couple of days. Perhaps he could come to her house for lunch, so they could talk about it.

To Kathy, 'talk about it' meant breaking up and ending the affair once and for all, but she realized that to Mark, 'talk about it' meant fucking her some more; she would correct that on the day. Kathy explained that she couldn't hang around right then as she and Dillon had plans that night but promised a lunch together at her house soon. With that, she spun around and walked out. She knew he was looking after her, admiring the swing of her hips and the outline of her panties through the business skirt she wore. He was that predictable. But her resolve stood to end it between them.

That night she planned to cook a steak dinner with a bottle of red wine, and if Dillon played his cards right, she would let him make love to her. In anticipation, during her lunchtime, she had bought some new lingerie, which she planned to put on after her shower and before Dillon got home, as a surprise for him. She felt quite lightheaded and giddy as she was planning what she would be doing later. She stepped out of the office building and squinted in the evening sunshine, dug her sunglasses out of her bag, and slid them on. If anything good had come from her affair, it was that Mark had helped her realize again that sex was fun and should be enjoyed, albeit with her husband only going forward.

She noticed a tall man wearing a Football Club cap follow her to her car park, but he walked on past her as she unlocked her car. Back at her home, she opened her garage with the remote and drove in. She was singing in her head to a song that had been on the radio.

Two days later, Mark sat alongside her on the couch in the family room of her home as Kathy explained why they couldn't see each other anymore, other than at work, of course. She tried to be gracious and kind to his feelings. She had loved their time together, but it was over. She had rekindled her love with Dillon, and she hoped that he would understand that. Mark had been there when she needed someone, and she would always be grateful to him for that. It was time she grew up and took care of her responsibilities, especially her husband. Kathy fervently hoped he would let her go gracefully and move on to another lonely housewife—there were lots of them. She knew he was a player, and that was his nature.

Mark went to work on her, and she realized what he was doing. He was playing on her guilt, but she felt relieved when he told her he respected her and would let her go without a fuss because he *did* care for her. He said he wouldn't make trouble, she meant just too much to him, and that he would be content staying good friends and work colleagues. His hand was on her thigh, and he'd slowly rubbed and caressed her as he'd spoken, lulling her with his voice and slowly working higher. He was gently sliding her skirt up with gentle strokes, and as soon he touched her panties, she knew they were damp. Her body betrayed her as he gently tugged her left thigh away from the other and rubbed her through the thin satiny material.

Why does he have to be so damned sexy? she sighed to herself, while unconsciously moving her hips in time with his finger motions as he tried to push her panties gently inside her body. She was relieved he had taken it so well and grateful he would let her go back to her normal life without making the sort of fuss she had dreaded. She could go on knowing Dillon would never find out. She believed she owed Mark something for that, didn't she, one last time for old time's sake?

His hands were all over her, and she became more turned on by his touch, knowing she should stop him, but he had been so good about it all. Oh God, he'd pulled her now soaking-wet panties to the side and entered her with first one finger, then a second. So many emotions raced through her mind, and feelings through her body. He'd kissed her, and she'd kissed him back as he'd stood and pulled her to her feet. He'd held the kiss as he'd lifted her top and bra over her breasts and began pinching and squeezing her nipples in his strong hands.

Breathless, she'd broken the kiss and told him, "This is the last time, Mark. We cannot do this ever again, you agree?" He'd nodded and then kissed her again, and all of her resistance had melted away as she knew how much he wanted her, one last and final time.

Ten minutes later, they were both naked in her marital bed, him on top and thrusting inside her. Kathy's eyes were closed as she writhed in ecstasy. Suddenly Kathy became aware of a warm, wet gushing over her chest and breasts. She looked up and saw Mark's head being held up by his hair. His throat had been cut, and blood had squirted and rained down all over her upper body while he twitched horribly. She screamed in panic and tried to break free from his now dead weight pinning her down. The knife had descended on her, cutting her deep in one smooth, practiced motion.

In the seconds it took to realize she was dying, she thought Dillon had come home early and was enraged at what he'd found, that he had done this to them. But then a head loomed over her, wearing a purple cap, and a gruff voice had called her a "fucking slut." The lights went out.

Chapter Fourteen

Journal Excerpt # 6, Amanda, my wife.

The next six months went agonizingly slowly for me, although in some ways, looking back, it also went by in a blur. Every day I lived to write to or speak to Amanda, or best of all, see her face on Skype, and I did every chance I got. I even bought a satellite phone just to hear her voice on those occasions we were away from base and the internet.

She seemed to be as overjoyed as I was when we did speak. I couldn't go into specifics of what we were doing there, yet she was always so genuinely interested in what I could tell her, and ending each call was hard on us both.

She was as beautiful as ever, and every day I yearned to see her radiant face and hear about what she had been doing since we had last spoken. Naturally, the time difference and her working at the travel agency or me out being a soldier did sometimes mean it could be days between conversations, but when we did talk, the time just sped by. I loved the sound of her voice and could listen to her for hours chatting about mundane things, such as the customers who she had helped that day or nights out with her friends.

Of course, I was worried. She was a beautiful woman, and every day I expected her to tell me she had fallen for another, more readily available man; yet every day, she didn't.

It was still a marvel what Amanda saw in me and why she would put up with me being away from her for months. She seemed genuinely happy to speak to me, and while I knew what I saw in her, I could never, ever get my head around why such an amazing woman could possibly feel the same about me. It was one of the mysteries of the universe, and when I asked her about it, she would shrug it off and call me silly and say that she wasn't the special one—I was!

She loved that I was fighting for our way of life, risking my life for others, while she was 'just a travel agent.' That fried my brain even more than what I was doing actually meant something important to her, yet I had never thought that way; it was just my job, though one I loved doing.

I was given a date for the end of my tour and booked one month's leave. I so looked forward to being married to this incredible woman, and the closer it came and the more we spoke about our plans, the more surreal it all seemed. Each night when I went to bed, I worried that either I would wake up from a dream and realize it had never happened, or worse, that she would change her mind about me because the separation was too much, or she had met someone else. She was such a bright, bubbly person that I knew the temptations she would be facing and the many men that would want to be with her.

I must admit to some dark thoughts at times that maybe she was seeing other men behind my back. Jealousy was something I had never experienced before, and on some occasions, it drove me to distraction and made me irritable. I easily lost my temper with guys in the unit for very little reason. I don't know why it was easier to think she was being unfaithful than to believe in her loyalty, but there it was. As hard as I tried to hide it on my worst days, she saw through me, as she always could. One evening she asked me what was wrong and wouldn't let up until I told her. She must have sensed this was a watershed moment for me.

On the one hand, I was scared to tell her the truth, in case I was right, and she admitted it when confronted, so then we would be over. On the other, I was so scared of offending or hurting her feelings by making an accusation that was untrue. As delicately as I could, in my ham-fisted way, I told her.

"Babe, sometimes being stuck over here in this depressing shithole of a place, I worry that you will be stolen away from me by someone else. I know you are an amazing woman, and I never got what you saw in me anyway, so I wouldn't blame you. Some days I just worry that it's all going to end, and I won't be there to try to change your mind, or stop it happening. I know I shouldn't feel like that, yet I do. I'm sorry." I watched her eyes, which welled up with tears. How like her to not be angry but understanding.

"Oh, Tank, you big dork. Can't you see how much I love you? Of all the men I've ever known, you are the most interesting, the most caring, and you are so into me. You listen to me and are genuinely interested in what I say, do, and think. Do you know how rare that is in men? Most just want to fuck, drink beer and watch sports. You are so much better looking than you know, and when we make love, you do it because you care, and you love me, and it shows. Nobody has ever made me feel the way you do. I'm yours, Tank, and I always will be. I would rather be here alone waiting for you than with anyone else.

You've spoiled me. I've had the best; anyone else is second rate. Get it through your head; I belong to you!"

After such a speech, how could anyone not believe her? And at the moment, I did, yet still, those feelings came back, against my will, from time to time, and I struggled to hide them from her. I found myself asking her questions about what she had been doing, then asking the same questions later and try to trip her up in a lie. She saw through that too and just smiled and shook her finger at me. She never got mad.

Often she would just change the subject to sex, and sometimes we would have incredible times together. She knew I adored her breasts, and that was where she always started her teasing. She would be talking of something innocent while touching her nipples through whatever she was wearing. She would offer to show me her breasts while she played with them, then would beg for me to show her my body. We would both orgasm watching each other, saying how much we were in love. It might sound dirty to some, what we did, but it wasn't that way at all to us because it allowed us to express and show our love.

Over the years of army service, I had saved a considerable sum of money. I didn't have much to spend it on as my life was pretty simple, and the army provided for all of my needs. My bank balance was healthy, and I didn't really care about money too much. If I wanted something, I bought it, but my possessions were pretty meager, really, with one notable exception.

My only indulgence for myself was my love of weapons. My collection was the most expensive thing I owned. In the army, there was a negligible cost to smuggling them back home. I had some guns, ammunition, and other mementos I had picked up on my travels or bought from other returning soldiers. They were sitting in a safe in a self-storage locker in Redcliffe, about twenty-five kilometers from the Swanbourne Barracks, with a long-term lease, paid up.

Why did I buy them and have them smuggled back home? I didn't really know. I just loved guns and thought it would be kind of cool to have some. The fact that they were highly illegal added to the thrill of owning and using them.

There is an awful lot of bush in WA and a never-ending supply of wild pigs, goats, donkeys, and horses, all deemed to be vermin to farmers. The laws governing weapons being what they were in Australia, it was all too hard to buy them and keep them legally. That would involve landowners giving written permission for you to shoot on their property, and certain calibers or styles of weapons were just not allowed, no matter who you were. In Afghanistan and Iraq, they were ten a penny, so the only hassle was getting them back into the country. There are plenty of black-market operators in the army, and a few hundred dollars to the right people made it all too easy.

At Swanbourne, there was an outlaw gun club—we even called ourselves outlaws—and groups of us would often take off somewhere in a 4x4 or two. We would head into the bush and just have some fun. I don't think people realize that if you take men and highly train them in death and survival, they need to have an outlet that involves shooting at live targets. The guns were nothing more than a way of letting off steam to us. The more exotic and illegal the weapons were, the more fun it was. Fully automatic guns were common, and it was something else to see a pig disintegrate with twenty-five rounds in just over a second or two. For us, it was just good times with good mates, a few bourbons, and fire off some rounds; no big deal.

So, money-wise I had no expenses and a very good wage coming in. I lived in the barracks when home, so it seemed natural to me to give her access to my bank account and to tell her to do what she wanted with it. My friends said I was mad to trust someone that I had only known for a few days with my money, but I knew her, and they didn't, end of story. Luckily for them, when they saw how angry I could get at anyone who said a bad thing about her, they pretty much kept their opinions to themselves.

Proof that I was right and they were wrong happened when I sent her out to buy her own engagement ring. I placed no restrictions on her as to the cost. After all, what did I know about such things? I knew that other men spent a lot of money getting the right ring for their bride-to-be. It would have been wrong to keep her waiting to wear one until I got back when we were going to be married. I wanted her to feel engaged, for others to see her wearing a ring, and to know I was waiting for her, as she wanted me to know she was waiting too.

Amanda had few savings. She said she never earned enough to have any, and her life cost just too much to live it. That was her attitude, but she was always very careful with mine. I wanted my savings to become our money and told her so. It meant nothing to me, while she meant everything, absolutely everything to me.

When she showed the ring to me on our next video call she acted very nervous and was worried I would be mad at her for spending so much. I expected some outrageous figure, but the cost was irrelevant to me, and I told her not to worry. I told her it was as beautiful as she was and that she deserved something nice on her finger, I didn't ask what it had cost because she'd chosen it, and it was stunning. I expected her to say that it had cost thousands, as it really did look amazing on her and sparkled brightly in the light. She sheepishly said she had hunted everywhere for a jeweler who had a sale on, then she had negotiated hard, gaining sympathy from the shop owner by telling him her fiancé was overseas, fighting in the army in Iraq. In the end, after half an hour's haggling, she handed over only nine hundred and fifty dollars.

Once the figure was out, her fear of me being cross was obvious in her face. I laughed my head off and wished I had been there to hug her. Amanda was just so incredibly beautiful in looks, mind, and spirit. What did my stupid cynical friends know? Nine hundred and fifty dollars was a fraction of what I'd thought it would have been. She could have spent five thousand, and I would not have batted an eyelid.

Amanda asked if I wanted her to contact my mother to tell her of the wedding, and for the first time, I showed displeasure with her. She saw the change in me instantly and apologized. I had to take some deep breaths to dispel the horrible images of my mother that reared up in my head out of the blue. Then I noticed Amanda was upset that she had made me angry. My heart melted, and I told her how sorry I was. I reiterated that I hated my mother and would not want her at my wedding, no matter what. I told her that it was not open for debate, and the last thing I would ever want was that bitch poisoning Amanda in any possible way. I had no intention of ever seeing her again for the rest of my life. She was already dead to me. On rare occasions, I would still wake up in a cold sweat from a nightmare, remembering what she'd made me do to her all those years before. The more time I spent with Amanda in a normal relationship made me realize how terrible what my mother had done to me.

On the other hand, I loved her mother and was so pleased to hear she was as thrilled as her daughter at the upcoming marriage. They would spend hours on end together working out invitations, who would be coming and who would sit where, the location of the reception, her dress, bridesmaids and all of the other hundreds of details to make sure our day was perfect. I was only sorry that Amanda's father wasn't around to walk her down the aisle, as I knew that would have made her day complete. While my father was the biggest asshole in the world, hers had been the kind of father every daughter wanted, and it was sad that he wouldn't be there.

I picked up my first wound that tour, though it was not enough to send me home, unfortunately. A ricochet went under my body armor and nicked my shoulder, and I bled like a stuck pig. I didn't miss when I returned fire and saw the guy drop. There was another by his side, and neither would be going home as I would be. Seven stitches, and I was back on duty the same day. I didn't mention it to Amanda. There was no point in making her worry even more than she already was. The pain was minimal, and it didn't restrict my arm movement. Really, it was nothing, just a part of the job.

The longest we went without talking that six months was nine days, which was the length of one particular mission, and any communications were strictly banned. I barely slept for worrying that she would be angry and worried at my absence. While the mission succeeded, we had lost one of our team to a sniper, so it was a very sobering time.

I had changed my will and noted Amanda as my next of kin so that if something happened to me, the army would have notified her ahead of my mother. I know she worried nonstop during those nine days, and when we did finally reconnect, it was a fantastic and truly memorable session.

When the chopper set us down back at the compound, I raced out of it to my room and called her on the phone at her work. She answered immediately as if waiting for it to ring. She cried, overjoyed I was there, and again I marveled that someone so incredibly wonderful could be so in love with me. I never felt worthy of her; it was just that simple.

The long days turned into weeks, and they turned into months. Missions came and went, and I think I killed over twenty that tour, but you could never be really sure. It could just as easily have been thirty or more. I never stopped to count.

Perhaps it was because I had changed since falling in love, but killing didn't hold the same fascination and enjoyment anymore. Shooting the enemy still didn't bother me; after all, who cared if there were a few less of the enemy in the world? My days and nights were filled with hopes and dreams of getting back to Amanda and holding her and making love with her. Everything else I did was just passing the time and doing my job.

Finally, I was airborne and heading for home and to my wife-to-be. I swear I have never felt so excited before or since. Johnno was beside me on the plane. He had agreed to be my best man, and my excitement the *closer we got to Sydney was palpable. He would try to talk to me, but all I wanted to talk about was her, and I realized he was fed up and bored with me doing that, so most of the trip was spent in silence. Me with my thoughts of Amanda and being with her, he with his of gambling, women, and booze, which he had been talking about for weeks.*

I had grown some facial hair this tour. We all did, don't ask me why. It was a phase we went through to grow a beard. I intended to shave it off on arrival. I was sure Amanda wouldn't like it up close, though, of course, she had seen it grow during our internet calls. Before I could get rid of it, she surprised me when I saw her at the airport. She had taken time off work to meet me, and she raced through the crowd to get to me. She whooped loudly and jumped into my arms, wrapping her legs around me. Oh my God, it felt so good to be back in her arms.

It took long minutes for her to want to let go. She was crying tears of joy while people swirled around us, tut-tutting as we held them up. We didn't care; she belonged right there, her body wrapped around mine.

Later, when I told her the beard was coming off, she asked me to leave it, at least until the wedding in four days' time. Then when we met at the altar, I would see her in her wedding dress for the first time, and she would see me unshaven. I just loved the way she thought of things like that. I never would have, and her romantic streak balanced out my pragmatism.

I must admit I loved her other request a whole lot less. That was that we didn't make love until our wedding night. With her, sex had always been fantastic, and she had a healthy and avid appetite for it. Some of our sessions had nearly melted my laptop computer they had been so hot. She had very few, if any, inhibitions, but to her, marriage was a sacred thing, and even though we had made love numerous times when we were together six months previously, this was different. Surely we could wait four days and make love as man and wife, and that the wait would only make it all the more special?

I wanted her. I had thought of not much else while away and was disappointed by her request, naturally. But, at the same time, I could see it was important to her, and really, couldn't I wait four days, and yes, wouldn't it be all the better when we did? I could make that sacrifice for her; there was simply nothing I wouldn't do for her if she asked. I wanted her, and the whole sanctity of marriage meant less to me than it did to her. I admit I didn't understand loving relationships and what were the right and wrong things to do. After all, I'd never had one and was learning more every day. So, I agreed to her wishes, as I could see that it mattered, and anything that mattered to her, I would agree with.

Poor Johnno had to cram into the back seat of her little Mazda and listen to us prattling on all the way back to the hotel she had arranged for us. To his credit, he took it all with a smile, and not for the first time I realized what a true friend he was. To be among so much death and destruction one day and crammed in a Mazda listening to lovebirds the next kind of put the war into perspective for him, he told me.

She, with her mother and sister, had organized everything for the wedding, and worked tirelessly to do so. But she had left two jobs for me so that I wouldn't feel left out. I adored her for doing that, but at the same time, I felt scared that in letting me have a part in something so important to her, I was bound to muck it up. She wanted me to arrange the hotel for the wedding night and the honeymoon destination.

I was torn over this, agonizingly so. While it was fantastic and so typical of her wonderful nature that she trusted me to do these things, it was terrifying for me. What if I chose somewhere she hated, or that turned out to be terrible? What if it rained every day? I tried to talk her into giving me some idea of what would be enjoyable for her because, after all, she was a travel agent.

She held my hands, looked into my eyes, and said, "Tank, I'm going to be Mrs. Williams, and whatever you plan, it will be amazing. Don't panic. It could be a tent on the Gaza Strip or a motel above a men's club in King's Cross. So long as I am your wife and with you, it will be brilliant. If it rains every day, it would be more reason to be in bed with you, so I trust you. Now go do it." She laughed that magical laugh she had of her pure unadulterated joy of life. I laughed too, and suddenly I knew what I had to do.

Back in my Swanbourne training days, one of the guys had gotten married. We weren't close, but on an overnight exercise one night, we spent some time together chatting. I asked him about where he'd gone on honeymoon, and he raved about Hamilton Island in the Whitsunday Islands the Queensland coast. It was near the Great Barrier Reef and staggeringly beautiful, he had said. They'd had their ceremony in a little white chapel there and honeymooned in the resort. He had made it sound absolutely idyllic. Nothing but blue skies, azure seas, snorkeling, sailing, and long walks on white sandy beaches, and, in a luxury five-star resort with views of the Whitsundays from every room.

I went to a city travel agent, told them that my wife-to-be was also a travel agent herself, but I needed a surprise for our honeymoon. The woman I dealt with, Rose, applauded my choice, so it was booked, flights arranged, and all at a pretty reasonable price. For the wedding night, she recommended the Shangri La at the Rocks, overlooking Sydney Harbor, and she got me a good rate in a bridal suite with champagne and chocolates. She even arranged for the bed to be covered in rose petals. When I paid, I gave her a large tip, gladly, because I would have been lost without her and wanted to show how much I appreciated the help.

The rehearsal went well, and we both picked up the rings, again with Amanda being the frugal one. I smiled as I watched her negotiate with the rather surprised jeweler, who I think wished she were his daughter. He was the same one she had bought her engagement ring from. He said he was pleased to meet a returned soldier, much to my pleasant surprise. Some people liked us, while some hated us and thought of soldiers as warmongers—from the safety of their own bed, of course. Go figure.

It was a busy time. I needed a suit, and Johnno and I were not easy to fit, but eventually, things turned out all right with two simple black suits, bow ties, and very pale lilac shirts, which I had been told would complement the bridesmaids' dresses. I would never have thought such a thing was important, which was yet another example of my blindingly obvious ignorance.

In total secret, Johnno had somehow arranged a surprise for me. No man ever had a better best man with what he thought to do for me. He took me away in a cab, shushing my questions, to a private house near Ranford, to meet this wonderful elderly woman of Scottish descent. She had a crazy accent that made it fun just to listen to her. He had found her on the Internet, and she taught me to dance. Johnno knew I wasn't anyone's idea of a dancer, and I had been crapping myself with fear, knowing I had to dance in front of everyone for the bridal waltz. I was petrified of making Amanda look as if she had married a loser. For the next two and a half hours, she put up with me, stepping on her feet as I learned not to look and feel like an idiot while dancing. She was amazingly patient and alternately cajoled and applauded me with lots of "'Och's" and "'Aye laddie's," and for the first time in my life, I was a "Bonnie lad." When we left, I couldn't thank my best man enough for his thoughtfulness and took him to a small specialist bar for several very stiff and rather expensive bourbons and a cigar.

That night he took me out for my stag night, such as it was with just two of us. It was fun, and the alcohol soothed my nerves. We ended up at a strip club, but Johnno could tell I wasn't interested in looking at naked women anywhere near as much as he was. There was only one body I yearned for, so we left to go to a supper club, which was, in contrast, very civilized.

We drank outrageously expensive straight bourbon and ate equally expensive tapas while some quiet jazz played in the background. It was a good night with a good friend, topped off with another very large Cuban cigar. I had never, before or since, had such a great friend. I wasn't to know then, of course, but Johnno would die in a roadside bomb blast only two and a half months after that night.

****

The big day came, at last.

Everything was perfect, except that I was so nervous I stumbled over my vows, but Amanda and the priest both smiled at me, and somehow I got through it. When we kissed, I knew I was married to the most amazing woman in the world.

It wasn't a huge ceremony and reception. How could it be? From my side, it was only Johnno and myself. There was no family that I wanted anywhere near. None of my other army mates could come—they were on missions and unavailable—but it was the happiest day of my life. Amanda looked dazzlingly beautiful in a full white dress, veil, and train, and her mother cried her eyes out as we said our vows. I knew my life was perfect and complete at last.

I've thought to myself a million times since, if only it could have stayed that way.

Chapter Fifteen

Dillon was at his desk working on his computer, reviewing the day's interviews from the phone room when he noticed he had a new email with an attachment. He was going to ignore it until later when he noted the sender's email address. Intrigued, he opened it, and his life changed forever in that instant.

From—The Ripper (theripper1@hotmail.com.au)

Subject—Your slut wife

Attachment—pic 1.jpeg

I've done you a favor, even though you don't deserve it after insulting me. I've got rid of your wife, who is like all of the rest of them and nothing more than an unfaithful slut.

My mission is just and set in stone. It cannot and will not be stopped by the likes of you. Do not insult me, my mission, or my sanity again.

Have a nice day.

With an overwhelming sense of fear and impending doom, Dillon clicked on the attachment, and a scene from hell opened. He was looking at his own bedroom. A man was on top of a woman, there was blood everywhere, and in the blood, one word was written above the bed head on the beige-colored wall.

SLUT

Dillon stood and screamed, "Kathy, no, no, no, no, *nooo!*"

His only thought was to save his wife. He ran out as other officers stood and stared after hearing the distress in his voice. Mike Knowles saw the picture on Dillon's computer screen, and he took off after his boss and caught up to him on a lower landing. Together, as one, they burst through the car park door and into Dillon's car.

Traffic meant nothing. Neither did the speed limit, as Dillon was vaguely aware of Mike yelling into the radio's microphone, calling for all possible cars to converge on the house and gave the address of Dillon and Kathy's home. They knew the killer would long be gone but hoped upon hope for a miracle.

****

The internet was an incredible invention. It really was. Once I had put the cop's name in the search engine, lots of links had come up. The most recent featured me, of course, which I read avidly along with all the others. One mentioned his wife by name and the charity she worked for. There were pictures of the happy couple at events, including the Black-Tie Fundraising Ball last year. He was dressed in a tuxedo, and she in a glittering gown. Apparently, the ball was the major event for a charity she was the head of. From there, it was an easy jump to find where the charity offices were and all sorts of other interesting information that I read and soaked up like a sponge.

I knew it would be really useful to know where the good inspector lived, and if necessary, I could pay him a visit if it looked like he was getting too close. I thought I could slow the investigation by killing the interfering cop to gain enough time to complete my mission. My plan felt right in my aching head. Follow his wife and find out where they lived, which was a perfect and logical step. After all, I knew a soldier could never have too much information about his enemy. So, the next day I camped outside her office block, waiting for her to come out. Naturally, I was well disguised.

The first time I spotted her, she was with another, clearly younger man. I followed them into the city then waited for them to come out of an expensive hotel later that evening. *Perhaps they have some sort of charity meeting,* I thought. When they exited, imagine my surprise when they both looked around furtively and then kissed goodnight. It was more than just a peck on the cheek, and I watched him feeling her ass, even lifting her skirt for passersby to see her underwear. As she walked away from him, I saw the look of lust in his eyes and realized the obvious—they were fucking.

It could not have been any better, and the irony was fantastic. I almost laughed out loud with glee. *The man charged with hunting me for killing unfaithful sluts was himself married to one; beautiful!*

I lost her in the city that night, but that didn't matter as it was only a couple of days later she came out of her offices looking very smart in a business suit and silk shirt. This time I followed her straight to her house, where I drove past so I wouldn't be noticed. Knowing where they lived, I went back to my place and thought what I would do about it.

That day my headache was a lot better for some reason, and a plan came together in my mind. It was funny how life could sometimes throw curveballs and work out so much better than a plan. Sometimes, with all planning, things could go horribly wrong, but in this case, it went better than I could have hoped. I had taken up station outside her offices, intending to find out where the boyfriend lived, as I had decided to kill him first and watch her suffer and try to hide that they had been lovers, which would be a hoot. The following day, I would pay Dillon's wife a visit and kill her, but only after I had been to visit Helena's sister. It had now been long enough for the police to lose any interest in her as a family member, and it was high time my mission began again.

I realized that killing Bradley's wife would play havoc with the investigation. He would have to stand down, and that would give me more time to find Amanda while someone else took over and be brought up to speed. Once I had caught up with Amanda, nothing else mattered to me, and if I died in a blaze of glory, I didn't care.

I had just sat down in a nearby café for lunch when they both came out together and headed toward the car park. My car was close, and I followed, not wanting to lose them. Not that I needed to worry; they seemed very interested in each other. To my great delight, they both went back to her house.

They drove into the garage and put down the electric door. I parked in the street behind, in a spot I had picked earlier after my recon, where I thought the car would go unnoticed when the time came. But now, it didn't matter to me if it was seen as the number plates had been lifted the day before from a van I had come across in a shopping center car park loading zone. If I could kill them together, a white sedan parked two streets away wouldn't be remembered, I was quite sure. But, even if it was noticed by locals, it was a very common model car with the wrong registration plate on it, so impossible to track back to me.

I quickly donned a cap and common brand trainers. I slipped out of my jeans as I had shorts underneath, and my T-shirt was plain and innocuous. I then took off back down the street, trying to resemble a jogger with a bandage on my arm.

I had returned late at night previously and done a complete circuit of the house and grounds and knew that the garage was open to the side garden. I hoped that in their haste to get inside and fuck they hadn't locked the adjoining door from the garage into their hallway. If they had, I would improvise, as I always did. I quietly slipped down the neighbor's driveway and, using a lemon tree as an aid, jumped the fence. Within seconds I was in their garden behind the garage. Having learned the hard way, I already knew there was no dog this time; I would never make that mistake again. My arm had become red and inflamed over the last couple of days and was a problem I would have to solve very soon as I realized infection had well and truly set in.

The gods were with me, and the door was unlocked. After putting on my latex gloves from the ever-present backpack, I eased open the door and stepped inside. I crept up to the corner and peered around. They were kissing while sitting on the couch, and just for a moment, I felt sorry for Detective Inspector Dillon Bradley. His wife was cuckolding him as mine had me. Perhaps he, too, would appreciate my work once he found that out.

I watched them and waited patiently. Soon he picked her up and carried her to the bedroom. How brazen this whore was, I thought, to fuck in the bed she shared with her husband. God, she made me so angry. My thoughts were clear, the headache was bearable, and the voices calmed as they knew I was about to kill.

The sounds of them rutting like dogs filtered down the passage. I slipped off my shirt, shorts, shoes, and socks, not wanting to get blood on them, and, dressed only in my underpants, went to the bedroom. *How funny will it be if they see me near-naked in the room with them?* I wondered. *Probably the slut will want to fuck me as well*, and that thought wiped the smirk off my face, as it was just too disgusting.

I could have been playing a bugle, and I doubt they would have heard. She lay with her depraved legs spread wide for her lover, and he was plowing her frantically. By the grunts he was making, he was close to finishing, so I decided it was time.

Her eyes were closed, and in one movement, I grabbed his hair, lifted his head, and cut his throat. I watched, enthralled as she opened her eyes to see her lover bleeding and twitching above her, and as the bitch started screaming, I cut her throat too.

Just before she passed, I had the pleasure of calling her what she was, a dirty fucking slut. I showed her my face, so she knew who was killing her, and she died knowing that she had been caught and killed for being what she was—a whore.

I felt good and sure in my heart my work would now be appreciated for what it was, a clean-up operation of these tramps who lived among us. I was sure that once my hunter got over his shock, and the embarrassment of his slut wife being in all of the papers caught with her lover, he would acknowledge my mission. *Perhaps*, I mused, *he might like to join me.* I doubted that, but you never knew how people would react. Time would tell.

I picked up the slut's panties off the floor, dipped them in her own blood, and wrote on the wall for the entire world to see what she was.

SLUT.

Then I crossed the bedroom carefully to her ensuite bathroom and cleaned up. Not too much blood had splattered on me, and what there was washed off easily enough. Once done, I went back to my clothes and dressed. I carefully looked around to make sure I had not touched anything, not that it really mattered anymore now that they had my DNA from the dog. But still, it paid to be prudent. I also had a good look around to make sure they didn't have a camera system that had taken my picture. If they did have one, I was sure it would have been turned off, especially with what she had been doing, but I wanted to make sure. He was a police detective, after all. There wasn't one that I could find, just a good alarm system, which she had naturally turned off when she had come home.

I was about to walk out the door, still thinking of cameras, when I had a fantastic idea. In the internet search of my nemesis, I had noted his work email address. Wouldn't it be fun to not only warn him to watch his mouth when talking about me to the press but also send him a pic of his wife? Oh, I loved the idea, and I laughed out loud. Sometimes my brilliance surprised even me. I snapped a picture of the lovers on my phone, then I was quickly out the front door. I glanced up and down the street, my cap pulled down and shoulders hunched.

****

Once I got to the footpath, I took off at a jog back to the car. This was a quiet area, and while I didn't know if anyone was watching me through a window, there was certainly no one on the streets to see me. People, in general, liked to mind their own business these days, thankfully.

I drove back to the city, parked in a multi-story car park on the top floor, waited to be alone, then quickly swapped plates with the car alongside. I drove down to a lower level and parked again. I redressed and put on a disguise. I was going to the same Internet café I had been to before. *Which is entirely appropriate,* I thought. When there before, I had taken note that they had no cameras and the person behind the counter was more interested in the computer game he was playing than seeing how his customers looked.

Once the cops got the email, they could trace where it had come from via the ISP address; I knew that, so the disguise was warranted. I got there with enough coins to operate a machine without approaching the counter and went straight to Hotmail to create an email address, smiling as I used the nickname the newspapers had given me. Of course, all of the information they wanted to set up the account was rubbish. I was smart enough to get past those safeguards. *Besides, this account will be used only once,* I thought, but that didn't stop me being theripper2, or three if I chose to keep taunting them into the future. I paid a few more coins to use the scanner, uploaded the picture, then sent it to my new anonymous email address. Then forwarded it to Mr. Dillon Bradley with a short note to be careful what he said in future.

Once done, I lost no time in getting out of there and heading back home. I parked the car in the garage and got inside just as the headache returned. This time it was a shocker. My eyesight became cloudy, tinged with red around the edges, the color of blood, and I collapsed in bed. I slept the sleep of the just for fourteen hours straight, and when I awoke, it was with a purpose. I had to get back on Amanda's trail. I looked forward to our date with destiny.

But there was a problem. I felt like crap. A fever from the infected dog bite had set in, and again, I cursed my stupidity as I was sweating profusely and my arm felt like it was on fire.

Chapter Sixteen

Journal Excerpt #7, The Honeymoon and return to Sydney

What an incredibly beautiful place Hamilton Island is. We had a fabulous spa room overlooking the Whitsunday Passage, which is a group of islands, mostly uninhabited, creating a cruising mecca as they formed a natural passage through the inner and outer Great Barrier reef in tropical Northern Queensland. We had flown there direct from Sydney after our wedding night, which was, as promised by Amanda, breathtakingly wonderful, having waited that extra four days to make love together.

The weather was kind to us, and every day was in the high twenties to low thirties Celsius, with clear skies and a gentle breeze. For someone such as Amanda, who had spent her whole life wanting to travel, it was a paradise on Earth. She was born to see the world, and to experience such an exotic location made her even more radiantly beautiful. When I pointed it out to her, she said it was my doing, not the travel—that being married to me had made her happier than at any time in her life. While I could agree with that sentiment because I felt the same, I also thought the location for our honeymoon played a part.

On our first night in bed, she traced her finger over the small raised scar on my shoulder and she asked about it with a touch of concern in her voice. I told her about the firefight from start to finish, and she listened with rapt attention. I always thought a woman, especially a woman such as Amanda, who possessed the gentlest soul imaginable, would not be interested in the vulgarities of a dirty war in an Arab country. Yet I was wrong, she found everything fascinating and continually asked questions so she could better understand what life was like over there. For those of us fighting, it was just our job, which we did for varying reasons. For some, it was patriotic—some because they liked being a soldier and some for deeper, darker reasons.

For myself, I enjoyed my army life, but then, considering what life I'd had before the army, that was hardly surprising, and it gave me a family that had been sadly lacking in my life. But then came what I called my LAA—Life After Amanda—when everything changed for me. I wanted to be home with her. Killing terrorists did not have the same appeal for me anymore. I did it and would continue to do so as well as I could, that was my job, but my focus had changed.

She tenderly kissed the scar and spoke softly. "Tank, you be careful out there, won't you? Always, always, make sure you come back to me. I couldn't bear to lose you." In that moment, more so than any other time before, I finally realized this woman, who I idolized, loved me with the same depth of feeling as I had for her. That was a wondrous eye-opening moment in time for me. To have someone care for me was something I was not used to. Yes, I had mates, maybe they gave a toss about me, maybe they didn't, and family? What family? In battle, you supported your teammates, and we watched each other's backs. But this was different—

somebody cared whether I lived or died and more importantly, wanted to be with me; I was loved. I may be a slow learner, but it was an earth-shattering moment for me. She had been my first and only girlfriend. I had nothing, no prior experience, to gauge these feelings by.

I took her hands in mine, stared deeply into her eyes, and vowed, "Honey, I promise you that no matter what, I will always come back to you. I will never leave you. You are my life." She wrapped herself around me, and we made the most beautiful love. She cried out when she came in a torrent of passion. I made that promise to her and myself, that nothing and no one would ever keep me away from her, ever.

I knew from that point on, when I went back to fight, it would be different for me, significantly so. I would become like most of the other people I fought with, and that was a sobering thought too. LBA—Life Before Amanda—in the army, for me meant killing full stop. While I didn't want to get killed, I went into situations really not caring if I did or didn't. I was a machine on autopilot, and I think that made me particularly good at my job. But I knew when I went back to war for a third tour, it would be different. I wanted to come back alive, with everything intact, and spend as many days as possible with my one and only true love.

We lived by the pool or on the beach. We hired a small catamaran, learned to sail it, and spent time dancing from wave to wave, seeing fish and dolphins every day, and we made amazing love together every night.

We gained incredible suntans, Amanda noticeably more so than myself, as Iraq was a pretty hot place to serve, so I was tanned before the wedding. She was stunningly beautiful with blonde hair, and with her tan, wearing a bikini, she was breathtaking to look at, which I never tired of doing.

We did a day trip out to the reef, saw some whales, and snorkeled amid the amazingly colored coral and fish life that abounded everywhere. We held onto ropes that trailed out from the stern of the barge our boat was moored to and watched huge fish come up to be hand-fed.

Amanda had an array of different colored bikinis that could make people think she was a movie star. That day she wore a bright yellow one that drew everyone's eyes. She looked like a model straight from a photoshoot. At one stage, I felt jealousy bordering on rage, as a couple of Swedish backpackers couldn't take their eyes off her and made it obvious. Not that I blamed them, she was the hottest woman on the tour by far, but I didn't like them ogling so openly and nudging each other as if she were a piece of meat. It was disrespectful to her, and that was unforgivable. The bright yellow tiny triangles of material perfectly complemented her long silky blonde hair and tanned skin. I tried hard not to get angry at the ogling and their crude, murmured comments, but was failing badly. I wanted to hurt them and could feel myself building up to a rage. I was ready to do just that.

Amanda noticed, of course. I was sitting on a bench opposite them on the boat, taking a break from snorkeling, when she came and stood in front of me and blocked my view of them. I glanced up at her smiling face, then she sat astride me, lowering her body so there were only two pieces of very thin material between the two parts of our bodies that had become very well acquainted since our wedding night. Softly and slowly, she rocked her hips, so we were touching in the most intimately teasing way.

She put her hands on my shoulders, her right hand being over my recent scar, and stared me straight in the eyes. "Hey, big guy, what's wrong? Are you mad at me? You know a smile suits you so much better than a frown." Then she kissed my nose, and I knew, I just knew, those two clowns were checking out her ass.

"I'm not mad at you, honey, but those two guys are really pissing me off." I put my hands on her hips, loving the feel of the elastic sides of her bikini bottoms under my fingers. I was tense with a smoldering anger, but she could always relax me in a moment. I melted under the come-to-bed promise in her eyes and the relentless teasing of her body rubbing against mine. My penis hardened, and I lifted my hips imperceptibly as I strained to touch her, to get back inside her where I belonged.

"I've seen them checking me out, babe. They are so obvious I couldn't miss it, could I? But guess what?" She had an impish grin on her beautiful face, and my bad mood was dissipating fast. "Later tonight, while they are fantasizing about me, probably wanking because neither of them will pick up a woman, I'm going to be naked and making love to my husband. Now think carefully before you answer, who would you rather be, them or you?"

She had me, and she knew it. I grinned back and pulled her tight against me. "Okay, we need to go for a swim now, these bathers are not made for hiding a hard-on." I kissed her, her breasts pressed against my chest, the damp bikini top making her nipples hard, or was that her love and desire for me? I knew the guys were watching, possibly drooling, but it no longer mattered. She had chosen to be with me, and that was more than *enough.*

The next day we took part in a sailing race with fifty-odd other tourists to what must be the most beautiful beach in the world, Whitehaven Beach. We sailed two fifty-foot schooners. Thankfully the two backpackers were not there. Maybe they couldn't afford the one-hundred-fifty dollar per person fee, or maybe they had gotten lucky and picked up two women. Who knew or cared?

I say it was a race, but no one was interested in which boat won or lost. The weather was perfect, and it was as much fun watching the other yachts tacking and dancing across and through the waves as it was being on one feeling it.

Once we arrived at the finish line and disembarked, we all went for a walk while the crews set up a fantastic seafood barbecue lunch, complete with large foam ice chests full of bottles of wine, beer, and soft drinks. The coconut palms reached down to the water, silver whiting, and other fish swam in the shallows, and it was just idyllic.

We joined a group of people and played volleyball with a net set up by the crew, both of us laughing as we dived in silky white soft sand to get the ball. Everyone was covered in sweat and sand, and when we were called to lunch, Amanda and I dived into the water to cool down and wash off first.

I had the best ice-cold beer of my life, sitting in the sand, the sun beating down, eating skewered prawns and Moreton Bay bugs with salad. I was looking across at the most stunningly beautiful woman in the world, today resplendent in a black bikini that contrasted with her oiled skin and blonde hair flying in the breeze. Amanda sipped on white wine with ice cubes in it to help keep it cool. Occasionally she would shake her head to flick her hair from her eyes in the breeze and look over at me and smile.

After lunch, we had an hour before the yachts left the cove to head back, and we took off alone. We followed a small stream into the dunes and palms until we found a spot where it widened out to make a small pool. We sat in it and drank the two beers we had sneaked away from the coolers, and within minutes I was on my back while she was above me, her black bikini removed, and she rode me to yet another earth-shattering orgasm.

We could easily have drifted off to sleep in the afterglow of lunchtime alcohol, the sun, full tummies, and contentment, but fortunately, we got back just in time. We swam out to where the sterns had ladders reaching down into the water and very unwillingly left Whitehaven. We participated in round two of the yacht race back to the Island Marina.

The skipper let Amanda take the helm on the return voyage for a while, and I have a beautiful picture on my phone of her steering the yacht. The evening sun was close to the horizon. She had a look of steely determination on her gorgeous face as her desire to help our boat beat the others back shone through in all its splendor.

All too soon, the ten days came to an end. We were both well-tanned and reluctantly left our island paradise to head back to Sydney—the traffic, hustle and bustle, and normality. We had some decisions to make about where we were going to live, and that presented us with our first dilemma.

I was based at Swanbourne in Perth, some four and a half thousand kilometers from Sydney and Amanda's mother and sister. She did want to travel in life and would be happy to follow me anywhere, so Amanda leaving Sydney and moving west wasn't an issue in itself. I also thought she would like the weather and relaxed lifestyle over there. But, if she left her Sydney job and transferred to Perth, then I got posted, and there were already strong hints I would be going back to Afghanistan, she would be alone in a new city with no friends or family support for as long as my tour of duty lasted.

She didn't really care about her job—in fact, she hated it—and she was pretty good, so could get a job in her field anywhere. It would just be the upheaval and loneliness when I was posted overseas. I had less than two weeks left of my leave and some decisions to make.

I thought about it long and hard. I wanted to come up with a solution that would make her happy, so one night, in bed, where we had most of our long discussions, I put my idea to her.

"Babe, why not do both? I can move us into married quarters on the base, and you can work or not work—that's your choice. There are plenty of travel agencies over there, or try something else if you like. But, if, or when, I do get posted, you could move back over here and you would be close to your mum and Jayne. We could rent an apartment here and leave it empty while we are gone. When you come back here, get another job again, or not, depending how long I'm posted for. Now I know what you're thinking and we can easily afford it because it's virtually free to live on base."

Then, as an afterthought, I had a blinding moment

of sheer brilliance. "What about Jayne?"

Jayne was her younger sister, another gorgeous woman with an equally lovely personality. They looked remarkably similar, and I have this awesome picture of the three of us with me in the middle, and it's like being between twins—a thorn between two roses is how I captioned it. Of course, Amanda had poked me when I did.

"We could get a two-bedroom apartment, and she can move in with us. It would give her somewhere nice to live, and she can watch the place while we are in WA. I wouldn't want to charge her rent or anything to help her get back on her feet."

Amanda stared at me for a couple of minutes, a look of wonder on her face, before hugging me tightly. "God, I love you, you big hunk. That's perfect, and it helps Jayne too. I've been so worried about her after that moron dumped her and broke her heart. You deserve a reward for being such a good boy." And, giggling, she moved lower down the bed and gently took me in her mouth. I felt like a very good boy indeed; she was exquisite.

I finished my leave in Sydney and helped her with all of the practical things we needed to do. We found an apartment. True, it was nothing flashy, but it was nice with a decent outlook. Two bedrooms, two bathrooms, and a big balcony to watch the sunset from. With two bathrooms, Jayne had her own privacy and space, and she was overjoyed with our offer for her to move in with us. She could get out of the dump she was in, and she treated it like a fresh start.

When we were alone, she gave me the biggest hug and said, "You know, if you hadn't married my sister, you could have had me." I slapped her behind and told her how tempting that was. But we were both joking. There would never be anyone else for me. I was hooked for life, and Jayne was fully aware of that.

I had hired a small moving truck for the day, and when we were all moved in, Amanda and I fell into bed tired and content. We were in our very first place together as a couple that night, and we commemorated in the way we celebrated everything. We ordered pizza to be delivered and ate it with cold beers, naked in bed, and it was fantastic.

Soon after, I headed back to the barracks in Perth alone to get things organized there while Amanda finished out her notice at her place of work. She also got Jayne settled in and said goodbye to her friends. Two weeks later, I met her at the airport in Perth and introduced her to the life of being an army wife on the base.

Like everything else she did, she took to that like a duck to water. She made good friends with other wives quickly and picked up a job in, of all places, a jewelry shop in Fremantle. She was working for a seventy-year-old Jewish guy who just loved her bubbly personality. After one week, he wanted to adopt her as his granddaughter.

Life was good. Better than good—it was fantastic.

But nothing ever stays good for long, does it?

Unknown then, black clouds were on our horizon, and in only a few short months things would turn very dark indeed. What we had at Swanbourne before I went away again was the last of our great times. If I had known what was to come, I would have gone AWOL.

Chapter Seventeen

My arm was burning up, the headaches were back, and I alternated between shivering cold and sweating buckets. There was no avoiding the facts; I had a serious fever. All of this I knew within minutes of waking up after getting back from the internet café. I'd spent the night throwing bedcovers off only to pull them back over myself when I'd become chilled. When I pulled the bandage off the wound, it was weeping yellow muck, and the veins around it were bright red as poison traveled up my blood stream. I knew I needed antibiotics, and quickly. The dog bite had become badly infected, and I realized I had left it way too long.

Naturally, that presented problems. I couldn't walk into a doctor's consulting rooms or hospital ER without questions being asked. The cops knew I had been bitten, and they would have told hospitals to watch out for all canine bite wounds that required treatment. I would be caught and locked up, and I couldn't have that—the mission was far from complete—but I needed a doctor badly.

I made it to the kitchen, took a handful of painkillers with several glasses of water, sat down with pen and paper, and thought it through slowly and calmly. The fever was making it difficult to concentrate, so I decided making notes might help.

Problem. I needed antibiotics from a doctor or

pharmacy. If I broke into one after-hours, how would I know which drugs to take? If I attempted it during opening hours, I risked capture. They all had CCTV, and some even had security guards, and there was no doubt I was in a weakened state, so I could have a problem defending myself.

Solution. I need someone to tell me what to take and when, and who doesn't present a risk of capture.

Problem. Where and how do I find a doctor who won't report me?

Solution. Kill him afterward to ensure his silence. This was obvious, and it made sense, but where did I find one? A doctor's office offered the same problems as a pharmacy with security and witnesses. If I called for a doctor to visit me here, there would be a log of where the doctor had gone and why. Clearly, I couldn't use my apartment, so it had to be elsewhere, but where? I thought long and hard and slowly, a plan evolved.

I suppose I should have experienced some sort of guilt for thinking of killing a doctor. You could blame me for that, and I would have to accept it. But my choices were limited, and I couldn't afford to get caught before I had finished my mission and found Amanda. I had no remorse. I had never enjoyed that emotion and didn't really know what it was. Killing was a way of life for me, just something I did when needed, and to be completely truthful, I'd felt nothing at all when I killed in the army or since, so a doctor was just one more casualty of my personal war; collateral damage, if you will.

The newspapers called me a sociopath, so I guessed that made me one, and even if I wasn't, if I were to be labeled thus, I may as well act the part. Who was I to argue with those clearly cleverer than me? Murdering the man who would help cure me was a task that needed to be done for expediency. Like any other job, if something came up, I'd been trained to adapt and move onward, always onward. So that was what I was going to do. Was it my fault I had no conscience or the army's?

My arm had another problem in that it was stiffening up. I had lost quite a bit of use in it, and I should rest it until it was fixed. If I got into a fight with an able-bodied person, it could pose a problem, and that was an unacceptable risk. Linked to the fact that my knife work had become my calling card, perhaps for this job, it would be worthwhile to change my M.O. In doing so, it may keep the police from linking his death to, so a bonus that would help get me more time to complete the mission. I needed to gain as much time as possible to find Amanda.

My storage locker in Redcliffe entered my head. I didn't know why I hadn't thought of it before. I had guns aplenty stashed there. Time to start using them for the reason they had been manufactured.

A couple of hours later in Redcliffe, I unlocked the roller door and opened it one-handed. I stepped inside the cool shadows and slid the door down for privacy. I turned the overhead light on so I had light to go to the chest against the wall and unlock it. Under the lid were towels, which I removed, displaying an array of firearms gleaming in the light.

I lovingly took out my Heckler & Koch USP nine-millimeter pistol and held it for a few moments, loving the way it fit in my hand—it just felt so good. From alongside it, I picked up a spare magazine and a silencer, which had been modified to fit the handgun and was a Special Forces adaption. I slipped it into my shoulder holster, which had provisions to clip the silencer and spare mag to it. From the drawer below, I took out a box of nine-millimeter hollow points and put both items into my backpack. A silencer didn't make the weapon silent, but it did reduce the noise and change its dynamic enough that a gunshot no longer sounded like a gunshot. I knew that could come in handy.

I was about to lock the box but stopped and thought about the other guns I owned. If through some fluke, the cops did get close to me, I might well need some firepower to get away, or at least to go down, taking as many with me as I could. I knew I wanted to give them a good fight if and when that time came. Death held no fears for me. With nothing to live for without Amanda, I would take as many of the cops with me as I could. If it happened before killing Amanda, then I would be happy that she would know she had been the cause of all the killing, pain, and suffering. It was all on her, not me. I took comfort in thinking that if it went down that way, she would spend the rest of her life not only feeling guilt for everyone else's death but would know her actions had killed me too. She'd always loved my tales of battles, but I doubted she would enjoy this one quite as much.

I took out the Heckler and Koch MP5 submachine gun and three curved magazines already loaded with the same nine-millimeter ammunition, but I packed another box as well. The retractable stock made it easy to fit in the backpack, and I wrapped it in a towel with the mags and tucked it inside. I also grabbed three hand grenades, but the other guns I left behind because I figured that if I couldn't get away with these, then the rest wouldn't matter. There was always the possibility, too that I may need a secondary stash. It might not pay to have all my weapons with me, so it made sense to leave some here.

I locked up and headed back to Scarborough, sweating and shivering, my backpack on the floor on the passenger side. It was good to have the weapons with me, and despite the fever, I felt able to continue. I had the ever-present headache, which came and went in waves, sometimes mere ripples, other times giant breakers I couldn't surf down. They didn't help the fever and my general feeling of lethargy. I ached all over and struggled to stay awake as I drove. I sipped slowly from an apple juice container. The fever had given me a thirst I couldn't seem to quench, but I knew that evening I would solve the problem. I could hardly wait.

Just after I had returned to Perth to hunt for Amanda, I went to a medical clinic to try to get some more powerful headache pills. I left once they'd started asking more questions than I was prepared to answer. I knew if they saw the scars on my head and heard the circumstances of how I came by them, they would want to ship me back to hospital for tests. *Like that was going to happen!* I was never going to be sent to another one of those places. That was where everything had gone wrong for me, and I was content knowing I would die before ever going back again.

While I was sitting in the waiting room, I noticed a poster for an after-hours doctor service that made house calls and made a note on my phone of the number, just in case. Well, it was *just-in-case time.*

I jumped online after my visit to the storage shed and looked at houses to rent that were currently vacant, and, during the afternoon, I had driven around until I'd found one that looked just right. It did not have a *For Rent* sign out the front yet. It was in a quiet street and from the front had no indication it was empty. Being an older style home on a large block, the gardens were untidy but not overly so, just a typical nondescript rental.

I waited until late evening. I ate a hamburger in the car on the way to the house, listening to the radio, then found a nice quiet spot to park nearby. Dressed like a jogger with a red cap and glasses, I arrived at the house. The toweling stopped the guns from clanking together in the backpack I carried. There was a couple walking a dog on the other side of the road, so I knelt to tie a shoelace as they went by, my head bowed. When they were out of sight, I raced down the side of the house through the gate and around to the back. I then stopped and checked to make sure no one was watching me.

Like a lot of rentals, this house wasn't terribly secure, and after one really good shove with my shoulder to the wooden laundry door, I was inside. The striker plate of the lock lay on the floor, and I shook my head at how easy it was. I put on my gloves and switched on a couple of lights before making the phone call to the doctor's service from my mobile. While it was ringing, I went to make sure I could open the front door easily from the inside, which I could. The owners hadn't seen the need to provide their tenant with a deadbolt, just a twist latch.

I made the call and spoke to a woman, telling her that my son had cut himself on some barbed wire a few days ago, and the wound was red and angry, and he was feverish. They asked for a Medicare card, and I explained that we had only just moved in, and I thought it was packed, and we hadn't come across it yet. I would be quite happy to pay an account in cash direct to the doctor and make a claim afterward to my health fund.

She told me it would be approximately a forty-five-minute wait. That was how simple it was to lure a doctor to his death.

An hour later, an older European car pulled into the driveway. I watched through the window as the doctor, carrying his traditional black bag, climbed out. I opened the front door to his knock and thanked him for coming so quickly. I shut the door behind him with my wounded arm. The other held the silenced gun behind my back.

He was probably in his late twenties and dark-skinned, perhaps Indian or Sri Lankan. I showed him the pistol, and his eyes widened. "I don't carry narcotic drugs," he said in an unusually British accent.

I shook my head and beckoned him into the empty living room. He thought I was a junkie—perhaps the red eyes, sweating, and flushed skin from the fever made me appear that way. I couldn't blame him, really. I knew I looked dreadful. Possibly worse than I felt, though I doubted that. I motioned him into the empty kitchen, where the lights were brightest, and to the breakfast bar. He stood on one side while I moved to the other. He placed the bag on the top between us and waited, quite calm under the circumstances.

I held out my bandaged arm to him. "I picked up a dog bite a few days ago, and it's infected. I need help." Understanding dawned in his eyes, and suddenly he was very scared.

"You're him, the Ripper. Why should I help you when you will kill me anyway? They say you are a butcher. I don't want to die." He started to back away, and I just moved the gun from being aimed loosely in his general direction to his chest and cocked it.

"This house is an empty rental, so there is no way to

find me or link me to it because I broke in and have gloves on. I have no reason to kill you and won't if you help me. On the other hand, I will be able to find you because I'm going to take your driver's license when I go. So, if you tell the police about me, I will kill you and your family. The cops already have a description of me, so there is nothing you can tell them that they don't already know, but I am going to insist you don't speak to them anyway. You have nothing to fear from me if you do as I say because you are not part of my mission. So, you have a choice, either fix me up and I will let you go, and pay for your time in cash, but minus your driver's license. Or I can kill you now and find another doctor. It's your choice."

The look of relief in his eyes was laughable. "I also need the strongest painkillers you have on you for headaches and lots of them."

Then I waited a few seconds while he thought about it. He nodded, opened his bag wide, and took out some instruments. Firstly, he cut away the bandages. He looked carefully at the wound, which was weeping greenish-yellow pus and was very red and inflamed. Now there was a deep red line snaking up my arm. He spent a few minutes cleaning it with cotton swabs and a strong antiseptic that stung like hell, but I didn't flinch; I'd had worse in my past.

He redressed it before speaking again. "Do you have any allergies I should know about?" I shook my head, and he took out a disposable hypodermic needle, a small glass vial, and two boxes of pills, one larger than the other. He crossed to my side, lifted my T-shirt sleeve, and injected me. He then held out the box of tablets to me.

"I've given you a penicillin injection, and these tablets are amoxicillin. Take one three times a day with food till they are finished. The other box is all I have for headache pain. They may help, or depending on what's causing the headaches, they may not. They should at least take the edge off. If the arm doesn't get better soon, you will need hospital treatment. You must keep a close eye on it. Gangrene is always a possibility. This is as much as I can do here. Please let me go. I promise I won't tell anyone."

I knew he was lying, of course, and shot him once in the chest. A heart shot at that range was easy, and using a hollow point meant he had no chance. *Doctors*, I thought, *so brainy yet so gullible.*

He fell to the floor and was dead almost instantly. I crossed to the back door, opened it quietly, and listened for any signs that the soft barking noise from the gun had been heard. It hadn't. People went on with cooking their dinners, watching the news, or whatever people did at that time of night in suburban Perth.

While death came quickly for the doctor, the hollow point had made a mess, and I couldn't be bothered to do anything about it. I picked up the used bandages, folded them in on themselves, and shoved them into my backpack along with the syringe and other stuff. The warm gun followed suit after I removed the silencer. One last look around to make sure I hadn't left anything behind, then I turned off the lights and went out of the front door onto the darkened entry porch. Once again, my luck held, and the street was empty, so I started to jog slowly down the road. I tried to look the part of someone tired and at the end of a run. I certainly couldn't have looked the part of a fit, athletic guy out for a jog.

The headache was killing me, and the fever was no doubt making it worse. I had one thought in my mind, to get home and sleep it off.

Once there, I crashed again and slept through the night. It was a troubled sleep full of nightmares and vivid dreams of things going wrong and bugs crawling all over me. At one stage, I woke, and the sheets were soaked with my sweat. I drank several glasses of water and went onto the balcony to let the cool night air chill my skin. Soon I started to feel cold, and once the shivering started again, I went back to bed and slept till after ten.

I stayed home all that day, eating whatever I had left in the fridge and cupboards. I didn't want to go out, and I didn't trust a pizza delivery man not to recognize me from the pictures still being plastered all over the press and TV. By lunchtime the day after, I felt a lot better. The drugs had worked well, and I was once again ready to get back on track with my mission.

Feeling human again, I was hungry, so I went to a busy Woolworth's supermarket three suburbs away. In the unlikely event someone recognized me through my latest disguise, they wouldn't know I lived in Scarborough. I spent big and did a large shop so as to minimize my time out in the public eye. I ate two pies from a busy Asian bakery while I shopped, and I instantly felt better again. The late doctor had done well. It was a shame I'd had no choice but to kill him, but that was life, or in his case, death.

In my time, I've found that most people just lie. The doctor couldn't have kept quiet. He would have tried to be the hero who helped catch the Ripper. That was human nature. I could not take the chance on his silence. It would have been an unacceptable risk. He was just one more piece of collateral damage as part of a bigger mission.

Once I was back home, and the shopping had been put away, I changed the dressing and squirted antiseptic all over it. The wound itself looked a lot better. In fact, it was well enough that around two a.m. that night, I went to the sister's house in Morley to question her about her friend Suzi and, more importantly, Toni, or as I had always known her, Amanda.

Everything went smoothly. I knocked on the front door, and the husband answered, opening it but leaving the security fly door locked. That was very wise in these days of high crime and violence. Unfortunately for him, security screens won't stop bullets, and once he saw the gun pointing at his chest and I told him to open up, he did.

Once inside, we rounded up his wife, and I got her to use the cable ties on hubby and cover his mouth, as I didn't want to listen to him begging. Then I took her and tied her to her bed. I no longer needed the gun, so I put it away and took out the knife.

Once hubby was taken care of, I sat alongside her on the bed and pulled off the tape covering her mouth. I held the knife to her throat and told her what I wanted. She realized the significance of my questions and knew I was the one who had killed her sister and others. Stupidly she thought she could bargain her life for the information, but once I started on her, it didn't take too long. Of all my victims thus far, she had the most spirit, but naturally, I couldn't spare her, and once I was sure I had gotten everything from her, I turned her over, so I didn't get covered in her blood and killed her.

Knowing that she too was a slut—after all, she was

female, wasn't she?—I treated her like the others. I was tiring of killing these women. Amanda was the one I wanted. Perhaps it was the tail end of the infection, but I felt so tired of it all. But the one shining beacon I had left was that I had to find and kill Amanda, and I was now one step closer to my Holy Grail.

Chapter Eighteen

Life seemed to go forward in slow motion for Dillon. It was a nightmare he couldn't wake up from. The love of his life, wife of twenty-seven years, mother of his daughter, and someone he'd thought he would grow old with had been butchered in their own bed. Just to rub salt in the wound, she had been murdered with a younger man she had been having an affair with.

Dillon could feel people staring, sympathizing, or laughing at him, and along with his own personal grief of loss, the sexual infidelity aspect took it to a completely different level. He alternated between grief at her loss and rage against her being unfaithful, even though he himself had been seeing Marci. To him, that was different because, he figured, had Kathy still wanted him, he would not have gone with Marci.

Reporters wouldn't leave him alone; his phone rang constantly, and everyone was too embarrassed to look him in the eye. Worse, they had no idea what to say to him or how to say it. People who knew and loved Kathy where shocked and saddened by her death, naturally. They were equally shocked and amazed that she had been having an affair, especially with one of her employees, who was considerably younger than her. Dillon believed her friends would blame him that she had looked elsewhere. Maybe that was even true. Probably it was his fault.

He realized also there were people who would automatically think he had killed them both. Or had them killed and made it look like the work of the Ripper. That was just human nature to think the worst, and with one or two cryptic comments in the papers, there was a groundswell of rumor and innuendo around him that that was what he had done.

He didn't understand how to act or feel. Should he be angry at Kathy for being unfaithful or heartbroken at her being killed, or was it okay to feel both? He spent his time with wild mood swings and depression, and the only place he could find solace was in a bottle. He drank constantly, only finding sleep when he passed out blind drunk.

His daughter and family were around, but all he wanted was to be left alone. The house was a crime scene, and he'd had to move out, not that he wanted to stay there anyway. He had lots of offers from people to move in with them for a while, and some of them may even have meant it. As genuine as they'd sounded, he didn't feel he was really wanted. That would be far too embarrassing all around, and he elected to move into a motel alone and try to hide away from everyone and everything.

He understood people's attitude toward him. Just exactly what did you say to someone whose wife was killed in that way? It wasn't easy for anyone, least of all him.

He was immediately placed on leave and removed from the task force, and he understood that. Even if he wanted to work, how could the head of the force be seen to be objective when his wife and her lover had been murdered by the man they were hunting? He wanted revenge in the worst possible way, but any lawyer could have gotten someone off the moment it came out in court that he was incapable of being clear-headed.

The funeral was arranged quickly, and over two hundred people attended the cemetery. He hated every minute of it. Kathy had been well known and liked. Friends, family, and a lot of people from work he knew were all looking at him with such sympathy and pity he just wanted to scream. If he could have, he would have run away to hide and get drunk again. He didn't know how he got through the day. He was robotic and hid behind dark sunglasses, his daughter clinging to his arm.

He couldn't bear to make a speech. He wore his sunglasses even inside to hide the rage, tears, and pain he felt. Afterward, he hated shaking hands, listening to people endlessly offering him anything they could do to help. He thanked them, over and over again, like an old broken record. It seemed as if it would never end, so even though a wake had been arranged by her family at a nearby hotel, he didn't attend. He went back to the motel, threw himself on the bed, and cried in pain and anger.

An hour later, he was sitting on the world's most uncomfortable couch, a bottle of scotch opened and half-drunk without a glass in sight. He had his gun in his hand, turning it over, looking down the barrel and thought, *just one more drink, then I'm going to put the end of that gun in my mouth and pull the trigger*. It would be so simple and would put an end to the myriad feelings he was suffering from. His whole life had been turned upside down, and there seemed no way out for him except the peace and eternal quiet a bullet would bring.

His life was over, ruined by a maniac killer he hadn't been able to catch in time. That was bad enough, but perhaps if he hadn't spent so much time trying to track down the killer, he wouldn't have ignored his wife and the menopause she was struggling with so Kathy wouldn't have taken a lover. He should have been there for her in her time of need, been more of a husband and less of a cop. Was it any wonder she'd taken a younger lover who could make her feel special when he, Dillon, worked night and day? To add to his guilt, there was Marci. Rather than fix his marriage, he had avoided the problem and relieved himself with a hooker, for Christ's sake! He railed against himself and saw no purpose to life and nothing left to live for.

And, while he was on it, if he had listened more to the psychologist's advice, who had tried to warn him against being antagonistic in the press, perhaps she would still be alive. If he hadn't insulted the killer's delicate state of mind, he wouldn't have been goaded into taking revenge and taking Dillon's beautiful wife from him. No matter how Dillon looked at it, everything was his fault, and he deserved to die, not her, and die he would after just one more drink.

He was interrupted in his thoughts by a loud knocking at the door. He heard the unmistakable voice of Mike Knowles. "Boss, it's Mike. I need to see you."

"Go away, Mike. I'm not in the mood right now. Come back later." With that, he picked up the bottle and took another swig from it.

"I can't, boss. There's been another two murders. We need your help, and we need it now. Let me in. We need to talk."

Dillon shook his head sadly. *Why, oh why, won't they leave me alone?* "I'm no good to you, Mike. I'm no help at all. I'm on leave. Just go away, please, just go away."

"Boss, listen, please, I know how you feel, but you are the only one who can help. I shouldn't even be here. I've been ordered not to, but you have to let me in and let me explain. Five minutes, no more, then I will go, I promise."

With a heavy sigh, Dillon stood and, still clasping the bottle, opened the door and went back to his seat. Mike entered and saw the gun on the coffee table. He turned and closed the door before pulling the straight-backed chair out from what passed as a desk and sat down.

For two or three minutes, they looked at each other, both knowing the gun was going to be used if Mike couldn't stop it. He took a deep breath. "Yesterday, Georgina Smart and her husband were murdered. The same MO as her sister, Helena, tortured then throat cut. Her husband also had his throat cut while tied to a dining room chair. Hubby worked at the same plant as victim number eight." He paused and let that sink in through Dillon's alcohol-fogged brain.

"We have been taken over by Assistant Commissioner Gordon Blunt, and it's not a coincidence it rhymes with cunt." He paused again.

Dillon groaned. Gordon "Lightfoot" Blunt was worse than Pollock and from the same university. Intellectually trained, with no less than two degrees, he suffered from a complete lack of practical police experience. In fact, they had both been poached from the Victoria after a scandal rocked the WA police and the commissioner of the day. He at least had been old school and well respected by all who'd worked under him, but he had been implicated in a wrongful conviction case of a well-known brothel madam years before and had had to resign.

Neither of the incoming bosses knew their asses from their elbows as far as catching criminals went, but they were both excellent at budgeting and greasing political cogs. They had never done anything wrong, and it was felt by the whole force they were very much political appointments.

"Mike, I'm sorry, I've been relieved of command and am on leave. I couldn't help even if I was capable, or even wanted to, for that matter." He took another swig from the bottle. "I'm outranked and compromised. I can't help you, and you know it. If I helped in any way and that led to an arrest, the judge would throw it out, saying I wasn't objective. I'm sorry, mate, it can't happen."

"Boss, you are the only one who can. Blunt has told us all to ignore the army angle and focus on Helena Smart's sister and husband. He thinks because there is a link with one victim, there will be others that we have missed. We are all chasing our tails and wasting time, for fuck's sake. I've tried to tell him that if there was a link, why the torture again? Surely that means this prick is on the hunt for someone specific, but all he says is the guy's a head case and to focus everything we have on the husband and find the missing links. His opinion is they were having an affair, but so what? Even if they were, that doesn't get us any closer to a serial fucking killer. The guy is a complete moron."

Mike opened the bag he carried, took out a laptop, and placed it alongside the gun on the table.

"You know as well as I do, boss, the army is our best hope, and no one is looking into it now. Blunt has said it would be a waste of time without any evidence. You and I both know so many things point to that kind of mentality, and the army finally came through with the discharge files. They won't give us DNA, constitutional rights, and all that garbage, but they have given us all the files for discharged soldiers nationwide over the last five years, including blood types. I've loaded them on here. You have to help look through them, and if you see something, let me know. I can always pretend I found it on my own time after hours. You can stay out of it. I am being ordered to leave all this stuff alone and do as I'm told. I've risked my job giving you this, but you are the only one who can do anything about this madness before more people are killed."

The silence hung heavy and dragged on and on. Dillon thought about it all. Really, could he be bothered? Should he get involved? His life was ruined, his reputation gone, along with his wife; he had lost everything. Slowly, as he considered his life, the self-pity and loathing were replaced with anger at the man who had done this to him. While it was true he could have done more for his wife, he hadn't committed the murders. That bastard had, and once the idea of taking revenge set in, he saw things in a different light.

He had Mike on the inside to give him information. If he did track down the killer, he could do something about it himself and kill him. Why not? He stood, put down the bottle, walked to the window, and looked down at the car park, at the people going about their everyday lives, and knew he had to do something.

"Okay, Mike, you win, tell me everything, talk to me about the other two murders and pass on to me everything you think is relevant, but this stays between us and only us, agreed?" For the first time in days, the dark cloud that had been over him started to lift. Depression changed to a slow-burning rage. He would find the Ripper, and he would kill him and damn the consequences.

The more he thought about it, the more he began to see that Kathy had made her choices. Now he should make his. Yes, he had to agree he hadn't been the ideal husband, but he hadn't been the worst either. She had been a grown woman who'd found some fun and sex with a younger man. That burned him up, it was true, good old male pride, but he himself had had sex with Marci on numerous occasions. In the final analysis, he was no better, so who was he to blame her for doing the same thing?

Had Kathy come to him and wanted a divorce, he would have been saddened, of course, but not suicidal. He would have reasoned, why would he want to stay with someone who didn't want to be with him? He would have moved on with his life, as many other people did in the same situation. Maybe the marriage had been on the rocks, but maybe it hadn't. Once she had come to him and admitted the menopause situation, their relationship had changed. She'd been wonderful. He had been more understanding too, and he'd barely had a thought about Marci after that time. Possibly he never would have again. Perhaps he should give Kathy the same latitude. Maybe she had been in the act of finishing things with her guy too, but the Ripper had stepped in, and the rest was history.

The bottom line was that he was no longer prepared to roll over like a dog and let this maniac get the better of him. He was going to fight back. Killing Kathy had been laying down a challenge to him, and the task force having been taken over by an idiot only made things easier. It was a challenge he would accept.

Chapter Nineteen

It was an unshaven, disheveled Dillon Bradley who finally got through the nine thousand and eighty-eight files from the army and went to bed. His head and eyes ached from staring at a laptop screen for far too long. His tongue was furry from too much coffee, and he could smell his own body odor, but all that could wait. He was exhausted and needed sleep.

With the wall-mounted air conditioner humming, he collapsed onto the bed and was asleep within minutes. He dreamed of army soldiers chasing him through a forest of trees that went on and on forever to the crisp, sharp noise of twigs snapping behind him as they closed in on him.

He now had about eighteen hundred men remaining from the first sweep of the computerized files who were Caucasian and over one hundred eighty-five centimeters tall. They were the first two criteria he had used to filter by. The rest could wait for the next day; he was so tired. Although his grief and anger still simmered below the surface, he was glad to be working again, if only as a distraction. His Glock was back in the bedside drawer and would stay there. The dark cloud of depression had passed, for now.

He slept well, despite the dreams, for the first time in days. He felt as if he had achieved something, even if that was only to discount around seven thousand men from the manhunt; it was a start.

After he showered and shaved, he went down to the motel restaurant for breakfast. Once he had eaten, he felt good and ready to get back to work. Next, he would be looking at pictures, searching for resemblances, and depending on how many he then had, the final clincher, he hoped, would be the blood type. He had thought to go for blood groups first as that would likely reduce the number dramatically, but he had cautioned himself against that. While the circumstantial evidence did point to their killer being the person bitten by the dog, it was by no means conclusive. He did not want to risk missing the real culprit if the dog had bitten an intruder who coincidently had been there earlier on the same night as the murders. He needed to be thorough, and that meant slow, painstaking work. The height, skin color, and general looks were known, the blood type only assumed.

He had listened intently to Mike's summation of the latest murders. As usual, there was no trace of the killer or mistakes made by him—again suggesting precision in planning and execution. This time the murders only differed in that the husband had been tied to a dining chair with cable ties and murdered, while the wife had been tied to the bed, also with cable ties. Once the husband had been dispatched, she had been tortured before being butchered. It was assumed once he gained entry, the husband had been tied up first with tape put over his mouth, then the wife taken into the bedroom and secured before the killer had returned to silence and kill the male. This would have given him time with the woman to torture her for whatever information the killer had been after.

Mike had wondered why *The Ripper* hadn't broken

into the house as he had previously because clearly, the victims had let the killer in through the front door. The husband, Ben—a plant operations manager for a company making plastic moldings, where an earlier victim had worked on the production line—had had his throat cut by a person standing behind him with a left to right action. This led them to believe the attacker was right-handed, as per the previous victim's deaths. At this stage, there was no evidence of the husband even having known the earlier victim, let alone having had an affair with her. However, they were being exhorted to pursue every tiny aspect of their lives.

Georgina O'Brien had the same numerous stab wounds as her sister, and her mouth had been covered with tape from the same roll as had been used before. Similarly, she had been turned to face the bed and had had her throat slashed, which obviously was the cause of death. Also, from left to right from behind, presumably to minimize the arterial spray hitting the killer.

Assistant Commissioner Blunt's opinion was this was just an escalation of violence and was typical of a deranged killer becoming more unstable. He did not share Bradley and Mike Knowles' opinion that it was a clinical search for a specific target and that the torture was to gain knowledge of someone else. In his opinion, quite simply, the killer was mad and was growing more insane by the day—end of story, or "period," as he liked to say.

The time of death was between nine and ten p.m. for the husband and approximately one hour later for the wife. They had eaten the same meal, satay chicken and rice, and the rate of absorption helped with times of death. The killer had left the same way he had entered, and the bodies had been discovered by a friend, Bettina. She usually took Georgina to work, and the next morning, when the front door hadn't been answered, she'd taken a casual glance through the window. That look would ensure she suffered nightmares for the rest of her life.

Georgina had only just returned to work after taking time off to grieve for her sister. The funeral had been the day before, and she had been trying to get her life back on track. Like every other case, there was nothing new to go on. The murders seemed to have been carried out in a very calm, deliberate, almost professional, and dispassionate way. There seemed to be no anger or panic. It was all purely clinical, apart from the mutilation wounds, which like previous occasions, did show a manic frenzied attack. There were fourteen stab wounds in and around the woman's vagina, inflicted after she had been killed.

Mike had stayed for two hours, and together they had reviewed everything they knew so far. When he'd finally left, Mike promised to update Dillon if there was anything new. They both felt confident that if there was something in the files, Dillon would find it, and Mike could then take the information to Blunt.

****

Since the release of the pictures, the phone rooms had taken hundreds of calls about men who resembled the artist's impressions. These tended to be from those who had a neighbor, a friend, acquaintance, or someone they worked with who they thought was *a bit funny* in addition to having some resemblance to the pictures. In some cases, when followed up, the person looked nothing like the sketches, and police felt the report had been made for malicious reasons. One report ensured the police were sent to see someone who was short, overweight, and Aboriginal. The witness reporting him was sure he was violent and was *just the sort of person to commit the crimes.* Every possibility had to be investigated and interviewed, but to date, nothing concrete had come from the interviews.

The task force members were stagnant and dispirited. Since Kathy Bradley's murder, everyone believed they were being dragged in the wrong direction by the new senior officer in charge. They also shared a sense of impending doom, a feeling that there were more murders to come. It was a dreadful time for the team, with hundreds of man-hours spent interviewing people but getting no closer to the killer. Mike Knowles noticed his fellow officers were disorganized and unmotivated as more and more outrageous claims were reported about people who couldn't possibly be the Ripper but which had to be investigated anyway.

Then came the confessions. Unbelievably, officers had to waste time performing background checks for eleven men who confessed to the murders. Each had to be investigated and discounted, and the offenders were charged for wasting police time and attempting to pervert the course of justice.

The usable DNA sample taken from the dog's teeth didn't match anyone in the database of known offenders nationwide. Neither had they recovered DNA at any of the previous murder sites that could be compared to the sample, which was troubling. It suggested that the man bitten by the dog might not be the same person who had carried out the killings. They also had no fingerprints recovered from any of the scenes that were unaccounted for.

Every lead turned into a dead end unless they could find someone that they could match the DNA sample to. It was true to say that some of the team were scared that their wives could be targeted by the killer, as Dillon's had been. Some had been sent away for a while to stay with family. Such was the fear even in the police force *The Ripper* had caused. Three senior officers had requested transfers out of Major Crime, citing fear for their families as the cause. Gordon Blunt refused each request, telling the men to: "Buck up your ideas, or resign, Man up you morons," and in one case: "Grow some balls." Such comments only ensured morale in the squad dropped even lower.

The psych profile suggested a history of earlier sexual assaults or cruelty to animals, and records were being searched for similar prior offenses around the country, which were all avenues that had been gone over previously. If anyone complained or questioned the rework was a waste of time, Lightfoot's answer was to "Do it again, and more thoroughly this time," as if they had been slipshod before.

Dillon imagined Blunt reporting to the commissioner, blaming his predecessor for poor management and the growing body count. Dillon knew that was unfair, as he was very well respected by the team before his wife's murder, so the insults had been politically motivated.

To make matters worse, while the overworked and unappreciated task force members felt they were going around and round in ever-decreasing circles, the army possibility was dismissed out of hand because it lacked any credible evidence. Assistant Commissioner Blunt was not the sort of man to waste resources on one man's hunch, and everyone was ordered to drop it. He had even belittled Mike in front of the team for such a stupid and time-wasting initiative, leaving Dillon as the only resource to check it out. He was a secret, one-man task force looking into nine thousand suspects.

Such was the complete disarray of the task force hunting *The Ripper* since the murder of Dillon Bradley's wife and her lover.

****

Journal Excerpt # 8, Living at Swanbourne

Amanda and I had seven weeks of bliss together at Swanbourne, and she fell in love with the relaxed lifestyle in Western Australia, as I thought she would. The weather was fantastic and the beaches pristine, and she enjoyed her new job. For the first time, Amanda felt she was appreciated at work by a boss who treated her more like a daughter or granddaughter than an employee. In the mornings, I watched her dress for work and marveled at her body. There is something very special about observing a beautiful woman dressing for work. Maybe I am weird, but in a way, it held greater pleasure, certainly in a different way, to watching her undress. The latter being sexual, while the former was a thing of beauty to behold. It was a simple pleasure, but the simple ones are often the best, I think. I seemed to spend most of my time in a permanent state of arousal whenever I was around her.

Amanda began to work out with me, and her fitness level increased. Her body, incredible as it was, took on a more toned appearance, and her skin was radiant with her newfound tan. We took long walks, jogs, and runs along Swanbourne Beach, part of which is a nude area, so there was always something to see, and we would spend a lot of time giggling like schoolchildren at what we saw.

There wasn't a single person who met Amanda that didn't like her instantly. She was fun, bubbly, and wanted to live life at breakneck speed. Unless we were in bed, making love, then she liked it slow, mostly.

We sneaked away to Rottenest Island, which was a short ferry ride from Fremantle, for what we called a dirty weekend. While it was nothing like the Whitsundays and Hamilton Island on our honeymoon, we had a lovely time swimming and snorkeling on the reefs and got untidy drunk at the one and only pub. Getting back to our villa was fun as there were no cars. We either had to walk or ride our hire bikes the two kilometers. We got there finally and had been laughing our heads off all the way. I never knew anyone else in my life that I could laugh with so easily. We shared a silly sense of humor, where the more ridiculous a situation, the funnier we would find it.

We saw the gun emplacements built into the cliff there and learned of the range of such guns to protect the entry into Fremantle Port, known as Backstairs Passage. Fortunately, they had never been fired in anger.

Rottenest has some rather unusual inhabitants, which Amanda fell in love with. She squealed in delight the first time she saw a quokka, and when we ate at a café, she bought more and more food to feed them. They looked like huge rats, hence the island name, Rottenest, which translated from Dutch meant Rat's Nest. While they did look like enormous rats, they were marsupials and were very calm and tame. Amanda wanted to take one home with us, which was strictly forbidden. I have a great picture of her sitting cross-legged on a path feeding the creatures with a look of incredible beauty and serenity on her face.

We vowed to come back as often as we could when we were on the ferry heading home, but as it turned out, we never did. Other things got in the way, including my final tour of duty, back to Afghanistan, where when things went wrong, they really went wrong. My life unraveled, and it's true to say it was the beginning of the end.

Chapter Twenty

For the first time in quite a while, I was in a buoyant mood. The headaches were better, down to a manageable roar thanks to the pills, which I used sparingly, only having the box of thirty. I was able to find some relaxation playing computer games again, and I found them fun and a distraction while waiting for my next stepping stone to Amanda. I couldn't get a stupid song out of my head. It came to me all hours of the day or night, *Wake Up, Little Susie*. I even found myself singing it, and it was so annoying I had to Google it to see who it was by. The Everly Brothers from the nineteen-fifties! I had no idea where that came from in my head.

The woman herself, Suzi, was on holiday in Bali, her best friend had told me, along with her home address, where she worked, and everything else she knew about her. Unfortunately, she herself hadn't known much about Toni, though she had instantly liked her when they'd met for lunch. She was Suzi's new friend, and they had gotten on like a house on fire. I had nodded in agreement; everyone loved Amanda at first meeting.

I toyed with the idea of going to Bali for a few days myself, not that I thought I could find her there. It would just have been good to get away, but it would have been fraught with problems, not least of which would have been getting out of the country on my passport. There was always a risk I could be recognized from the pictures of me by immigration. I would have been surprised if my picture was not at the airport on a watch list. Best to play it safe, finish the job at hand, then think about where to go and how best to get there.

Driving across country seemed to be the best idea once the mission was finished, and perhaps fly somewhere from Adelaide or Melbourne after spending some time there. I knew I might not have lots of time left to live, but once I caught up with Amanda, I intended to make the most of the time I did have. One place I would never go was back to Hamilton Island—too many painful memories.

I had phoned Suzi's work to confirm when she would return and had been informed that she was away for a further five days. When asked if anyone else could help me, I hung up. Five days? That was nothing. I had been waiting so long since I'd left the hospital to catch up with her. Another five days I could do easily.

****

Journal Excerpt # 9, The Third Tour, Afghanistan

When things go wrong, they go wrong in bunches, don't they? It never seems to be just one thing, but a series of things, or in my case, an avalanche of things that went wrong.

I left Amanda crying as we said our goodbyes on a warm morning, without any idea that, as I boarded my aircraft, it would be the last time we shared any kind of normal relationship. She was very sad, as I was, to be apart again, and she worried for my safety. But she was also fiercely proud and told me to 'Give the bastards hell' when she cuddled me on the tarmac. She had picked up a lot of the way SAS spoke about people, and she had fit right in as an army wife. Amanda was always like a

214

chameleon, picking up other people's words and mannerisms if she spent time with them. If she had asked me to, I would have left the army, but she didn't want that, even though she didn't want the separation either. She supported me entirely, or so I believed.

She had not told me she had missed a period, and she thought there was a chance she was pregnant. In her mind, it was likely to be the change in lifestyle, leaving family and friends in Sydney and starting a new life in Perth, which could have thrown her cycle out of sync. She hadn't said a word to me about it before I left, and when she did tell me later, she said that she hadn't wanted to say anything only to then find out it was a false alarm. Apparently, it wasn't unusual for her to skip the occasional period. It happened from time to time with her and generally was no big deal. Always the practical one, that piece of information was still a few weeks away and would be delivered by video call, but with how things turned out, I wish I had known at the time. Both of our lives could have been different.

So, off I went to hell again, and while the deaths and danger never bothered me, I did miss Amanda and thought about her constantly. With the time difference and her working at the jeweler's, we couldn't speak as much as I would have liked, so time moved very slowly.

Still, the biggest fear I lived with was her getting bored alone and finding fun with someone else. I hated that about myself, but I was powerless to stop the negative feelings. As I had never been strong on self-confidence, losing her to another man was always something I worried about. I didn't mistrust her as such. It wasn't like that to me. I suppose it was just a fear of losing her. When I faced those terrors, I felt a rage inside, and though I would tell myself not to worry, of course, I worried all the more. She was a beautiful woman and would have no shortage of men chasing her, especially on an army base where every man resembled a TV advertisement for a fitness gym. What on earth could she see in me to make her wait for me to come back?

Was she faithful to me during that time? I never knew for sure, but with how things turned out later, I think that she did take other lovers. Realistically I couldn't really blame her for that while I was away, and that was a complex issue for me. I knew my mother had been unfaithful to my father when he was away because she made me her lover. Therefore, what was normal behavior for a woman? I had no concept of that kind of loyalty. I know I think all women are unfaithful sluts now and cannot be trusted, so when I think back to me being on tour, I believe it would have been normal for her to find other men to alleviate her boredom. It wasn't that I knew for a fact she was unfaithful, just a worrying fear I had.

Did that have any bearing on things going wrong that tour? Was I in some way off my usual game and more susceptible to making errors by being distracted? Now, I don't think so, but I do think it was always her nature to be unfaithful, and I was the stupid sap who fell for her charms. But, at the time, though I worried, I also had faith in her, and I was the problem, so was torn.

I shouldn't even have been on the mission that went so horribly wrong, but my opposite number in one of the other groups had supposedly been cleaning his rifle while tired and had left a round in the chamber of his weapon. Naturally, fate had stepped in, and the night before departure, the obvious happened, and it went off. The sound firstly frightened the crap out of everyone else in the barracks but also blew a hole in his hand. He had to be airlifted to a hospital in Germany for surgery to try to save it.

There were some who said he did it on purpose because in the lead-up, he had become more and more antsy and was showing signs of distress. This wasn't entirely unusual with guys getting close to going home, and he was due for rotation soon. So, though we all noticed he wasn't himself, we thought he would be okay. When he got back, he could then recover or get help if he needed it. We all felt he just needed some rest and to get out of the shithole we were stationed in.

We all witnessed varying forms of emotional distress; that was just part of the job. Not that anyone suspected he would shoot himself to get out of going, but no one was entirely surprised when he did. I don't want to put shit on the guy—maybe it was a genuine accident—but there was a lot going on around the place, and everyone was permanently on edge, so anything was possible.

It had only been recent that one of the local trainees turned out to be an insurgent. He had let loose in the compound, shooting three men dead and wounding two others before making his escape. Everyone was pretty much always on edge and distrustful of the entire local population after that. The constant vigilance required and the looking over your shoulder had got to his nerves, causing him to either forget to unchamber the round or deliberately shoot himself to get out of a tour of duty. Only he knew what was going through his head just before it happened, but I will say there were quite a few *accidental wounding's that year, and they all got to go home. In hindsight, I should have done the same.*

Each group had a specialist in different fields who complemented the others. Communications, explosives, weapons, language, medical, and the like. I was the match for their man and available, so I was seconded to his group until they flew over a replacement.

It was that night before we were due to leave camp at dawn that, Amanda told me that she had been pregnant with our child when I flew out. She had miscarried only two days prior to the call, which was how long it took for her to pluck up the courage to tell me. She was unhappy, upset, and confused, with no idea how I would react to her having a baby and whether I would want it or not. She, too, hadn't considered it, with her dream of travel before children not having changed. She had spent weeks feeling terrified of what might happen to us when she told me she was expecting. Children were not something we had ever discussed, and she knew that my childhood resembled a horror movie. She had been scared to tell me for fear of what I might say. She had even considered aborting while I was away and never telling me at all. She had no sooner decided against that when fate stepped in, and she'd miscarried.

I was stunned into silence while she talked nonstop between sobs and dabbing at her eyes with a tissue. I wasn't angry, not at first anyway. I only felt complete shock. I knew Amanda was on the pill. The packet was forever on display in her messy bedside cabinet. Had we talked about having children, or if I'd had any inkling it was coming, I would have reacted differently. To my shame, though, at that point in time, I was dumbfounded—me, a father?

I had never considered myself father material before that call. Hell, sometimes I'd struggled to fit in with people just as a man, but a father? No Way. In my heart, I now know that if it had happened, I was damn sure I would be a good one. I knew I would never raise a hand to my child, unlike my father had to me, and I didn't think Amanda would make our son her lover either, so, given a chance, I think we would have been good parents.

I was shocked on several fronts at once, and quite simply, I didn't know how to react. I just stared back. I'm a complete dummy, I know, and I was silent for too long. I tried to take in what she was saying, what she meant by it and what it meant for our future together. Part of my thinking, in my addled brain, was worrying why she hadn't told me straight away, why hadn't she done that? Didn't she trust me? That seemed wrong. To my mind, she should have told me when she thought she might have been before I flew out, then, I could have shared that experience with her, and we could have discussed it then. She chose, for whatever reason, to wait until I was thousands of kilometers away in a war zone while she struggled with the emotional concerns alone rather than discuss them with me.

I could have applied to stay behind at the barracks on compassionate grounds and not come back to the shithole I was sitting in had I known. Whether that request would have been granted or not, I will never know. But if she had told me at the time, I could have tried, and again we could have avoided all the terrible things that happened in our future.

If I'd been able to stay behind with her, I think we would have been stronger as a couple for sharing the experience. As it happened, she'd miscarried, but even then, we would have been together to console each other. But, there seemed to be, for the first time in our relationship, a level of deceit.

Next, she considered aborting our child without telling me? I really didn't know how to react to that, but I felt shocked and horrified she could think I would condone killing an unborn child of our own. Yes, I killed people in war—yes, I wasn't the most caring person in the world, I agree—but how dare she think that I would be all for her murdering our own unborn child? Anger did start to creep in at that stage in my mind, wrongly, I realized later, but in my defense, all of this was new to me.

The final straw was that she had miscarried and only afterward told me. Despite that, I could see she was hurt and emotional. Stupid me was stunned into silence for too long. I had to work through everything in my muddled brain. She then became upset with me, thinking that I was angry with her when really I was just confused and needed time to process everything. Once she lost her temper, I admit I did get angry back, but not rage with what happened. I'm sure of that now. I was only angry that she got angry with me when I had done nothing wrong except be so dumbfounded and too slow to react.

I should have been more caring about her and her state of mind and feelings, I admit that. But I didn't know what to say and even how I was supposed to react, never having been in any similar situation. I was always conscious not only of being wrong in the way I felt but that I shouldn't feel wrong in the first place. At love, I was still a dummy and hopelessly inadequate.

It was our first major disagreement, and by the time I tried to tell her I wasn't angry at her being pregnant or miscarrying, she was enraged with me. Amanda cried. I was cruel, she screamed and then hung up. My screen went dead, and I was left sitting alone for minutes on end, thinking it was an accident and she would call back, yet she didn't.

I tried to make contact later that night, but she didn't answer. Clearly, she was still too mad at me. All I could do was send an email, telling her how sorry I was for being an idiot and begging her to forgive me. I hadn't even had a chance to tell her I was leaving for a mission the next morning, so I did in the email. It was quite long, and I wrote well into the night, finally hitting send and hoping things would be fine by the time I got back from the mission, and we could make up. I knew I had screwed up and was desperate to make amends and to know she had forgiven me for being an idiot. Sadly, we were robbed of that possibility, and with all that came after, the subject was never discussed again.

I don't know to this day if she forgave me or whether her staying angry helped cause the breakdown later. Who can say with any certainty at what point in time the wheels fell off our wagon; but they did fall off.

By first light, I had not slept and determined that the moment the patrol got back, I would let her know I was all for being the kind of father mine never was, and if she wanted children, I was for it one hundred percent. I wasn't scared of that kind of commitment, that she, Amanda, was the one who I wanted to spend my life with and raise a family with. All of this I had put in the email, but I wanted more than anything for her to see my face and for her to read in my eyes the absolute sincerity of my words.

I had also decided this tour would be my last, that

once I got back to her, I would never leave again. She had changed me and my life, and I valued her far higher than being a soldier. I would resign from the army, and while I had not figured out what I was going to do with the rest of my life, that life would be with her, full stop. Fate then stepped in and took that chance away from us, and I never got an opportunity to tell her any of that, either.

We left in choppers just after dawn for a top-secret mission to go and bring a supposed top Al Qaeda informant back to safety. He was going to give us the names and locations of several senior terrorists in his cell in exchange for his safety and a new life in the West. Military intelligence—now there is an oxymoron— said this would be a walk in the park. We were to be dropped five kilometers from a small village where he was in hiding, go get him, then straight back to an evacuation point, then back to base in less than a day.

There is only so much you can plan for, and as any soldier would agree, things often go wrong even with the very best of plans. When it does, you adapt to changing circumstances as best you can. The rest is up to luck and chance. My luck had run out, plain and simple, and I had no chance.

Book Two

I watched the sparkle leave your eyes.
Remembered again the many lies.
The lies of love, the pain, deceit,
Not foreseen when we did meet.
Then with rings, the promises made
So soon to break, the men you laid.
My cause is just, the army trained
My heart was broke; my vengeance reigned.

Chapter Twenty-One

It took four long coffee-filled days and sleepless nights, but finally, Dillon had narrowed his search to seven distinct possibilities. He celebrated with his first drink since he had begun, a tumbler of straight whiskey and ice.

Of the seven men, one hailed from Tasmania, three from New South Wales, two from Victoria, and one from Queensland. Seven men who had been discharged for various reasons from the army and whose pictures, though they had been taken years before, could possibly be the man they sought.

Dillon had emailed Mike, requesting current addresses from DMV departments in each state and contact phone numbers if known. That information was not in the army files provided. While he waited to hear back from Mike, he packed up his motel room. The forensics team had finally cleared his house, and he moved back into the home he had shared with Kathy.

Taking on the search and getting back to work, although unofficial, had given him his direction back. He felt anger at Kathy for her affair but a much more powerful rage at her life being taken so callously by *The Ripper*. The need for vengeance against her killer outweighed the anger for his late wife for her betrayal. He was moving forward with his life and felt grateful to Mike Knowles for kicking his butt and giving him a reason to stop wallowing in self-pity.

He knew he had all sorts of challenges ahead without Kathy. There was a list of practical things he had to do and even learn how to do. For example, he had to learn how to pay bills. For as long as they had been married, Kathy had always taken care of that. Life was not going to be a walk in the park, being alone after all the years together, but he decided he was up for the challenge. There were other things to learn to do too, but Dillon thought he had the strength of character to survive, no matter how long it took; he believed he would be fine. At times he wondered if her having an affair did make it easier for him to get over losing her? Possibly it helped rationalize that maybe she had been getting ready to leave him anyway; he would never know what her state of mind had been.

His career was another issue, and he had to make some decisions there. In some ways, he felt it was already over, having been removed from the highest-profile case ever in Western Australian history. It could be very difficult for him, and he would need to wait and see what developed as to whether he would even want to stay with the force, assuming they wanted to keep him. He would have to face a barrage of tests and counseling before they would let him work again, and he respected their need for that. If the same tragedy had happened to one of his men, he would be the first to require a psychological evaluation, and he did not want to be hypocritical.

Currently, Dillon was on extended leave, and under the circumstances, he knew he could drag that out as long as he wanted if he said he felt stressed. He supposed that, within the next couple of weeks or so, the commissioner would want a meeting to discuss his psychological assessment for a return to work. Then he would make suggestions as to his placement. At that time, Dillon would decide what he would do.

He hadn't thought of money, but he and Kathy had earned a good living, their house was paid for, and they had some modest investments. Then there would be her life insurance and accumulated superannuation when he could bring himself to look into it. In an idle moment, it had occurred to him that he wouldn't need to work for monetary reasons once her insurance was paid. So, if they gave him a transfer he thought could be interesting, he would look at it favorably, and if not, he would resign.

Dillon qualified for a pension, having served twenty-five years, and he could have a relatively comfortable life if that was what he chose. But first and foremost, in his mind was being involved somehow in catching up with the Ripper and stopping him; the rest could wait.

He supposed that as his wife was murdered due to his job, it could mean some form of compensation. For the moment, he couldn't bring himself to think that losing his wife equaled gaining money, but in the back of his mind, he knew that day might come.

The first stop back at his home was the laundry, and he put a load of washing on from a large plastic bag with the name of the motel on the side of it. Then he took a long, steaming hot shower in the main bathroom. He had put off going through the master bedroom until later when he plucked up more courage.

As a courtesy to him and his rank, the subcontracted police clean-up people had been in, and the bedroom smelled of bleach and disinfectant. All traces of the two horrific murders had been erased. Even the mattress, which had been beyond saving, had been removed. The bed, sans mattress, waited for a replacement, but Dillon didn't think he would be sleeping in that room any time soon. There were way too many painful memories.

Later, as he stood in the bedroom doorway looking in, with another strong whiskey in hand, Dillon remembered the scene he had come home to. He felt he needed to face up to it rather than emotionally run away. His butchered, beautiful wife and her lover had been in the throes of sexual union, then had had their throats slit in a blood bath. He needed this to face his grief, guilt, and anger alone in his own time. He stood for a long while, sipping his scotch, just looking, remembering, and thinking. Finally, he sighed, closed the door, and walked back toward the family area of the house.

He had put off another job for long enough. He felt terribly guilty for all but ignoring his daughter since the funeral. He had hidden behind his grief and anger and worked on his search for the killer, oblivious to everyone else's pain and suffering. She, too, must have hurt and hurt badly. He knew he should have been there for her, as she had tried to be there for him, but when she had contacted him on his phone, he had fobbed her off, saying he was okay.

It had always been Dillon's way to suffer in silence, and he couldn't speak of it to her then, but he had assured her that he would soon, when he felt he could. Then he had buried himself in his computer files, searching for the man who had brutally taken Kathy from them both. Now the time had come to talk to Louise. Dillon wandered into his study, poured another drink, and picked up the phone.

During the next two hours, he stopped to wipe tears from his face on several occasions, and he knew his daughter did too, as slowly he rebuilt the bridge between them. At first, she was distant with him, deep in her own grief and resentful of his selfishness. Gradually, he was able to help her understand his distancing himself was because he needed it for his own sanity and not because he didn't care about hers. She had always known him to be the strong, silent brooding man he was and so eventually relented, understanding his need to suffer in silence.

They would both miss her mother, naturally, and while he cursed himself and always would believe it was ultimately his fault, he discovered that she didn't blame him at all. Louise had been told by her mother days before her murder of the menopause and the effect it had had on her and her treatment of her father. The problems within the marriage she had believed to be her mother's doing and not her father's. That Kathy had blamed herself and the emotional trauma of menopause, not him, for the rut which occurred between them made it easier for them both. Of course, Kathy had failed to tell Louise of the lover she had taken or why. That was understandable, and whether that relationship had been at the start or the end, they would never know.

Louise knew her father well and understood when he explained his need to help find the killer, even though he was now suspended from duty. He told her the department had gone in a different direction to that which he felt held the most promise. There was a lot of Dillon in her, and she offered support and help if needed, which he would never accept. He appreciated her offer nonetheless. He had lost a wife, and he would never risk losing his daughter, too, by putting her in harm's way. Until this maniac was caught, or killed, which was his hope if he had any choice in the matter, he wanted her as far away as possible from even the tiniest risk. Dillon promised to call in and have dinner with her and her husband soon in Melbourne, that he would come to visit for a few days and spend time with them when he was able. He loved her and always would, and again he was sorry for ignoring her after the funeral.

After Dillon hung up the phone, more tears came, but not from depression. The talk with Louise had been therapeutic for them both, he believed, and it had been the first time he had voiced any of the feelings he'd felt since the murders. While Louise had the support of her husband, which had been fantastic for her, Dillon had needed time alone. That had always been his way.

Dillon stayed in the same chair until he heard the message tone of his mobile chime. He picked it up and saw that Marci had sent her deepest sympathy and hoped he was all right. She would always be available if he needed her as a friend. Dillon smiled faintly when he saw she had signed off with a sad emoticon. He went to bed in the spare room without replying.

On the home answering machine was a message from the Police Department Counseling Service. Corinne Stapleton offered him help and was available to him any time he felt the need to talk about his loss. She sounded kind and considerate, but Dillon no longer needed counseling. What he needed was to be sighting down a gun barrel at the killer. That would be all the treatment he needed.

****

Mike Knowles received Dillon's email and went

back into the offices after everyone except the night duty data inputters had gone home. Their job was to log all of the interviews made during that day and information from the phone room. Correlations could then be made much quicker if some information crossed with something else from a different detective's report. They were data analysts, not police officers, and were there to ensure the officers on duty in the morning had all of the information from the day before at their fingertips.

While they tapped at their keyboards, Mike sat at his desk and went to work sending official requests for information to the different state police departments for background information on the seven men his boss had come up with. He did not request for them to be interviewed, not wanting to bring up any red flags at that stage. Just some basic, discreet information, and anything relevant such as their recent arrests, assuming they had any.

Because it was a request made with low priority, it could be some time before anything came back. As he had been ordered not to pursue this line of inquiry, Mike could not afford to raise any interest by asking for urgency. It would take as long as it would take the overworked officers at the other end of his emails to get to.

Mike was in the elevator to go down to the car park when his mobile phone pealed its rock song ringtone. It was a friend of his, Larry Daggonville, another homicide detective who was not attached to the task force. Larry asked if he wanted a quick beer and a chat; a strange case had come up, and he wanted Mike's thoughts on it, as he personally had reached an impasse.

Mike looked at his watch. He was going to be late

home anyway, so another hour wouldn't hurt, and he very much fancied a beer or two. He agreed to meet him at his local pub, which wasn't too much of a detour from his home and wife.

Mike had long held the belief in life, and marriage in particular, that it was easier to seek forgiveness than permission. If he called Bettina to tell her he was going to the pub, and she got mad, as she probably would, he would have to decide whether to cancel his mate's request for help or upset his wife. She usually won those arguments. But if he didn't call, dinner would be late, she wouldn't talk to him, and any thought of a special cuddle in bed later would go right out of the window.

As he walked to his car, he decided on the compromise and sent his wife a text saying he had been called to a meeting and would be an hour to an hour and a half late home. He hit send, then climbed in his car and headed to the pub. He didn't see that as an act of cowardice, just common sense. Why have a fight if he could avoid it?

He spotted 'Daggs' propping up the bar in the corner. It was a relatively quiet night, and he ambled over.

He ordered a light beer from the voluptuous barmaid wearing a T-shirt with strategically placed tears, so her black bra showed, and said, "What's up, Daggs?" Then he grinned as it sounded awfully like saying, 'What's up, Doc?' and he considered saying it again in a Bugs Bunny voice.

"Hey, Mike, good to see you. Thanks for dropping by. I caught the strangest case, and it baffles me. Hope you don't mind me running it by you. I need a fresh set of eyes. I have a doctor shot dead in an unrented house and zero, I mean *zero* evidence, and no idea why." He took a sip of his beer and watched Mike pay the girl, admiring the woman's overly large and barely concealed breasts.

"What's the details, mate?" Mike took a long drink once she had gone to the till, and they were alone.

Daggs raised his left hand and counted off the relevant details by pointing at a finger each time. "One, Dr. Suryanna, from an after-hours call-out service, got a call to visit a child with an infected cut from rusty barbed wire fence. No Medicare details were taken over the phone because the boy's father sounded distressed and said that they had just moved in and couldn't find the card. He promised to pay the account in cash on arrival."

He pointed to his second finger. "Two, the good doctor attended an empty house that we know was advertised for rent in the paper but had no *For Rent* board out the front. Naturally, the doctor didn't know the house was empty when he arrived, and the killer let him in through the front door. He had broken in through the rear himself earlier."

For some reason, Mike began to get an itchy feeling at the back of his neck as Dags raised another finger. "Three, we don't know for sure what happened, but we know that intravenous penicillin and pills were taken, as well as some painkillers. Apparently, they keep a check on inventory, and those items were missing from his bag. Four, the doctor was shot dead at point-blank range by a nine-millimeter hollow point, dead center of his heart. He would have died instantly."

He paused to take another long draught of his beer. "Five. Neighbors saw or heard nothing but did note the doctor's car in the driveway. They just thought someone was moving in. Six, there was no evidence left at the scene whatsoever, and if drugs were given there, the syringe was taken away by the killer. Seven, the good doctor appears to have had a happy home life, a recent baby boy, and it seems he was quite the proud father. There were no marital problems we can find and no other reason to be at the house other than a genuine call-out. Eight, there is no eight, that's it, nothing at all to go on. It is a mystery. And you know what I keep coming back to? Why no one heard a gunshot."

Red lights and warning bells were going off in Mike's head as he thought. *Could it possibly be?* His mind was racing with variables as an idea crystallized. Then out loud, he said in an excited voice, "Daggs, tell me how this sounds and whether you think I'm going nuts. Several days ago, our *Ripper* serial killer, while in the act of killing five people, got attacked by the owner's dog. Big bastard mongrel of a thing, and we know it bit his arm. We think he put it up to fend off the dog, then while it was biting him, he calmly slit the dog's throat, cool as a cucumber. We got blood and tissue from the dog's mouth, and he must have bled like a stuck pig. We found the garden hose uncurled and running, which had washed his and the dog's blood away, and no fingerprints anywhere. He methodically used the hose to wash his own blood away and clean himself up. Items were missing from the washing line that we think he used as bandages. We sent out bulletins to the doctors and hospitals to report anyone presenting with a dog bite wound, but so far, nothing."

Detective Daggonville's eyes opened wider as he suddenly got where Mike was going. He started nodding as Mike continued, speaking quickly, his words rushing out. "Let's say our guy's bite gets infected, and he is getting sick. What can he do? There is no doubt he is a lunatic, but he is one fucking smart lunatic who the psyches call a fully functioning sociopath. So, we know he can plan things out just fine. He would know he can't walk into a hospital, doctor, or chemist without a report being made. This guy is so good. He never leaves any evidence. This dog bite and the DNA we got from the dog's mouth is his first and only mistake. So, if he was getting sick from the infection, what does he do? Maybe gets a friendly doctor out to an uninhabited house and kills him to hide the evidence." He suddenly grabbed Dagg's arm and said, "Oh fuck, he's got a gun! He's got a fucking gun! Up till now, it's only been a knife he's used. And nine-mill hollow points? Jesus fucking Christ, *he is military!*" His mind was racing as he thought through the possibilities.

Nine-millimeter hollow-point shells were common, especially in police and army circles, because of the mushroom-type expansion on impact. There was much less likelihood of a bystander or innocent person being hit by a standard wadcutter bullet going straight through the intended target and into someone else. Hollow points caused a lot more damage on impact to the victim than a standard bullet because the expansion of the shell meant that the wound itself was much bigger internally. Resultant shock and blood loss meant, technically, it was banned even for military purposes because it was deemed to be inhumane. A soldier who might otherwise be wounded by a normal round would almost certainly die from a hollow point. But Mike knew, from his own personal experience, certain Australian Armed Special Forces still used them widely so as to cause death *rather* than wound.

Nine-millimeter was also a readily available caliber throughout the world. It could be for any one of a hundred guns that fired it. He knew most police officers used nine-mill Glocks, while Australian military used Heckler and Koch, but there were many other brands of handgun that also used it. Colt, Smith and Wesson, Barretta, the list was endless. Due to strict Australian gun laws, pistols were hard to get unless you were a drug dealer or underworld figure. So, Mike mused, how would the killer get such a weapon with hollow-point bullets? To Mike, again, this pointed to a military person, or another thought occurred to him. *Fuck, what if it's a cop?*

Without another word, he took out his mobile and phoned Dillon and told him of the murder. Then he called Blunt. He explained hurriedly that, in his opinion, the Ripper had claimed another victim, a male doctor. He also pointed out their target was now armed with a gun, probably a silenced one. More than ever, the use of a gun, especially this gun, with this round and this accuracy, screamed ex-military to him. He hoped upon hope it would now for Assistant Commissioner Blunt too.

Chapter Twenty-Two

Mike Knowles desperately tried to calm his anger the next morning in the incident room while sitting at his desk. At least Blunt, the stupid prick, had listened before telling him his imagination was running away with him. *That at least is some consolation,* he thought.

He didn't know if the Assistant Commissioner's motivation was stupidity, politically motivated, or maybe just dumb pride that wouldn't allow him to change a decision he had already made. If that were the case, losing face was more important than catching a killer, and the task force had no hope.

In a loud, aggressive tone, Blunt had agreed that *possibly* it could be their offender who had shot and killed the doctor. Yes, the M.O. was *suggestive* of a cold-hearted, calculating, *possibly* army-trained assassin who had gone bananas and switched weapons from knife to pistol, but where was the *fucking evidence?*

Surely it was also *possible* the doctor had been lured to his death because a junkie wanted drugs he thought the doctor would be carrying, or *possibly* the doctor owed money to some unsavory characters, as yet for reasons unknown, *possibly* he was involved in an illegal immigration racket, *possibly* he was a closet gay, and a lover was angry at the recent baby, *possibly* his wife had had him murdered…

"Do you want me to continue, Sergeant Knowles? I

can come up with a hundred scenarios, if you like, and make any one of them fit the facts. The use of a gun *suggests* it wasn't our man because he has hitherto *always* used a knife. So more likely, it's a drug deal gone wrong or criminals falling out with each other, you imbecile."

Blunt made it very clear to everyone listening to Mike's debasement that he didn't want *any* leak by *any* member of the task force that this murder was in any way, shape, or form connected to *The Ripper* hunt unless any direct *evidence* was forthcoming that linked them. Standing nose to nose with Mike, he asked if he understood that. Desperately trying not to reach out and throttle his superior officer, Mike nodded, not daring to speak.

With as much sarcasm as possible, which was a lot from a man who used it every day, Blunt almost screamed at Mike, "Do you remember what *evidence* is? It's the stuff we use to convict people with and lock them up. Sergeants' opinions don't do that, only *evidence*."

Mike held his tongue, knowing it would be useless to argue, and from a political point of view, he could see why Blunt would not want this linked to their murderer. It would add to the growing list of victims the task force was already looking into. Most especially, being so early into his tenure, it would make him look bad to the commissioner.

But Mike was furious as, in his heart, he knew it was all wrong and that it still meant he would not permit anyone to look into the military angle. More than ever, Mike knew that their man was army, in some way. The use of the gun was highly suggestive of Australian Army, as it would be easier to bring into the country a souvenir from a posting overseas than a foreigner smuggling one in through customs. Yes, it was true they had no evidence, but how would they find any if they didn't look? And it wasn't as if they were finding evidence to the contrary. In fact, they were finding no *evidence* at all. It seemed to Mike that because it was an avenue put forward by his predecessor, that in itself was the very reason it wasn't being pursued. He couldn't get his head around the blind-pig ignorance and wondered for the hundredth time; *how did this clown get to be an assistant commissioner?*

Far from being congratulated on a job well done and appreciation of the after-hours work he had put in uncovering the other murder and linking it, he was ridiculed. He was accused of wasting time and that his efforts could be better used to find the *real* psychopath, not the *imagined* one.

Seething with rage, he opened his email, intending to let Dillon know that he was, for the time being, still the only person investigating the army personnel. He then noticed that he had a response from Victoria, with information on the two men living there plus the one for Tasmania. He forwarded the information to Dillon with a brief note explaining what had happened. He also sent him a text message, telling him that he had an email, then Mike went back to work.

****

Journal Excerpt #10, Wounded in Battle
The only thing that went right with that mission was the chopper flight to our landing spot. We arrived on schedule, and we dropped to the ground and dispersed, taking cover in the rocky terrain, and watched it fly back the way it had come. My mind was still very much with

Amanda and hoping upon hope she was okay and had forgiven me once she read the email. I cursed over and over again the timing of things that saw me on a mission while she was so upset, both with losing the baby and thinking I was angry with her for doing so.

The weather, as usual, was hot with clear blue skies and no breeze. The ground was loose shale with scrub and bushes but very few trees for shade. It was very hilly and uneven ground to walk over and held a million places for an ambush from any of the cliffs or ravines.

Once we had taken our bearings, we took off at a brisk pace but had gone no more than a kilometer when one of the guys, Ramsey, slipped on some shale over a hole in the ground and twisted his ankle. He fell, writhing in pain.

Within minutes it was swollen and painful for him to walk on, so he had to be aided by one of the others because an injury like a twisted ankle would never stop us from completing a mission. We were trained to push through pain, but there was no doubt it slowed us down. With the lower pace and continual caution for a potential ambush in the inhospitable terrain, we were over an hour late for the meeting at the village.

When we arrived, we took up observation spots from the hills above and watched for anything unusual. Our uniforms blended in with the scrub where we hid,, and we kept very still and quiet. After ten minutes, we saw no signs of life at all, which seemed by itself strange, as there should have been some movement. Yet there was nothing but smoke spilling out from a single chimney. It was as if we were looking at a ghost town.

The captain made a decision to move in and, using sign language, ordered our injured man plus two others to watch from the rocks above, which would aid us in a hasty retreat if required. He led us down the paths into the village to check it out. If we had been smart or blessed with hindsight, we would have quick timed it back to the evacuation point and gone home. But 'Who Dares, Wins' is not a motto earned by giving up and going home at the first hurdle. We spread out and moved slowly, using any cover we could, and made our way down the slope and into the unknown.

As we drew level with the first house, I peered through a window and saw the inhabitants dead on the floor, their bodies riddled by gunshots and lying in bloody pools. I knew then it was a trap, and we were in trouble. I gestured to the others immediately.

Just as we dropped to the ground, hell broke loose. All around us, hundreds of bullets hit the walls and ground from several of the other buildings at once. A young guy I barely knew, on only his second sortie, named Jimmy Buckley, was hit with several bullets. For a moment, he resembled a dancing rag doll in midair as he was struck by machine gun fire. He fell dead in the dust.

We returned fire and got cover where we could, then slowly retreated to get back to the others hidden above us in the craggy rocks. They provided cover for us and laid down a barrage of gunfire and grenades that gave us some smoke and, I'm sure, stopped the enemy from overrunning us. The guys above us were the only reason we were not all slaughtered right there. The firepower they launched helped us beat a retreat and at the same time, pinned our ambushers down.

The incessant chatter of enemy AK-47s and the occasional rocket exploding around us was deafening.

The noise reverberated from the rocky hills surrounding us while the smoke from explosions aided us in our slow retreat back up the hill.

Seven of us had gone down to the village. Five made it back to the scrub thanks to the covering fire. Two of us were wounded. I had been shot in my right side. It felt like a clean through-and-through hole in the flashy part just above my hip, which hurt like fire, but was manageable. I doused it in antiseptic powder to clean it and help seal the wound, and was ready to press on. One of the other guys caught a graze across his neck that fortunately missed the main artery, though you wouldn't have thought it by the amount of blood over his shoulder and down the front of his uniform and body armor.

Two lay dead in the dust, one in the village and the other a third of the way up the trail, both hit numerous times and beyond any attempt at saving. We were very lucky to lose only two with the firepower they had rained upon us. Had they been a well-trained army, we all would have died, of that, I had no doubt. But their inaccurate shooting showed they were militia or rebels. Heavily armed, yes, but poorly trained. We were unhappy leaving our dead there, but we knew we were too heavily outnumbered. We would have been slowed down too much had we dragged them with us. Plus, it's difficult to fight if you are carrying a body.

We made contact with base and were informed help and evacuation would be around an hour at best. We chose one of the prearranged backup evacuation spots to try to get to. Of all we had considered, this one would be the easiest to defend from the hoard intent on killing us. It was a spot chosen so the choppers could more easily get in and pick us up.

Quickly, we got underway, stopping now and again to fire and keep them off us, but they were slowly and relentlessly coming up the hill, no doubt eager to kill the infidels. We had to think they were sending troops ahead if they hadn't already, so we dared not stay to fight.

Often, in the past, the enemy forces we came across were uncoordinated and lacked the communications and numbers to launch a major attack. However, what they missed in skills they more than made up for with sheer weight of numbers, a fanatical devotion, and enthusiasm for killing us. The running battle that ensued was the worst I had ever been in, with several more wounds taken by our group. There was also one other loss of life—our radioman, nicknamed 'Tinpot.' We reached our goal, took whatever cover we could, and settled in to wait. Despite our best efforts and their losses, they just kept coming, thankfully in dribs and drabs, rather than a full-scale attack.

Cumulatively we were all running low on ammunition and had to make every shot count, but we dug in deeply and would not go down easily. Surrender was not an option as we knew they did not take prisoners. They usually beheaded anyone they took, and that was often after torture.

They never rushed us for some reason, even though we were dreadfully outnumbered. Had they done so, we would have all been killed. I don't know why they didn't, but possibly they thought we had more numbers than we did. Even so, we were under heavy fire for what seemed like hours on end, but of course, it was a lot less than that. Finally, we heard the approaching choppers in the distance. Though we were wounded, battered and bloody, we now knew we would make it. The choppers would lay down a barrage of covering fire while one came in and picked us up.

It was right at that moment that the enemy began firing mortars. They somehow got their range about right. Rockets came in and hit our hidden positions, and numerous rounds fell all around us. I have a vague recollection of a blast alongside my head, but then everything went black.

When I awoke, I was in the chopper, my only thoughts of Amanda, but everything was fuzzy and distant as if any noise was coming from far away. My vision was like looking through a kid's kaleidoscope, but I could still see her face, though it was distorted, and I remember reaching for her to hold me. I faded out again as I felt nauseated, then sometime later, I woke momentarily, and everything was white. My vision and hearing were still not right, and I realized I was in hospital. I remember Amanda's smile. She was laughing with me on the beach, but I couldn't hear her. That was my last thought, and the next time I woke up, five weeks had gone by. I had been in a coma.

Chapter Twenty-Three

The fifth call Dillon made after all of the contact information had come in from Mike Knowles was to Sydney. It was picked up by a woman who answered with just a simple but happy-sounding "Hello?"

"Hello, could I speak with Paul Williams, please?"

There was a long silence before a quiet and more serious voice said, "He isn't here and hasn't been for a long time. I'm sorry."

He had the feeling she was about to put down the phone, so he hurriedly rushed on. "I am Detective Inspector Dillon Bradley from the West Australian Police, calling from Perth. It is very important we find out where he is and speak with him on a rather urgent matter. Could you please let me have a contact number for him? May I also ask who you are, please?" There was something in her voice, melancholy, sadness, and something else he couldn't put his finger on.

"My name is Jayne McMahon. My sister was married to him, and I live in their apartment. But neither of them has been here for quite some time."

There it was again, Dillon noticed, something in her voice. Something was off-key, and his interest grew. "May I call you Jayne, please? Jayne, I'm Dillon, and I promise you this is very important. I really need your help to talk to him."

"I'm sorry, but you are just a voice on the phone.

What's all this about?" she asked.

She sounded still wary but at the same time interested, and for the first time, he realized her voice had a slightly husky note to it.

"Jayne, to be fair, I can't really tell you because it is to do with a serious ongoing investigation. It may, in fact, have nothing to do with Mr. Williams at all. But his name has come up, and, really, I just want to eliminate him from the inquiry. I can tell you it is really important, and I wouldn't be phoning and bothering you if it wasn't vital I speak to him. I know he did spend a lot of time over here in Perth with the army, didn't he?"

Her voice broke then, and with a mixture of anger and sadness, she said, "I don't know who you are but let me tell you this. Tank didn't deserve what happened to him. It was so unfair, and he's such a good man. I'm not going to tell you anything over the phone. You could be anyone for all I know. If you're genuine, you send someone in uniform so I can see them face to face."

Now she was crying openly. *Why did she call him Tank?* he wondered, but before he could ask, she added, "Why don't you just leave him alone. Didn't he give enough for his country?" Then she hung up on him. A very mystified Dillon sat staring at the phone in his hand, trying to figure out what had gone wrong.

He frantically ripped open the laptop and looked again at Paul Williams' file. Like all of the others, it was scant, as the army only wanted to give out minimum information on its ex-servicemen, and in particular, SAS. He had been honorably discharged on medical grounds, and he had received commendations for bravery in Afghanistan and Iraq. 'Wounds received in battle' was the reason given for the discharge, but nothing specific about what those wounds were. But from what this woman had said, it sounded serious.

There was no mention of post-traumatic stress. What information there was seemed perfectly normal for a decorated soldier who had been wounded and discharged. His home state was New South Wales. His father was Colonel Jack Williams, and mother Gwendolyn. He had been in officer training for a while, then joined the SAS, stationed in Perth with three overseas postings.

There was nothing that stood out. His picture did resemble the artist's rendition, his build was similar, and the blood type was O negative. Possibly all coincidences, but something just didn't *feel* right to Dillon. His spine was tingling, and he always trusted his instincts. Again, he looked at the pictures and build, the fact that he had been stationed in Perth, and that he had been discharged after being wounded. There was nothing, yet then again, his instincts told him there was *everything*.

Dillon remembered Mike had told him nine-millimeter hollow-point bullets were used unofficially in Special Forces. The SAS were the most special the Australian Army had. His radar was jangling. Could this possibly be the killer?

Every instinct he had told him it could be, no, scratch that, that he *was*. He opened another window on the laptop and called up Qantas. He was going to Sydney to find out. He had nothing to give Mike to make it official. It could well be a dead end and if it was, he would stop in Melbourne on the way back and visit Louise, as promised.

****

"Wake up, little Suzi. Wake up," I sang to her,

smiling at my own humor as I tapped the side of the knife blade against her cheek. I wondered if her men friends woke her up in the mornings with such sparkling humor. Probably not. Mine was a special talent. She woke with a start, and I clamped my hand over her mouth before she could scream. Then I shook my head, showed her the knife in my other hand, and waited patiently until she mentally processed the danger and came to her own conclusion she should stay quiet. She stopped wriggling and looked up at me with eyes wide open and pleading.

"Shush, Suzi. Do exactly as you are told and keep very, very quiet, and you won't be hurt. Now turn over and put your hands behind your back." Her eyes flashed wide at my use of her name. I tried to sound gentle and calm, but I am sure my excitement showed through. After all, she was going to tell me where Amanda lived.

I took my hand away from her mouth, and her words rushed out in a hushed torrent, "Please don't hurt me. I don't have much money here but what I do have is in my purse in the kitchen."

I touched the flat side of the blade to her lips and said, "Shush now, I don't want your money. Now turn over and put your hands behind your back. I won't ask nicely again."

This time she did roll over and obediently held her hands behind her back, but she couldn't help herself. She had to try again. "Please, I will do anything you want. There is no need to tie me up. If it's me you want, just promise not to hurt me, and you can do what you want to me. Please don't hurt me."

Now she was sobbing and crying, but it made no difference to me. I slipped the two cable ties already looped and joined together over her wrists and yanked them tight, then flipped her back over and pulled the tape I had torn off earlier from my jeans and placed it over her mouth.

She scanned around the room frantically, then back to me. She was searching for any help or escape. I just sat beside her on the bed, staring down at her, taking a few minutes to appreciate what I was seeing.

She was cute, no question. The T-shirt she wore lay flat over her full, round breasts, which, with gravity, pulled to her sides. She did have a plain but pretty face and long blond hair with a darker brown stripe where the lighter hair had grown out. I wasn't there for anything other than information, of course. But of all the women I had come across since coming to the west, I had to admit there was something about Suzie that could have had some appeal in different circumstances. She had a certain air to her. It was hard to put your finger on, but I just thought she could have been special. I sighed as I realized that she was probably just like all of the rest of the sluts in the world.

She kept her little house very clean and tidy, with her only company a small tortoiseshell cat. Suddenly, I realized, to my shock, my mind was contemplating letting her live! Common sense had to prevail, though. Just because she *seemed* like a nice woman didn't mean she was. I sighed again. It wasn't like me to get maudlin, and I had to stop it.

"Suzi, you have a friend. Her name is Toni. I have been looking for her for a long time, and I want you to tell me where she lives, where she works, and who she lives with. If you lie to me, I will hurt you. Do you understand? Please nod if you do."

She did, so I took the tape from her mouth, and out

it came in a flood. "I don't know her that well. I only met her about six weeks ago when she booked my holiday to Bali. She is a travel agent and works at the agency in Belmont Forum Shopping Center. I don't know where she lives. I haven't been there. She is pretty secretive about it, but I know it's close to her work because she walks to and from every day. She is a really nice, fun woman and I like her a lot. We have been out a few times for a couple of drinks and stuff like that. She did speak once or twice about her ex-husband, that she is hiding from...Is that you?"

I nodded. She deserved that. I knew she was being honest. There seemed little point in trying to get much more from her, but she had a nice voice, and I must have seemed sad as she carried on. "She is trying to get back on her feet. She's only been in Perth for a few months. I do know she isn't living with anyone other than her two housemates. The Forum Shops are near where I work on Belmont Avenue, which is why I went to her agency to book my holiday. We just sort of clicked. I really liked her. She's good fun, and we went out a couple of times— drinks, a lunch, a concert, just girls' stuff. She doesn't seem interested in dating men. I like her a lot. She's nice, and we are just becoming good friends."

She was repeating herself, trying to delay the inevitable. She took a breath and then really shocked me when she said, "She said you became violent with her. That's why she left you; she was scared of you."

She flinched as I immediately lost my temper. My rage welled up inside me. How dare she blame me for being violent? How dare she? It was her who was seeing other men, her who was screwing my doctor, good old Doctor *'Call me Charlie.'* And the other guy, too, and probably lots more even though she'd denied it. I'd seen her while I'd been recovering, learning to talk and walk again. She was fucking everyone in sight. And she says I was violent! I was never violent with her. I worshipped the ground she walked on, loved her, and would have given her anything.

Rage coursed through my body, making me tremble, and I suddenly realized I was out of breath. My sight had turned a cloudy blood red, and my head pounded unbearably. I closed my eyes and fought to get my breathing back under control, all the time screaming to myself, *the fucking, fucking, fucking lying bitch; how dare she say I was violent.*

Eventually, I calmed down, and the freight train of a headache eased. I opened my eyes. Suzi was dead. Her upper body was a mass of angry stab and slash wounds, and stupidly my first thought was someone else had done it. I looked around for the offender, jumping up, ready to fight whoever it was. Then I noticed I was covered in her blood. Then the realization hit me—it had been me. I had killed her and didn't remember doing it!

The control I had worked so hard to maintain for years, I had lost through a fit of temper. I shook my head, saddened for her and angry at myself. I had quite liked Suzi in the very short time I had known her. She had seemed a genuine and caring person who had told me the truth and who hadn't sniveled and begged more than you would expect anyone normal to do while being threatened by a knife.

I knew she had to die so she couldn't interfere with my mission to find Amanda, but she had deserved better than she'd received. I would have treated her with respect and killed her quickly. What I had done would have been horrible for her, and I truly felt sorry for the poor woman. With a touch of panic, I realized I hadn't heard her scream. Surely she must have. The number of stab wounds she'd suffered she must have made quite a lot of noise, yet I didn't remember hearing a thing. Perhaps what I remembered of my own angry screaming had been hers. That kind of made sense in my muddled brain, not that thinking clearly with such a bad headache was easy.

Am I losing my mind? I searched my inner feelings, stared down at the grotesquely bloodied body, and it slowly dawned on me that I felt something, and I couldn't put my finger on what exactly it was. Was it guilt? That gnawing sense of wrongness, that feeling I had done something terrible, that was something new for me.

I explored my feelings further, and after a few calming minutes, I shrugged. What had been done couldn't be undone, and I had found where Amanda worked. That was all that mattered. When I caught up with her, I would teach her a lesson or two. For one thing, she had told other people I had been violent to her, the bitch. And for another, I blamed her for my temper attack on Suzi. Yes, I had done the deed, but only because she had told me I had been violent with Amanda. I had never hurt her and never would have. That said, there had been the episode with the scissors, and gnawing away at the very back of my mind, there was something else that was out of reach. I had suffered some very dark days in hospital, and there were patches of time I couldn't remember. Had I been violent to her then and forgotten about it? I didn't think so, but I didn't want to dwell too much about those times because they were too painful. I had to get moving as time was ticking away, and the screams might have brought unwelcome visitors.

There could be police or nosy neighbors here any minute, but I was so incredibly tired, and yes, I admitted to myself, a little depressed. I really just didn't care right at that point in time. If they came, let them come and catch me. *They could take me in a blaze of glory, gunfight at Suzi's place just like the gunfight at the OK Corral,* I mused.

The attraction to that was that only then I would find peace from the headaches and thoughts of death and the voices commanding me to kill. A few minutes were all it took, and I shook myself out of my malaise and decided to get back to work. The police or nosy neighbors hadn't come to check on her, and once again, I would get away, call it luck or what you will.

I yanked back the bedclothes, exposing her lower half, intending to use my knife again on her like all of the others. I wanted to show the world what I thought of unfaithful bitches. The quilt had tangled around her legs in her death throes, and it took a few seconds. Her T-shirt had ridden up, and I saw she wore plain white cotton knickers. Not at all slutty but simple and nice, like her. Seeing them made me stop and think again. She may have made me angry, but I didn't think she was a slut.

In that moment, I realized she wasn't like all of the others, and I decided not to cut her up. I really did feel ill, almost like vomiting, and the headache was ebbing and flowing but heading to a major one. I thought I had to do something to let the police know this was a mistake and that it wouldn't have happened like this if I hadn't been provoked.

On the bedside cabinet, there was a box of tissues. I

pulled out a wad and balled them up, then dipped it in her blood. I wrote on the wall above her dead body a single word—*SORRY*—to show my remorse. I then dropped the tissues and left her bedroom, still not feeling myself, but better for leaving the message.

I cleaned up in her bathroom, washing the knife and my bloodied gloves and arms. I stopped and looked in the mirror at the person looking back at me, a murderer. That murderer deserved to pay the ultimate price for Suzi, and I knew in my heart I would. But not just yet. If the doctors were right, that would come soon enough anyway.

Amanda was so close now, I could almost taste her, and she had to be my number one priority. She was and always had been my mission, and missions had to be completed come what may. I had been trained over and over to never stop until the mission's goals were achieved. As I stared into the abyss of the person's eyes in the mirror, I began to feel better about Suzi. After all, she had been a stepping stone, a part of a greater picture that was titled 'revenge.' Collateral damage, as the Americans called bystanders in war.

I would kill Amanda, finally, and only then think about my consequences for Suzi. On that thought, feeling better than I had in quite a long time, I cleaned up and got ready to leave. I put on a light jacket, pulled my cap low, and left the house after first carefully listening and looking for any signs of life outside. I was not quietly whistling a song as I walked back to the car, but I could have if I wanted to. I just didn't want to right then. After all, the day after tomorrow was Monday. The travel agency would be open, so Monday would see me at the

Belmont Forum Shopping Center. The end of the mission loomed closer.

Chapter Twenty-Four

Journal Excerpt #11, The Fight to Recover
I should have died on that hillside. There is absolutely no doubt about that, and perhaps it would have been better if I had. Most people would have, and even weeks later, I still could have easily died during one of the many operations I had.

When I finally woke from the coma, I was dazed and confused, fading in and out of sleep, and the pain in my head was intolerable. It took quite a while before I could even understand where I was and what had happened. I do have vague recollections of Amanda being there, but nothing concrete. I found out later that I had been drifting in and out of consciousness for a few days. Once I became aware of my surroundings and people, my problems were far from over.

Doctors, nurses, and Amanda all tried to talk to me. I tried to answer back, and in my mind, I was making perfect sense. Unfortunately, the words wouldn't come out, and if they did, they were jumbled or made no sense at all to them. When I knew they couldn't understand me, I became agitated and angry.

I was drooling constantly out of the side of my mouth, and when I tried to wipe it away, my hand wouldn't move. I was paralyzed, it seemed, although at first, I thought my hands were tied or handcuffed to the bed, which only seemed to anger me more.

For all intents and purposes, I had woken up a complete vegetable, unable to move of my own accord or speak. I couldn't even wipe away my own dribble. My thoughts were reasonably clear, but my continuity wasn't. I forgot things and didn't recognize some people—worse, I lacked the ability to do anything except lie in bed.

It was horrible, and for a long time, I worried that I had gone insane or had reached a place there was no coming back from. Time had no meaning for me, and my best friends seemed to be the forty-seven white ceiling tiles above my head. I had counted them hundreds of times, and that was my reference point. So long as each time I got forty-seven, I thought I was still sane.

Doctor—good old 'Call Me Charlie' McGovern—was a tall, lanky guy with sun-bleached blond hair, so he resembled a surfer, not a doctor. He spoke in a relaxed 'I just want to catch the next wave' kind of way. He was sitting by the side of my bed when I woke up feeling, for once, reasonably lucid. I have no idea when this was in relation to how long I had been there. It could have been hours or days after I initially woke as I had no way of telling the passing of time. When he was sure I was awake and paying attention, he spoke.

"I'm Dr. McGovern. Please, just call me Charlie. It's okay, don't try to speak. I know it's difficult for you. I think you can understand me even if you can't talk coherently yet. Can you blink your eyes? Try once for yes and twice for no." In a panic, I blinked rapidly time after time, not knowing if I was blinking or not.

I was greatly relieved when he smiled and said, "Okay, I can see you blinking, slow down, Paul. That is excellent. So, you have some motor control, and you can hear, think and understand me. That's great news and is a good start for what is going to be a long road back for you. But, I think you are up for the challenge, aren't you?" I blinked once, and he smiled again.

"I have answers to some questions I'm sure you must have, and I'm going to try to help you understand what has happened. You survived what was a mortar or rocket blast right alongside your head, and you have suffered the most catastrophic injuries most surgeons have ever seen. That blast would have killed anyone else. I am quite sure about that. That you are even awake now is, some would say, a miracle. Yet here you are back in the land of the living. I think you will regain a lot of your movement and speech in time, but I cannot be absolutely sure of that. You've rewritten the rule book, do you understand?"

I blinked.

"After the base camp hospital, where they did what they could to stem the blood loss and stabilize you, you were airlifted to Germany. There they operated to remove as much shrapnel as possible and patch you up as best as they could. You were operated on by the best surgeon in Germany, and he really has done remarkably well. Again, the fact you are awake is testimony of that. They gave you just about zero chance of living. One day you will have to tell us your motivation and how you came through everything, but we are guessing your level of fitness has clearly been a major contributor, though I suspect your need to survive stems from somewhere else, somewhere in your mind you refused to let go.

"From there, when you were up to it, you were brought back here to Sydney. You are now in the Royal Prince Alfred Hospital, and you've been here just over

four weeks. We've done scans and some more surgery as your signs strengthened. We put a plate over the big hole and did some cosmetic surgery, so your head resembles the same shape as before. We then put you in an induced coma to help you recover from the trauma. Are you still with me so far?"

I blinked slowly so he could see I understood. I tried to say yes, but to me, it just sounded like a moan.

"Your beautiful wife has been here just about every day, waiting for you to wake up. She sits with you, holds your hand, and has been talking to you constantly. She is an amazing woman, and you are a very lucky man."

I blinked profusely, and tears welled in my eyes at the thought of her. He had no way of knowing that Amanda had been my motivation for coming back.

"It's okay. She is just outside, waiting for us to finish our chat. I'm told that you are SAS, so you're tough and fit. That has helped you so far. For sure, a less fit man would have died. Are you ready for some home truths?"

Naturally, I blinked again and waited.

He stood and walked around to the other side of the bed. I tried to move my head, so I could keep looking at him and nearly passed out from intense, white-hot pain through my neck, head, and eyes. Everything turned red and milky, and all I could hear was the sound of a rusty spring going boing, boing. Somehow I clung on to consciousness.

When it cleared, he was staring down at me and seemed very sad. "There is very little information about your sort of injury, I'm afraid. The main reason for that is that usually, people don't survive, so nothing I say is hard and fast true. Some things we know, some things we think we know, and some things that we think we know

259

could turn out to be completely wrong. One thing I can tell you for sure is you are in for a world of pain and suffering to reach any level of reasonable recovery if, in fact, you can recover at all.

"The fact is we cannot remove all of the bits of debris inside your brain. There are some that are just too deep and too close to critical areas. For now, we decided to leave them. After all, we were not really sure you would wake up in the first place, let alone recover any further." He paused, then carried on.

"One day, no matter how well you recover, one of those bits could move to the wrong spot, and you could die. We just don't know, and we need to do regular scans to see if they are moving and where they might move to. Your neck has some major ligament and tendon damage, most of which we have repaired, but it will take a long time to get better. Your shoulder also suffered some shrapnel wounding, which has also affected your spine. We did remove a couple of bits of metal from right up against vertebrae, but we think all of that will heal and that you will come good in time and regain movement."

I was struggling now to keep up. Was I going to live or not? And if I lived, would I be normal?

"At the moment, we have you on morphine, a lot of it. You will be on that for some time, but then slowly, we are going to have to reduce the dosage—we don't want to turn you into a junkie. I am afraid you are going to have to learn to live with pain. One of the people who will work with you closely is a pain specialist. I think the headaches will continue, but how bad, how often, I don't know. We will have to monitor that closely. Your eyesight may fade in and out, or possibly one day, just stop working altogether. You will suffer from mood swings

and possible personality disorders and changes. You will lose your temper easily. Please know this and try hard to maintain calmness. I believe learning meditation will help you here.

"The wound, skin, and bone damage will heal, but the hair will never grow back normally, and the scarring will be permanent. I'm sorry. That's about it for the bad news. Are you ready for some good news?"

I blinked.

"We have some very good people here who are going to work with you. Neurologists, physiotherapists, and a speech therapist, they will all want to write a paper on you and make you their number one priority. They see you as a miracle man to have lived through what you have, and we all feel for you, having suffered this injury fighting for your country. They will want to make you their pet project, to help you talk and walk and do pretty much anything you like in as short a time as possible. Naturally, all this depends on how hard you are willing to relearn all of the skills that so far in your life you took for granted."

Once again, I blinked rapidly.

"You will not be able to continue on in the army. You will be discharged due to your injury. I believe you will receive an ex-gratia payment from the government to help with your rehabilitation and start your new life, plus you will be receiving an invalid pension. All of your treatment won't cost you anything, okay?"

I blinked. Money was the farthest thing from my mind.

"Slowly, we are going to put you back together again, just like Humpty Dumpty, and I want you to realize you've been given the gift of life. We don't know

how long it's going to last. As I said, one of those bits of metal in your brain may or may not put an early end to it. But it's up to you and how hard you work as to what quality of life you regain."

Hard work had never been a problem for me in the past, and I was absolutely positive it wasn't going to be one now. If I had a chance to walk and talk again, I would work my backside off.

Of course, in my naivety, I had no idea how hard or painful my road to recovery was going to be. I also had no idea how angry I would get with the world, and everyone in it, including Amanda. But I just knew no matter what it took, I would do it to get back to normal. More than anything else, I needed to be with her again.

****

Slowly, over the weeks and months, I got some movements back. My physiotherapist worked hard with me, and eventually, walking, and the use of my hands and arms did return. It was much longer before I could talk coherently, but even then, I would get words wrong. In my head, I was saying one thing, like 'can you, please open the window,' but the nurses would tell me what I actually said was 'open the fucking cat.'

I don't know why I took to swearing so much; I never did it consciously, that was not my nature, and no one could explain to me why. But when I got angry, which was often, I swore at anyone and everyone. It took a long time for me to realize I was getting some words wrong. To me, they all sounded right. This would lead to frustration and anger from me, and I would be repeating the same thing over and over, getting louder and louder. I would be swearing profusely and wondering why the stupid nurse wouldn't open the damn window for me, while she would be wondering what cat I was screaming about.

My doctor, Call Me Charlie, explained the issue was twofold. Firstly, the blast had been close to my head, which had caused physical damage to that side, and also, shrapnel and bits of rock had been blown into my neck, shoulder, and deep into my brain. Secondly, the blast had caused me to bang the other side against the rock wall of the crevice I had been crouched in, causing more harm. That blow caused a contra-coup injury to the brain. I should have died; I really should have. In many ways, with what came later, it would have been a lot better if I had.

For a long time, they thought I wouldn't recover at all, but then they didn't know me or my determination to win at all costs. I fought hard to gain back everything that had been taken from me, one small victory and then another – that is how a battle is won. I was brain damaged, and no matter how hard I tried, it took a long, long time before I got anywhere near being 'normal' again. The embarrassing dribbling seemed to last forever, then one day, it just stopped, and it took me a couple of hours to realize it was gone. That was a major victory.

Only when it looked like I would recover did they start the regular X-rays and discovered there was some progression in the small parts of metal they couldn't get to. No one would tell me what that meant. It was all "ifs" and "maybes." They could still stop moving altogether, though more probably, any one of them could shift suddenly and cause, who knew what? Blindness, deafness, or even death. Maybe they wouldn't move anymore at all, and I might live a long life, carrying around in my head an Afghanistan souvenir. Amanda was always hopeful and upbeat, but to me, it didn't ring true, and I felt she was holding back information.

Call Me Charlie, though, in some of our long and deep discussions, led me to believe he had no doubt they would kill me; he just didn't know when. He would stop by when he finished work with two long black coffees and sit with me awhile and just chat. His opinion was that no one should be able to walk around with that much 'scrap iron' in their brain and that one day it could be a strenuous movement, fall, or accidental blow to the head, and it would be lights out. He was particularly concerned with my temper and fits of rage, and I appreciated that he never pulled any punches. He treated me with respect and called a spade a spade.

He never made any secret of his admiration for Amanda, and I could see in his eyes that he liked her whenever we spoke of her. For example, if I had been particularly angry with her that day, at visiting time, he would chide me. At that time, I thought he was nothing if not professional and speaking to me like my father never had. But I later came to believe they were having an affair. When I looked back on those conversations, it made more sense, even to my twisted brain.

Not too long before I discharged myself, I found out that one of the bits had moved considerably and was edging ever so slowly closer to a spot they felt would kill me. It was just a matter of when not if. He used that to urge me to be kinder to my Amanda, but I didn't really get it at the time. I thought I was being fine and that it was her who had changed. Before I found that out, though, I had to endure months of rehabilitation and physiotherapy. I was learning to talk coherently, to walk unaided, and use my hands to grip things without either dropping or crushing them. The swearing took a long time to go. Most of the time, I didn't even know I was doing it, especially when Amanda was visiting me.

She would often leave in tears, and Nurse Jacobson or Call Me Charlie would tell me off and, quite angrily, tell me some of the things I had said to her. They were the only ones who stood up to me and would reprimand me instead of fawning all over me like the other doctors and nurses; all they ever did was treat me like an invalid.

One day I wanted Amanda to take me outside and to get me a wheelchair so we could go, as the sun looked so nice through the window. I had asked her to 'get me my fucking cricket bat.'

She asked me what I meant. And I replied, "My fucking, fucking cricket bat so I could sit in it and go outside."

"How can you sit in a cricket bat, Tank?"

"Don't be fucking stupid. I don't want to sit in a fucking cricket bat. I want my fucking cricket bat so you can take me outside."

According to Nurse Jacobson, by now, I was shouting over and over how I wanted to go outside and to bring me my fucking cricket bat and for her to stop being stupid and get it for me. I know now it sounds mad, but I just couldn't stop myself from being cruel to the one person I adored. Most of the time, though, I didn't know that I was getting my words wrong; everything I said made perfect sense to me in my addled brain.

What made it worse was even when I did know I had said something horribly wrong and been insulting and offensive about it, I seemed incapable of apologizing. The next day I said I was sorry to her and tried to explain that when I asked for my cricket bat, I didn't mean an actual cricket bat but a cricket bat with wheels that I could sit in and be wheeled outside in. She said, "Oh, you meant a wheelchair," and smiled condescendingly at me. No matter how hard I tried to stop it, that would make me angry all over again, and once more, she would leave in tears.

She hadn't signed up for a life of being abused verbally by an invalid she'd once loved, but then I hadn't asked for the head injury either. She could have been more understanding about it instead of blaming me for things beyond my control. She could have tried to be more forgiving. If only she had been more patient and held on because I did recover eventually. We could have had a good life while it lasted. The army had given me a large payout that sat in my bank account. We could have gone anywhere, seen the world together, and lived like we had lived before at Hamilton Island.

Yes, there would always be limitations in what I could or couldn't do, and there was always the risk everything could end at a moment's notice. But from when I did get better until the end, we could have had a great life and traveled as she had always wanted to do.

As I now know, though, she sought solace in the arms of other men rather than be patient and caring. It seemed she had forgotten her vows of better or worse, sickness and in health. I became suspicious of her, and when I could move around of my own volition, I kept it from her for a while. I used that secret mobility to watch her, and I saw her in Call Me Charlie's arms in the corridor hugging. If I'd had a gun or knife, I would have used it.

I later told myself to be calm and keep watching.

Maybe I had been wrong and mistaken a friendly hug for a lover's one. But once that seed had been sown, I saw more and more signs of her growing discontent with me and happiness with him. There were little glances and smiles when they thought I wasn't looking. I tried to hide that I knew, but it all made me more and more angry.

Days stretched into weeks, and they turned into months. It took a long, long time to get better. And then, when I really was better, Amanda had become very distant, in fact downright cold with me. I had been hell to be with, and I suppose I had taking my frustrations out on Amanda, even though I loved her with all of my heart. I could only look at her and get angry as if, in some way, it was all her fault. She was healthy, and I was not. The doctor tried to tell us that the anger was a symptom of the injury and that it would get better, and for Amanda to try to ignore it because I didn't mean it. She would nod and agree with the doctor and squeeze my hand, but then later run off crying because I was yelling at her, just because I wanted her to do something she couldn't understand.

I was off the morphine but did have some pretty strong tablets to take as and when I felt I needed them. The headaches were dreadful and would come and go without warning, and that too would make me angry. Sometimes the edges of my eyesight would be tinged red as if my eyes themselves were bleeding. It seemed to me that everything made me wild, and I developed a habit of throwing things.

And so it was, on what turned out to be my final day in hospital, I had been doing a therapy exercise cutting different-shaped animals out of a child's coloring-in book with a small pair of orange-handled kids' scissors.

I was trying hard not to cut over the lines. I tired of it and went for a walk and found myself at the windows looking out over the enormous car park when I saw a late-model car pull up at the drop-off point. Amanda got out of the passenger side, and a man I didn't know got out of the driver's side. They hugged before Amanda turned and walked into the building. I turned to ice and went and got back into bed, picked up the book and scissors, and waited for her.

She entered and came to the bed and kissed my cheek. A far cry from the days when she wrapped herself around me, I thought. She sat in the chair alongside me, and without preamble, I asked her, "Who's the guy in the luxury car?"

She looked startled, and before she could think about a lie, I said, "I was at the fucking window and saw you get out and hug him. Are you fucking him too?"

Her eyes twinkled with tears. The anger welled up in me, and I clenched the scissors tighter.

She shook her head sadly and said, "That's Greg, the boss' son. He was coming this way and offered me a lift."

She had gone back to work at the travel agency, so it was possible she was telling the truth but did she expect me to believe she would hug the boss' son? She reached for my hand, and I flinched when she touched me. Why did I flinch? Was it anger, or did she just take me by surprise? I couldn't say for sure, but as I did, I stabbed her wrist with the scissors, scratching her and bringing a spot of blood.

"Ouch!" she yelled and snatched back her hand, raising her wrist to her mouth to suck out the blood before it stained her pretty white blouse. She looked at

me with horror, as if I had done it on purpose, and that made me wild, and I screamed at her.

"It's not enough for you to fuck my doctor, but now this guy as well? Stop whinging, you stupid bitch. If I wanted to hurt you, I don't need these stupid fucking spiders, I mean scissors." With that, I flung the damn things across the room to clatter against the wall. I gained some pleasure in noting the point had dug into the paintwork and scratched it.

She stood up crying loudly and screamed back, "Since I met you and fell in love with you, you big fucking ape, I haven't fucked anyone but you. How could you think I would do that? You're sick if you think I would fuck your doctor when he has been so wonderful to you, and he has been a comfort to me. And Greg is just Greg who was kind enough to give me a lift. Yes, he does want to fuck me, for your information, but that doesn't mean I would. Yes, I hugged him. I hug lots of people, that's just me being me, remember? I am a hugger. I come here every day and have you yell and swear at me while I give you support and try to get you back to the man I fell in love with, and now this? Tank, how could you?"

She cried uncontrollably, and just for a moment, I believed her, but before I could say anything, she said, "I'm going away. I'm not sure for how long. I'm going back to Perth, the army has been in touch and offered to have our stuff boxed up and sent back, but I don't want them going through our private things. I think a break will do us both good."

I sat there stunned. She was leaving me? Going back to Perth? I was speechless, and she turned on her heel and walked out of the room. I wanted to call after her to come back. I tried to, but the words wouldn't come, then *she was gone. The more I thought about it, the more convinced I became that she was lying and had run away because she now knew I knew she was a lying, cheating slut. The anger seethed inside me, I finished the whole bottle of painkillers to ease the massive headache I was feeling, and that was when the voices started.*

"Find the bitch, kill the bitch find the bitch, kill the bitch." Like a mantra in my head. The sort of mantra I could relax to while trying the meditation good old Call Me Charlie had recommended. I barely slept that night, waiting for her to come back and reassure me. I kept expecting her to walk in and apologize, and every time I heard a footfall in the passage, I looked up, but she didn't come.

I waited until lunchtime the next day, then I dressed in the clothes Amanda had brought in for me, including a red baseball cap to hide my scarring. I walked out of the hospital without saying a word to anyone. I didn't trust myself not to attack good old Call Me Charlie had I seen him, so perhaps it was fortunate I didn't. I left, not knowing how long I had to live but determined that before I died, I would track down Amanda and kill her. Amen to that.

Chapter Twenty-Five

Mike Knowles had been plodding on with the exhaustive checking of family and friends' backgrounds of the two murdered sisters and families. The body of Suzanne Delvechio was discovered by detectives following up with friends from Georgina's address book. She, too, had been slaughtered in her bed while tied to the bedhead.

While this had undoubtedly been committed by the same killer, there were stark differences in the way she had been murdered. That and the lack of mutilation of her vagina caused Assistant Commissioner Blunt, and therefore the task force under his direction, to come to several conclusions. The scope of these decisions set them back even farther than they already were.

The only person who believed they were on the wrong track was Mike Knowles, and he was furious to the point he risked his career and made his feelings known. Such were his vehement arguments to the contrary, he was accused of not being a team player. Worse, if he didn't change his attitude *pretty fucking quickly*, he would be transferred out of the unit forthwith and would face disciplinary charges, Blunt had told him with his usual utter lack of diplomacy.

Mike considered asking for a transfer anyway, but that sort of thing tended to follow you around in the force. Those who gained a poor reputation seldom got other opportunities for advancement, so he bit his tongue and hoped upon hope Dillon was making progress in the right direction.

Blunt hypothesized that the changes in M.O. meant that Suzanne Delvechio had been the killer's intended victim all along and that now he'd murdered her, the killings would stop. Of course, Mike pondered, Blunt had no idea why she'd been the original intended victim, but common sense seemed to make little difference; it was his way or the highway. Mike was astounded by the stupidity of this claim. It seemed that Blunt's focus wasn't on catching a serial killer anymore but to celebrate that he was not going to murder anyone else. The relief coming from "Lightfoot" was contagious and almost seemed to set off high spirits in the team; if the boss said the killings had stopped, it must be true.

Mike had never seen anything quite like it. He tried to point out that this woman did not strongly resemble the profile of the majority of the victims, especially the first ten of them, but he was ridiculed for voicing his concern. She did not have long blonde hair, good looks, and short stature but, by the same token, could be said to have been a very plain woman, while earlier victims had been stunningly beautiful. Delvechio was a little chubby with mousey brown hair, dyed blonde, who wore glasses and apparently was gay. Blunt accused Mike of looking for shadows that weren't there, and he suggested the first ten victims' resemblance was just coincidental, which Mike tried to point out completely went against the psychological profiles done at the time. Mike wondered *If you weren't going to listen to expensive consultant profilers and psychologists, why have them in the first place?*

"Furthermore," Blunt said, "just because a lunatic starts out with a preferred type of victim doesn't mean he had to stick to it. He is, after all, a madman, so can't be predicted. That's why he is a lunatic." This small-minded attitude seemed so ridiculous as to be laughable, and Knowles wondered, not for the first time, how this clown had become an assistant commissioner.

The frenzied stabbing and slashing suffered by the victim pointed to a rage, and Mike agreed with that. To Blunt, that suggested that this was the final victim, but to Mike, it made more sense that something had triggered the anger, perhaps something Delvechio had said which set him off. It was that which tipped the killer over the edge once he had the information he was after, and *that* was more likely why he had written *SORRY* in blood on the wall above the bed.

"Rubbish," was what Blunt thought of that. He took the writing of the word as further proof that the spree had finished and the killer had finally experienced some remorse and guilt for his actions.

Mike believed nothing *The Ripper* had done resembled guilt. The psych report stated he was a sociopath with psychopathic leanings and therefore incapable of feeling that emotion. He seemed to have no remorse for anything he had done, so it made no sense to think he now suddenly felt sorry for the twenty or so murders he had committed. Yes, something had made him write that he was sorry but sorry for losing his temper seemed much more likely to Mike Knowles.

Finally, the lack of mutilation to the victim's vagina, which every other woman had suffered, was the last link in the chain for Blunt. What else could it mean but the end of the chase? Anyone who thought differently was an idiot, he said, looking right at Mike when he said it, who just shook his head.

Mike no longer cared if Blunt believed him an idiot or not. If his and Dillon's theory was correct and this was an ex-Army killer with some psychological trauma leading him to find one particular woman or facsimiles of one woman, then the lack of mutilation, the frenzied stabbings all linked with the use of the word *SORRY* showed regret at this particular killing only. While the reason for the regret could only be surmised, it seemed logical to Mike that on this occasion, *The Ripper* had lost his temper at something and, in a fit of rage, had murdered his victim in a way he would not normally do. When he'd realized what he had done, he'd felt regret and said sorry in the only way he could, firstly by not mutilating her any further, and secondly by telling them he was sorry in blood. Mike's theory fell on deaf ears; Blunt was already writing his press release, stating that *he* had stopped the Ripper single-handedly.

More than ever, Mike thought the murderer was getting closer to his target. Suzanne Delvechio had known her or known of her, and perhaps the Ripper now had the information he had been searching for to find her. Mike would not stop looking for him just because Blunt told him to. He prayed Dillon would find some information in Sydney that could lead them to stopping the killings once and for all. Nothing would please Mike more than capturing the murderer and showing Blunt just how good a policeman he was despite the woeful management he had received.

****

On his third knock on the door, it was opened, and Dillon did an immediate double-take. Standing there, without doubt, was an amalgamation of the first ten victims. The overall resemblance was uncanny. He was staggered and stared open-mouthed.

"Yes? Can I help you?" the rather short, blonde-haired, and stunningly beautiful woman said. She wore an amused smile at the obvious shocked look on his face.

Dillon quickly recovered, took out his identity card, and showed it while trying to smile back. "Hi, sorry about that. You reminded me of someone else. I'm Inspector Dillon Bradley from the WA Police. We spoke on the phone about Paul Williams, and I thought I would come and see you myself. It's so impersonal over the phone, isn't it?" He smiled his most disarming smile, and it was her turn to look shocked

"You flew over from Perth just to talk to me? Wow, aren't I special? You better come in. Would you like a coffee?"

He followed her inside the pleasantly decorated but small apartment, looked around, and spotted the pod coffee machine on the kitchen cupboard top. "You know what? That muck they serve on the plane is just dreadful, isn't it? If it's no trouble, I'd love one thank you, Jayne, isn't it?"

She nodded and pointed to a stool at the breakfast bar while she went and turned on the machine. Dillon, still grieving as he was for his wife, couldn't help but admire the looks and body of the long-haired woman standing with her back to him. It had been many years since he had been knocked off his feet by a beautiful woman, and she was simply breathtaking.

Dillon put his briefcase on the bar top and wished he was single and twenty years younger again, then winced as he realized he *was* single. He choked back the pain and anger at Kathy's murder; he needed this woman's help, so he forced back his grief and made himself smile again.

"So," she said over her shoulder, "you better tell me what this is all about. It must be serious to drag you to Sydney just to talk to me about Tank. What is it you think he has done?"

He realized in that moment he liked her very much. Her voice was soft, sexy, and she seemed genuinely lovely. He had always been pretty good with his first impressions of people, and he was rarely proved wrong. In a different world and time, he would have loved to have gotten to know her.

He sighed inwardly. "Do you mind if I call you Jayne? I have to tell you first that this is an unofficial visit, and you don't have to talk to me at all if you don't want to. Just ask, and I will leave. You are in no way under any investigation, and I don't want you to worry that you are in any sort of trouble. You are not. I have no authority in this state to question you, and I promise you I'm not here to hound Mr. Williams or you. But the fact is his name has come up in relation to some very serious cases in Perth. First and foremost, I would like to eliminate him from those inquiries. I have the utmost respect for our returned soldiers, especially those wounded, so please believe I have his interests in mind. No one would be more pleased than me if I can eliminate him entirely and move on. Why do you call him Tank, by the way?"

He saw her shoulders drop with relief, and he knew he had taken the right approach with her by being friendly rather than officious. He thought she would respond to slow, gentle questions, and he needed to find this man she called Tank, who Dillon now had no doubt was the one they were after. If her sister was his ex-wife and they looked alike, then he thought he had found the motivation to kill anyone who resembled her. Something must have gone horribly wrong between them.

She shook her head, her hair settled around her open-necked top, and he caught just a glimpse of a purple bra strap on a milky white shoulder. Another distraction for him. How did beautiful women have the knack to knock men off their game so easily? She turned to face him with two empty coffee cups in her hands, smiling and with the pride and admiration obvious in her voice, she explained: "Tank is the nickname given to him by his friends in his unit after he saved all of their lives when he single-handedly took out a tank, although he is so modest he said it was more of an armored vehicle. I met two of his mates, and they idolize him. Apparently, they were pinned down and would surely have all died if not for his bravery, which he just called a moment of madness. He was given a medal, not that he ever bragged about it. That's just not his way. Tank is an awesome guy, one in a thousand. Believe me, I've known the other nine hundred and ninety-nine assholes." She grinned at her own humor, but that grin had a hint of sadness too, and Dillon felt himself being more and more attracted to her.

"Okay. I can tell you like him. He sounds like the sort of man I'd like to meet and buy a beer. Like I said earlier, I respect men like him, so let's see if we can eliminate him straight away, shall we? Has he been in Perth to your knowledge in the last twelve months or so, and does he live there now?"

She had been smiling, but suddenly her face

saddened, and her lovely blue eyes went misty.

"To be honest, Inspector, I don't know, but I'm pretty sure he did go back there a few months ago. But I don't know how long he stayed or if he is still there now. It's possible that by now, he has died from the injuries he got in the war, or he could be in Timbuctoo partying like there is no tomorrow. I wish I knew." With that, she broke down and cried soulfully.

Dillon stood up, took the cups from her, and guided her to the sofa. "Let me make the coffee, and if you would, I'd love you to tell me all about him. How do you have yours?" He waved one of the cups at her, then walked back to the machine, which was now warm.

"Just a flat white for me, no sugar. That's the light brown color pods. The long black are the red ones. Thanks for helping. I'm sorry, I'm being silly, I know, but what happened to such a wonderful man is so sad. It's all just so unfair."

She cried again, and Dillon thought it best to let her go and let her get over it. He was sure this story, once he got it, was going to be a good one. He made the coffees, took them over, set them on the coffee table and sat alongside her, and waited for her to begin, which she did while dabbing her eyes with a tissue.

"You know, I'm a sucker for a good romantic story or movie. I'm just a born crybaby, sorry, but I could never write a story as beautiful as Tank and Amanda's. Paul and my sister met by chance in a bar after she finished work on a Friday night. They instantly fell in love. He was on leave here in Sydney because he'd just finished a tour in Afghanistan. He was with the other two guys I told you about from his unit.

"I wasn't there when they met, but I know they were

just made for each other. I've never seen Amanda happier in her life before meeting him. He just swept her off her feet, truly love at first sight. And while Tank did seem a bit strange at times, that was understandable when you know his history. He had never had a girlfriend before Amanda, would you believe? And his childhood, from what little I know, Amanda said was like a horror story with his father being a domineering monster who beat him with a cane all the time. Tank would never speak about his mother. He hated her with a passion you wouldn't believe, so much so he would not invite her to their wedding."

Dillon's ears pricked up all the more with news of his childhood problems, which the profilers had said he would have.

"He had a heart of solid gold, and he was really good for her. He told me he fell in love with her at first sight too. They were together for ten days before he had to ship back, and they spent every minute together. Amanda even threatened to quit her job if they wouldn't give her time off so she could be with him. He proposed to her at the airport on the day he was leaving. She had given him a lift so he could go on his next tour of duty to Iraq. Isn't that romantic? The proposal, I mean, not going to Iraq." Her tears flowed freely as she spoke; there was no restraining them. Periodically she dabbed with the tissue and smiled at him as if apologizing for being such a crybaby.

"You would think six months' separation after knowing each other only ten days would be the end of the relationship, wouldn't you? Well, it would have for me, with my luck with guys anyway; men always seem to dump me. But not for those two. They used to video call and phone every chance they got. Amanda never had any shortage of men chasing her, but she was off the market for good because she said she had experienced roast beef, so would not accept hamburger anymore. She waited for Tank, and for Amanda, it was almost like waiting for him was a badge of honor, which she wore with pride. Mum and I helped her arrange everything for the wedding, and that happened four days after he got back from Iraq. Inspector, it was just beautiful. You have no idea. Tank is such a big doofus of a man, a real gentle giant. And Amanda is like me, small, but with bigger boobs." She smiled and winked her red left eye at him to show she was joking.

"Jayne, please call me Dillon, and go on. I'm really enjoying this story. I'm a sucker for a good rom-com myself." He smiled back to encourage her while thinking that really, her mentioning her breasts was a tease and a very good one.

"They honeymooned in Hamilton Island, Queensland, and had an amazing time. The pictures they brought back were just fabulous. They both just kind of glowed with an inner peace and happiness. Then they hit me with the surprise of my life, and this will show you what an amazing guy Tank is. You just won't believe it. Now, bear in mind he hardly even knew me then. You see, I had just been through a pretty bad breakup with a married man, and I had contemplated suicide a few weeks before. Yeah, yeah, I know, stupid me." She shrugged her shoulders, giving Dillon another glimpse of her purple bra strap. "That's the story of my life, always picking the wrong man. If only I'd met Tank and not Amanda." She paused a long time as if she were thinking of the possibilities before shrugging again and going on.

"Tank was based in WA, where all the SAS are. A place called Swanbourne, have I said that right?" He nodded and smiled at her. She had the most enchanting way of speaking.

"Of course, Amanda wanted to be with him over there, but he knew he would be going on at least one more tour. That would likely be for six months, and he was worried Amanda would get lonely away from family when he went away. So, they rented this place here, which has two bedrooms and two bathrooms. But then they asked me to move in, rent-free, to look after it for them while they were away. Amanda told me it was actually Tank's idea. See what a sweet guy he is? Naturally, I jumped at it—the place I was in wasn't anywhere near as nice as this, and it was expensive. I didn't want to move back in with Mum, so I jumped at the chance. While they were over there in Perth, I was here, all alone, but if or when he went away and she came back to Sydney, she would have somewhere to stay. Here's the really amazing thing. Neither of them have been here in such a long time now, and still, Tank is paying the rent. It comes out of his bank account automatically. I never hear from the agent apart from rent inspections, of course. They are just a pain in the bum. Seriously, can you even imagine any other man being that thoughtful? No offense, if you are, of course."

He laughed and said, "No, Jayne, no offense taken. I agree that he sounds like a really good guy, as you said. One in a thousand for sure, and I'm sure from what you are saying, he isn't our man. So, what happened a year ago?"

He cursed himself as she broke down in tears yet again. This time tears of anguish, and he couldn't help himself. His heart went out to her, and he hugged her before he could stop himself.

It was only afterward that Dillon thought, *what am I doing hugging a witness?* But he had to admit, it was the right thing to do, and she did hug him back, apparently glad of the comfort he offered. He was somewhat in a daze. She felt so warm and soft. Her hair smelled nice, and with a shock, he realized he wanted her. He was immediately angry at himself. He should not be thinking that way about anyone, least of all a witness, and especially so soon after his wife's murder.

Eventually, she pulled away. "Thanks, I needed that."

She smiled sheepishly at him, and not for the first time, Dillon was struck with how beautiful she *really* was. He had to remind himself, yet again, that he wasn't there to arrange a date. He was there to track down a serial killer, and he needed information from her. But Jayne possessed such a gentle spirit and kind personality he couldn't help but feel sorry for her. He knew when she found out her *'Tank'* was a murderer, she was going to be devastated.

"If you just hold my hand, I will try to get through the rest of this without breaking down again," she said.

Against his better judgment, he took her small hand in his and squeezed it softly. It just felt incredible to be there.

"Tank was on a mission. He never spoke about it, but half of his squad were killed, and he was horribly wounded and very lucky to have been airlifted out. The doctors were amazed he even survived and said anyone else would have died. I mean that he shouldn't have lived through his wound. But, do you know what I think,

Inspector, I mean, Dillon? Promise you won't laugh at me?"

He squeezed her hand gently and realized he didn't want to let it go, ever. "Jayne, I promise I won't laugh at you. I would never do that. Please tell me what you think."

"Well, just remember you promised." She squeezed his hand once more. "I truly believe that the only reason he didn't die from his injuries was because of his love for my sister. That love kept him alive and drove him to recover just to get back to her. He once made a vow to her that no matter what, he would always come back to her from battle. I wish, just for once in my life, to have someone love me one-tenth as much. A mortar went off close to his head. For God's sake, who else could survive that?"

She broke down all over again. Dillon hated himself at that moment for making her relive what clearly was a very painful memory. But there were now no lingering doubts in his mind that Williams was the one. There were far too many coincidences to discount this Paul 'Tank' Williams. Even without one shred of evidence, everything screamed at him that he was *the Ripper*. He now knew why the killer always wore a hat, wig, or cap; to hide his scars. The evidence would follow; he was positive. No matter how much he would like to protect her memory of him, that was not going to happen. Her faith was going to be destroyed.

Soon, she recovered and went on, with him still holding her hand. "They brought him back here to Sydney after some surgery in Germany, still in a coma. His skull was barely in one piece, and he had shrapnel buried deep inside his brain, neck, and shoulder. They got a lot of it out, but not all of it. They couldn't. Some they had to leave behind. When he woke up, he had no movement in his arms or legs, he couldn't talk, and he dribbled nonstop. He was a mess. Oh my God, it was so sad. Amanda was distraught and did everything she could to help nurse him back to the man he was before, but he had changed so much.

"The doctors told us he may or may not recover some or all movement. He could suffer brain damage, personality disorders, mood swings, depression, and temper tantrums. They just didn't know. But Amanda thought her love for him would help him through it, and for a while, it seemed like she did."

Dillon was fascinated. It seemed to be the story of a true Australian hero and a love story like no other, the kind of love he couldn't imagine. But Dillon knew the story was going to turn bad, and he squeezed Jayne's hand to urge her to go on.

"They worked on him nonstop, operations, therapy, and specialist after specialist. He was like a charging bull. He never stopped trying to get better; his determination to recover to be with Amanda was phenomenal. At least, that was my belief; it was all so he could be with Amanda. A weaker man would not have survived. He learned to walk again and talk, his incessant dribbling stopped, and the doctors were amazed with the speed of his recovery. But, oh, Dillon, it's so *fucking* sad. Mentally he was never the same again. His anger was scary, not that I personally ever saw him at his worst. Mostly, he didn't even know he was angry, but apparently, a lot of nurses didn't want to care for him because he was so rude to them and could snap at any moment, and being such a big guy, they thought he would hurt them. He would get words wrong and not know that he had, and no one knew what he was talking about. So, he got angrier and angrier and blamed everyone else because they couldn't understand him. He was moody, God, was he moody! Even with me sometimes when I visited him and with everyone else most of the time. But then it got worse. Jealousy sent him over the top with Amanda. He accused her of seeing other men while he was stuck in the hospital. It was totally untrue, of course, and then he attacked her with a pair of scissors. That was the end of it for her; she had to get away for a while.

"She thought a break would do them both good, give her time to calm down, and give him time to get over his jealous rages. The doctors told us it was likely to be a temporary thing, although there was no guarantee of that, of course. Everyone was flying blind. She believed it would help him if she stopped seeing him, and that's when I fell out with her. She was wrong. That was when he needed her the most, and she abandoned him.

"The army had paid him out when they discharged him, quite a lot of money. For services rendered or some such shit, small price to pay for what they did to him. It just seemed like they wanted him gone. Not only that, but they had also been on to Amanda to go back to Perth to clear out the quarters they had lived in at the barracks. She thought it was the ideal time to go over for a while, pack everything up, say goodbye to the friends she had made there. Then she intended to come back to him to try again, hoping he would be better by then, she said.

"She called me in tears on that last day. They had fought, and that was when the scissors thing happened. She said that in her heart, she knew the Tank we knew was gone and that while he had not tried to kill her with the scissors, the look in his eye was that one day he would. She thought if they went on the way they were, sooner or later, he would lose his temper and hurt, if not kill her. I never saw that side of him myself, and I told her so. She thought she had to get away from him and give him time to recover without her being the focal point of his anger, but I thought she should stay and just deal with it. She told me she was going to Perth and wasn't sure when she would be back. She even asked me to look after Tank and visit him, and tell him she loved him no matter what, and for him to give her some time away. I loved my sister, but I was so mad with her for abandoning him. I have never been lucky enough for a man to love me the way he loved her, and I would have fought harder for him when he needed me the most. Even the doctors said they thought his moods would pass, that he wasn't really responsible for them, but she left anyway.

"The next day, I took some time off work to visit him in hospital at lunchtime, but he had packed up and left. He just walked out, and the doctors were very worried for him. No one saw him leave. I've not seen him or heard from him again, though I kept hoping he would turn up sometime, but he never has. I would just love to give that big hunk a hug again. I called Amanda from the hospital and told her he was gone, and we argued. I'm sorry now, but oh, I was so mad at her."

Dillon noticed Jayne's face had an angry, determined scowl to it, which only made her look cuter.

"I called her a selfish bitch when she said she was still going to Perth even though Tank was missing. I regret that, but goddammit, she should have been by his side and not on the other side of the country. He still suffered massive headaches, blurred vision, bad moods, and dizzy spells. Not to mention he could get very angry very quickly. He was nowhere near recovered, and he just vanished. Amanda hung up on me after saying some not very nice things back, and I haven't heard from her since. Neither has Mum because she agreed with me. Amanda's phone was disconnected a few days later when I tried to make peace with her, but it's like she just ran away from us all. I miss her, and I miss Tank, they were just so good together, and it was so horribly sad. None of it was Tank's fault."

He left her cry it out, sitting with her, holding her hand, not trusting himself not to hug her again. He knew he had to talk to her and ask her some very painful questions, which would upset her more, but what choice did he have?

After a while, she pulled herself together, and as gently as possible, he began. "Jayne, do you think he took off to Perth to find Amanda?" he asked, and she nodded enthusiastically.

"He had to. A love like that doesn't just die, especially for him who had never been in love before, had never even had a girlfriend, remember? He would have chased her to the moon. He had been brain-damaged, and it may have given him some sort of temporary insanity because of the trauma, but he was a fighter. Inspector, he would have fought his way back to be with her. He loved her with everything he had. He wouldn't, just couldn't, stay here thinking she had left him to go to Perth. Yes, I think he would have followed her."

"Do you have any idea at all where I might be able

to find him or Amanda?"

"No. But he had his payout, so they had money. Amanda always had this dream to travel since she was a little girl. I think he probably found her, and they made up. Perhaps they are traveling the world, maybe sailing in the Caribbean, or skiing in France. They told him he may not have long to live. Those fragments in his head were moving. So, I think they would have taken off together to enjoy what time he had left." She now smiled at Dillon, her eyes still sparkling with unshed tears, and he thought she looked radiant. "Here's the thing. They were doing regular scans and X-rays before he ran away from the hospital, and one or two of the bits left behind in his head were too deep to operate and remove. The feeling was sooner or later, one would move to a spot, and he would die or lose some motor functions. It was just a question of when."

Dillon nodded slowly, thinking deeply, then said, "Jayne, that is an incredible story, and as much as I think it's amazing, it's also very troubling. Would you mind if I show you something? It's really why I'm here, and I think you need to know. But I have to tell you right now it's not going to be pleasant."

She gazed into his eyes and looked worried, if not even angry. She took her hand away from his and nodded warily.

He went to his briefcase, took out the pictures of the first ten victims, and slowly spread them out over the breakfast bar. "Please have a look at these women and tell me what you think." He moved back and gave her room to see the pictures clearly.

She stood and slowly approached, looked at the pictures, raised her hand over her mouth, and screamed.

"Oh my God, what does this mean? What are you showing me these for? They all look like Amanda." She turned on him, angry, as if he was playing a sick joke on her.

He shook his head sadly. "I'm sorry to tell you this, Jayne, but over in the West, we have had a serial killer; you've probably heard of him. The press calls him *The Ripper.* Over the last several months, these were his first ten victims. What I think is that Paul Williams, in his diminished state of mind, thinks he keeps finding Amanda and killing her."

He jumped toward her and caught her just before she hit the floor in a dead faint. He very gently lowered her down the rest of the way, protecting her head, and went to find a bathroom and damp cloth.

Chapter Twenty-Six

Once Mike Knowles got the call from Dillon, he went straight to see Blunt. He knocked and walked in without waiting for an answer. Mike was not known for his tact, and he was triumphant and felt superior that his theory had borne fruit, and Blunt was an idiot. He was also incredibly angry and lost no time in showing it.

"Thanks to Inspector Bradley, we now know who the killer is. He has been working from home on the army angle, which you wouldn't let us investigate, and he has identified him. We need to pull out all the stops to find him now before he kills again, and I need your permission to release it to the press so we can find him quickly."

Blunt sat as if in silent shock. Mike watched while he slowly bridged his fingers together under his nose and obviously thought how best he could handle the information Mike had brought him.

"Just so I'm clear on the facts here, Sergeant, we have a senior commanding officer whose wife was murdered by the suspect while in the act of having sex with one of her employees. He was, quite naturally, relieved of his command and put on leave." He held up his hand to stop Mike from interrupting.

"Now, if I'm reading this right, he has been fed information by you from this task force against a direct order from me. To make matters worse, he has been carrying out an unauthorized investigation with information acquired illegally. He has identified someone who, even if we arrested him now, would be released with his case thrown out of court because of that illegal investigation?" He held up his hand again to stop Mike from answering back. "Wait! I haven't finished. What, pray tell, *evidence* has Super Cop unearthed that we dunderheads have missed?"

Mike's heart sank. He could tell this was going to end badly. Fuck him. He was a complete and utter imbecile. As best as he could, he controlled his growing rage.

"He manually went through all of the files from the army and identified several people with the right blood type who, by the pictures supplied, resembled the artist's impressions of our man. One by one, he worked through that list until only one was left, a Sergeant Paul Williams, discharged wounded in Sydney. He is ex-SAS who was based at the Swanbourne Barracks. Dillon flew to Sydney and went to his address, and met his sister-in-law. Williams came back from Afghanistan with a severe head wound and psychological trauma. He suffered mental issues and personality disorders along with severe temper outbursts following his recovery. His wife left him, and she came back to Perth apparently to clear out their possessions at the Barracks. Dillon says she is a dead ringer for the first ten victims. She and her sister are almost twins in looks, apparently, and she has given Dillon the full background. According to Inspector Bradley, it is an incredible story, right down to the childhood abuse the profilers told us our guy would have. Williams discharged himself from the hospital to find his wife before he was well enough to be released and hasn't been heard from since. Being SAS he would have access to the nine-millimeter hollow points and weapons. Dillon has no doubt at all he is our man, everything fits."

Blunt still had his fingers bridged and stayed silent a long time before saying, "I asked what *evidence* he has. Sounds like he has none at all. But you want to besmirch the name and reputation of a wounded returned soldier who had a bad childhood all because his wife, who ran away from him, is blonde. And you want to go to the press and plaster his name and picture all over the place. Are you fucking mad?"

"Yes, I do want to, and no, I'm not mad. You stopped this department finding out all this ourselves and getting the evidence you want. We can find the evidence if you let us look." He was shouting, giving full vent to his anger. "If you refuse to go public, I will go over your head. This investigation has been a complete fucking shemozzle since you took over. The maniac is still out there and is hunting his ex-wife. The profilers said it would be something like this. Clearly, Suzanne Delvechio knew her and how to find her, and now so does Williams. We have to go public and save her from the same fate as the others."

"And you know this to be a fact because?" Unlike Mike's raised voice, Blunt's was quiet and cold.

"Because this guy is ex-SAS. I was in the army, and I knew some of these guys. They are the most highly trained troops we have, like British Commandos or American Seals, and they do not fuck around. They don't stop, even when wounded—they are trained to ignore pain. They will keep going, no matter who is in their way or no matter what hurdles are thrown up. That is what they are trained for. Paul Williams, because of the head injury, physical and emotional trauma, and his wife leaving him, sees himself as being on a mission. Remember the note he sent Dillon? He said his mission was just, and to SAS a mission is like it's from God himself. Williams is a mentally unbalanced, highly trained, cold-blooded killer who thinks his ex-wife has wronged him for leaving him when he was wounded. For fuck's sake, what will it take to convince you? It's not like you have had a single better idea since you took over. You've had the whole team chasing their tails since you arrived."

Blunt nodded, stood to his entire diminutive height, and hitched up his pants by his stressed belt. Face red, voice now equally trembling with rage, he said, "You listen to me, you little pipsqueak. I've had enough of your insubordination and your demoralizing attitude. No one likes you in this squad, and I bet you didn't know that, did you? You can consider yourself relieved of duty pending an inquiry into your and Inspector Bradley's behavior. You've both ignored direct orders, supplied sensitive information, and carried out an illegal, unauthorized investigation. You will pass over all information you have of this Williams character, and he will be investigated along with every other suspect we discover. That's called *police work*, you fucking moron. We will not slag off, in public, a wounded national hero until we have some *evidence* and not just the opinion of an overzealous detective trying to gain promotion and a grief-stricken inspector. He at least has an excuse. He cannot possibly be thinking straight after his adulterous wife was murdered by the very suspect we are trying to catch. You may think you've been doing good work, but you haven't. Now clear out your desk and go home. You are suspended." He sat down and went back to his paperwork while Mike Knowles stared at the top of his head, trying hard, *very hard*, not to punch the arrogant stupid fuckwit.

He walked out of the office, slamming the door as he left. He didn't clear out his desk, did not stop to pass on any information to the team, but went out to his car. He sat inside and punched the steering wheel to relieve his frustration. Suddenly his knuckle doubled in size, and the pain hit him. *Fuck!* Now he had broken his hand, could today get any worse?

He dialed Dillon's mobile number, hoping to catch him before he boarded his plane to come back to WA, and listened to the prerecorded message telling him he had missed him and switched to his message bank. "It's me, boss. Blunt has suspended me and will look into Williams *in due course* because we have no fucking evidence. I've found his address. He rents an apartment in Scarborough. It's 4B 222 Seaview Parade. I'm going there to see if I can find him and tail him. Like you, I'm very worried he is on the track of this Amanda woman. Ring me when you get in."

He hung up, started the engine, and headed off to Scarborough. It was just after three p.m., and he hoped he wasn't too late.

****

When Jayne recovered, Dillon helped her to her feet and to the couch. She was so small and light he could have carried her but thought it best not to, for fear of her feeling he had taken advantage. She was as white as a sheet.

"It doesn't make sense. It just doesn't make sense," she said over and over again. "He wouldn't do that. He just isn't like that at all." She shook her head and turned-on Dillon, her eyes blazing with suppressed rage. "You lied to me. You said you were on his side and wanted to exclude him from the investigation. Tank loved her; he would have died for her, and he would never hurt her. And he certainly wouldn't kill someone who looks like her. You're wrong. I'm sorry, but you just have to be wrong."

He gently replied, "Jayne, I didn't lie to you. I never would do that. Firstly, I don't tell lies to anyone, and secondly, I like you and especially wouldn't lie to *you*." He smiled as warmly as he could and tried to show his sincerity.

"I had hoped it wasn't him and that I could exclude him; that's the truth. But the more you told me, the more I realized he fits the psychological profile we have of the killer." He raised his hands and counted on his fingers. "One, we are looking for someone with a very disturbed childhood. Two, someone who isn't deterred by violence, and three, he was murdering women who resembled someone who hurt him emotionally. Our killer has now killed twenty-two people that we know of, including my wife and her lover. Plus, he shot dead a doctor who treated him for an infected dog bite. He has no remorse, no guilt whatsoever. He seems to be a killing machine. Four, someone who was killing with a purpose. Now, we didn't know what that purpose was, but with the first ten victims, each one looked very similar to your sister. You can't ignore that, Jayne. Lastly, we suspected a person who was psychotic, and you've told me he had severe mental and personality issues after the head injury, before Amanda abandoned him, which may well have made him worse.

"You've told me he was badly wounded and was prone to fits of rage and jealousy. You've told me he fell in love with Amanda and she was his first and only love. Don't you agree it's more than possible that when he took off to Perth to find her, he was angry with her, thinking she had dumped him for someone else and had run away with this mystery man? Then when he thought he found her, in a psychotic rage, he killed her. But, later, when he found out it wasn't her, but someone who looked like her, he looked for her all over again and again. Each time in his mind, he is killing your sister for leaving him when he needed her the most." He was pleading with her now, needing to convince her that everything clicked into place and made sense.

"Jayne, he also mutilated the female victims in a horrible way. I won't describe to you what he did because it was so gruesome. But we suspect in his warped mind he believes all women are adulterous sluts, and he thinks he is on a mission to rid us of them. Unfortunately, in the case of my wife, she *was* being adulterous, not that I knew, of course." Dillon gave a crooked grin. "He told me by email he had done me a favor by killing her, but he set out to punish me because in a TV interview, I upset him by insulting him. But, the thing is, in his warped mind, he ended up helping me and expected me to be grateful." He stopped, momentarily choked up as he recalled the sight of his murdered wife and her lover.

She reached for him and hugged him, wrapping both arms around him and whispered in his ear, "I'm so sorry for your loss, Dillon, and I can understand why you want it to be true. The way you say it, I can see why you would think it was him. But you don't *know* him like I do. He is gentle. Yes, he is a big tough man and trained to kill, but is it possible your judgment is clouded by your loss? I just can't compare the man I know to the one you describe."

Dillon nodded in the crook of her shoulder, enjoying the fact that she was still hugging him, unwilling, it seemed, to let go, as they sat next to each other on the couch. Her left breast pressed against his chest, and again he was aware of his attraction for her.

He understood her dilemma. She liked her memory of Paul Williams, and Dillon could understand why. He seemed like every woman's dream of a knight on a white charger. True, he didn't have any evidence that proved he was the mass murderer; everything was theory and circumstantial. But, he hoped that the police could find him and ask some questions, maybe even search his home and find the evidence they needed. Perhaps they could locate the trophy underwear he always took as a souvenir, for example. Dillon thought they would soon find the proof once they located him. Most importantly, he hoped they got to him before he found this beautiful woman's sister. He pushed her gently away from him but held her by her upper arms, both thumbs imperceptibly touching the sides of her breasts, and looked into her eyes.

"Jayne, can I be honest with you? I should not be saying this, but I'm going to anyway. I think you are a wonderful woman, and I wish I was twenty years younger and you weren't a potential witness in an ongoing murder investigation. I wish my wife hadn't recently been taken from me, but she has, and I'm single again after nearly thirty years. I'm only human, and I would love to know you better. But I completely understand that even if we didn't have all this hanging over us, there isn't the faintest possibility you would be interested in me, and that's fine."

He smiled at her and noted the change of look she gave him. Initially, she looked a little confused, but then as if he was wrong, that she would be interested in him. He pressed on. "Maybe you're right, and I'm wrong. I hope I am. With the information you've given me, we can at least try to track him down now, and if it's not him, I promise I will let you know. No one would be happier than me if I could give you good news. I think you deserve that. Tell you what, I will come back to Sydney and take you out to dinner at the best restaurant you name as my way of saying sorry if I am wrong. In the interim, while we check him out, could you please do me one really big favor?"

She stared at him with wide-open eyes and nodded. "Jayne, I'm serious about this. Please, until I get back to you in a day or two, would you please go and stay with a friend? Someone Paul doesn't know, just to be safe. If I *am* right, and he is our serial murderer, and he thinks you have betrayed him..." He let the pause hang in the air. "Perth is only a four-hour flight away, you know."

Eventually, she nodded, though she looked deep in thought. "Dillon, I am not used to men caring for me. Mostly when they say they do, they're lying to me to get me into bed, so I will do as you've asked. I don't have a good track record with men and relationships. You are talking as if you think you are not good enough for me or too old and decrepit, but you are so wrong. I can see the depth of feeling you have for your late wife, and you are obviously a good man. Forgive me because I haven't known too many of them, other than Tank."

He stood, embarrassed and feeling flustered. "I really should be going. I want to thank you so much for talking to me, Jayne. I will be in touch with you soon, okay?"

She stood too and looked down at her feet. Holding her hands together in front of her, she appeared angelic, if not a little schoolgirlish. "When are you flying back?" she asked.

"I fly out at eleven tomorrow. I wasn't sure when I could catch up with you, so I booked a later flight." He started to gather up the pictures and stopped in his tracks when she softly spoke.

"I said I would do you a favor, so you have to do me one in return. That's only fair, isn't it?"

He had to agree it was. He turned to her and waited. "I don't want to be alone tonight. I'm very sad and worried now. I don't think you want to be alone either. Please stay with me, and I will take you to the airport tomorrow morning. Then I will go to a friend's place for a few days as you've asked."

The invitation was there. Her eyes were clouded with emotion, and he was torn. Yes, he wanted her. Who wouldn't? It wasn't just her looks. There was something so gentle, so lost about her that made him want to protect her. There was no doubt in his mind he should leave that minute and run away from her as fast as he could, if only because his wife had been killed the week prior. Jayne was way too young for him, and she was the sister-in-law of his prime suspect. There were at least a hundred reasons to go and only two or three to stay, yet he wavered. He was about to tell her that would not be a good idea when, sensing he was about to refuse, she crossed to him and threw her arms around him.

"Please stay with me. I know you want me, and I know you think you shouldn't, and I like that about you. I think you are one of the nicest men I've ever met who is doing a really tough job. Tonight, just for tonight, I think we need each other, especially if you are right about Tank."

He dropped the photos on the floor as his hands came up to hold her. She fitted so well against his body, like two spoons in a drawer. In a flash, they were kissing as she stretched up to reach him, one leg cocked in the air behind her. He enveloped her in his arms, and all thoughts of leaving disappeared. Both of them were wounded souls, and both deserved one night away from the madness.

Chapter Twenty-Seven

I felt more alive than I had in weeks, knowing I was close to the completion of my mission. The headache was a bearable throbbing over my temples, and my eyesight was reasonably normal. I had woken up early, driven across town to Belmont Forum Shopping Center and sat in the car park, and eaten a breakfast burger. I watched an entry door from a distance. I had hoped to see her arrive but if that didn't happen I would wait for the customers so that I could enter and mingle with them. Then I could find the exact travel agency where Amanda worked.

I wore my blond hipster-style shaggy wig, circular glasses, faded jeans and a plain white polo shirt and trainers. I had to be careful not to get too close to her in case she recognized me through the disguise, but I hoped she wouldn't. After all this time and her leading her *new life* without me, I thought I could escape her detection so well disguised. I hoped I was the farthest thing from her mind while she was always the nearest to mine.

Balanced against my hatred of her and what she had done were always the nice memories of when things had been great, like on Hamilton Island. That was a favorite for me. I relived the perfect life we'd enjoyed there time and time again in my mind.

I needed to locate the travel shop where she worked and discover what exit door she would use to leave at the end of the day. My plan was to go back at closing time and follow her to her home. Suzi had told me she lived only walking distance away, so it was important to know which door she would take because it was a big mall.

I knew she had only housemates, and she wasn't dating any men at this time, so there was no real threat there. Once I knew where she lived, I would go there that night and look into her eyes as I killed her. I would also kill her housemates, one last final statement about how unfaithful sluts should beware. Then, I would be free, at last. I shivered at the expectation and knowledge my mission would be ending soon.

I looked at my watch. It was nine-thirty-seven and time to go for a walk as she had not arrived at work through the door I was staking out. I grabbed the backpack with the pistol inside, took the gun out, and tucked it under my shirt in the small of my back, where I would be able to grab it if needed. There, the backpack should hide the bulge once I put that back on. I didn't think I would need the gun, but in shopping centers these days, there were always security guards. As this was about to be the end of my mission, nothing was going to stop me, and I would kill anyone who got in my way. If Amanda confronted me, I would shoot her dead inside her place of work and anyone else who was there who tried to stop my retreat.

I had no idea how much longer I had to live. The headaches didn't seem to be a guide by themselves. They came and went. The intensity and frequency varied, and that said, recently, I had noticed that when they were bad, they were *really* bad. Worse than I could ever remember them being before. Sometimes I had to close the blinds and stay in bed in the dark until they passed, and that often took many hours. I hoped to have some time to travel and see some of the world before they got much worse, or things ended suddenly. I thought I deserved at least that once my mission was concluded. I felt like going to America. Now there was a country that liked their armed forces and the public bearing arms. I would fit right in there.

I sat in the car for just a few minutes longer and thought about all I had done since I'd come back west in search of Amanda barely ten months before. I relived the steps that had brought me here.

I tried to catch her at the barracks, but I missed her. She had been and gone, and the guys had no idea where she was staying. I found the Scarborough apartment and rented it, paying cash, to use as my base of operations. I then sat around for days on end, wondering how I could catch up with her. I tried her mobile phone time and time again. I vaguely remember speaking to her once, but that memory is clouded in fog. After a few days, her mobile just gave a disconnected tone.

I shunned the guys at the barracks who wanted to socialize with me and told them all I had to go back to Sydney. I didn't want contact with anyone from my past and, in particular, the army. I started working on disguises, realizing I might have to kill others to get to Amanda. I was also determined to make things as difficult as possible for the police because I knew I may need time to find her. Also, I did not want to spend whatever time I had left in jail.

The final reason for changing my appearance was that knowing once I did catch up with her, and I was in no doubt that I would—the ex-husband would be the first person suspected. To that end, I began building an escape plan because a good soldier always has an escape plan. This included pulling a lot of money in cash from the joint account and stashing it with my weapons cache at the storage locker. I hid spare clothes, my passport, and other things I might need for a hasty getaway. I purchased a second car for cash but didn't register it in my name. I also had a good stock of canned food and bottled water as I was not averse to going into the bush to escape capture. I could live there very well if need be—I had been well trained in survival and living from the land. In some respects, I hoped that happened because I could give any pursuing police a battle they would long remember.

I had found an old but low-kilometer nondescript diesel 4x4 wagon. It was for private sale at a cheap enough price, and I negotiated with the owner to include renewing the registration, which was close to expiry, for a further twelve months. I gave him a fake name and address, then got it serviced and checked over and put in a new battery, and treated it to a full tank of fuel. I parked it in the lock-up storage facility in Redcliffe.

Then I was set. If I needed to get away in a hurry, I could escape Perth by killing anyone who tried to stop me. I thought I could drive either north to Darwin or east across to Melbourne through the bush or outback roads, then lose myself in another state and begin my new life. Planning was everything, as was adapting if the plan went wrong.

One day, I noticed Amanda had withdrawn money from our joint bank account at a branch in Fremantle. I staked out the bank day after day, waiting for her to go back there for more cash. When she did four days later, I followed her to her home and murdered her.

I returned home and waited for the headache to subside, which took a day and a half. When I emerged from my darkened bedroom, I saw the news that identified her not as my wife but another woman! In my haste, I had made a mistake and somehow—and to this day, I don't know how—mistook the woman for Amanda. Her name was Melanie Trotter! But when I was stabbing her, I was positive it was her, even though she denied it. I just figured she was lying, as I would have expected her to do.

I panicked a bit but soon recovered, thought long and hard, and realized that maybe my perception was off, and I saw Amanda in this other woman because I wanted to see her. My head injury perhaps had caused some sort of breakdown, and in my desire for revenge, I had mistaken Melanie Trotter for her. I would need to be more careful, I thought, but then again, I had come to the conclusion that all women were not to be trusted, and so what if I killed a few more on the way to my real target?

I visited the Jewish jeweler she had worked for. He told me she had visited him to say goodbye and had mentioned she was staying at a holiday rental resort called the Breakwater on the River at South Perth. I felt no remorse killing him and making it look like a robbery. I had visited at closing time, so when I vacated the shop, I latched the door on my way out and left him in a puddle of his own blood and piss. I went straight to South Perth, where I threw away the jewelry I had taken to make it look like a robbery.

I found Amanda the following day and stabbed her in her apartment. I just forced my way in, but she denied she was Amanda too. Once again, I thought she was lying. Don't all women lie to save themselves? But, she hadn't been lying, which I discovered when I read her name in the papers the next day. Julianne Reynolds was vacationing at the resort for a wedding she had come down for from Geraldton. That was about four hundred kilometers north of Perth. She was to have been in the bridal party, and just for a moment or two, I felt a little sad remembering my own wedding.

That was when things just went a little crazy for me, and it's true to say I saw her everywhere I went. I realized I couldn't trust my judgment anymore, but I had to keep killing her until I got the right one, didn't I? Anyone could understand what I had been through, surely?

Once or twice, I arranged a date with them, wearing a disguise which I had become very adept at, and engineered a chance meeting somewhere, which was a bit of fun, before killing them. I was very careful to study their movements for a while so I could plan their execution. By then, the papers were full of stories about a killer walking the streets murdering blondes. They even called me the Perth Ripper because I took to cutting them up a bit after I'd killed them so that the world would realize they were sluts who only used their feminine charms to trap and then cheat on their men.

It was a journalist for the local newspaper who coined the Ripper name when he likened me to the famous Jack the Ripper of olden days. That was a bit spooky, as my father's name was Jack! Within a day or two, I found it all so funny, and I enjoyed reading all the wrong things they printed about me.

I took my time from then on. Still, more than anything, I wanted to find Amanda but didn't lose any sleep those times when I killed a facsimile. It didn't matter; to me, each was a good substitute. I knew in my heart sooner or later I would get her. There was no more rushing for me. I took time for more strategic planning and adapting more disguises. Even though there were some times when I realized an intended victim wasn't Amanda, I killed them anyway. After all, they looked like her and probably acted like her.

****

I came back to reality, sitting in the car, a sweat forming on my forehead as it was a warm day.

I now believed all women were sluts, just like my mother had been with me when my father had been away. No wonder he used to whip me. Knowing what I did now, I forgave him. He must have realized his wife was fucking their son every time she got drunk when he went away. I shuddered at the horrible memories of my mother's naked body and what she had made me do to it. It still made me want to vomit every time the images came to me. But with what I knew about Amanda, those memories did put my father in a different light. *Like father like son,* they say.

Then there was that cop's wife. What started out as a means to gain more time turned out to be a revelation; wasn't she just a typical whore like all the others? There was no doubt in my mind that while my mission in life was to kill Amanda, any women I got along the way were just collateral damage.

An idea came to me out of the blue, which made me feel so much better. Once I had dealt with Amanda, I would go back to Sydney one last time and kill my mother. I smiled broadly at that plan and wondered why I had never thought to do it before. What better way to exorcise my demons than killing the woman who had started it all?

Then, while in Sydney, there was one other person I should go and see, the fucking sister Jayne! Really, she was no better than Amanda and probably worse. She got into all that trouble that I helped her out of because she had been fucking a married man! How much more proof did I need? Every single woman I had ever come across in my life was nothing but a filthy slutty whore who deserved to die.

When I pondered deeply, I realized the only exception to that rule, I had to admit to myself, was both the girls' mother. She was a sweetheart, loyal to her husband even after he'd died. She had never dated another man that I knew of. I wouldn't kill her. I always wished she had been my mother and not theirs.

I looked at my watch when I noticed how the gun was digging into my back. I was shocked to see it was now ten-seventeen. *Where did that forty minutes go?* I had been so deep and lost in my memories I'd lost track of time. Maybe I was getting worse after all! *Time to get back to work,* and I got out of the car, locked it, and slipped on the backpack. I made sure the gun was hidden and headed off across the car park into the center, trying to look like every other *normal* customer.

A ten-minute circuit later, I was fuming and very angry at myself and realized my own problems may well be worsening. I had been stupid. Belmont Forum was a big sprawling shopping center over a huge area in three different blocks with walkways joining them together. It had seven entry-exit doors with three fucking travel agencies in three entirely different locations! *Why, oh, why did I not question little Suzi more closely?*

How many people in this area went on holiday, for

God's sake? The worst thing was that try as hard as I might, I could not remember the name of the agency Suzi had told me Amanda worked at. If, in fact, she had told me the name at all before I lost my temper. I couldn't remember clearly, but I seemed to recall she'd just said '*the travel agency.*' Didn't that imply there was only one?

The three of them were Holiday Universe, Holidays R Us, and Blythe Spirit Travel. How could it possibly be that I had forgotten such a key thing as which one she worked at? All I could remember was her referring to the travel shop in Belmont Forum. I was sure that was correct. Was I making other errors and not remembering? I was furious with myself and the head injury which was causing my lapses in memory. I went back to my car and considered slowly and carefully what options I had.

I could have peered into every shop through the window to see if I could spot her, but that was dangerous as she could have seen me looking in. Plus, they had security guards wandering around; I'd noticed one snooping around, acting like he owned the place. True, he was pretty elderly, but maybe they had more. He'd had a radio clipped to his belt with an earpiece and microphone attached. So, I didn't want to be thought of as a loiterer or stalker and cause a scene.

The only other alternative I could think of—and granted, at that time, I wasn't thinking clearly about anything as I was far too angry—was to come back at closing time. I could pick an exit and watch it and hope she left through it. If I was wrong and she didn't appear through that one, there was always the next morning when I would watch another door. Then that night, a different one again and so on until I found her. Granted, that could take a day or two, but I thought I had plenty of time, and rushing might mean I spooked her if she saw me. If she ran, it would all start over again, so I had to calm myself. She would have no idea I was this close, and I could take her by surprise so long as I took my time.

I discounted another plan, which was to phone each shop in turn and ask for her, then hang up. But what if she answered the phone and recognized my voice?

This close to my prize, and I had no doubt in my mind that finally I had found the real Amanda, and I was not going to risk everything by rushing and making a mistake which would stop me exacting my long-overdue revenge; she deserved everything she had coming. The decision made, I left the center and returned home. It was a lovely day. *Maybe a swim, lunch, and long walk on the beach before heading back to Belmont later on,* I thought. After all, I had all the time in the world as the reports on TV and in the papers showed the police were no nearer to catching me.

****

Mike Knowles sat in one of the visitors' parking spots, looking up at number 4B, waiting. There was no sign of life. The curtains were open, but from this angle, he couldn't see inside properly, so he didn't know if Williams was there or not. He decided to go up and knock on the door. If Williams answered, he would pretend to be looking for the caretaker and a place to rent. If not, he would look in through the window to see what he could see. Waiting had never been his strong suit, and he was worried that as he sat watching the apartment, Amanda Williams could be being murdered elsewhere.

He was still raging inside with anger at Blunt. He

wanted nothing more than to arrest Williams and take him in single-handedly and prove what a dickhead his boss was and what a good cop Mike was.

****

I had just returned from my beach walk and, always vigilant, noticed a man who had cop written all over him sitting in a car on a hot day, looking at my place. There could be little doubt he was obviously there for me, and I wondered what I should do about it.

The guy was by himself, and I recognized him from the many TV reports I had watched as being part of the task force to catch me. But as he was alone, clearly he wasn't here to arrest me. They would have had a lot more than one cop sitting in a car if that was the case. What to do about him was the question, and I backed into the shadow of the corridor between the beach and the car park and thought about it.

Obviously, they were closer than I thought. Perhaps I was a suspect, but not a very strong one. Otherwise, they would be here in force. But one thing was for sure—my time left was limited, and Amanda had to be my number one priority; the mission had to be completed.

All I was wearing were bathers, T-shirt, cap and sunglasses. Everything else I had was in the apartment. My first job, I determined, was to get inside and grab whatever I could. I backed down the passageway to the rear of the block, which was facing the ocean, and climbed onto my balcony quite easily. I had done that once before after I had lost my keys in the sand when I had gone for a swim. I entered through the sliding door I had left partly open to let some breeze through. I didn't like air conditioning; I preferred the sea breeze to cool the place down.

Once inside, I went into the bedroom, quickly dressed, and crammed things I thought I would need into the backpack, intending to get back out the way I had come in. Suddenly there came the sound of the doorbell. Too late, I realized I had left the bedroom door open, so if whoever was there peered through the window, they would see me as I packed. I turned and saw it was the cop. But luckily, for the moment, he wasn't looking at me. I slipped the gun out of the pack and, keeping it from sight, quickly screwed the silencer to the barrel and slipped it down the arm of the recliner rocker facing the couch. I walked past on my way to the front door to face my fate; I was quite looking forward to it.

****

Mike peered in through the window and spotted a man inside looking as if he was packing a bag in a room across from the living area. Without further thought, he backed away and knocked on the door. After two minutes, it opened, and he came face to face with the man he knew, without a shred of doubt, to be the serial killer. His gray eyes were dead and soulless. He showed no emotion whatsoever, and there was horrific scarring on the side of his head through his short spiky hair. Mike realized why every account they had of him stated that he had been wearing a cap or wig. That, plus his overall size and fitness made him look like one scary fucker.

Mike's insides turned to water, and fear, the likes of which he had never known before, hit him. He cursed himself for coming alone. What had he been thinking? He made a decision to forget the caretaker bluff he was going to use as he realized it wasn't going to work. This guy was far too smart for that.

"Paul Williams? I'm Detective Sergeant Mike

Knowles. Would you mind if I came in and asked you some questions?"

****

Dillon turned his phone on after landing at the airport and read the voice-to-text message from Mike. He cursed out loud, *"Fuck!"* That caused nearby passengers, who were turning their phones on around him, to look up. He hastily dialed Mike's number.

It rang, and he silently urged him to answer, but after five rings, it went to the message bank.

"Mike, I've landed. Ring me urgently. Do not—I repeat *not*—approach this guy alone."

He hung up and stood. He took out his ID card as he excused himself and pushed through the people queuing in the aisles. He clutched his overnight bag, thinking over and over to himself, *Come on, Mike, ring me back, fuck you.*

****

I was totally calm, but I could tell in an instant he was frightened, which meant he realized who I was, *and he knows my name.* The cop's voice was quavering; his body language reeked of fear, and his eyes were darting all over the place. All of these things showed me that he knew I was the one he was looking for. Perhaps before he saw me, he only suspected; *now he knew.* In that moment, I knew he had to die.

"Sure you can. Can I see some ID first, though?" I said nonchalantly.

He pulled a wallet out of his left-hand jacket pocket just as his phone rang in the other. In the time it took for him to open it up and show me his ID, which I then took my time in reading, his mobile stopped ringing.

I stepped back from the door and pointed to the

couch. "Come in, grab a seat and tell me how I can help you."

He sat down as a message tone sounded from his phone. I knew he wanted to take it out and answer. Probably he would scream for help if he did, I could tell, but he didn't. He looked at me as I stared into his eyes. This was going to be fun.

Chapter Twenty-Eight

Dillon knew he had no official standing in the investigation and was smart enough to know that the last thing he should do would be to race around to the suspect's house and confront him. If he did that, it could cause all sorts of legal problems down the track in court if Williams had a smart lawyer. After trying Mike's phone several times, he knew something was wrong, and he was very afraid of what that would turn out to be. There really was only one thing he could do, and he called Assistant Commissioner Blunt, who answered on the fifth ring.

"Sir, it's Dillon Bradley calling. I believe there is an urgent situation I think you need to be aware of regarding Mike Knowles," he began.

"Ah, if it's not *Super Cop* himself. Thanks for phoning in. You've saved me calling you. I trust you are well after your recent bereavement? It seems you've kept yourself busy, and yes, I know all about Senior Detective Knowles. He has been suspended, *as are you,* in case you'd forgotten."

Dillon took a long, slow deep breath and thought quickly how best to get this idiot off his back enough to listen to reason. Sadly, he realized there was probably only one way, and that would be to agree with him and grovel.

"Sir, I know what you are about to say. I've just now

only flown back in from Sydney, and I wanted to come and see you immediately to personally apologize to you and explain what had gone on and why. I realize I've perhaps not done the right thing, but all I can do is ask you to please consider what you would have done if it had been your wife murdered. Please accept my sincere apologies. I assure you I did what I did with no intention to undermine your operation but to complement it. The truth is, sir, I did it as a kind of therapy. It stopped me from going mad or even worse." He let that hang in the air. All police knew the suicide rate among detectives was particularly high.

"Well, I must say your attitude is a lot healthier than your underling. He has been impossible to work with, disloyal, arrogant, and rude."

My God, the egotistical son of a bitch, Dillon thought, but still, he had to work with this prick and not against him. "I know, sir, he is a hothead, but remember back when we were that rank? I'm sure you made errors of judgment too. A good cop like yourself always does on his way up the ladder." He had to choke back the bile that rose because of what he was saying. Fawning to someone with less than half the brain and dedication of Mike Knowles was tough, but it had to be done.

"Hmmm, yes, well, you may or may not be right there, Inspector. All right, well, we need to get together so you can bring me up to speed with your somewhat unorthodox investigation. Let's see, it's getting late in the day now. How about ten a.m. tomorrow, my office?"

Dillon thought that if he was right about Mike, they would be seeing each other much sooner than that. "Absolutely, sir. I would be happy to do that and help out in any way I can. I will be there in the morning. That aside, there is a problem with Knowles, sir, and *it is* urgent. I could be wrong, but I think he has gone off to confront the prime suspect I came up with after you sent him home. I fear he may be in trouble, if not dead, sir."

Mike accepted that while Blunt may be an idiot, he did care about his officers and fully realized the danger they placed themselves in every single day.

"Talk to me, Inspector, what has he done?"

"He left a voicemail message for me after I had boarded the flight to come back to see you. The message says you had dismissed him and our conclusions about the killer, and he sounded very angry. When he couldn't get a hold of me, he said he was going off to this guy's apartment in Scarborough. His intention, he said, was to follow him as he is very concerned, as I am, for the safety of his next and original intended victim. His ex-wife, whose name is Amanda Williams, née McMahon, appears to have been his target all along. I've tried to contact Knowles several times since I landed, and he isn't picking up. I've called his wife, and she hasn't seen or heard from him. I have a very bad feeling. If he has come up against our man, who is a highly trained and decorated SAS soldier, I fear for his safety. Williams was discharged for, among other serious injuries, mental and personality disorders after recovering from severe trauma. I strongly believe this man is our serial killer, and if I am right, by now, Mike could well have been murdered by him too."

"Give me the address. I will get a car round there right now. But for your information, Inspector, I didn't dismiss your theory. I said we would investigate it. What he wanted me to do was go public and possibly ruin the name and reputation of a wounded returned soldier. That

I would not do without evidence. Give me that address now, Inspector."

****

Dillon was told to stand by his phone, and it was some forty-five minutes later he got the call from Blunt. As usual, he did not beat around the bush.

"I don't know if this is a wild goose chase or not, Inspector. There is no one home at that address, the unit next door seems empty, and, in fact, the whole place looks like holiday residential apartments. It's out of season, so it looks pretty quiet. Without a warrant, we can't enter, but we did find Detective Knowles' car in the car park. You said you thought his intention was to follow the suspect. We can only conclude he is doing that. Possibly his mobile phone is off, or the battery is dead, making him uncontactable. There is nothing to do but wait. I've posted an officer in the car park to wait and report back if either return."

Dillon's thoughts raced ahead. He knew how hard it would be to get a search warrant after hours without strong evidence. What Blunt said, he reluctantly had to agree with. He promised Blunt he would call back if Mike did make contact and was given his private mobile phone number to use should that happen. They agreed that if Knowles hadn't made contact by nine a.m., they would apply for a warrant and break the door down to effect a search. Beyond that, Dillon agreed to come into headquarters in the morning to go through all the information he had from his trip to Sydney. Before Dillon could respond, Blunt had hung up.

****

I closed the door quietly behind him and went to sit on the recliner armchair opposite him. Like a lamb to the slaughter, he sat where I had pointed, and I waited patiently for him to begin.

"Mr. Williams, I am part of a task force that is investigating the serial murderer who the press has labeled *the Ripper*. I'm sure you've read about it?"

He smiled at me, but I could see right through that. "I've heard of him. Who hasn't? But that doesn't explain what that has to do with me?" I asked innocently. Yep, butter wouldn't melt in my mouth.

"Well, this is somewhat embarrassing, but we have been displaying composite pictures of the man we would like to talk to. You wouldn't believe how many people call in saying they know him, and of course, they all have to be checked out. We have had a call by someone, it seems, who thinks you resemble our suspect."

He smiled again, and I knew he was lying. But still, maybe he wasn't. That would explain why he was here alone. "Really? Was it a neighbor? I bet it's Mrs. Campezie from number six, isn't it?" I said, showing a bit of disbelief in my voice. There was no Mrs. Campezie or a number six. I had made that up. I was having fun. I slipped my hand down the side of the chair and gripped the gun. My thumb automatically found the safety and clicked it off. I moved my hips and settled in the seat further at the same time to hide the light clicking noise.

"I'm sorry, Mr. Williams, I'm not at liberty to say. I'm sure this is a waste of both our time, but as you can appreciate it's such a serious matter, we have to follow up every lead. I have a list of dates and times. Can I ask you please to cast your mind back and tell me where you were and what you were doing for the ones that you can remember?"

I glanced at my watch and realized with utter dismay

I was never going to make it back to Belmont in time. This prick was going to make me late. "What makes you think that?" I asked. He looked confused, the poor lad.

"What?"

"That it's a waste of your time?" I pulled the gun out and calmly aimed it at his chest. "How did you find me?"

He visibly slumped in the chair. I could see the cogs turning as he fought to think of a way out.

"I'm ex-army too, though unlike you, I never saw service."

What a dope, I thought, *as if that would appeal to me*, but I still couldn't resist joke. "Oh really, is that so, what area?"

"I started in infantry, then finished in artillery," he said with more than a little pride.

"I hate artillery. You bastards stay out of harm's way while the rest of us plods get hit by your friendly fire." I shot him three times with perfect grouping, dead center of his chest. The silencer reduced the sound to a coughing noise. He slowly slipped to the left and ended up lying on his side, dead, on my couch.

I didn't bother picking up the casings. I had most of my stuff pre-packed, allowing for just this type of situation, but I did take his wallet, and his driver's license would help me book a cheap motel for the night. There were masses of them along the highway near the airport, which was also close to Belmont and Redcliffe. There was one I knew of which catered for short-term stays, and if they had a vacancy, they wouldn't even ask for ID. They catered to prostitutes. Some of the guys at Swanbourne used them, but I, of course, never had.

I also grabbed his police ID card, which could come in handy in the morning at Belmont Forum. Clearly, I was now out of time, and things had to happen quickly.

I looked down at him and realized I had to get him out of sight, and he was a pretty big guy. Damn, I should have taken him to another room before shooting him—dope! I manhandled his body, and half dragged, half carried him into the bedroom and got him onto the bed. That left me dizzy and my headache roaring like a waterfall. I sat alongside him and waited till the pounding in my head and vision cleared.

I had to change my shirt as it had blood on it. Once done, I grabbed my backpack and other bits and pieces and left my apartment for the last time. I had enjoyed my time being right on the beach. It always reminded me of Hamilton Island. Tomorrow would be my last day in Perth. I had to finish things with Amanda and get out.

Chapter Twenty-Nine

"Hi, Jayne, it's Dillon. How are you doing?" he said as she answered her mobile phone. Despite his concern for Mike's safety, he couldn't help but smile as he remembered what a wonderful night they had shared, though he still felt terribly guilty at times, being so soon after the murder of his wife. Dillon was amazed that he could find some happiness and even more surprised that he had been up to the challenge of making love to Jayne as he had. On the flight back, he had come up with an adage he liked that summed it up, 'the better the canvas, the better the art.' Jayne being the canvas.

Life goes on, he thought to himself, and the opportunities for him, at his age, to meet someone as lovely as she was were going to become less and less likely into his future. Of course, no amount of rationalization could stop the guilt and sadness that plagued him at odd times when he least expected it. Again, Jayne was incredibly understanding of his fragile emotional state.

"Hello, Inspector," she said huskily.

He could tell by her voice that she, too, was smiling at the memory of the night before. "Are you calling to take me back to Perth in handcuffs and put me under house arrest in your bedroom?" She giggled, and he loved the sound of that.

"Oh, I'm going to sell the house, then find another

before I take you to my bedroom, Jayne. You wouldn't want to spend time in there at the moment. In fact, I don't go in there myself unless I have to, but the thought of having you in handcuffs is appealing."

"Oh, Dillon, I'm so sorry. I was just kidding. I didn't mean to upset you. God, I can be so stupid and insensitive sometimes. Please forgive my thoughtlessness," she pleaded.

"It's fine, don't worry. I'm sorry for being moody; I'm a bit distracted at the moment. What you said wasn't a problem, and you handcuffed to a bed is interesting. Don't worry about that," he said, regretting putting a dampener on her mood. "I want to see you again—if you want to see me, that is—and if we do, I don't want this to be a no-go zone between us. It happened, my wife was unfaithful to me, and she was murdered with her lover in our bed. We can't skirt around something like that. That just wouldn't be right. So please, don't worry, you keep joking with me; I need that, and I wouldn't want it any other way. Now on to more serious matters. Did you do as I asked and find a friend to stay with?"

"Yes, I did. I told you I would, and I kept my word. I'm staying with one of the girls I work with—Laura. Tank doesn't know her, and she thinks it's all rather exciting. It's nice sharing with her and talking girlie things about you."

She is giggling again, and that's good, Dillon thought.

"I still don't think it's Tank anyway, but I like having you worry about me. It makes me feel wanted and cared for. That's, umm, not something I'm used to. Have I told you how much I enjoyed last night?"

"I think you did mention it once or twice, and you

know I did too, right?"

"Mmmm, yes, I gathered that when you wouldn't let me get any sleep. So, Inspector, please, don't stop worrying."

He smiled even though every professional bone in his body told him he should not be flirting—correction, sleeping—with a witness. *I may not have a job soon anyway, the way things are going, so fuck it,* he decided. Life was too short, and he should roll the dice and see how they landed.

"Honey, I like worrying about you, and I won't stop. That's a promise. But I need to tell you something, something bad, and I had to know you were safe, okay?"

"What's happened?" she asked immediately. "Have you caught him? Is it Tank?"

She sounded frantic, and he reminded himself she was a gentle soul *and* she liked someone whom she was slowly discovering was a murderer. She would be a mess of nerves and emotions for a while. In addition, her sister was still missing, which was adding to her worry.

"No, Jayne, calm down, we haven't caught him, but I do have to tell you that more than ever, I'm positive it's him, which is why I want you safe. One of my officers took it upon himself to go to Tank's apartment alone once he discovered where he was living, while I was flying back. The stupid idiot couldn't stop himself trying to prove to his new boss he was right all along. Williams is in Perth, Jayne, and has been all along. That officer is now missing, and I think he has been murdered by Tank."

She was silent for a long time.

"Are you okay, Jayne?"

"I'm fine. Look, I have an idea. Hear me out before

you try to change my mind, which, by the way, you can't do. You better get used to that, lover. If I make up my mind to do something, I will do it, so just you shush a minute and listen."

This was a new, determined Jayne he had not experienced, and he did listen. He understood how serious she was, but it was more than that. It was her 'I want' attitude, and on her, for some reason Dillon couldn't put his finger on, it was incredibly attractive.

"I have to assume, because I know you wouldn't lie to me, that you are right, Dillon, and everything I felt and thought I knew about Tank was wrong. So, maybe he did lose his mind, and he has been out there killing people. Now, if you think I am in danger from him, then I must accept I probably am. If not now, then one day in the future. If you know anything about him, you have to know he won't stop. He *can't* stop. I doubt I will be safe here no matter where I stay or who I stay with. In fact, I could well be putting Laura at risk too, and that I will not do, Dillon. Am I right so far?"

"I'm sorry, but yes, I think you are right. I think you are in serious danger from him."

"Okay, so now don't jump down my throat, but I'm going to come over to Perth. Tonight, right away, now, in fact. You can protect me over there. I know we've only just met, but I trust you, Dillon."

He started to interrupt, but she stopped him.

"No, no, shush, just listen to me. This makes sense. Firstly, I do trust you to protect me from him. Second, if I'm there, I can help you. You have no authority anyway; you told me that, so there is no reason we can't be a team. There is so much you don't know about him that I can help with, like, for example, you have to know he will have guns. He is a nut for them. He told Amanda he has lots of them stashed in a storage shed somewhere, but I can't quite remember where. He won't go quietly, you know that, right? If you corner him, he is a soldier. There is no telling how many of you he will kill. But, if you have me with you, I can talk to him. I have some of her clothes here. I could even dress like her, and at a distance, he will think I am Amanda. I can calm him down; he liked me. Trust me, you have to say yes. You know it makes sense. Oh, and if you say no? I will come over by myself anyway and go to the papers and TV and make him come to me, but then you won't be able to protect me."

As crazy as it sounded, Dillon knew she was right. He absolutely didn't want to put her in harm's way, but she had stated that she was coming anyway. At least here, he could control her, or at least try to control her. He knew that he did want her with him, and she made a very good point that she could be invaluable in talking him out of a bad situation.

"Okay, I agree. Everything you say makes sense, Jayne. But here's the thing, you must agree to do everything I say, no ifs or buts or questions. If you agree, I will pick you up from the airport, disagree, and you are on your own." Of course, it was a bluff. He wanted her with him for more reasons than one, but he hoped he could impress on her the seriousness of it all *and* for her to do as he said.

"I'm on my way to the airport now. I agree with your terms; I always would have. I will do anything and everything you tell me to." Her voice had gone husky again, and the double meaning wasn't lost on him. "You can always handcuff me if I'm naughty, Dillon."

She had a beautiful giggle.

"So, we agree. I'm leaving now. I'm already packed. Can you please book me a flight, and text me which airline is the quickest one to get there, and please be there to meet me. Oh, and, Dillon?"

"Yes, babe, what is it?" he asked, already looking forward to seeing her.

"Please don't be mad at me, I know I shouldn't say this, but I think I'm falling for you, madly." With that, she hung up.

Dillon sat with the phone in his hand for quite a while and had to admit to himself, he was falling for her too.

****

It was just after ten that night I woke up. I had fallen asleep on the couch while watching a crappy TV movie. When I moved, I noticed my nose was bleeding. My T-shirt, which had been blue, was now red. It was still dripping out of my right nostril, and when I raced to the bathroom to clean up, I looked in the mirror, and my right eye had blood inside it. Just in the corner, right where I would rub if I was tired. In this case, though, I knew I hadn't rubbed it; a blood vessel had burst and leaked inside.

I looked at my reflection in the mirror, knowing full well what this meant. One of the bits of shrapnel had moved around in my head, just as good old Dr. *Call Me Charlie*, the wife fucker, had said it would. Possibly it'd happened after I'd struggled with the dead cop's body; he had been heavy after all. I'd had to no choice but to manhandle him out of sight from the window. Nothing says *'break the door down'* quicker than seeing a dead body through the window, but it seemed I had damaged myself doing it.

I held a cold, wet hand towel over my nose and went to lie back on the bed and wait until the bleeding stopped, assuming it did stop, of course. Maybe this was it, the beginning of the end, and this shitty room would be where I died.

No, fuck it. I hadn't come this far to die quietly bleeding to death in a flea-bitten motel within five kilometers of Amanda's workplace and home. No, that was not going to happen. That was *not* how this story was going to end; of that, I was damn sure.

I mentally surveyed my body to see if anything else had changed. My hands, arms, legs, and feet all worked, with no twitching or loss of strength that I could detect. I was relieved to find nothing else had gone wrong. On a scale of one to ten, the headache was a nine; nothing new there. So, a bloodshot eye and bleeding nose may be a warning of things to come, but it was not the end of the road, not yet.

If only there was some way to know when the end would come, I mused, but of course, there wasn't. Did I expect the worst and plan for it or carry on as normal and risk dying before I reached my objective? It didn't take too much thinking, really, plan for the worst and act accordingly to ensure the mission's success. That was how it would end for me—and if it was time to die, let it not be in vain.

I thought about how I would dress in the morning. I had a light bomber-style jacket. *How appropriate.* The two side pockets would hold the grenades, and at that, despite the nose bleed, I laughed out loud. The jacket would also hide the shoulder holster, gun, and the spare magazines tucked into my jeans belt at the back. The sub-machine gun would be in the backpack, with the flap open so I would be able to reach it in an instant.

The plan, such as it was, was pretty simple now. At ten in the morning, I would go into the shopping center and go from travel agency to agency, find Amanda and kill her along with anyone who stood in my way. Then I would wait for the police and take as many of them with me as I could. That thought was my last for the night.

I fell asleep with my nose still bleeding and my mind happy with the plan. I felt secure in the knowledge that tomorrow morning, come hell or high water, Amanda would be dead. The fact that I probably would be as well didn't matter or change a damn thing.

Chapter Thirty

During her flight to Perth, Jayne had done nothing but marvel at her feelings and, though sadly not for the first time in her life, wondered if this time she had found the right man. One who could, in time, love her and give her the safety and security she so desperately yearned for. He was older than her, but she saw that as a good thing. He was mature in thought and deed. He was a man's man and strong, but not cruel. Most importantly to her, he had a vulnerable side. She could tell by the sadness he showed when he spoke of his wife, which was only natural, but the fact he blamed himself rather than her showed he was a kind and considerate man.

Last of all—*but by no means least*, she'd marveled, snuggled into her seat, pretending to watch a movie—the sex the night before had been amazing. When they had made love, he'd been the type of man who was very rare in her experience. He cared. She had slept in his arms, exhausted and glowing contentedly, knowing in her heart this man was a diamond.

She wasn't stupid. She knew there were lots and lots of things against them ever being any more than they already were. His job, the death of his wife, the hunt for her brother-in-law, and the fact that his daughter wasn't too many years younger than she was. That was a hoot, and she smiled at that, but in a good way.

She understood he most likely wasn't ready to settle

down with her and wouldn't be perhaps for a long while, especially being straight after his wife's death. He would need time and perhaps a lot of it. But for her, there was no rush. She knew that. More than anything, she wanted to give him that time and be there for him when he was ready, hopefully, for her.

Also, not to be forgotten was the fact that they lived in different states four thousand kilometers apart. That alone would make things very difficult, plainly. But one thing her father had taught her was that anything worth having was worth the effort to go and get it. For all of the potential problems and hurdles they would face, when she thought of him—and she found herself doing that all the time—she *just knew* he was 'the one.' She'd felt so excited to be on her way to see him again.

She cautioned herself that she had to go slow and steady. Try not to be clingy, demanding, or needy. She would just be herself, which he seemed to like. Then, see where it led to, just one step at a time. He had shown the night before he wanted her, and not just as a sex object. He cared. That caring made her glow inside and feel rather wonderful.

****

Sitting in the airport bar, nursing a light beer, Dillon was fighting with himself. He was tormented by his own fears and misgivings but found that he was incredibly attracted to Jayne. His pulse quickened every time he thought of her, which was often. In his logical police brain, he tried to muddle his way through and sort his feelings into compartments where he could examine them one at a time.

One, he was too old for her, and she would be far better off with someone in her own age bracket. If he had any common sense at all, right there was reason enough to make sure this went no further. But…easy to say, not so easy to do. She was incredible, and he wanted her, and she seemed to want him too.

Two, she was stunning, and he couldn't help but keep coming back to that. Not only was she beautiful, she had a wonderfully gentle spirit. He felt she needed to be loved and wanted, and there was nothing so incredible for any man to have a beautiful woman want and need him.

Three, how could he be sure that if he permitted himself to have any feelings for her, she would return those feelings for him? Would he be dumped and left like a love-torn adolescent?

This was a major point to him, and he needed to examine it. They had been thrust together under very unusual and potentially dangerous circumstances. Her brother-in-law had murdered Dillon's wife, and he knew at some point in time she could be in danger from Williams. That sort of danger and intrigue could easily make her feel something for him which wasn't real. Again, he didn't want to end up down the track as the sort of man who had fallen for a much younger woman and looked like a dope to everyone around him. But at the same time, he didn't want to risk losing her if it was real. Sure, she seemed genuine, and he believed deep down in her sincerity. The clincher, for him, was that it sounded like she had had a run of bad luck with the wrong men; incredible though that seemed.

Four, he had to think about the sex, and he'd found himself doing so often in the last few hours. In his life, he had slept with a total of nine women, not a huge number by any means. He had always tended to be loyal, and the only time he had been unfaithful to Kathy was with Marci. But then, that had only been because life had become unbearable at home. He had always loved sex, obviously, and he supposed, like most men, he wanted it as often as possible. Marci was a hooker and a damned good one. While she was very—how should he say?—technically gifted and uninhibited, she didn't *feel* anything for him other than a sense of gratitude for helping her out of a bad situation. He hadn't *felt* much for her either, other than enjoying using her body whenever he wanted. So, the sex had been satisfying but hardly earth-shattering.

Last night with Jayne, the sex had been, for him, mind-blowing. He felt it was more than the emotionally charged situation that had made it that way. They seemed to just *fit* together in all the right ways. Things he liked to do she loved and vice versa. Yes, it had been one night only, so far. That couldn't be ignored, but what a night it had been.

He looked at his watch and began counting down the minutes till she arrived. He felt excited. His hand had a slight tremor to it. She had bewitched him; he knew it, and really? He could plot, plan and compartmentalize his feelings as much as he liked, but why shouldn't he go along for the ride? *Enjoy life*, he thought; maybe he deserved a bit of that. Just take things as they came, and if something worked out with Jayne, fantastic. If it didn't, then he would have had an incredible experience and memories to keep of a beautiful woman who, for a while anyway, wanted him as a man. In the final analysis, he felt he could live with that.

At eight fifty, the plane landed, and they hugged for long minutes on end as soon as she appeared through the arrival gate. Dillon grabbed her suitcase, and they headed for the car park and his car. He explained that he was taking her to a hotel in the city to stay rather than his house. They had been walking through the terminal when he told her. She stopped dead in her tracks, unhooked her arm from his, and folded both of hers across her breasts. Her face turned steely, and she developed what he recognized as her 'I want' pout.

"Don't you even begin to start thinking you can dump me at a hotel and leave me there, mister. I came here to be with you and help you, and I do mean *be* with you. I'm going to be with you at night, and you are going to make love to me, *lots*. And during the day, I'm going to be with you helping to find Tank before he finds Amanda."

He couldn't help it. He burst into spontaneous laughter and hugged her tightly. He loved how strongly she felt about him and her dedication to risking her own safety. There was no doubt in his mind she was an incredible woman, a *keeper* as his mother used to say.

"Calm down, honey. I have no intention of dumping you anywhere. And I want to be with you as much as you want to be with me, you goose. I will be staying at the hotel with you, too. Let's not forget your brother-in-law knows where I live. He killed my wife there, so that's not the place to take you. And if it's okay with you, I'm not yet ready to take you there even if I thought it was safe," he said, a bit more seriously. "Jayne, I think you're wonderful, and I hope we can make something work between us, but you have to give me some time before I take you to the house I spent all those years in with her. That's no reflection on you, it's a reflection on me, and I hope you understand that."

She hugged him back and whispered in his ear, "I like it when you call me a goose. Of course, I understand not going to your house. I like you even more for that. I'm sorry I got uppity with you. I do want to be with you, and I'm sorry for thinking you were getting rid of me."

He picked up her bag in one hand and guided her with his other arm toward the car park. Once in the car, they kissed long and deeply before he broke off, slightly breathless.

"Did you eat on the plane, or are you hungry?"

"Yes and yes," she answered. "Yes, I ate on the plane, and yes, I'm hungry for you. Now take me to the hotel and make love to me. I've missed you."

He smiled at her response, and the mental image of being in bed with her made him hard, but there was one thing he wanted to do first.

"I've missed you too, and I want you as much as you want me, you goose. But, before we do that, do you mind if we go check something out? I've already booked into the hotel, so we can keep your bag in the car. I've got the room keys here. I thought we would do a drive-by of Tank's apartment and see if Mike has returned there to pick up his car. He is still not answering his phone, and we can't get a search warrant until tomorrow. Are you okay with that?"

"Oh definitely, I'm into that. Do you have to deputize me or something? Do I get my own handcuffs?" She grinned at him and clicked on her seat belt.

"I keep telling you, babe, I've been relieved of command. I'm just a private citizen now, so no, I won't be deputizing you. But you can borrow my handcuffs if you like. I kept them." He winked.

He started the car, and they left, heading toward the

west to Scarborough. Her hand was high on his thigh as he drove, and every so often, her finger splayed out to touch his crotch while she looked ahead innocently.

Suddenly, out of the blue, she said, "Dillon, serious question. Are you armed? If we see him, he may or may not recognize you, but he will certainly recognize me. You know he will be armed, don't you? I remember the three of us went to a shooting gallery once, and he taught us how to shoot handguns. It was a lot of fun. Amanda was brilliant at it. But, he never missed, not once. To him, in the army, killing was a way of life and his job. He won't stop. He won't think the way you would. He will just shoot, and it won't bother him at all."

He took her hand in his, picked it up, and guided it to his hip, where his gun sat in its holster under his jacket. "Yes, babe, I am armed. I'm not SAS, but you know what? It won't worry me one bit either to use this if I get the chance. I will kill him if I can, and I won't be losing any sleep over it. I hope that's okay with you."

Jayne nodded determinedly, which he saw clearly by the dashboard lights, and she put her hand back in his lap, this time much higher, and gently squeezed. "If it comes to it, don't miss, will you? He won't, so don't give him a second chance. If you get a shot, take it and come back to me, please?"

****

Silently, with lights dimmed, Dillon pulled into the visitors' car park of Paul William's apartment complex and parked alongside Mike's Commodore. He looked around but couldn't see an officer on duty in hiding anywhere. *Maybe he went home*, he thought. He looked toward the four apartment blocks, which showed little life anywhere apart from the odd light poking through closed curtains. The place seemed pretty deserted other than two vehicles farther down the car park.

He was looking at the letter boxes when he realized something was off, and it took a minute or two for him to realize what was wrong. When it came to him, he said out loud, "Oh fuck no." He grabbed his phone, opened it, and brought up the message from Mike. There it was; the apartment number in the message was 4D, but if that was the case, why was Mike's car sitting in front of the apartment block containing 1A & B, 2 A & B, 3 A & B, and 4 A & B? The next block along had the same numbers but were C & D. With a sinking heart, he suddenly knew what had happened. The voice-to-text could have changed the message from a B to a D. Then, the cop car sent by Blunt would have gone to the wrong apartment.

"What's wrong?" She asked three times, each time louder than the last, while he thought things through. He quickly explained to her what he thought had happened. He made a decision instantly what he should do next.

"Sit here in the driver's seat and keep watch. If you see anything, anything at all, you honk the horn two or three times. If Williams comes out without me, just drive away as fast as you can. I have to go up there and look into this, and your brother-in-law may be still inside. Take my phone. I've put it to Assistant Commissioner Blunt's mobile number. If I'm not back in five, all you have to do is hit dial and tell him what's happened. Tell him it's 4B, not 4D, and I went to check it out, and he should send the cavalry, okay?"

She nodded. She would do exactly as he'd told her to do, but she did throw her arms around him. "Please, please be careful."

"Jayne, I am literally crapping myself here, but I have to do this. I will be careful, don't you worry. And, one last thing? I'm glad you said it first, but I think I'm falling for you too." He kissed her quickly to show he meant it.

Before she could reply, he jumped out of the car, took his gun out, and crossed the car park to the stairs. He climbed to 4B and without hesitation, knocked loudly and called out that it was the police before jumping to the side. He waited for God knew what—the door to be flung open or a hail of bullets to come through it—but nothing happened. The place was as silent as the grave. He looked in through the window. Inside was dimly lit, with the only illumination from the outside lights. But other than the shape of furniture, he could see nothing out of the ordinary. No one appeared to be home.

He had two choices—he could go to the hotel and make love with Jayne, which certainly had appeal, or he could take the law and his job in both hands and break in. He only thought for a matter of seconds before making a decision. His job, which had been his life up until recently, had cost him his wife. He had been relieved of command, and the stigma of all that had happened would follow him, whatever he did next. There was a very real possibility he might not go back to work, and even if it killed him, he was determined to do whatever it took to find *the Ripper*. He turned the gun around in his hand and smashed the glass window alongside the door, reached in, and unlatched it.

Cautiously, he pushed the door open, the gun held in front of him, and flicked the light switch on. He stepped through the threshold, crouched low, scanning left and right, ready to fire at anything that moved.

The place was deserted. Dillon crossed through the living area and looked through to the dining and kitchen area. Everything seemed tidy and neat, other than a game controller on the floor in front of the TV. He turned three-hundred-sixty degrees and only then noticed the massive bloodstain on the couch, and his heart sank.

Dillon assumed the first door to his left led to the main bedroom and when he opened it, there, lying on the bed, was Mike Knowles' body. He felt for a pulse, but he was long since cold to the touch. Knowing the rest of the place would be empty, he left the body to check anyway, which took only minutes. Paul Williams was long gone.

Back in the living area, he was startled by a voice from the front door. A neighbor called out at the same time as the horn honked to warn him.

"Hello, is everything all right?"

Dillon turned to see an elderly man holding a very large torch as a club. He thought, unkindly, that the only offender to be scared by that would be a ten-year-old. He tucked the gun back into the holster and took out his ID card.

"Thanks for being a good neighbor, sir, I am Detective Inspector Bradley, and you are?"

The man's eyes turned huge, and he all but dropped the torch when he saw the dead body through the bedroom door. "Hubert Winkler, people call me Hub. I live in 4A. I heard the glass smashing and came to look. Is that Paul?"

"I'm not at liberty to say at the moment, sir. Did you hear anything unusual this afternoon at all?"

He shook his head. "I never hear a peep out of Paul. He is as quiet as a mouse, no visitors ever, no parties. I hardly even hear his TV."

Dillon nodded. "Please go back to your apartment, police officers will be here shortly, and they will want to talk to you in more detail a bit later."

Once the neighbor had left, Dillon went down and sat in the car with Jayne. He took his phone back from her and called for a cab.

"I found my missing officer, Jayne. He's been shot dead. Your brother-in-law is long gone. I have to report this and wait till the troops arrive, then answer a lot of questions. I've called a cab for you. There is no point complicating things with you being here, okay? When they ask you tomorrow, I picked you up from the airport and took you to the hotel. It's the one on Adelaide Terrace, by the way. Then I came here alone. In the morning, I will take you to headquarters, where you are going to have to make a statement about Paul. Wait for me tonight, and I will be with you as soon as I can."

She nodded, crying softly. "I still hoped it wasn't him. Stupid, aren't I?"

"No, babe, you are far from stupid. What you are is loyal, and that is a quality I value. Will you be okay by yourself for a couple of hours or so?"

"I will be fine, don't worry, you do what you need to do. With the time difference between here and Sydney, I will probably be asleep when you get there. It's pretty late for me. But please, make sure you wake me, no matter what time it is when you get in."

The cab drew up into the car park, and Dillon got her case out of the boot of his car and transferred it, then opened the cab door for her. She slid into the cab, and he kissed her softly. He passed her one of the two electronic door keys for room four-twenty-two. Then he gave the driver a fifty-dollar note and told him where to take her, then watched as they drove away.

Once they were out of sight, he went back up to the apartment and dialed the number in his phone, dreading the conversation he was about to have.

Chapter Thirty-One

Dillon's night at the crime scene had not gone well, which he knew it wouldn't. For the first time, he experienced the full wrath of the assistant commissioner, who seemed to be even more angry than normal. Perhaps it was because he had been called out during the night, like a regular police officer, when he was more used to the nine-to-four-thirty hours he usually kept.

He took it as an affront that an officer on his watch had been murdered. Not that he could be blamed, it was Dillon's fault for getting the message wrong. He would not accept it was a technical glitch with the way the message had been delivered. It was also Knowles' own fault he'd got killed. If he had followed orders and gone home, he would still be alive.

Blunt refused to countenance that it was, in fact, he who had stopped the army link being investigated in the first place. He couldn't acknowledge that it was his fault for not taking Mike more seriously and sending him, by virtue of that, to his death. Dillon was angry. He pointed out that if the task force had been investigating rather than him by himself, they could have identified the man much faster and probably caught him well before then.

Blunt totally ignored that and told him it was unforgivable that Dillon had broken into the apartment to find the body. He had been suspended and had no warrant—did he not understand the law?

Gritting his teeth, Dillon told a lie for the first time in his police career. He said that the bedroom door was open, and he could see the body through the window, so he felt he had grounds to break in. And, what did Blunt expect him to do when he saw that, and there was no response to his knocks?

Blunt blustered some more but must have realized he was losing the debate. There seemed little point in inflaming the situation any more. Whether the door was closed or open, to Dillon, was irrelevant. Mike Knowles had been murdered. *That* was relevant.

The bullets used were nine-millimeter, the casings on the floor were that caliber, and the mess on impact showed they were hollow points. That strongly implied the doctor's murder had been committed using the same gun, and Dillon took pains to point that out too. Blunt had chosen to ignore that murder when Mike had brought it to him, and that was yet another thing that made Blunt look incompetent. Dillon noted that Blunt seemed to slowly realize he was not going to look good when this all came out.

Dillon was livid with Blunt's stupidity and ignorance. The best cop on the task force, who had been right about everything all along, was dead, while the biggest idiot on the force still lived and was blaming everyone else for his own shortcomings.

Dillon was sure the inquiry, which was bound to follow, would destroy Blunt's career and possibly reinstate his. Though for obvious reasons, he could not officially be involved in *the Ripper* investigation at any point in time for fear of compromising it in court later. But it was Mike Knowles and Dillon's dogged determination in the face of Blunt's unbelievably poor decision-making that had identified the murderer and his car. Both of which were now the subject of an urgent statewide hunt.

William's bank account could be located and frozen, every way out of the state was being watched, and it must only a matter of time before he was in custody because they knew who they were looking for. A driver's license picture was going to be released to the media first thing in the morning, along with his name, and all stops would be pulled out to catch him.

Had Dillon, of his own volition and expense, not gone to Sydney, even without authorization as he had, who knew when the killer would have been identified? Possibly never. But rather than thank him and congratulate him for his dedication, Blunt continued to berate him for acting without authority and permission. There was also breaking and entering and risking any evidence being thrown out on technicalities and, of course, for getting the address wrong in the text message. The reality was that even though technically he was correct, there was no possible way a judge could throw out the evidence they now had—the dead police officer in the killer's apartment negated any possible technicality. But, as always, Blunt was only concerned with his own position and refused to listen to common sense.

Dillon wondered how many police officers over the years had been tempted to punch this idiot in the face. He was sure the list would be long and distinguished.

A search of Williams' apartment yielded little. He lived frugally. However, they did find what they believed to be the earlier victims' missing underwear in a bedside drawer. DNA would confirm that later. The only other thing of interest was a torn-off sheet of notepaper found in the bin that listed three travel agents at Belmont Forum Shopping Center and the name Toni. Blunt seized on this as proof that the killer had finished his murderous spree and was talking to travel agents to get a flight out of the country. Williams' name and passport details had already been sent to customs and immigration to halt him at any airport or port nationwide.

The three travel agents would be spoken to tomorrow, but there seemed little urgency to do that as all airlines had been contacted, and the name Paul Williams was not booked on any international or local planes in the next seven days. This led Blunt to think Williams would now flee by some other means. As he was SAS and trained to live off the land, perhaps he would disappear into the bush to hide out. With the description they now had of the car, driving interstate would be unlikely due to the full-scale manhunt. Blunt believed it wouldn't take long for the police to track Williams down; he had to be on the run.

Eventually, Dillon was dismissed and ordered to bring Jayne into police headquarters, where she would be questioned in the morning. Formal statements would be taken from both.

Tiredly and in a rather depressed and angry mood, he drove back into the city through deserted streets to be with Jayne. She was the only ray of sunshine in an otherwise very cloudy day. He was forbidden from doing anything else in the investigation. He'd offered to go and speak to Mike Knowles' wife but was instructed not to do so. That would be taken care of by Blunt himself.

****

I stirred around three a.m. and was instantly awake,

in agony. The pain was blinding, by far the worst I had experienced. So much so that I knew there would be no more sleep for me that night. The headache had increased in intensity with a vengeance, the pounding between my ears was horrific and the voices were chanting in my head.

Slowly, I lurched my way to the bathroom and found what was left of the tablets I had taken from the doctor. I put four of them in my mouth and scooped water from the running tap to swallow them with. I knew that I had almost taken the last of them, but as of tomorrow morning, I wouldn't need them anymore, not where I was going.

Tiredly I looked in the mirror. The nosebleed had stopped for the time being, but my top lip and nostrils were caked in dried blood. Gently, I cleaned my face, careful not to hurt it and start the bleeding again. The eye was worse. While I could still see out of it, there was no white left at all. It was blood red, and I knew I had a major problem. *I just need to hold on a little while longer and finish the job, then I can sleep,* I told myself.

There was a chair and table on the tiny balcony, and I went and sat outside in the cool night air to wait for morning. I took my laptop with me so I could bring my journal up to date. I wanted to leave it behind to tell my story and for my tale to be as accurate as possible.

****

Dillon gently woke up Jayne when he returned. He had spent two or three minutes watching her sleep simply because she was an incredibly beautiful woman. The way she hadn't complained and had done everything he'd asked without question, in what were, to say the least, unusual circumstances, impressed him. Could he possibly be that lucky that amid the horrifying times he had been through, he could find the woman of his dreams? He shook his head; that was a question for later. For now, he had to live in the moment and let whatever happened happen.

He was sitting on the side of the king-sized bed as she woke, and without hesitation, she sat up. The sheet fell to her waist, and she pressed her naked breasts against his chest as she hugged him tightly.

"Thank God you're okay. I was worried sick before I fell asleep. Are you all right?" she asked, one hand on the back of his neck, the other holding his shoulder, her feelings for him evident in the anxiety in her voice.

"I'm fine, babe, but tired. It's been a long day, and I've just spent two hours with the biggest dickhead in the world. That bed looks *so* inviting. Can I join you?"

She threw back the covers, showing him her body. "I will be mad if you don't."

Within minutes, he, too, was naked, and he snuggled into her. Dillon realized she wanted to know what had transpired and felt he needed to talk to her too, but they both had a greater need. She was warm and welcoming, and the next forty-five minutes were spent clinging together, making frantic, passionate love.

They didn't have the conversation they wanted and needed because, in the afterglow, they both drifted off to sleep, mentally and physically exhausted, wrapped in each other's arms.

****

Paul Williams sat three kilometers away in the darkness, planning to murder his wife, and as many people as possible, in a few short hours. He especially wanted to kill all the women he could find at the shopping center because he felt that would be a fitting end.

He was in pain, tired, and ready to die and face whatever came next. He was just fed up with life and the misery he had suffered throughout. He knew were it not for his mission, he would have ended it before he got to the level of pain he was feeling right then.

Chapter Thirty-Two

At seven-forty in the morning, Dillon and Jayne were in the restaurant on the top floor of the luxury hotel, enjoying a buffet breakfast. Earlier, they had showered together and made love standing up under the cascading water. Her body was so diminutive he could easily hold her while her legs were wrapped around his hips, and she clung to him, biting his shoulder to stifle her orgasm. As they dressed, Dillon pointed out that he had not eaten the night before, had only an hour or two of sleep, and he was famished.

They sat in a window seat looking out over the river as he ate bacon and eggs heartily while telling her all about what had transpired after she had left in the cab, and she listened with rapt attention. He knew Jayne had never been to WA before, and while Sydney Harbor was spectacular, she told him how much she enjoyed the scenic view across the Swan River. She ate fresh fruit and yogurt, followed by toast and marmalade, which she ate in small pieces while watching the boats and ferries in the morning sun.

Dillon warned her what she would be in for from Blunt when he took her into the station later, and they talked about how the interview would be conducted. He could not be with her as he would be giving his own version, which protocol demanded, which Jayne understood and seemed willing and able to handle the questioning.

Then, he mentioned the note listing travel agents in the Belmont Shopping Center, which he pointed out to her was pretty close to the city and near to where they were in the hotel. It appeared Williams was speaking to someone named Toni at one of them and that while Blunt was a complete fool in his idea that the killings were over, he did appear on the face of it to be correct that the killer must have been making arrangements to flee the country.

Jayne sat quiet for a moment, then asked a very astute question as she sexily licked some marmalade off her finger. "Hon, why would he go from all the way over in Scarborough to find a travel agent in Belmont?" While she didn't know the geography of Perth at all, he could see how it might seem a long way to go from their drive last night.

"Good question; you're learning." He smiled and winked at her. "I don't know, possibly this woman Toni is someone recommended to him, or she may have looked after him when he was in the army before. Maybe he was just being cautious by doing it so far from home, but it is strange, I agree," he answered thoughtfully, then sipped his coffee.

"Oh, you mean Toni is a woman, not Tony as in a man. I didn't realize that." She suddenly looked worried and shook her head.

"What's wrong, babe? You look like you're troubled about something?"

"Oh, it's probably nothing. I'm sure you guys know what you're doing." But she still frowned.

Dillon reached for her hand and said softly, "Hon, if I have to kiss it out of you, I will, you know."

She laughed. "Mmmmm, well, only if you promise. Look, you sexy man, I feel silly saying it, that's all, but then again, maybe you didn't know... Amanda was a travel agent when they met each other. She had been one since she left school. When she was here, she worked in a jewelry store, a place in...is it Fremantle? Is that how you say it?"

He nodded, interested in what she was saying.

"She quit when Tank was wounded and came back to Sydney, obviously, and got her old job back. There is one other little thing too, but again it's probably nothing, and I feel idiotic mentioning it."

"Babe, I didn't know she was a travel consultant, and it *is* very interesting. Go on, what else?"

"Well, our dad had a bit of a thing for French women's names, so my middle name is Danielle, and Amanda's name is Antoinette. We both love our middle names, and when we were younger, and we played dress-up, we both used to pretend. I was Danni, and she was Toni. She loved that name. You don't think that Toni, the travel agent at the Belmont shops, could possibly be Amanda in hiding from Tank, do you?"

Dillon stared at her for a few minutes, processing the information when she broke his train of thought.

"No, that's stupid. Why would she call herself Toni? I'm being daft, don't worry about it." She picked up her toast again and looked back out of the window.

Dillon thought on. Could it possibly be that the last victim, Suzanne, had identified Toni as Amanda to Williams and told him where she worked, in a travel shop in a Belmont Shopping Center? And was that why he had it written on a piece of paper? He thought hard. Something was gnawing away in the back of his mind that Mike had told him. What was it? Then it came to him—Suzanne Delvechio had not long come back from a holiday in Bali before she had been murdered. Just suppose Toni had organized that holiday for her, but then okay, even if she did, what did that mean? It still didn't make sense.

Still deep in thought, something else occurred to him. Just suppose Toni was Amanda hiding from Williams. She probably didn't realize she was being hunted and that her ex-husband had become a serial killer. Surely if she had, she would have come to the police? If she knew she would, but still it had to be a possibility that she had just tried to evade Williams and start a new life by changing her name. What if she was living with another man now and just simply didn't want her ex to find her and spoil it? If it was her, she might go back to what she had always done for a job—travel. If it *was* her, she was in danger, great danger…if Williams knew, of course.

There was only one thing for it, he decided, and hurriedly pulled Jayne to her feet. "You're right, it's probably nothing, but let's go to the shops ourselves now and find out if this Toni is Amanda just trying to have a new life. If it is your sister, we need to get her out of there and into safety. C'mon, let's go."

Again, Jayne didn't question or argue; Dillon had said to go, and he appreciated that she agreed without fuss.

****

At first, I thought I'd been sitting too long in the same position. My left leg had stiffened up considerably and ached with a dull pins-and-needles kind of soreness. I had left the balcony a while back and gone and sat at

352

the desk and brought the journal up to date. I knew there would be no more entries after I left the motel, and I wanted people to know my story after I went out with a bang. I wanted everyone to know what had driven me to take the actions I had.

My leg wouldn't seem to do what I wanted it to, and on standing, I fell over and hit my head on the edge of the desk. It didn't knock me out, and my headache was already a blitzkrieg raining bombs between my ears. I lay dazed for a while but then found I had trouble getting up. After a few minutes, it eased, but my leg still wouldn't work properly.

The irony was not lost on me. I'd used to use a limp to help disguise my walk and height, but here I was now with a real one. It wasn't painful, not like my headaches were painful. It was more numb and achy. I also didn't have full use of it, but I knew I wasn't going to be running anywhere. At least the nosebleed had stopped, but the bloodshot eye was now making sight out of it difficult, as if there was a red haze across everything I looked at.

I lifted my left hand to rub and massage it, and that was when I noticed the tremors. I quickly lifted the right to compare it, but that one was normal, which was something at least. *Early stages of Parkinson's?* I wondered. I shrugged, knowing I would be able to shoot straight with my right, though I was literally quaking with the left. I sighed deeply, knowing for sure my remaining time was limited and could worsen further at any point. I decided I absolutely had to get to the shopping center, and quickly. Maybe I only had minutes left or hours; I had no way to tell. I just knew this latest development was not good news and that I was deteriorating fast. Interestingly, I felt quite calm.

Slowly I dressed for what I knew would be the last time, struggled on with my jacket with the grenades in the pockets then made a decision to call a cab rather than risk driving. It made sense—not only couldn't I trust my driving ability, but the car was also registered in my name, and by now, the police would be searching for it. I had my dark sunglasses to hide what my eye must look like to others and had to hope that would be enough. I made the call for a taxi to pick me up and noticed that my voice didn't seem the same. I sounded like I'd had too much to drink, and my words were slurred slightly. They understood what I wanted, though, so it wasn't *that* bad.

****

Journal Excerpt #12, Goodbye, Sayonara, Farewell
So, this will be my last entry. I am about to grab my things and make my way down the steel staircase, through the car park, and out to the reception to wait for the cab to arrive.

I can hear through the open balcony door that the traffic is already building up and getting hectic on the highway. Being so close to the city on the one hand and the airport on the other, it does get busy. I know it won't be too long before my ride arrives. I will sit on the low brick wall out the front and wait. I wanted my last journal entry to be something deep and meaningful. But I'm so tired, and in so much pain, I just can't be bothered.

****

Battling the morning rush hour traffic wasn't too bad coming out of the city, as the bulk was going into it. But once Dillon turned onto the Great Eastern Highway and headed toward the airport, it slowed dramatically. He wondered if there had been an accident farther ahead, which made the usual slow-moving traffic even worse.

Dillon was torn between reporting Jayne's theory to Blunt that possibly Toni was her sister and the object of Williams' search or doing what he was and checking it out for himself. If it was Amanda, then she could well be being hunted. If that was the case, not only was she in danger but anyone else that she was with could also be targeted. If the task force head had been anything other than downright rude to him the night before, and if he didn't feel so tired, he probably would have thought more clearly. Had he done so, he would have erred on the side of caution and reported it. Then it would be armed Tactical Response Group officers going to the shopping center.

Blunt is an idiot. Dillon decided and realized that the time it took to convince him to get the TRG mobilized would be a lot longer than getting there himself and getting Amanda out if, in fact, she was there. If she wasn't there, then the detour wouldn't matter, and Blunt need never know. It all made perfect sense.

Having Jayne with him was good and bad, too, Dillon mused as his car crawled through the traffic jam. She could identify her sister immediately, though as they looked so similar, he could do that himself, but there was always the chance if she was in hiding, she had changed her appearance. And if Williams was anywhere near, Jayne could point him out too, so that was good. But he really did care for her and was concerned for her safety first and foremost, so that was bad.

He calculated they were no more than ten minutes or so from the shopping center, and it was still fifteen minutes before opening time. *That should be time enough to get her out of there,* he decided. Then he could contact the tactical guys or plain-clothes officers to stake out the center and wait for Williams, but only after she was safe. If the woman Toni wasn't Amanda, he would look like an idiot for calling out the TRG. And that would give Blunt more ammunition against him in the political shitstorm that he knew was coming.

As he sat waiting in the queue for the traffic lights to turn green, out of the corner of his eye, he saw a cab pull out of a motel car park and thought nothing of it. *Someone off to the airport?* He mused, then glanced down at the amazing sight of Jayne's bare thigh.

Dillon made the decision that if he felt it was needed, he would call the TRG direct from the center rather than risk an argument with Blunt. He would do that just as soon as he could establish who Toni was and assess any risk. That would save time in the long run, though make an even bigger enemy of Blunt, though Dillon didn't care too much any longer. He would make that call first, then Blunt second. He would deal with his wrath knowing that the best of the best, the most heavily armed police, the Tactical Response Group, were in transit, and they should be a match for Paul Williams if or when he showed up. Dillon was armed and was sure he could handle anything that came up until the troops arrived. His biggest concern was to keep Jayne safe, and he had made her promise she would sit in the car and wait for him while he entered and made inquiries at the three travel shops.

Dillon parked the car near the multistory car park under the shade of a small tree, kissed Jayne, and told her to sit tight. He entered through the Belmont Avenue entrance, walking briskly, having already undone the retaining clip on his holster.

Dillon went straight to Blythe Spirit Travel and tapped on the glass door as he could see two women inside.

One of them approached. "I was just about to open the door. You're nice and early. I'm Donna. How can I help?"

"I'm looking for a lady named Toni. Does she work here?" He showed his police ID card.

"No, there's no one named Toni here, sorry. Are you sure I can't help you?" She smiled back at him.

"No thanks, it has to be her. Can you point out the other travel shops here? She must be at one of the others."

"Sure, well, if you go this way to the food court and turn left, out the door and down the covered walkway, and into the other building, Holiday Universe is there. Or back this way and turn right at the corner, go through that passage and around the front there are shops and restaurants between here and the cinema complex. Holidays R Us is there."

"Thanks for your help. I appreciate it." He turned and took off toward the cinema.

"Any time, Inspector," she called out to his retreating back.

****

I paid off the cab and entered from the other side through the Wright Street entrance, limping but still moving quickly enough. Years of SAS training wouldn't permit a limp to slow me down too much.

For once, I didn't wear a cap. I was going into my final battle proud of the ugly scars on my head. I didn't care if people saw them. The shops were beginning to open, and even at that early time, there were quite a few people arriving and milling around.

I limped to Holiday Universe, a large organization with nine desks for consultants and protected by a linked security grill, which was still down and locked. All the lights were on, and I could hear several female voices coming from inside, toward the rear of the store, behind some partitioning, laughing and giggling with one another. *No doubt they are talking about the men they were with last night,* I thought.

My eye was now so full of blood it throbbed horribly, and I couldn't see out of it very well at all, which ruined my depth of vision. I could still see fine out of the other, so it would not affect my aim. I knew I was fading fast; the limp was worse, and the shopping center was filling up with more people. I knew I had to finish things now. It was my last chance.

I thought for a second of taking out the machine gun and shooting the bitches through the partitions, but I still had two other shops to get to, and once I opened fire, I knew it would be mayhem with shoppers running everywhere. I took out one of the grenades, pulled the pin, reached in through the grill, and tossed it across the shop, so it rolled and settled near the partition. Then I took off as quickly as my limp would allow. I got around the corner when the explosion occurred.

****

Dillon was only a short distance from the second travel agency when he heard the blast. With a sinking heart, he turned to run back the way he had come, drawing his gun as he hurried. His path was partially blocked by people leaving shops and trying to flee the center through the door he had come out of, and they slowed him down. Even though he kept screaming that he was the police, there was a blind panic, and no one made way for him.

****

Jayne heard the explosion and, without a thought, opened the car door. She stumbled in her haste in her high heels and almost lost a shoe before regaining her balance. She ran as fast as she could to the door, which now had people rushing out. Jayne didn't know what had happened but feared the worst. As she ran, she raged the word *no* over and over in her head. She had finally met the right man, and she knew her brother-in-law had killed him. Tears of anger, fear, and sadness welled in her eyes as she ran, not caring for herself. Her only thought to get to Dillon and try to help.

****

The glass door of Blythe Spirit Travel opened, and Donna stuck her head out to see what the commotion was. She saw a man thirty meters away as he pulled a gun out of a shoulder holster and fired toward her. The bullet hit the door frame in line with where her head had been as she ducked back inside, screaming. Her coworkers panicked and ran with her, seeing the tall limping man with a gun in his hand approach the front door. He shouldered it open as they disappeared into the staff room, slammed the door behind them, and twisted the lock. They heard something clatter to the floor near the door.

Once he tossed in the grenade, he turned and limped off quickly toward the third and final travel shop. He tucked the gun in his jeans waistband, pulled the backpack off his shoulder, and hurried to get his machine

359

gun out as he ran. With that and spare magazines in his hand, he dropped the bag, extended the stock, and primed the slide back, so it was ready to fire. Years of practice and training made it a smooth operation even though he only had one good eye. He could have done it blindfolded.

****

Dillon skidded around the corner and saw Paul Williams hurrying toward him only meters away. In a split second he took in the dropped backpack and the ugly-looking machine gun in his hand and his heart sank. They recognized each other at exactly the same time, and both raised their guns. With years of combat training, Williams was always going to be quicker.

****

Jayne had pushed through the last of the fleeing crowd through the entry door and had drawn level with the travel agency when she saw Tank and Dillon raise their weapons. With no thought for her safety, she screamed, "*Tank, no!*"

Then the grenade in the shop went off with a deafening roar.

The blast knocked her from her feet as a hundred shards of glass hit her like javelins. She was flung sideways to the tiled floor, unconscious and bleeding from more than fifty wounds. Most were minor, but a large dagger-sized piece was protruding from her neck. Blood slowly pumped out around the deadly shard as she lay on a carpet of a thousand other pieces of glittering glass.

****

Williams heard his nickname being screamed out, and he could have sworn it was by Amanda. He would know her voice anywhere. Although he had been trained to ignore any distraction, the shock of hearing his name shouted by the very voice of the woman he was hunting momentarily made him pause. That split-second delay saved Dillon from being torn apart from a hail of 9mm bullets before he could aim and fire. Both weapons discharged together.

Paul Williams was close to suffering a massive brain aneurism, his parting gift from months before in Afghanistan. His death would not be listed as a consequence of the war, and his name not placed on the plaque of fallen soldiers. Only minutes before that would have happened naturally, Dillon's one and only shot hit 'Tank' Williams in the middle of his chest.

The hollow-point slug knocked him backward, and his head hit the tiled floor with a crack that by itself would have killed anyone. The remainder of the shots from his machine gun were fired with his finger frozen on the trigger. The bullets traveled in an arc from Dillon, then up and across the ceiling until the magazine was empty. The ejected shells fell raining, hot and smoking, around his prone body.

His last thought was disgust that with all of his training, he had been shot by a cop while they were both running. That was bullshit. For a cop, that had been an almost impossible shot to make; he had just gotten lucky. Williams knew he would die, not knowing whether he had killed Amanda or not. He had failed his final mission.

Having killed over twenty people while with the army and over thirty since he had been discharged, Paul 'Tank' Williams died.

****

Dillon was hit twice, once in the shoulder, which spun him to the left as the bullet smashed through bone and muscle and almost tore his arm from his body. The second hit his hip, breaking it in four places before it ricocheted upward into his stomach.

He was thrown backward by the impact to the floor and lay conscious, not realizing he had been shot or how much he was bleeding internally. He wondered why he was lying on his back and unable to move his legs to get up. Shock had set in as the ever-widening puddle of blood expanded around him.

****

A security guard named Ryan Hebberling arrived on the scene. He was a jovial, gray-haired, portly man whom everyone working at the shopping center thought was lovely. He was known to be very brave because he had once gotten his name in the local newspaper for saving a woman from three Aboriginal attackers. They had been robbing her outside the very shopping center he still worked at for forty-four hours a week, including overtime. He knelt on one knee by the wounded man's side. "Don't move, mate, you've been shot. I've called an ambulance and police, and they are on the way. You're bleeding quite badly, so best you don't move," he said earnestly.

Beyond that, Ryan didn't know what to do, as he had never seen a gunshot wound, and his first-aid training did not cover the massive amount of trauma he saw before him.

The man croaked, "I'm police. Take my gun. That's *the Ripper.* Make sure he is dead or immobilized and take his gun away from him, and please, please try to save that woman. Her name is Jayne. She saved my life, and I think I love her." Then he was gone, unconscious or dead; Ryan didn't know which.

Without a thought, Ryan picked up the gun and, with his usual fearlessness, raced over to the other body lying on the floor. One look told him he was dead, but he kicked the machine gun away, just in case. The fallen man's eyes were open and staring, although one was full of blood. *He's an ugly bastard with all that scarring on his head*, the guard thought before taking off at another run to check on the woman.

She was unconscious, too, and looked to be in a bad way. Blood was pumping and bubbling from a wound in her neck, along with numerous other less serious ones all over her body. Ryan knew enough of first aid to see she was bleeding to death.

He knelt among the glass, which crunched under him, and turned her onto her side in the recovery position. Her wounded neck now faced up, and he grasped the shard and slid it out. Blood squirted upward and Ryan placed his balled-up handkerchief, freshly laundered by his wife, over the wound and applied pressure to stem the flow. He stayed that way until help arrived a few minutes later. He knelt over her, saying her name and telling her over and over that her man told him to tell her he loved her, and she was to hold on.

Epilogue

Over the weeks and months that followed the bombing at Belmont, the newspapers and current affairs TV shows pulled Paul 'Tank' Williams' history to pieces. It became the talking point of just about everyone in Australia around water coolers, in restaurants and bars, and between family and friends. Everyone had one question—how could such a thing happen? How did one man, a national hero, deteriorate to such an extent that he became one of the most notorious serial killers and mass murderers in the nation's history?

There were those who took the simplistic view that it was post-traumatic stress disorder and that politicians had to do more for our returned soldiers. Others thought it was a mental breakdown due to emotional reasons because his wife had left him, and others stated it was a combination of the two.

During a current affairs TV segment, time was devoted to his childhood, and the only ever interview with Gwen Williams went to air. The well-known female presenter tried to delve deeply into her son's psyche as a child. The nature of the questions caused her to break down in tears for her 'dear Jackie boy.' It was thought to be great investigative television. She left the studio sobbing, went home, and committed suicide by swallowing over two hundred tablets of varying description while drinking a bottle of white wine, which had always been her first choice of alcohol.

Some thought it was guilt and that it proved she must have been a bad mother, while others thought she had been hounded by the media and was just another victim of intrusive interviewing and paparazzi journalism. It was only much later, when Williams' journals were released to the public, that the full implications of his tormented childhood and incest became known.

The Belmont Forum Shopping Center stayed closed for two weeks while structural and other repairs were carried out. Seven people had been killed in the grenade blasts and three wounded. The most relieved people were the ones working at the third travel agency, Holidays R Us, once it became known that the killer had been on his way to that shop to continue his killing spree. One of the women working there fainted when told she was the intended target of the maniacal Paul Williams.

Toni Billingsgate had absolutely no idea why she had become Williams' prey, and became a media sensation. She appeared on several TV chat shows and was featured in magazines and newspaper articles. Everyone, it seemed, wanted to interview her. At the time of the attack at Belmont, she hadn't known Suzi had been murdered. She rarely watched the news, and the police had not interviewed her. Having run away from her abusive ex-husband, she kept a low profile so he wouldn't find her. She hadn't associated herself with the sisters' murders as she had only met them once. Suzi talked her into going to a concert in the park, and they had lunch first. It was a complete mystery to her why Paul Williams was intent on killing her.

The Independent Crime Commission held a full

inquiry on the task force and looked at the long list of errors made by Blunt after Dillon had been given compassionate leave. He resigned from the police force to avoid embarrassment. Blunt was completely disgraced in the media, with *'informed sources'* inside the task force telling of his abrasive nature and complete disregard for Mike Knowles' work which led to his suspension and subsequent death. There was some talk of charges of negligence being brought against him, but those rumors died in time. His wife of thirty years left him.

Ryan Hebberling received a bravery award for being the first on the scene and ensuring Paul Williams was disarmed. His jovial face was suddenly considered to be perfect for marketing, and he made several TV commercials for the shopping center.

****

Louise Bradley was distraught when told the news of her father and flew over immediately from Melbourne in shock. Having had her mother murdered two weeks prior, she could not bear the thought of losing her father too.

Dillon's heart stopped through shock and loss of blood, and he died in the ambulance as its sirens blared on the way to the hospital. He was revived and kept alive by a frantic paramedic, who received his training with the British Army and had also been stationed in Afghanistan. He had seen gunshot trauma before and performed his job perfectly. Dillon was rushed into emergency surgery at Royal Perth Hospital, where he spent nine hours in theater.

Dillon Bradley could have died at any time in the days following and gave the doctors and nurses many scares. He was constantly monitored in intensive care, with Louise watching through the window, willing him to wake up. He had been placed in an induced coma while his broken body healed. His shoulder and hip had been smashed and had numerous plates and pins inserted. There were serious doubts he would ever walk unaided again.

He very slowly recovered from the injuries, shock, and blood loss. His arm was secured to his body to ensure he did not move it while the bones knitted. His leg was similarly anchored to help the healing process in his hip after the trauma the two expanding bullets had caused. His trip back from the brink of death was slow and torturous. It would be a long time before he would be able to walk or use his arm for anything significant, and he would have to suffer through many painful physiotherapy treatments for months.

Dillon Bradley was hailed a hero in the media and theater of public opinion but initially considered less so within the police force. The fact was, his detractors believed, he should have reported his suspicions, and the TRG should have been sent immediately. Whether they could have got there any quicker than Dillon was debatable, and the extent of delays from an antagonistic Blunt would never be known. Naturally, he denied that and led the charge in blaming Dillon for the deaths that occurred that fateful morning.

In the bedside interrogation after he had been awake for a few days, some three weeks after the explosions, Dillon argued that the time he spent on the phone to Blunt would have been time that slowed him getting there. There would have been far greater loss of life, not only from the third travel agency personnel but anyone else who got in Williams' way. When the journal entries were deciphered, and investigators read that Williams had vowed to take as many police and public as possible with him in his final battle, it reinforced Dillon's position, and Blunt's incompetence became the focus for blame.

Dillon thought long and hard about his future as a police officer and whether he wanted it anymore. But the decision was made for him. He was told he was being discharged on medical grounds. His injuries were far too severe for him to ever be classed as fit enough for duty. He was offered a settlement and full pension for the rest of his life, plus all medical expenses covered. It was an easy choice to make, but he was smart enough to engage a lawyer, Peter Best, to negotiate on his behalf a fairer payout. It took time, but he signed an agreement to take the money and only be complimentary to his old employers. He knew he had financial security, no matter what he chose to do.

Dillon accepted the medal and commendation presented to him by the commissioner, the state premier, and governor general at a ceremony in his honor. Though he was in a wheelchair, he smiled when Commissioner Pollock almost had to bow to him to place the ribbon around his neck. Later, at another ceremony, he was given the key to the city of Perth, which he found very humbling.

In her long vigil, Louise had also become very friendly with the other person frantic for him to survive, Jayne McMahon. Ryan Hebberling had saved her life by stopping the blood loss when he had, and she never once forgot to send him a birthday or Christmas card to thank him until he passed away many years later.

Jayne had suffered a concussion, a perforated eardrum, and a total of forty-seven stitches for cuts from the flying shards of glass. Much later, Dillon nicknamed Jayne Pin because he always joked that she became a human pin cushion from the blast. Fortunately, she had been side on to the travel agency when the grenade exploded, so her beautiful face was virtually unmarked, though the ugly scar to her neck did require some cosmetic surgery, but she recovered quickly.

When she awoke, her mother was there from Sydney, and her first question had been if Dillon had survived. She openly cried when she was told he had, but at that time, he was in intensive care, clinging to life by the thinnest of threads, in a coma.

She demanded to be taken to him, and after bodily threats to nurses and doctors, was wheeled to the viewing window in a wheelchair, her drip bottle in tow, where she met Louise for the first time. She would only leave the window at the doctors' and her mother's insistence but spent more time there than in her hospital bed.

When Dillon finally woke up, Jayne and Louise had become friends for life, and they were both permitted to see him. There was no doubt that Jayne shouting out Williams' nickname when she did, had not only saved Dillon's life but hers and possibly lots of others as well. She was alongside Dillon when he received his medal before she received her own.

****

They stood on a marina wharf as the sun was setting at Airlie Beach in Northern Queensland. They were awaiting the return of the forty-five-foot yacht Wave Dancer. The vessel was owned by a cruising charter company and had been out for a ten-day charter through the beautiful islands of the Whitsunday Passage.

Jayne clung to his arm tightly and could barely contain her excitement while Dillon leaned heavily on his walking stick. He also shared her nervousness but wished there was somewhere to sit. His hip ached like a bastard, as it always did in the evening, especially if he had been on his feet for too long during the day.

The three of them had been communicating for a week by email, but this was the first opportunity to catch up personally after Dillon had tracked her down. The yacht had been on a charter, and Jayne and Dillon had to wait for its return. They had flown in from Perth two days prior.

Finding her had been no mean feat, and later the search would be the catalyst for Jayne pushing Dillon to open a private detective agency for the two of them to run together. His profile, experience, and his contacts would ensure their success, and he jokingly said they could call it Beauty and the Beast. She punched his good arm lovingly and told him she loved him, and he was more than good looking enough for her.

****

Amanda Williams had hidden away after escaping from her husband. She had planned to hide for the rest of her life, and refused to own or use a phone from fear Williams would track her down. She had never recovered from the trauma of the vile threatening phone calls and voice messages sent to her by 'Tank,' when she had first gone to Perth, which she intended would only be for a respite.

The man she'd once loved with every fiber of her being had gone into intricate details in several phone calls about how he would cut her up, burn out her eyes

370

and stab her in her unfaithful cunt, for being a slut and running out on him.

She had initially gone to Perth feeling sad, lonely, and guilty for leaving Tank in the hospital bed, but she had had to get away for a break from him. For months on end, she had spent hours every day with him, trying to help put him back together and reassure him of her love and devotion, while he constantly yelled and swore at her for no good reason. He was always getting his words mixed up, and the more she couldn't understand him, the angrier he got. Every day had ended up with him screaming that she was nothing but a useless whore, or worse, over and over again, until he broke her spirit.

It was strange how he'd never mixed up his swear words; he always got those right. But, he had been getting worse with her, throwing things, cursing her, and spying on her because he'd just *known* she was screwing other men.

His doctor, Charlie, was a wonderful man who at first tried to tell her things would get better, that his outbursts were a symptom of the injury, and to be patient with him. But the longer it went on, the angrier Paul became with her, and she'd grown to fear him. Then even Charlie agreed he doubted 'Tank' would ever completely recover. She'd begun to dread visiting him, but if she'd tried to make excuses to not come to have a breather, he would be incensed and accuse her of wanting time away from him so she could *'fuck her boyfriends.'*

Before he'd been wounded, Amanda used to love 'Tank's' eyes, and she used to especially love the way he'd looked at her. It was as if every time he saw her, it was for the first time. No man had ever treated her as he had, and Amanda had adored him for it. After the coma, though, his eyes had been dead and lifeless, except for just one time. That was when he had turned the scissors on her and stabbed her wrist. Then his eyes had been ablaze with passion, and she had known right then, he gained pleasure from hurting her. Worse, she had known for an absolute fact that he would want to hurt her more and more, and maybe one day even kill her.

His specialist eventually agreed with her that Tank had become psychotic and had offered her comfort. He arranged advice on having her husband committed to a secure psychiatric ward, from where he wouldn't get out again. He had been concerned that the temper fits were becoming more frequent, louder, and had the potential to be violent. Amanda made the mistake of giving him a friendly hug for understanding her plight, but they had been seen by Tank. Then her husband's jealousy knew no limits.

She was informed that Tank wasn't going to live too much longer. They told her he would likely have less than two years left, but it was difficult to be precise. Charlie told her he should never leave a secure hospital because of his erratic behavior. Secretly, Amanda had begun to wish he hadn't fought so hard to come back to her; she would have preferred her memories of the man he had been rather than the horribly wounded animal he had become.

But she loved him with all of her heart and prayed every day for the Tank she'd fallen in love with to find his way back to her. Even though his doctors told her he wasn't going to, that the damage was too great, she held on to that hope. Amanda dreamed they might be wrong, and Tank's love for her would bring him back from the brink.

He had taken to accusing her of being unfaithful every day she visited. If only he could have known how impossible that would have been for her. She adored the man he had been. There was no one else and never could be. While he lived, there was hope, and she had clung to that as long as she could.

The army had wanted to empty their belongings out of the rooms they lived in at Swanbourne. She thought it would be the ideal time to use it as an excuse to take a break from the stress and pain of watching her once-wonderful husband become more estranged from her. Charlie had instantly agreed that not only would it be good for her, it just *might* be good for him too. It could have given him something to look forward to when she came back. They'd thought it might help him overcome the hatred and jealousy he had seemed to have developed for her, but how wrong they were.

She wanted to talk to him about it calmly and reassure him she would only be away two weeks. But she walked out crying after his attack with the scissors and left for Perth sad, lonely and depressed, worried that perhaps she shouldn't stay away for two weeks, maybe just three days, time enough to pack up their belongings and get back to him.

That had been when he started the phone calls and messages. He wouldn't listen to her. All he'd wanted to do was tell her he was going to slit her throat and cut her up. She knew he meant it and had been terrified. She'd tried to reason with him, sometimes spending up to an hour on her mobile with him, trying to convince him she loved him and she was coming back. She repeatedly told him that she wasn't with another man, but he just screamed at her that he was coming for her and he was going to kill her.

When Jayne phoned Amanda and told her 'Tank' checked himself out of the hospital, she became scared that he would do what he said he would and hunt her down. Then Jayne got angry and blamed her for running out on him. After her sister yelled at her and the nonstop threats from him by phone, Amanda broke down. She'd hung up on Jayne and thrown her mobile phone into the ocean vowing never to own another. She took some time to get her head together, withdrew twenty thousand dollars from their joint bank account, and left. She had no plan but had to hide from him and everyone she knew to protect them from 'Tank's' wrath. Amanda needed time to get over her guilt because she blamed herself for everything. She had been the one who had ruined Tank's life, not the mortar round that exploded near his head.

Amanda had fallen in love with Northern Queensland on their honeymoon and thought she would try to get a job at Hamilton Island doing something—anything would do. She had to get herself together, hoping he would never find her there. She'd thought if she stayed away for a year or two, she would make contact with her mother and Jayne and see if they had forgiven her. Amanda's fear, lack of self-confidence, and guilt had been so overpowering it was the only thing she could think to do.

Arriving at Airlie Beach as a starting point to get to Hamilton Island, she lucked into the perfect job. She began working on the Wave Dancer as a general hand, serving drinks and meals, cleaning, and looking after guests. She loved it, and the owners of the yacht appreciated having her. They let her live on the boat and most of her days had been spent cruising in paradise while she shunned the outside world.

Amanda had no idea of the death and mayhem going on in Perth in her wake because she never watched TV or read newspapers. She had been horrified when Dillon tracked her down and told her. Amanda spent hours with Jayne and her mother on video calls, blaming herself for the murders and wished she had stayed and let him kill her. *At least then everyone else would have lived,* she believed.

Slowly, they calmed her and made her realize none of it had been her fault, that 'Tank' had been mentally disturbed and horrifically wounded. Dillon and Jayne made plans to fly over and spend time with her. Now that she had been found, she would face a media frenzy, and they wanted to be there to help her through it.

****

The Wave Dancer appeared through the heads. Dillon and Jayne saw her on the bow waving at them. While Dillon could not wave back because his good arm held him up on his walking stick, Jayne raised her left arm and waved frantically, tears streaming down her face.

The dying embers of the sunset glinted off the large diamond engagement ring she wore.

****

Dillon and Jayne will return in *Repo*, a fast-paced thriller about a restored muscle car, high stakes poker, murder, and love.

Author's Note

Forever Night was the first book I wrote, and as far as story goes, it has always been my favorite. It was originally published by The Totally Entwined publishing house in London. Sadly, after signing with them, things happened beyond either of our control, and we parted company. But I enjoyed my time working with their wonderful editorial staff and will never say a bad word about them—they took a chance on a new Australian author, so sincerest thanks to them for that.

Inspiration for the plot came from one line in an amazing song by Leonard Cohen, called Nevermind, and I will always be indebted for that masterful poet and songwriter for starting me on a journey that now comprises thirteen published novels.

I have the utmost respect for our soldiers, who are highly trained to go off to faraway trouble spots, face unbelievable conditions to fight for our way of life and freedom. That said, I am a pacifist and would prefer if we could live in a world without war, and I live in hope one day we can. I have known two ex SAS soldiers, and while Paul 'Tank' Williams is a figment of my imagination, they gave me a lot of valuable information about their core beliefs and training regimen that makes the SAS among the best in the world at what they do. They are experts in death and survival.

Tank's story is a tragic one, and I wanted to paint a picture for you, dear reader, of a man who, through circumstances not of his making, endured to become a war hero, found the ultimate true love, then tragically lost it which led to him becoming a deranged serial killer. This story is not about the very real post-traumatic stress disorder many of our returning soldiers face. For me, it's about two love stories, one tragic, one successful. The murders and hunt for the killer were the vehicle to tell those two love stories. I hope I did it well enough.

Stephen B King
Perth Australia

A word about the author…

I was born in the UK, what seems like an epoch ago, and moved to Australia at age 16. I was a long haired rock guitarist and poet/songwriter, before real life got in the way, and I gave it all up for love.

I've always felt I had tales to tell and won short story competitions and published poetry in my wilder, younger days. More recently I've written and published fifteen novels. While they have mainly been Police procedural thrillers, often focusing on Serial killers, they all have a love theme running through them.

I believe love, and family are everything. Anything else you gain in life is a bonus.

I live in Perth, in Western Australia and am fiercely patriotic, and parochial. My wife is amazing in that she not only puts up with living with a writer, but encourages it. I've been blessed with five children, and I adore them all.

http://stephen-b-king.com